Sunrise at Seminary Ridge

JAMES A WYNNE

SUNRISE AT SEMINARY RIDGE

Copyright © 2024 James A. Wynne

Because of the dynamic nature of the Internet, any web addresses or links contained in this book may have changed since publication and may no longer be valid. The opinions and viewpoints of the characters created in the book do not necessarily reflect that of my own.

Library of Congress Control Number: 2024935464
                    Paperback: 979-8-89306-031-7
                    eBook: 979-8-89306-032-4

Printed in the United States of America

CONTENTS

CHAPTER 1

28 June, 1863

Jacob slowly opened his eyes. Even though it was still dark outside, he could tell by the crowing of 'Ol Jehosophat," the rooster that it was time to get out of bed. The moonlight was still shining brightly through his bedroom window, making it easier to him to find his things; his trousers, shirt, stockings, hat and a pair of black boots. He pulled his nightshirt off quickly, but unlike those mornings in the middle of winter, his room was already warm – almost uncomfortable. He walked to his dressing table and reached down, picking up two handfuls of water from the basin, and then splashed his face in the same motion. In any other household, this washing protocol might have been accomplished while standing in front of a mirror, but in this home, a mirror was considered an instrument of man's vanity. In one efficient sweep of his hands, he had washed his face and finished the process of waking up.

Jacob was careful to wash the sleep out of his eyes. He took a hairbrush and pulled it through his long, blonde hair, and then smoothed the long locks behind his ears. His bangs fell almost in front of his eyes. Jacob let out a great yawn. It felt good to get it out of his system, but it was also something which he would not wish to do in front of his father. The boy was naturally intelligent, and inquisitive. He often longed for a life away from farm life, but was pragmatic enough to know his place in the vast scheme of things. He was, after all, a young man who had just passed his eighteenth birthday.

The boy turned quickly to his rear, looking back toward the two beds that occupied the sparsely furnished room. His brother, Abraham, was not in his bed – which Jacob took as a very bad sign. This could only mean one thing; Jacob had slept past his normal rising hour. He was late for the morning chores.

Jacob dressed quickly then walked downstairs. His mother, Sarah, was preparing his breakfast as he walked into the kitchen. His father, Ishmael, was already sitting at the kitchen table, eating his meal. His younger brother, Abraham, had yet to come to the table, which meant that he was probably still attending to his chores in the barn.

As was typical of the houses occupied by the people of Jacob's sect, the house was painted white, with accents of black. There were none of the designs that had found their way onto the homes of those who had emigrated from Germany – the so-called "Pennsylvania Dutch." Most typically, these designs were incorporated in the geometrically balanced "Hex Sign," – a form of good luck charm which was placed on barns, out buildings, and even houses – and meant to ward off evil spirits, and encourage blessed spirits to enter the abode. The other design featured was called the 'distelfink' – an artistic representation of the goldfinch. The Zook family, and the tradition from which they had come, had strict rules against such artwork. Their lives were to be kept 'plain.' Having such artistic luxuries would be considered 'fancy,' and therefore against the rules, or, as they called it, the Ordnung.

"Morgen, Muti," Jacob said to his mother, gently kissing her on the cheek. Then, addressing his father, Jacob added, "Guten Morgen, Papa."

His father glowered at him, but then observed, "Du bist spät, Jacob!"

"I am sorry," the contrite boy replied.

"Do you expect me to do all of my work, as well as yours?"

"No, sir," Jacob answered, sitting in a chair across from his father.

"The sun is rising, and we still have cows to milk. I warned you that this might happen if you stayed out too late with those English friends of yours."

"Yes, Papa." The fact of the matter was that Jacob had no 'English' friends, as his father called them; he had very few friends at all in the town. He had spent the previous evening walking around the small town in which they lived …alone – if for no other reason than to escape the boredom he felt as of late in his own house. As much as he disliked fabricating the story to his parents, he had a feeling deep-down in the pit of his stomach that there was something more – something wonderful – to be discovered outside of his family unit. He felt that it was coming time to stretch his wings a bit – if only he could…if only they would allow it.

Jacob's mother bent over his shoulder, placing a bowl of oatmeal in front of him. "Here, Jacob – Eat! Quickly! Do not keep your father waiting!"

"Thank you, Muti!" Jacob answered, quickly lifting the first spoonful to his mouth.

"We have a great deal of work scheduled for us this day, Jacob," his father continued, as if his wife was not even present in the room. "We have some repairs to make on the cupola, and we have some varnishing to do on some of the desks."

"Yes, sir," obediently replied his son.

"Your mother will be spending some of her morning in the garden, then you will bring some of the harvest to the market in town – but that will not be until late in the afternoon. You may take Abraham with you."

"Papa?" questioned Jacob. "Why must I take Abraham with me?"

"And why not? Your brother wishes to go into town almost as much as you do!"

"But…but…" Jacob stammered, looking for a good reason to leave his fourteen year old brother back at the house.

"Don't begin this argument, Jacob! Just do as I say!"

"Yes, Papa!"

Ishmael Zook hated being called "Papa," or any other term of affection that was so commonly utilized by the "English" community in which they lived. And Jacob was well aware of his father's dislike for the term, in fact, he often used the word just to irk his father, so much so that it had even become second nature to him.

The Zook family had moved to this town in Southern Pennsylvania a few years back because there had been a great deal of dissention among the members of their community. They had owned a large family farm in the small town of Paradise. The land they had owned had been passed down from male heir to male heir within the Zook family for many generations. As the oldest of the Zook brothers, Ishmael was now head of the family – assuming that position after the death of his father, Isaac Zook.

Isaac Zook had been a taskmaster, and the Zook boys labored to make the farm profitable – which they succeeded in doing. Ishmael married Anna Miller in 1844, and they built a large and comfortable home on the family property. Anna caught diphtheria in the same year while she carrying her first child. She died in the early spring, taking her unborn child with her. Ishmael was inconsolable, especially in the words spoken within the Faith meant to comfort him. He found his own faith to be unwavering and harsh. Ishmael found consolation in the arms of a young woman who he had met at the market in Bird-In-Hand. Her name was Sarah – Sarah Loder.

Sarah was not of his sect. She was a Mennonite.

Isaac Zook expressed his opposition of any possible union between his son and this other woman. Ishmael threatened to leave the Paradise community, if only to be with the woman he had fallen in love with. Relenting, Isaac gave his blessing to the marriage, which took place in the spring of 1846. The newlyweds once again occupied the large home which had been originally built as a home for the Zook/Miller union. The community was outraged. The elders of the congregation threatened to shun Ishmael for marrying outside of the faith, but Isaac had used his influence to quiet these threats.

Sarah gave birth to her first-born, a boy, who Ishmael proudly named Jacob. Even this provided the community with a source of tongue-in-cheek humor. In a society that seemed to prefer the use of Old Testament biblical first names, Isaac had named his first son, Ishmael, after the half-brother of the Isaac in the book of Genesis . According to the Biblical story, before Abraham's wife, Sarai, could bear a child of her own, Abraham had a son with his wife's slave girl, Hagar. When, in great old-age, Sarai gave birth to Isaac, she begged her husband to send Hagar and her son away, which he did. On the other hand, Jacob was the second son of Isaac, but he was raised filled with guile and deceit, and it was he who attempted to rob his older brother, Esau, out of his rightful inheritance by confusing his aging father.

Oh yes, the community had a very good time laughing at the ambiguity of these names.

Isaac did whatever he could to insulate his son from the hatred of their neighbors. Sarah gave birth to a second son, Abraham, a few years later. The addition of another name from the Genesis story only further added to the problem.

And then, suddenly, in the winter of 1855, Isaac Zook died. With the family patriarch now gone, the community felt free to openly criticize the Zook family, so much so that, in the summer of 1857, Ishmael packed up whatever he could fit into a wagon, and left the Lancaster area, moving more toward the urban center of the area – Harrisburg. Even still, the Zooks felt out of place in the city climate. They still were clinging to many of the styles and customs of their ancestors. Their life had become intolerable. They had nowhere to go.

Being able to speak English and German fluently, as well as the dialect of German that was most commonly spoken back in Paradise, allowed the family to blend fairly well into a German Lutheran congregation in Harrisburg. Using his connections with the Lutheran Seminary, just a few miles away, the Pastor was able to secure a job for Ishmael as custodian at the school. The job was often overwhelming for Ishmael, but as his firstborn son, Jacob, grew in stature, it became a little easier. Moreover, the people were kind to them.

They had been assimilated.

Jacob Zook carried an armful of planking up the winding stairs that led to the cupola. The cupola was just about the tallest structure, which sat on top of one of the highest elevations in the area – Seminary Ridge. The ridge took its name from the Lutheran Seminary which had found a home on that tract of land. Founded in 1826 by Reverend Samuel Simon Schmucker, it became the first seminary to teach the principles of Lutheranism in the fledging country. The Schmucker family was in favor of the abolition of the institution of slavery, and the seminary building was used as a stop on the "underground railroad."

This philosophy suited Ishmael Zook, who was under the opinion that a man was born to do his own work and to tend his own crops. Ishmael felt that, as he would not wish to be a slave, neither would he have any desire to be a master of slaves.

This ideology was always being tested, however, as they lived precariously close to the border with the State of Maryland, which was considered a hotbed of controversy these days, being a so-called "border state." There were many slaves kept in Maryland, but there were also a number of free men, as well. Jacob wasn't really sure if the issue of slavery was the main cause of the war that was now being fought, but it seemed like many in the country seemed to think that this was a good reason to fight.

By ten o'clock in the morning, the repairs were finished on the cupola. The floor boards had been rotting away, so Ishmael had expertly replaced the failing timbers. Father and son climbed back down to the ground level of the seminary building to spend the next few hours varnishing some of the classroom desks. Classes were not in session for the summer, so this was the obvious time to accomplish all of these necessary tasks.

Jacob hoped to enlist his father into an academic debate about the war. "Have you heard the latest news from Chancellorsville, Papa?"

"Other than the tremendous loss and waste of human life, it does not really concern me, Jacob."

Jacob expected such an answer. He knew that his people had managed to stay clear of all forms of governmental entrapments, including military service, for many, many years. He was also well aware that his father intended to stay this course during this war, to insure that he, and his brother, would stay clear of service – even if it was to battle the evils of slavery.

But still he felt the need to needle his father. "I heard that thousands of men were killed in that battle, Papa."

"I heard that, too."

"And…?

"And what, Jacob? Do you think this will change my opinion of this war? That is what war does, Jacob – it kills the young men of the country….and for what?"

Jacob had heard these words before. "Still, Papa….there must always be other young men to replace the ones that fall." And with that statement, he had just stepped over a line.

His father put his brush down. "Replace? How? With you, perhaps?" "Papa! There are boys out there…on those battlefields…who are younger than I am."

"And they are dying, Jacob. Do you think I wish to hear that you have been killed in such a way?"

"No, of course not! But I do wish to do my part!"

"You are doing your part, Jacob. You are helping me varnish the desks for the upcoming semester. Why are you in such a rush to die?"

"Because it is my duty….sir."

"Your duty? A man may have to defend his own home against attack, but he must never pick up a weapon to strike down another, simply because another man has ordered him to do it."

Jacob twisted his father's words. "So….then….you would be in favor of defending our home, were it attacked by the rebel forces?" "Don't put words in my mouth, Jacob."

"I am sorry, Papa…I was just wondering if there were any exceptions to your rules."

"Enough of this talk. We should get back to work. You are much too clever with your tongue, Jacob; Too clever for your own good. You should finish up that desk and then get back to the house to help your mother. She will need help loading the wagon with the produce for the market."

"Yes, Papa."

The father and son finished their work in silence, but Jacob quietly looked forward to his adventure in the sleepy little town. He had several very good friends there, and he hoped to run into a least one or two of them at the market. It really wasn't much of a town, to speak of; just a few hundred residents, most of whom lived in wood-framed houses alongside the Emmittsburg Pike. What he most appreciated was the fact that the town didn't have a foolish name, not like his former place of residence – Paradise- or like some of the other towns in the area: Bird-In-Hand, Intercourse-Ephrata. This one had a very simple, very American name…

…it was called Gettysburg.

CHAPTER 2

The Same Day

Once again, the commanding General of the Army of the Potomac had been sacked. First, it had been General George McClellan, whose inaction and reticence to face the enemy had frustrated President Lincoln for the first half of the war. Lincoln then replaced McClellan with Ambrose Burnside, who then proceeded to lead the army to a disastrous defeat at Fredricksburg. Lincoln then handed the reigns over to Joseph Hooker, a hard-drinking, hard-fighting General – but even "Fightin' Joe" had his problems, and these were dealt to him in spades at the battle of Chancellorsville. Lincoln dearly wanted a General who could win against Robert E. Lee. The President next turned to General George G. Meade, to see if he was capable of leading the Northern Army. This latest shift in leadership came only days after the Union defeat at Chancellorsville.

The Army of the Potomac now was shadowing the Army of Northern Virginia. Lee, ever a pragmatist, hoped to make the war even more unpopular in the North by attempting, for the second time in the war, an invasion of Northern territories. At the same time, he was also hoping to gain an even greater advantage over his enemy, and considering the intelligence he was receiving concerning the Union strategy, his intuition told him that this would be an excellent time for such a bold move. His first objective was the Pennsylvania city of Harrisburg, but if the Union Army could not stop him there, he could easily mount a march eastward and attempt to capture Washington, thereby forcing the government to negotiate a treaty.

Lee was correct, certainly in one assumption; the Union Army was in total disarray. Following his appointment to lead the Union forces, Meade called together his Corps Commanders, anxious to assert his new position, as well as to point the finger at the defeats of the past.

Many of his senior officers had seen action in battle before this. Many had been veterans of the Mexican War, having fought under either Zachary Taylor or Winfield Scott. Many of the same officers not only knew of the reputations and abilities of their Confederate counterparts – in many cases, they were good friends, or even related to them, by blood or by marriage.

But some of the senior staff members were a younger, brasher type. Many had attended West Point, but others were simply, as the saying goes, "officers and gentlemen." In a day when only the privileged few attended colleges and universities, or even could read or write, military training and experience was considered important, but it was left to gentlemen to lead the troops – and to act as a role model for their behavior.

Then there were the political appointees.

A person well situated within a political machine could easily sue for a commission in the army – either army. As General Meade gathered his war council together, he noted the presence of one such man – a man who had received his commission as a result of his position within the ultimate political machine in the State of New York – Tammany Hall.

General Daniel Edgar Sickles was not a career soldier, nor did he attend West Point. He had received his first commission to lead a regiment, the rank of Colonel, as a direct result of his association with the infamous New York City political organization. He received the promotion to Brigadier General – from President Lincoln, himself – for his work, through the same machine – in recruiting soldiers for the war effort.

General Sickles talked tough, and acted tougher. He quickly rose from Brigade commander, to Division Commander, to Commander of an entire corps, the III Corps.

Sickles had been a close friend of his former commanding General, Joe Hooker. They were drinking and womanizing friends in arms. Under Hooker's command, Sickles misread the troop movements of Confederate General Thomas "Stonewall" Jackson during the Battle of Chancellorsville, mistaking the rebel flanking maneuver as a retreat. Sickles lack of experience on the field of battle directly led to a final blunder, which allowed the Union IX Corps, under General Oliver Howard, to be decimated by Jackson's Division. It cost the Union the battle – and his friend, General Hooker, his job as commander.

George Meade was not Joe Hooker, and he was not about to let this political appointee fail again. General Meade immediately commandeered Prospect Hall in Frederick, Maryland to call his Corps Commanders in for a meeting. Hooker already had the Army of the Potomac following Lee's advance into the northern states, and Meade, if he was to lead with efficiency, needed to quickly gain important information from his commanders,. Meade had not been Lincoln's first choice to replace Hooker, in fact, there were four other Generals who outranked him at the time, including General John Reynolds. Lincoln had asked Reynolds to replace Hooker first, but the General had refused the appointment. Lincoln then turned to Meade, who had disagreed with Hooker's tactics at Chancellorsville.

Fearing that Lee was about to attack Harrisburg, and knowing that his army needed to be placed between Lee and the Capitol, Meade probed his Generals to gain the upper hand. The Army of the Potomac currently consisted of the following Corps and Commanders:

I Corps – under the command of Major General John Reynolds Corps – under the command of Major General Winfield Scott Hancock III Corps – under the command of Major General Daniel E. Sickles
V Corps – under the command of Major General George Sykes VI Corps – under the command of Major General John Sedgewick XI Corps – under the command of Major General Oliver Howard XII Corps – under the command of Major General Henry Slocum
The Calvary Corps – under the command of Major General Alfred Pleasonton

Also in attendance at the meeting were members of Meade's general staff, including Chief of Staff, Major General Daniel Butterfield and the Chief of Engineers, Brigadier General Gouverneur Warren.

There was a mixture of animosity and relief in the room. Several of these senior officers had publically denounced the actions of General Hooker, most especially General s Slocum and Howard – although they could also find an easy ally in General Pleasonton, whose nature was that of a self-promoter and complainer. On the other hand, several of the Generals harbored a bit of resentment toward Meade, having witnessed his meteoric rise to the head of the army – some being passed over for the position. Meade was well aware that he was conducting a war council in a room filled with superegos.

Meade was first to address the assemblage. "Gentlemen –the President is aware of General Lee's movements north. It is his fear that the Army of Northern Virginia will continue to move northward through Maryland

and into Pennsylvania, thus beginning a second invasion of the northern states."

"It would be my opinion, George," observed Reynolds, "that Lee's ultimate goal is the capture of the Capitol."

"Perhaps Baltimore, too," added Sykes. "That would add to his momentum a great deal. That city has given Lincoln a hard time ever since he took office."

"Yes, I agree," answered Meade, "but at this present time we do not know the whereabouts of Lee's army. We do know that he has split his army into several large columns, but they seem to be wandering about in Western Maryland. Our Intelligence tells us that his army is in desperate need of certain items; his army is almost barefoot – so I would think he will take advantage of his invasion to re-equip his divisions."

"Granted," said Hancock, "but we all know General Lee. He doesn't move his army without a solid plan in place…"

"…And he seems to always find the high ground," added Howard. "Just once…just once…I would like to face Lee on the high ground." Howard turned his attention to General Warren, the Chief of Engineers, when he said this.

Warren returned Howard's statement with an icy stare. "General…I may only build defenses with what I am given by the Commander in the Field at the time."

"Gentlemen," interrupted Meade, "there is no need to debate this point. General Burnside was an expert Engineer…perhaps a better engineer than a field General…and this fact did not prevent the overwhelming defeat at Fredericksburg. Lee has outmaneuvered this army time and time again. If he manages to do so this time, I fear that he will move on the Capitol. Those of us who know Lee well know that he is no seeker of glory for himself; he seeks the end of the war."

"Were he only fighting on our side," added General Sedgewick. Sedgewick, perhaps the most senior of the officers present, at least in years, was a close, personal friend of Robert E. Lee. Lee's decision to resign his commission in the United States Army rather than take the role which Abraham Lincoln had offered him – the overall command of the Army of the Potomac – had been based upon his reluctance to take up arms against his home state of Virginia.

Many of the officers present nodded agreement at Sedgewick's remark, but that did nothing to change the tone of the meeting. "Lee has expertly made use of Jeb Stuart's Calvary Corps," observed General Pleasonton. "Those southerners have wonderful horses! If I had horses half a good as theirs, we would not be whipped at their hands over and over."

Meade quickly answered his brash new Corps Commander. "General Pleasonton…I am happy to see that you recognize this obvious strength in General Lee's command. Your first duty as Corps Commander of the Calvary is to track down General Stuart. You are to engage the General and his troops whenever and wherever possible, thus preventing him from providing Lee with valuable information – especially of the whereabouts of this army."

Pleasonton smiled at Meade and nodded.

"Furthermore," Meade continued, "you are not to engage or attack the main body of the infantry. Make sure that you tell your Brigade Commanders of my wishes. You are to keep Stuart occupied so that he cannot become Lee's eyes and ears."

"This is a good plan, George," added Reynolds. "Stuart has been giving Lee some very valuable information for many a battle. If we separate Stuart from Lee, he will be wandering around blind."

"I have taken steps to assist in this process, General Meade," the overly confident Pleasonton added. "I have just replaced or promoted several new Brigade Commanders within my Corps. I think that they will bring a great deal more aggressive behavior to our calvary."

"Please see that this is so, General," answered Meade. Meade was also knowledgeable of Pleasonton's own political leanings. He knew that he was connected within Washington circles, and that he had powerful relatives who were eagerly watching the young officer's career. But Meade wanted to control Pleasonton, and his actions. He recognized that, unlike the attributes given to Robert E. Lee, that Pleasonton was in the war for personal glory.

General Sickles, who had become more and more agitated with the proceedings of the meeting, now spoke up. "General Meade…are you saying that the purpose of this army is not to engage the enemy?"

Meade had been expecting a confrontation with Sickles, especially because of the General's friendship with Hooker. Meade also knew that he had several very strong supporters of his own within the room, including Sedgewick, Hancock, and Reynolds. He returned the barb issued by Sickles. "Daniel…I am not saying that we will not engage the enemy, but I am stating unequivocally that we must engage the enemy on terms of our choosing. Perhaps you are, as a less experienced field officer, less prudent about making these decisions, but there are still those in this room who are certainly able to do so, and without endangering the precious lives that make up our army."

Stickles bristled at Meade's reply. It had been a two-pronged attack; first on his own ability as a General, as second – on that of his friend, Joe Hooker. "You insult me, George!" he replied, his face red with indignation. "Everyone in this room knows that you rose from Brigade Commander to Corps Commander without much proof of combat experience. You are, like Burnside, an engineer, are you not? Other, more senior officers, were passed over by Lincoln before you were given this command."

Meade looked indifferently at Sickles, allowing him to hang himself with his own words, if need be. The other members of the staff merely looked down, uncomfortably avoiding being drawn into this inevitable battle of wits.

Sickles turned to General Reynolds. "John…you should have been the logical man to replace Joe. Didn't Lincoln offer it to you?"

Reynolds looked up at Sickles. "He did…and I turned him down." The other officers in the room seemed startled by this revelation, with the exception of General Meade, but including Daniel Sickles. "You seem surprised, Dan! Didn't you get that information from your friend, Stanton?" Reynolds was referring to the Secretary of War, Edwin Stanton, who was also connected to Sickles, under most peculiar circumstances. "I was first approached by the President after I had contacted him, complaining of the way that Hooker had run the army." Reynolds watched Sickles face drop as he revealed, for the first time to all present, that he, too, had voiced his displeasure in Hooker's command. "Lincoln's response was to offer me the job, but I also had my own codicil in mind. I told him that I would assume command, providing he gave me a free hand to run the war; that he, and Stanton, and even General Halleck should allow me complete control over this army – without interference from someone sitting behind a desk in Washington."

Sickles bristled at this statement again, for if that was the case, why hadn't his old friend, Stanton, persuaded Lincoln to offer to position to him?

"I suggested that George would make a fine commander, mainly because I know he is capable of riding this team of hotheads and blending them into a fine, unified body. In order to do this, Dan, we must all follow his orders…without exception." Reynolds was referring to the incident at Chancellorsville, in which Sickles had not followed Hooker's command, but rather tried to strike out on his own. The result was that his III Corps actually placed Howard's Corps in a vulnerable position, which allowed Confederate General, Thomas "Stonewall" Jackson to capitalize on the mistake.

Sickles now chose to keep his mouth shut, realizing that his allies in the room were very few.

Meade cleared his throat, wishing to put himself back in control of the meeting. "And on that note, Gentlemen, I must also mention to you that Thomas Jackson also fell in that battle."

"What?" asked General Slocum, the youngest General in the room. He was only thirty six years old.

"We have ascertained only today that General Jackson was shot by his own men; a victim of crossfire. He died yesterday from his wounds." Several of the Generals looked truly saddened by the news, for even though Jackson was the enemy, as well as a fearsome opponent, he had also been one of their friends.

"I do not wish to seem insensitive," mentioned General Howard, whose Corps had been most hurt by the fallen leader, "but Jackson's loss may also turn to our advantage. There will be a new Division Commander."

"I agree with you, Oliver," answered Meade, "which is why we must act quickly...but with caution. Our best plan would allow us to trap Lee's army in the North, where we can cut his supply lines and force him to surrender. That action would go a long way to help us end this damned war."

CHAPTER 3

The Same Day

By eleven o'clock in the morning of June 28, Rebecca Tilden had already finished her morning chores. The Tilden home was located on the uppermost end of the Emmitsburg Pike. At a little more than seventeen years old, Rebecca was already an accomplished seamstress, having learned the craft from her mother, Mary Elizabeth. Living within the closely knit buildings of the little town, instead of on the outskirts as part of the agrarian community, had afforded some residents the opportunity to augment the family income with small bits of commissioned work – and Mary Elizabeth and Rebecca were among the most sought-after creators of fine ladies' dresses in the area. Without a doubt, most of their work was a result of the female population of the town proper, as most of the women living on the adjacent farms were still quite handy with a needle and thread.

Rebecca gathered up her sewing basket, bade good-bye to her mother, and set off for her morning appointment – a little home just around the corner, on Baltimore Street. It was there that she planned to meet up with her good friend and fellow seamstress, Virgina Wade, as the two were working on a series of ladies dresses, with the thought of opening a dress shop somewhere in the town. Virginia, or "Ginnie," as she liked to be called, was at twenty years of age Rebecca's senior, but had been a good friend to Rebecca for many years, having grown up in close proximity.

Ginnie was now living at the McClellan house, the home of her sister, Georgia McClellan, who was expecting the birth of her first child at any time. This temporary move proved even more convenient for the two friends, as it had brought Ginnie even closer to Rebecca's front door. Ginnie was engaged to be married to a soldier fighting in the Union Army, Corporal Jack Skelly, but she was unaware of his whereabouts on that late day in June. Rather than allow her friend to design and create her dress for her wedding, Rebecca had offered to do this for her – with Ginnie's careful and meticulous eye lending some experienced advice every once and a while.

Rebecca walked with a quick and deliberate step. She was anxious to get to work on Ginnie's gown, almost as if it was her own. She approached the small side door of the McClellan house and rapped twice on the frame.

"Come in," answered a female voice from within. Rebecca lifted the latch and pushed the door inward. Ginnie and Georgia were both working in the kitchen, which was just inside the doorway. Rebecca had not seen Georgia for the last few visits and was immediately taken back by how much larger and rounder she appeared. Rebecca let out an audible gasp at the sight. "Now don't you even say it, Becky Tilden," Georgia admonished, seeing the expression on the young girl's face, "this is how we all look when the time for our deliverance draws near. Someday… you will look this way, as well."

"I apologize, Georgia," Rebecca replied. "I meant no harm. It's just that I haven't seen you for more than a month…"

"I am just joking with you, Becky," Georgia answered with a smile. "I know I must look a sight!"

Rebecca turned to the right and greeted her partner. "Hello, Ginnie."

"Hello, Becky," Ginnie answered. "Georgia is just about ready to burst. The baby should come any day now."

"You must be very excited, Georgia," Rebecca said, once again returning her attention to the older sister.

"Excited," she answered, "and terrified. That's why I invited Ginnie to come stay here with me. We have a midwife for the delivery, but I want a familiar face with me, as well."

Rebecca nodded, but secretly knew that she would not wish to be in Georgia's position. The entire notion of giving birth frightened her, almost to the point that she did not ever want to be in that situation. She moved to the small table that sat adjacent to the kitchen and began to unpack her sewing tools. Ginnie, too, was now moving away from the kitchen in order to fetch the dress which the two had been working on. But Rebecca's mind was still on the impending birth. "Georgia…pardon me for asking a question like this…all things considered, but….aren't you a bit concerned about bringing a new life into this world, especially with this war going on?"

"Concerned?" Georgia asked. "What is there to be concerned about, dear, other than the birth itself?"

"I was just thinking," Rebecca answered, gauging her words, "that it must be even more frightening to be bringing a new life into the world, when there is so much hostility around us."

"Life goes on, Rebecca," Georgia patiently answered. "Besides…the war is being fought in the South. It is miles and miles from here, so there's nothing more to worry about."

"I suppose you're right," answered Rebecca.

"Let's not talk about the war," interrupted Ginnie. "Instead…let's talk about the celebration of our independence….and the ball. It's only a few days away, you know."

"Not really a great year to celebrate," answered Georgia. "The country is so divided, and our army has been badly beaten over and over."

"But still," persevered Ginnie, "we need a little distraction from these problems; don't we?"

"And how are you so distracted, Ginnie ?" her sister asked. "What with Jack away fightin' for Lincoln, who are you going to dance with…even if you go?"

"I would not dance with anyone, Georgia," Ginnie replied, "I would just go to listen to the music."

"Nonsense!" exclaimed Georgia. "And what about you, Miss Becky?"

"Me?" an astonished Rebecca asked. "Why would I consider going to the silly ball? I don't have a suitor. Besides, I am only seventeen years old!"

"Just!" interjected Ginnie.

"Just seventeen," agreed Rebecca. "I have yet to find one of these Gettysburg rabble to be to my liking. I am holding out for a real gentleman."

"That's the spirit, Becky," assured Georgia, "but let us hope that the cream of the crop are not mown down in this futile war before you get your chance to pick one."

Rebecca and Ginnie worked on the wedding gown for two hours, all the while cheerfully gossiping about some of the other young ladies of the town, not to mention the upcoming 4th of July Gala. It was almost two thirty in the afternoon when Rebecca suddenly put her sewing down.

"Lord, I almost forgot! Mother wanted me to go to the market for some turnips!"

"You've got time, Becky," Ginnie answered. "The market is still open for hours."

"Yes," Rebecca replied, "the market is open, but Mother needs time to clean them, peel them, and cook them for our dinner tonight. I can't simply show up at five o'clock with a handful of raw turnips, now can I?" She started to put her shears back into her basket.

"I suppose not," answered Ginnie. "Can you come over again tomorrow?" "I think so. Yes, that is for sure."

Rebecca stood up, ready to head for the door. Ginnie also stood, but gave her younger friend a hug. "Thank you for coming today, Becky. We are making some real progress here."

"You're welcome, Ginnie. I will see you tomorrow."

Rebecca Tilden left the McClellan house and turned right on Baltimore Street, walking along the rough path until it again intersected with the Emmitsburg Pike.

She still had several streets to cross before arriving at the market, so she hastened her steps.

Her parents, John and Mary Elizabeth Baker Tilden, had moved to their present home on the Pike just after Rebecca was born, on July 15, 1846. It had been a difficult birth, and the doctor had cautioned Mary Elizabeth about having any future children; but they loved Rebecca – or "Becky," as she was affectionately known – unconditionally, as good parents should love their own. Becky was devoted to her mother, and had been a big help to her around the house, even from the time she was just a young girl.

Rebecca did have one secret longing, however. She most desperately wanted to see a big city, such as Philadelphia or New York. She had seen Harrisburg, but had left that city feeling somewhat let down by the experience. She had heard so much more about the big, new cities of the country, and Harrisburg – well, that just was not what she had heard.

She also longed for a proper education, even though she understood that, as a female, this was not likely to happen; only young men were permitted to attend a college or university.

Rebecca Tilden had reached the market. The area in front of the store front was filled with crates, barrels and other containers for holding the fresh farm produce. She quickly moved around the crates, looking for the object of her search – the turnips. The market was still very busy, even for this late in the day. Most of the produce arrived in the early morning, but some was delivered in the early afternoon, as it was often harvested during the mid-morning hours.

Rebecca could see the crate holding the turnips just to the right of the store front. A young man – or was it a boy? – was still in the process of delivering a fresh supply to the stand. Rebecca felt this was a good sign. Even if she was a little late in bringing the bulbous vegetable home to her mother, she could at least claim that the turnips were the very freshest to be had that day. She noticed that the farmer, or his son, was still in the process of removing the long, thin taproot from the bottom of the turnip bulb. The young man was using a small, sharp knife to accomplish this, cutting off the root and then carefully laying each individual turnip on the crate.

Rebecca reached over the crate to examine the turnip that had just been placed there. As she reached over the stand, the young man started to place the next turnip on the crate. As she reached in the lift the turnip, she inadvertently grabbed the top of his hand. In that brief moment, she thought that she was lifting a turnip, not a human hand – but then the reality of the situation became apparent. Not letting go of the hand, which was covered with grime from cleaning and paring the turnips, she looked up the arm, her eyes climbing further up until she looked into the stranger's face.

He had a very surprised look on his face, too.

"Oh!" Rebecca emoted.

"I am sorry," said the young man. "I could have cut you with my knife." "I am sorry, too," Rebecca answered. "I mistook your hand for a turnip." "An easy thing to do, I'm afraid," he answered. "Both the turnips and my hand are covered in dirt." And then he gave a short, dry laugh.

Rebecca looked a little more carefully at the young man. He seemed to be just a boy, perhaps the same age as she – maybe just a bit older – perhaps. But she did not recognize him, and that was odd, because she knew most of the people in the small town of Gettysburg.

She decided to be bold. "Are you from around here?" "Oh yes," he answered. "I live over by the seminary." "By the seminary?" she asked. "Are you a seminarian?"

"Me?" The young man gave the same dry laugh again. "I just live there." "You live at the seminary, and yet you are not a seminarian. Are you a minister?"

The boy laughed at this…twice. "I'm only eighteen years old!" Then the boy realized that he might have just insulted the attractive young lady and added, "No, nothing as grand as that. My father is the caretaker of the property, and my mother raises the vegetables in the garden. We sell whatever extra we have at the market."

"And you have lived in Gettysburg for a long time?"

"No," he answered, shaking his head, "only about two years."

"I'm sorry," she said, finally letting go of the boy's hand, "I have been prying into your personal life. It's just that…well, I thought that I knew just about everybody in this town…and now I have just met someone new to me."

"Don't apologize! Please!" The young man said, straightening up. "It is I who have forgotten my manners. I am Jacob….Jacob Zook; Son of Ishmael and Sarah Zook. It is a pleasure to make your acquaintance."

Rebecca once again reached forward and took the young man's hand, this time to shake it, warmly. "And my name is Rebecca Tilden. I live just down the way, right on Steinwehr. I am very pleased to meet you, Jacob." Rebecca then let go of his hand. "And we are just about the same age, you and I." And then Rebecca blushed, realizing that a young woman's age is always meant to be a matter of great privacy.

"So…um…you like turnips, I suppose," Jacob asked.

"Actually….no…I don't, really….but my father loves them." But then she added, "I'm sorry."

"Don't be sorry, Rebecca," he replied, smiling a broad grin, "I don't really like them, either. I much prefer potatoes." At that moment, Jacob felt a hand on his shoulder. Looking to the side quickly, he discovered that his brother, Abraham, had finished putting his share of the produce out at the market.

"Are you not ready yet, Jakob?" the boy inquired, somewhat annoyed.

"In a moment, Abraham," Jacob stalled. "Can you not see that I am busy with this young lady?"

"Is this one of your 'English' friends, Jakob?" the younger boy asked, his voice rising with anticipation and curiosity.

"Abraham…this is Rebecca Tilden," replied Jacob, "and, no, I have just had the pleasure of meeting her for the first time just a few minutes ago…just in case you are preparing to make this known to Fati."

Abraham leaned forward and cast a jaundiced eye in the direction of Becky, ever suspicious that his older brother might be attempting to pull the wool over his eyes. "It is a pleasure, Fraülein," he said, greeting her with his best manners.

"Jakob…I am getting hungry. Are you almost ready to go?"

"You go ahead to the buggy, Abraham. I will be there shortly." Abraham gave Rebecca another suspicious glance and then walked away, heading toward the wagon.

"Younger brothers can be awful sometimes; can't they?" mentioned Rebecca, with a slight laugh in her voice. "I have a younger brother, too."

CHAPTER 4

The Day Continues

Rebecca hurried home, having purchased a great many of the turnips that had been placed in the crate by Jacob Zook. She entered her house through the door by the kitchen, placing the canvas bag containing the vegetables on the work table. Her mother, Mary Elizabeth, was already in the process of preparing the evening meal.

"It's about time you arrived home, Becky, "she said, without looking up from the pie crust she was rolling out. "I was beginning to worry."

"I'm sorry, Mama. I really didn't mean to spend so much time with Ginnie. I lost track of time."

"Did they have a good supply of turnips at the market, dear?" "More than enough, I would say."

Mary Elizabeth turned to face her daughter, her eyes immediately falling to the work table. "Rebecca! There are enough turnips there to last us a month!"

"I know, Mama….I must have lost my mind…but, well…we can put the excess in the root cellar, can't we?"

"Well…yes…but I don't know whatever possessed you to buy so many," her mother complained. "I do hope they were at a fair price."

"A very fair price, Mama," Rebecca replied, and then smiling at her mother, she left the kitchen and headed for her bedroom. Rebecca closed her bedroom door behind her, removing her bonnet in the same action. She found the basin on her dressing table and splashed some water on her face. "Gracious!" she mumbled to herself, feeling the warmth that was radiating from her cheeks. She couldn't imagine why she felt so flushed. She understood that it was almost ninety degrees in the sun, and that she had walked home at a quicker pace than usual – but this? This was something very different.

Rebecca sat down on the side of her bed. She started to think about that young man again…Jacob Zook. Just the mere thought of him made her tremble, and she felt a twisting sensation in the pit of her stomach. She wondered why that was, and what could be done to make it stop.

But she couldn't get the young man's face out of her mind. Even now, she was trying to recreate it, and she so hoped that her memory was accurate – that she wasn't improving on his looks with her own vivid imagination.

No, she thought – he really was that handsome! Jacob had a ruddy complexion, probably from a good deal of work in the sunlight. He had sparkling blue eyes, and light brown hair. No, she corrected herself, it was more of a blonde color…and she liked the way it fell over his brow. He definitely looked Germanic – or Scandinavian! His face was smooth – with not a sign of any facial hair. And she remembered his smile; his smile presented a full set of white teeth. She also recalled that the boy was not overly tall; he only stood a few inches taller than she. She also remembered how polite he was; that he wasn't coarse or rude in any way – which she valued a great deal.

She wondered if she would ever have the happenstance to see him again.

She hoped that she would have that chance.

Rebecca spent the next hour in her room, thinking about the boy while working on her needlepoint. On most evenings she would be downstairs, assisting her mother with the preparation of the family dinner – but her mother was cooking a stew, which required very little extra help, so after checking to see if her help was needed – and it was not – she returned to her needlepoint…and her thoughts.

A short time later, she heard her father enter the house. John Tilden owned a dry goods store which was located just a few doors down from their home. Rebecca put her needlepoint away, knowing, with her father now home for the evening, that dinner would be on the table imminently. She rushed downstairs to greet her father, as well as to help set the table for their meal.

John Tilden was a tall, thin, balding man in his mid-forties. He tended to be overly serious about many aspects of life, but more than anything else in the world, he was very serious about his only child – his daughter, Rebecca. Rebecca fairly skipped over the kitchen floor to hug her father, and he returned the gesture with a kiss, placed squarely on her forehead. John then removed his jacket and handed it to Rebecca. Rebecca couldn't imagine why her father thought it necessary to wear a jacket on a day close to ninety degrees, but she would never, ever question the logic of her father to his face.

Never!

The small family sat down and the table to eat their evening meal. In addition to the turnips which Rebecca had fetched earlier that day, the stew also contained chunks of pork, some carrots, beans, and a few bits of potato. Her mother had also baked bread earlier that morning, and they all used a slice, or two, to sop up the gravy-like liquid that filled the bottom of the plate.

When and only when, her father had consumed his first plateful, could the conversation at the table begin. Those were the rules.

"Becky?" her father began. "Did you get a chance to see Mrs. McClellan today?"

"Yes, father," she answered, without looking up from her dish. "She looks about ready to…deliver."

"Is that your official medical opinion?" he chided, quietly.

"I can tell some things, father," she returned, raising an eye in his direction. "I'm not a child, you know."

"Oh…I am most definitely aware of that fact, my dear." John turned to his wife. "The stew is particularly excellent this evening, Mary. What did you do differently, do you think?"

"Nothing, John," she answered gently. "You must simply be very hungry." "Perhaps," he replied, "but there is a very savory flavor in the mix." "Perhaps," interjected Rebecca, "it is because of the quality of your favorite vegetable."

"The turnips?" asked her father. "Is there something special about the turnips, Mary?"

"Not from my point of view, John," Mary Elizabeth replied, "but Rebecca may be of another opinion."

Tilden put his spoon down on the table and looked side to side; first at Mary Elizabeth, and then at Rebecca. "Something is not being said. Am I to be kept at odds with the dinner conversation? Tell me, Rebecca, what is so special about the turnips used in this stew?"

"Nothing, Father," she said quietly, but then added, "except that they were sold to me by a most charming young man."

Tilden once again looked at his wife, who returned his gaze by slowly nodding. "Mother…do you know about this?"

"I assumed as much, John. Rebecca never said a word about it until just now."

"Well, Mary," he continued, "it seems that our little girl has grown up."

"Let's not be so hasty to get her married off just yet," his wife answered.

"Married?" Rebecca asked, with a shocked tone in her voice. "Mother!"

"You never know, dear," she answered softly. "People have been known to do many a crazy thing when there is a war going on."

"I just met the young man today," Rebecca responded. "He did not propose marriage."

A quiet fell over the dinner table. Tilden picked up his spoon and took in another mouthful of stew. "And what, pray tell, is this young man's name?"

"His name is Jacob," replied Rebecca.

"Jacob?" Her father nodded, refilling his spoon again. "A good, strong Christian name! Does he have a last name?"

Rebecca paused. She was worried that her father might not recognize the name as being from one of the established families in the town. She knew that her father and mother were not concerned with social standing, but she did know that they were concerned with the upbringing of any potential suitor. "His last name is Zook. Jacob Zook. He lives over by the seminary."

"Zook?" asked her father, an incredulous look on his face.

"Is there something wrong, Father?"

"Zook! That's what's wrong, Rebecca!" His face began to redden. "I don't understand, Father. What is wrong with his name?" "Did he tell you anything about his family, Rebecca?"

"No..only that his father worked as the caretaker at the seminary." "Hm."

"Is there something wrong with that, Father?"

"Not at all," he answered quickly. "It's a very good, honest living." "Then what is it?" Rebecca asked.

Tilden pushed his chair back from the table – the usual signal that he had finished his dinner. But this was not usual; not at all. He had something on his mind, and at this point it was clear to see that it was not concerning dry goods. "Zook is one of the most common family names that you may find if you were to travel to Lancaster County." Mary Elizabeth let out a sigh, knowing immediately what her husband was to say. "Unless I am completely mistaken, your young man is a member of the Amish community."

"Amish?" Rebecca asked. "What is that?"

Her father got up from the table and walked about. Rebecca could tell that her father was measuring his words. "The Amish are a religious sect, Rebecca. They are a devout form of Christianity. They are very much tied to the past, and they live as if our modern times do not exist. They do not believe in paying taxes, nor do they believe that they should serve in our military. They usually live in very tight-knit communities, and many of them are in Lancaster County."

Rebecca listened quietly to what her father had to say. When he finished his description of the Amish, he looked over at Rebecca, as if to ask for her input on the matter. Rebecca wanted to ask her father what was wrong with any of the attributes he had just mentioned, but she decided to down play her optimism. "Except for the taxes and the military, I don't know if the rest sounds all that terrible, Father."

"I know, Rebecca," he answered, with a gentle tone in his voice. "I am trying very hard to be kind." He thought again, pacing once more around the kitchen. "Let me ask you this, Becky…What did your young man look like?"

"He is very handsome, Father."

"That is very nice, Rebecca, but that is not what I am asking. How was he dressed?"

"How was he dressed, Father?"

"Was he wearing a hat?"

"Yes, he was," she answered.

"What color was it? What did it look like?"

She tried to recall all of the details from the afternoon. She remembered his hat. "It was a wide-brimmed black hat, Father."

Her father nodded his head in a knowing way. "What did his shirt look like?" "It was white, Father."

"No," he interjected, "did it have hooks, or buttons?" "What?" she asked.

"Did it have hooks or buttons?" he repeated.

Rebecca closed her eyes, as if she could see the boy's shirt clearer that way. "It had buttons,, I believe…but I think the jacket he was wearing was fastened with hooks." She opened her eyes and looked back at her father. "Why?"

Tilden shook his head, as if this description was enough proof of his suspicions. "The Amish believe that buttons are "fancy," - that they display a frivolous and ostentatious nature. Hooks are considered "plain," which conforms better to their way of life." He thought a bit more. "Did he drive a buggy?"

Rebecca answered quickly, "Of course he did, Father. He had to bring the produce to market."

"What did the buggy look like?"

Rebecca became frustrated. "Father…it looked like a buggy." "Rebecca! Don't sass your father!" Her mother implored.

"I didn't mean anything by it, Mother! The buggy wasn't anything special!" Tilden put his hand up, as if to ask for silence. "Rebecca, you have much to learn about the ways of the world. No good can come out of a friendship with this young man, for even if the boy is willing to call upon you, his parents would certainly not allow it. You are young…not too young to consider a beau, but then again…too young to become serious with one – especially if it is destined to hurt you in the end. It would be best to put the young man out of your mind."

"But, Father...."

"Enough, Rebecca," her mother added. "Your father has spoken."

CHAPTER 5

At the same time...

Ishmael Zook sat at the head of the table, his wife Sarah at the foot. On his father's right side sat his first born, Jacob, and on the left sat his second born, Abraham.

Ishmael Zook was a large man, measuring over six foot in stature. He had a full head of wavy dark blonde hair, the color of which he had genetically passed on to his eldest son – and a full beard of the same color. He wore no mustache, which according to his tradition, the Ordnung, was forbidden.

His wife, Sarah, wore a plain black dress which was wrapped to fit around her body, then held together with straight pins. She wore a kerchief over her head. She was an attractive woman, although years of hard farm work had caused her to look many years older than her thirty five years.

In a manner similar to that of the Tilden household, there was only sparse conversation at the Zook dinner table. Both boys were well aware that the family's sudden departure from Paradise the previous year had caused strife within their small family; that there were topics that were not open to discussion at the dinner table, or anywhere else for that matter. Jacob knew a little more than his younger brother, Abraham – at least he understood some of the problems. He understood that his father was unhappy to be away from the rest of his family – and he also understood that his mother considered this to be largely her fault. But Jacob was very aware of the tension in the small household, moreover… he knew that there was very little he could do about it.

Even though they were now shunned by the community in Paradise, they continued to practice many of the "old ways" and to live by the Ordnung. Sarah had made quite a few sacrifices to ensure that these traditions would carry on, even though she was not obligated to follow these practices, as she was a follow of Menno Simons – a Mennonite. Her husband had been a disciple of the sect founded by Jakob Ammann, the followers of which had become known as the Amish. Both sects had been known in Europe, prior to fleeing because of religious persecution by the Roman Catholics and other Protestant sects, as Anabaptists, because of their controversial viewpoint that adult members of the community should be baptized, not infants and children. Early on in their history, there was only a single doctrine that governed that Anabaptists, but dissention arose within the ranks over a number of principles. Chief among the differences of opinions was the issue of shunning – the social chastisement of the unfaithful to the Ordnung – the Order. Those shunned were forced to live outside the community- often for the rest of their life. The Amish believed in and practiced shunning – the Mennonites did not.

Ishmael Zook had been shunned by the Paradise Amish community. This shunning automatically extended to his wife, who was not a member of the community in the first place and therefore really didn't matter, even though she represented the reason for the shunning – as well as their offspring, which was currently represented by Jacob and Abraham. In the eyes of the Amish community, the boys were not born in a manner expressed in the Ordnung, even though they had been raised since birth following those principals. This made the shunning even more intolerable to everyone in the Zook family.

But the boys still didn't understand it.

Even after only a year in seclusion from the community, Jacob found his role in his family untenable and unexplainable. He did not understand why they had to continue the masquerade; if they were Amish that was one thing – but according to the Amish they were not…so why not simply adapt and move in a new direction?

This was a source of contention between Jacob and his father, Ishmael. Jacob felt that there would come a time when he would be forced to make a break from the family, if only for his own sanity. There were many days when he considered running away, but he could never actually bring himself to do it. He felt that he would be hurting his mother too greatly – and he also wanted to take his brother with him, and Abraham was still just a little more than a child.

Even still, living in Gettysburg had opened his eyes even more to the ways of the world. He was a smart young man, and could read and write in two languages – but any furtherance of his education was thwarted, and that was very difficult to swallow, especially in a little town which offered both the Lutheran Seminary and Gettysburg College. Now that they were out of Lancaster County, Jacob was continually frustrated to be forced to witness these other possibilities, knowing that he was being raised to become the next generation of his Amish father. Even an acquaintance of his, a young man who had assisted the family when they had first settled in Gettysburg, a man named Wesley Culp, had taken the opportunity to strike out and make a name for himself by moving to Virginia to learn more about the leather trade. Wesley's family owned a large farm in the area – a large farm which contained one of the topographical features of the area – Culp's Hill.

And then there was another thing....

...It was that girl. The girl he had just met this afternoon.

Jacob was of the notion, as of late, that it was time to go exploring; and he knew that the only way he was going to be able to explore any part of the country – outside of the small town of Gettysburg – was by taking a very drastic step.

He took another bite of his mother's schnitzel and took the first step on his irreversible course. "Fati?"

"Yes, Jacob," his father replied.

"How old were you when you and Muti were married?"

"This is a strange question, Jacob… one, by the way, that you already know the answer to."

"I am just curious, Papa….can't you tell me?"

Ishmael sat back in his chair, carefully eying his first-born. "I was eighteen years old. Your mother was seventeen."

Jacob nodded to himself, now aware that another question would quickly follow.

"Why do you ask, Jacob? Are you planning on getting married?"

His mother seemed to pale significantly as she listened to the conversation, but she held her tongue.

"What if I said 'yes' to that question, Papa?"

"Then I would say that you were asking the impossible, Jacob" "Why is it impossible, Papa?"

"Why?" Ishmael's voice quickly rose in pitch. "It is impossible because there are no other young women who follow the Ordnung in this town. Who could you possibly marry?"

"Why must I marry a woman within our community, Papa?" Jacob knew that it was already too late to turn back, so he decided to just forge ahead. "Look what happened to you and to Mother!"

"Jacob!" His mother gasped.

Ishmael remained unusually calm, under the circumstances, and spoke quietly to his son. "Jacob…it is my hope that we may…one day… return to our home in Paradise."

Abraham looked up front the table. "Really, Fati? When shall we be going?" "Not yet, Abraham," the father replied. "We shall go back when they summon us."

"Yes," answered Jacob, sarcasm in his voice, "when they summon us. That day may never come, Papa!"

"That is not for us to decide! That is for the council!"

"The council?" snapped Jacob. "Look at the people of this town, Papa. They don't listen to a council, and yet they are good people in spite of that. They are religious, too. You know that for yourself. You see it every day at the seminary. Does it really matter if they are not plain folks?"

"Jacob, I have been listening patiently to you…because you are almost a man, and soon it will be your right to express yourself – but I must remind you that you should be aware that you are speaking to your father."

"I know that, Papa," the boy replied, "and if I have offended you in any way I would much rather cut off one of my fingers than live with that offense, but…Fati…We are very unhappy living like this!"

"It is God's will, my son."

Jacob sat back in his chair and muttered to himself, "free will."

"You are only eighteen years old, Jacob. You have plenty of time to find your helpmate."

Jacob wanted to end this battle, but he also wanted to win it. "And what would you say if I told you that I already have met this girl?" The question caused Abraham to drop his fork onto his plate, as the events of the day flew back into his memory.

Ishmael leaned forward in his chair and looked directly into his son's eyes. "I would tell you to abandon this folly. If you were to take steps to find a girl outside of the Ordnung, then I would say to you that you would be shunned from this family."

CHAPTER 6

June 29, 1863

General Daniel Sickles had caught back up with his Corps, bringing with him the orders that would bring his III Corps into close proximity to Lee's army. Meade had ordered his Corps Commanders to move their divisions between the Confederate army and Harrisburg, but to avoid any engagement with the enemy until all of the army was in place. Meade also was relying on the fact that Lee's army was tired, having marched into Pennsylvania all the way from Richmond. Meade ignored the fact that his own army would be equally as exhausted, because they would now have to close the distance between themselves and the rebel army by marching – and they would need to cover distances of up to forty miles a day in order to do this.

Sickles dismounted his horse and walked to his command tent. He sent his orderly to find his Division Commanders, Major General David Birney and Brigadier General Andrew Humphreys. Stickles, never a quiet man, and certainly not one to take insult lightly, was still angry over the dialog at the meeting.

Humphreys was the first to arrive, along with the commander of his first brigade, Brigadier General Joseph Carr. Sickles had taken the opportunity afforded by the time alone in the tent to dig out a bottle of whiskey from a foot locker, as well as about six small glasses. He filled several of the glasses with the liquid. When Humphreys and Carr arrived at the tent, Sickles handed each man a glass of whiskey, but asked them not to drink until the other Division commanders arrived. This happened only moments later, when Major General Birney arrived with Brigade commanders Brigadier Generals Charles Graham and Hobart Ward. Birney had the duty of acting as second in command of III Corps. Stickles also handed each of the newly arrived officers a glass of the whiskey, and then raised his own.

"Gentlemen," he said, enacting a toast, "to Major General George Meade – the new Commander of the Army of the Potomac."

"General?" asked Birney. It had been a matter of debate over the new man in charge, but Meade's name had not even been suggested as a remote possibility.

"You heard me, Dave….it's Meade! Can you believe it?"

"What are our orders, Dan?" asked Humphreys.

"First order….drink your whiskey….remember, it's to General Meade…God help him!"

The men inside the command tent all repeated the same salutation, "To General Meade!" and then downed the amber liquid in one gulp.

"Now," barked Sickles, "ready your troops. We move immediately to the West to intercept Lee's army. Meade thinks that his target is Harrisburg. If he is correct in this assumption, then Lee will attempt to disrupt the railroad lines that converge there. But Meade also believes that Lee has a larger goal in mind."

"The Capitol?" asked Birney.

"It does make sense, doesn't it? Lee is a practical man, and he knows that there aren't many new southern boys gonna join his army too soon.

His only hope in winning this war is to make it even more unpopular than it is right now."

"Lee's army is still pretty big, Dan. I think he still has close to a hundred thousand marching with him, "remarked Graham.

"Yes," answered Sickles, pouring himself another glass of whiskey, "I do believe you are correct, General. But I happen to know that the Union has an almost unending supply of new recruits. We get thousands more every day – every time a ship lands in New York Harbor. Most of them are dirt poor Irish immigrants – but they are a hard-fighting lot, and we are signing them up as soon as they walk off the boat from Europe."

"That is…almost unbelievable, Dan," responded Humphreys. "Unbelievable…but true, I can assure you of that. I spent quite a bit of time working for the political boss up there in New York…a fellow named Tweed. He, more than any other man, helped get me these stars. Yes sir, men….the rebs are fighting the fight right now, but they cannot withstand a few good losses, so I am telling you right now…if George Meade can deliver a battle plan…if he is the man for the job…then we need to follow him…to the death. But if I see that he is being cautious…like McClellan was for almost two years….then I will strike out as my duty calls."

"Here, Here!" said Ward.

Sickles passed the bottle around again, allowing the officers to get another drink, while he, himself, took a third drink. Having done this, the men departed for their brigades in a hurried manner, knowing that they had a great deal of territory to cover by the end of the day.

Daniel Edgar Sickles was an interesting man. In addition to his political scheming, he was also an appointed and elected official, having served as an Ambassador to England, and in the State Senate of New York and the House of Representatives in Washington.

In 1859, just two years before the outbreak of the Civil War, Stickles murdered Washington District Attorney Philip Barton Key in front of Stickles own home on Lafayette Square. Key, who was also the son of the author of "The Star-Spangled Banner," Francis Scott Key, was having an affair with Sickles young wife, Teresa. Sickles, himself, had already been unfaithful to his wife, having taken up with a notorious prostitute, Fanny White, who had been brought to England and even presented at the Court of Queen Victoria. In any event, Sickles tracked the whereabouts of Key for several days, and then ambushed him in front of the Sickle residence, brandishing two revolvers. He shot Key some five times, including the coup de grace, which was a point blank shot in the chest. The attack followed a confession given by Sickles' wife, detailing the extent of the affair. The shooting was witnessed by at least twelve people. Sickles was immediately arrested on the charge of first degree murder.

But then, in a twist of fate, Edwin Stanton, who was on the staff of then President James Buchanan, decided to defend Sickles' actions, and made history by entering the first-ever plea of 'temporary insanity.' The trial achieved national notoriety, and popular opinion swung in favor of Sickles, who was viewed by many as simply defending the honor of his wife. In truth, the affair between Key and Teresa had gone on for over five years.

Now alone in the command tent, Sickles packed up his whiskey and glasses. He opened the flap of the large tent and walked outside. Sickles was in the army to repair his damaged reputation, but he was also in it to advance his own political causes.

Edwin Stanton, his former defense attorney – now Secretary of War under Abraham Lincoln – had made much of this possible. This was still an era that allowed for the rich and well connected to achieve battlefield glory as members of the senior staff. Sickles had definitely contributed to the war effort, and he was rewarded with a Generalship, first one star… and now two. Sickles had gone from a vilified murderer in 1859, to a leader of thousands of men in 1863. But Daniel Sickles was hungry for even more…

War…and the opportunity for glory on the battlefield, can sometimes propel someone, properly placed, into national prominence. Daniel Sickles hoped to be prepared, should that opportunity present itself.

CHAPTER 7

June 29, continued

Jacob Zook did not take his father's advice. He already felt disenfranchised, having suffered through the embarrassment of expulsion from the Amish community in Paradise just a little more than a year prior. He could not understand his father's loyalty to 'those people,' but he also could not understand why his father would also choose to alienate his own wife the way he did. He could have just as easily moved the family into a Mennonite community, where they would have been accepted very graciously. But, as Jacob well knew, his father was a stubborn man. Even though he and his family had been shunned by the Amish community, Ishmael had not given up hope that they would be able to return... someday.

Jacob felt this was an insult upon the family honor, and couldn't understand why his father did not share that opinion. And the fact that Ishmael had threatened his own son with shunning was proof enough to Jacob that his father had learned very little from his own experience. Clearly, Jacob thought, it was time to leave.

The only question remaining in Jacob's mind was....when he would do it.

This was not an easy decision to make; Jacob felt sorry for his brother, Abraham, and the problems that his leaving could cause for him, but he was mostly worried about his mother.

The young man decided to sleep on his decision. Things always seemed a little better in the light of a new day. But nothing had really changed when the boy awoke on the morning of June 29. His father was already working in the barn, and, even though Jacob had not slept past the crow of the rooster, his father made him feel that he was neglecting his duty to the family.

He really wanted to speak to someone about the problem, and early that afternoon went to seek the advice of Reverend Meier, one of the Lutheran ministers who taught at the seminary. Jacob liked the young minister – he was not like any of the holy men he had known in Paradise. He was clean-shaven, even though he was a married man. (Amish men always grow their beard out after they marry) He was also aware that Reverend Meier enjoyed talking to him – especially about his former people. Most people he met always found his past to be fascinating; the Amish were a curious and fascinating people.

But the good reverend was not to be found that day, so Jacob, his chores and responsibilities concluded for the day, did exactly which he was instructed not to do; he set off for the town, on foot, to seek out the young lady he had met on the previous day.

Jacob first stopped at the market in the fleeting hope that Rebecca Tilden would once again have fresh vegetables to purchase. She was not there. Feeling a bit downhearted, Jacob left the market and headed out onto the Pike, walking slowly and deliberately, his eyes darting from here to there, vainly searching for the young lady.

He crossed the dirt road to the other side of the street, turning a bit to the left when it intersected with Baltimore Street. He wondered if this street would actually take him all the way to the metropolis of Baltimore

– one of the oldest and largest cities in the country. He knew that the Emmitsburg Pike would take him to

Emmitsburg, Maryland – but Jacob really didn't have any desire to go there. Baltimore sounded like a wonderful destination – and about as far away from his father and the Amish as any boy could want to be. He knew that he could begin a life of his own in that big city – and he also knew that, wherever he might go, even if it were only to Emmitsburg, his father would never follow after him or search for him in any way.

He knew that his father would have dismissed him as…dead.

Jacob started walking up the slight incline that had started as soon as he stepped onto Baltimore Street. He continued to look for his young lady, but he also realized that she had mentioned that she lived on the Emmitsburg Pike, so he was, in fact, moving further away from where she lived. He wondered if he really could do it – could he just keep walking and not looking back?

Suddenly he heard a rapping. He glanced around quickly, looking for the source of the noise. The rapping continued, and it sounded… urgent. Jacob looked up the street and back down, but saw no one that appeared to be making the noise.

And then he heard it again.

It was the sound of someone rapping on a window sill. He turned to his left. He saw a small wooden framed house, and there, standing by a window…was Rebecca Tilden.

She was rapping on the window to him.

Jacob raised his hand and waved to the young lady, a broad smile appearing on his face.

But Rebecca was not smiling back, in fact, she looked frantic. Jacob shrugged his shoulders to her, as if to ask 'what do you need?' Rebecca responded by holding up an index finger – a tacet sign that he should not move an inch.

He waited patiently for her to emerge from the house. Rebecca breathlessly joined him outside of the house a few moments later.

"Hello, Rebecca," he said, still smiling broadly at her.

But Becky Tilden was not in the mood for pleasantries. "Jacob! I am sorry, but I am desperate! You live on a farm....do you know anything about birthing?"

"Birthing?"

"Jacob! Listen to me!" Jacob was a bit put off- not understanding the situation. This was not the capricious girl which he had met just yesterday. She seemed close to hysterics. "Have you ever assisted in the birthing of an animal?"

"Yes, Rebecca," he said, still wearing a bit of a smile, "but they can usually handle it pretty well all by themselves."

"No," she replied quickly, "you don't understand. My friend's sister, Mrs. McClellan, has gone into labor. The midwife was supposed to come, but she is busy birthing another baby across town. Georgia seems to be having a difficult time, and we don't know exactly how to help her."

"Gott in Himmel!" stated a shocked Jacob. "Did you send for the doctor?" "He can't come, either...and my Mama is not to be found. Can you help us?" "I don't know, Rebecca," Jacob replied. "I have witnessed a few animal births, but I never actually helped out."

"Please! Come with me!" she pleaded. Jacob took her hand and walked her back into the small house. Rebecca led the boy to the bedroom, where Georgia McClellan was lying on the bed, in obvious discomfort. Her sister, Ginnie, was cooling her forehead with a wet rag. "This is Jacob. This is the boy I was telling you about. I met him yesterday. He lives on a farm. Maybe he can help."

"I am not sure that I can help, M'am," he offered.

"Please..." hoarsely whispered Georgia.

"Alright," he agreed. "How long has her labor been going on?" "Since early this morning," answered Ginnie.

"I'm not sure, but I think that sounds like it's too long," he observed. "Can you feel where the baby is?"

"What do you mean?" asked Rebecca.

"Can you tell if it is coming out head first, or feet first?" "What should it be doing?" questioned Ginnie.

"Head first, and facing down toward the floor…otherwise….it's a big problem."

"How can I tell?" asked Ginnie.

"You've got to…," he paused, not knowing the right way to explain this procedure.

"Yes?" asked Rebecca.

"You've got to put your hand up inside her and feel around a bit," he said quickly.

"What?"

"If you feel the head, then you just have to wait it out, but if you feel a foot, then….well I don't know, Rebecca….I'm not a doctor, you know."

"I know….I know," replied Rebecca. "Ginnie….can you do that?"

"I don't know, Becky."

Rebecca was flustered. She turned to Jacob, "Can you do it?" "Me?"

"Jacob…answer me this…can the baby die if it is in the wrong position?" He nodded. "Can Georgia….well…you know?" He again nodded. "Then I suggest that

you do this, because you are the only one here who knows what to do." Jacob nodded.

He slowly approached the bed. Georgia was lying flat on her back, with her head slightly raised on a pillow. Her legs were just slightly spread apart, but she was still wearing her skirt. She watched the boy approach her, her eyes filled with terror – not of the boy, but of the other possibilities. Jacob began to lift the skirt back, but turned his head away, as if he would be able to perform this examination without looking.

Her skirt was already above her knees when a voice came booming from behind them. "What in heaven's name is going on in here?"

It was Mary Elizabeth Tilden.

"Mama!" cried Rebecca, running to her arms.

Jacob froze, still holding the hem of the skirt in his right hand, but looking fearfully at the angry woman that was standing just a few feet away.

"Who are you, young man?" she demanded.

"I…I…" he stammered.

"This is Jacob, Mother," Rebecca said. "This is the young man I spoke about yesterday."

"And what is he doing with Miss Georgia's skirt, might I ask?"

"I asked him to help out, Mama. Georgia is in trouble, and we couldn't get the doctor."

"Trouble?" asked Mary Elizabeth, who quickly moved to the side of the bed, but not before slapping the skirt out of Jacob's hand. "You two wait in the kitchen. Ginnie, you and I will see to this baby."

Jacob and Rebecca left the bedroom. Jacob was now certain, more than ever before, that he had an appointment in Baltimore that he had to keep. He wanted to run out of the house, but he had been commanded to wait by Rebecca's mother – so he waited. He did not have to wait for very long. Mary Elizabeth returned to the kitchen to inform them that the baby was, indeed, in breech position. She explained that she knew a few tricks regarding birthing such a baby, but it would be better to have the doctor present. She asked the two teenagers to search the town for the doctor and to bring him at all speed.

Rebecca and Jacob set out immediately; she running in the direction toward Seminary Ridge, and he running in the direction away from it.

They were both unsuccessful in finding the doctor, but it really didn't matter – the baby was born just the same. Mary Elizabeth had assisted with the birth as professionally as a midwife. Mother and child were both fine.

But by the time all of this was brought to a successful conclusion, it was already past dinner time, and Jacob was late to return to his home. Almost unwittingly, he had accomplished that which he had debated in his mind. He knew that he would be most assuredly in trouble if he dared to return late, and he would be in even deeper trouble if he dared tell his father that the reason for his tardiness was because he spent the afternoon with the young lady he had been specifically forbidden to see.

Jacob was sure that he could not return home, under the circumstances. He had considered running away – and now that had become a reality. He said his farewells to Rebecca Tilden and left the house, heading back onto the Baltimore Pike. He had nothing with him but the clothing on his back.

CHAPTER 8

June 30, 1863

Jacob Zook awoke around six o'clock in the morning. He had spent the night on a small hill on the opposite side of the town from the seminary. For some unknown reason, perhaps his own guilty conscious, he could not bring himself to travel any further than he had. But he knew that the little hill, which he knew by the name 'Sugar Loaf Hill,' was a good hiding spot. It reminded him a bit of the hill on the Culp farm. It was rocky on one side, and covered with trees on the other.

Ginnie had given the boy some food before he set out the evening before. His supplies did include a few loaves of her bread, and a jar of jam. He now took the opportunity to eat about half a loaf of bread, but he saved all of the jam for later.

Jacob stood up and walked to the edge of a rocky outcropping. He could clearly see the farmland below, especially a large wheat field, an orchard of some kind, and, if he squinted, he could make out the outline of the seminary building.

A flash of light caught his eye.

He looked across the large field, seeing into the distance perhaps a mile, as it was a particularly clear morning.

He saw another flash….and then another.

Then he understood what he had just seen. He had seen soldiers marching – their weapons gleaming in the morning sunlight. Jacob wondered which army had sent troops to his little town. More than that, he observed that they were not very far away from his home on Seminary Ridge. He needed to get a closer look, and then he needed to inform his family – no matter what they thought of him – if, in fact, those were Confederate troops.

Jacob quickly packed up his food in the little cloth which Ginnie had supplied, and set off down the gentle sloping hillside. He didn't quite run, because he didn't want to draw attention to himself – but he did move at a fast pace. He quickly covered several hundred yards, soon approaching a rough looking patch of ground ahead of him.

He shuddered when the boulders loomed into sight before him. Local legend had it that this array of granite boulders housed an immense snake – a monster. The large rocks seemed to be scattered, but in a tight area, as if some Titan had picked up a handful of pebbles in his gargantuan hand, and dropped them in the middle of an otherwise barren field. Even at eighteen years old, the sight of the place put a bit of a scare into Jacob's heart, although after the scare the previous day with the birth of Georgia McClellan's baby, he was sure that a pile of rocks really didn't appear as frightening any more. But just to be on the safe side, Jacob made sure to give the rock pile a wider berth than he had to give it.

But after passing the rocks, he would now be in the open field. In the distance lay his goal, a long tree line which formed a natural border between several large farms in the area, particularly the large McPhearson farm. Jacob wanted to break into a flat out run, but knew that would seem a bit odd to anyone watching him. Why, he thought, would a farm boy be in such a hurry to cross an open field – unless, of course, he was chasing a farm animal, like a cow, that might have broken out? So, in spite of his inclination to cross the field quickly, Jacob purposely took his time – even to the point of meandering. He remembered seeing the glint of steel several hundred yards up to his right, so he also considered the fact that perhaps no one was looking down in this direction.

If he was correct in that assumption, he never knew for sure, but in just a few minutes time, he reached the safety of the large trees that bordered the field. He still had a few hundred yards to cover, but now he felt much safer, knowing that he could hide behind the trees and brush. Even so, Jacob was careful to take his time doing this. The sun had already started to rise in the sky, and it looked as if it was going to be another hot, humid day. Jacob reckoned that it was already going on seven o'clock, which meant that there would be other locals out and about, seeing to their work of the day. But thus far, he met little to speak of, and was making progress through the trees. He stayed close to the edge of the tree line so that he could gauge his distance. He could still see that big pile of boulders by looking over his right shoulder, although they did seem to be more distant with every new hiding place.

It took the boy almost another half hour to advance to the point where he could now see the cupola on the top of the seminary building. His own house was just a bit down and to the right of that building, but he couldn't see it from this vantage point, as it was obscured by the trees on Seminary Ridge. Jacob looked over his shoulder again, just to get his bearings. He was now quite a distance from the granite rock pile, and he could just make out the outline of Sugar Loaf Hill – and then he could see the form of a much bigger hill, the one the locals called 'Round Top,' in the far distance. He knew that he was close to where he had seen those reflections.

He moved a few trees closer. He could hear some noise.

It was the sound of men talking.

Jacob moved quickly now, changing trees on the diagonal, but stepping as lightly as he could to avoid snapping the downed twigs that lay scattered on the ground.

He could still hear the talking, but could not make out any distinct words. Jacob changed trees again, moving toward the sound of the voices, but once again on the diagonal. Then he changed trees again.... and again.

He knew that the men were one hundred, maybe two hundred feet from where he stood, but the density of brush and trees prevented him from seeing them. He decided to stop and listen to what they were saying, hiding behind a very large oak. Jacob stayed motionless for a minute, listening as hard as he could for any recognizable word.

And then he heard it. He distinctly heard one of the men say the word, 'Lee.' "Lee?" he muttered to himself. He knew that was the name of the rebel General, but what did that matter? It could be Union soldiers speaking about the enemy, couldn't it? He also realized that he could have just picked up the end of another word, like 'naturally' or 'geographically' or 'historically.' He knew that he had to get the position of being able to see these men, but that would take him dangerously close.

Dangerous – Lee.

He spotted his next move, a large elm tree to his left. He waited for the men to speak together, as if in conversation, hoping that they wouldn't notice his noise.

But as he was about to start out, he heard the double click of a rifle being primed, and it had come from directly behind him. He turned around slowly to see a soldier. The soldier had his rifle trained on him. "Wot cha doin' there, boy?" the soldier asked. He spoke in a very clear southern drawl – but it really didn't matter if he did or he didn't – he was wearing a grey uniform.

Jacob instinctively raised his hands. "Nothing, sir."

"Nothin?" the man questioned. "Looks to me like you are spying on our position. That's hardly 'nothin.'"

Jacob felt his mind spinning. He looked at the man's gun. It wasn't a rifle…it was an old musket – and it had seen better days, at that. But even a musket, fired at this close range, would not need the accuracy afforded to the newer rifled guns. At five feet away, this gun would be deadly. "I live around here, mister." Jacob waved his left hand toward Seminary Ridge. "Up over there, by the Seminary."

"Yeah?" asked the soldier. "Why should I believe you? Maybe you're just a spy!"

"A spy?" returned Jacob. "Me?"

"Get movin,'" ordered the soldier, indicating the direction with the barrel of his gun. Jacob turned around and walked in the direction of the voices, now side-stepping all of the trees and following a much more direct route. In just a few moments the dense woods gave way to a clearing. A small encampment of soldiers was in the clearing. Most of them were eating their breakfast. Jacob noticed that they didn't have any tents pitched, and there were not very many of them, so he assumed that they were scouts. There were about twenty men, in all. "Look what I found, boys," announced his captor.

A soldier stood up and addressed the man behind Jacob, "Put your gun down, Travis, before you shoot the boy. What is the matter with you? Your knife would have worked just as well!" Then he turned to the boy. "Who are you, boy?"

Jacob felt his stomach turn. "Jacob Zook, sir." Jacob could now see that the soldier speaking to him had three stripes on his sleeve. "Sorry… ah…Sergeant."

"Hm," replied the sergeant, thoughtfully, "smart boy! Where are you from, Jacob Zook?"

"I live…with my family…up there…on the ridge." Jacob instantly felt as if he had lied to the soldier, especially about living with his family.

"Really?" asked the sergeant. "You don't say? Have you lived there your entire life?"

"No, sir," answered the boy, "only the last year, or so." "Do you know much about the town?"

And with this question, Jacob knew exactly what the sergeant was doing. He realized that he was trying to get information out of him. "It's just a town, sir. I spend most of my time at my home…doin' chores." Some of the other soldiers laughed a bit at this remark, as if they all understood the concept of 'doin' chores.'

"See any other soldiers lately, Jacob?" the sergeant asked, smiling and acting friendly.

"You mean Federal troops?" asked Jacob.

"So you get my meaning," answered the sergeant, "but yes…Federal troops. Have you seen any?"

Jacob wanted to tell the sergeant that there was a brigade stationed in the town, but he also knew that something like that could backfire in his face. It might be a trick question; maybe the sergeant was already aware that there were no troops in the town. "I haven't seen any Federal troops for weeks, sir."

"Good boy," replied the sergeant. "You gave me the right answer."

It had been a trick, Jacob thought. "What are you going to do with me?" "We could shoot you," answered the sergeant, "'cause you're a spy…but that would be too noisy." Some of the men laughed at the sergeant's witty answer. "So maybe we will just hang you from a big tree." His men laughed again.

"You don't want to hang me," said Jacob, trying to think quickly.

"Really?" asked the sergeant. "And why is that?"

"Because…because…I am not a threat to you, that's why. I have absolutely no interest in your war, or in the outcome."

The sergeant's eyes grew wide at this response. "What do you mean by that, Jacob Zook? How is it that you have no interest in the war? Why do you call it ***our*** war?"

"I have no interest in it….because….I'm Amish!" There! He said it! It was only half-true, but he had said it. The truth be told, Jacob did care about the outcome of the war, even though his father had preached otherwise.

"Amish?" asked a young corporal. "What is that?"

And then Jacob remembered that his sect was concentrated in only a few states in the country, particularly in several areas of southern and western Pennsylvania, and in Ohio. He wasn't aware of any communities in the south – and especially not the Deep South. "Sorry….I forgot that you don't have any Amish communities south of the Mason/Dixon line. We are a religious sect. We have nothing to do with the Federal government; we don't pay taxes, serve in the military, or go to school."

"He's like us," said a private. "We don't have anything to do with the Federal government, either." A few of the soldiers found this ironic and laughed.

"And you didn't go to school, either," added another private, laughing at the first.

"Hold on," said the sergeant. "Let me get this straight. Your people don't care about Abe Lincoln?"

"Not one bit," replied Jacob, once again lying to the man. In truth, Jacob admired Lincoln a great deal.

"Well I'll be," answered the sergeant.

Jacob felt the hands that were holding him relax, then let him go. "Well, if that's all you have to ask me, I will just be moving along. I have chores to finish."

The sergeant quickly replied to Jacob's comment. "Can't let you do that, Jacob. You are not really a prisoner, but we can't let you go back up to the town, cause you might mention us to other folk, and that would just about ruin everything…so….you're coming with us."

"Going with you?" asked Jacob. "Where?"

"You keep on asking questions, boy, and someone eventually is going to shoot you."

"But…my parents…"

"I know," answered the sergeant, gently, "they will be worried sick over you, but you will only be gone for a day, or so, and then you will have plenty to tell them about."

Their breakfast finished, the rebel scouting party quickly packed up and began the trip back to the main body of their unit, which was stationed outside of the little town of Cashtown, about eight miles away. The scouting party used the Cashtown Pike to return to the army, but would occasionally scramble off the road if they happened to notice any local traffic. It took the party almost three hours to return to their unit.

The sergeant escorted Jacob to the Cashtown Inn, which was now serving as the Headquarters for the III Corps of the Army of Northern Virginia. The sergeant held Jacob firmly by the arm as he entered the inn, and was immediately stopped by a young captain.

"Sergeant MacAllister, have you just returned from your reconnoitering of the area?"

"I have, sir," replied the now-named sergeant. "And who is this that you have brought with you?"

"This is a young local boy, Jacob Zook, who we found watching our encampment, sir."

"A spy, sergeant?" The officer seemed puzzled at the scout's actions.

"We are not sure, sir," replied MacAllister, "but we didn't want to chance him giving away our position…sir."

"Very good, Sergeant," the officer answered. "I will tell General Hill that you have returned." He turned and left the room. Jacob looked around the front room of the inn. This room had been used as a saloon and restaurant, but it had now been commandeered as a headquarters for a military operation. Jacob noticed that there was a great deal of activity going on, especially a constant parade of couriers – at least to him they looked like couriers. But he was also aware that the longer he stood in that room, the more he would learn about the rebel army, and that would only delay his eventual freedom.

The captain returned and addressed the sergeant. "Sergeant, you will be able to see to your men in a few minutes. Please accompany me, along with this boy, to speak with General Hill."

"Yes, sir," replied MacAllister. The two soldiers escorted Jacob Zook into the adjoining room which, like the outer room, had now been turned into a command center. Jacob observed that there were about a dozen high-ranking Confederate officers in the room, either leaning over a large table, which had a map of the area spread out on it, or standing around the room in discussion. The captain gestured to Jacob, informing him by doing so where he was to stand. A tall officer, wearing a full beard and mustache stood up from the map table and looked over at Jacob. Jacob could see the stars on his jacket. Jacob knew that the stars indicated that he was a General.

The man approached Jacob. "Hello, sir," he said, bowing to Jacob at the waist. "I am General Ambrose Powell Hill, Commander of this corps of the Army of Northern Virginia. We are your guests here in Pennsylvania for a few days. I understand that you are Mr. Zook?"

Jacob nodded quickly, awed by the presence of a real general. "Yes, sir. I live atop Seminary Ridge."

General Hill turned back to the map table, where another officer – another man with stars on his jacket, pointed out the location on the map. "Yes, yes…Seminary Ridge." Another officer now approached General Hill, whispering something in the General's ear.

"General Anderson wishes to know, Jacob, if you are any relation to General Samuel Zook?"

"General Zook?" Jacob asked, his voice filled with surprise. "There is a General Zook in your army?"

"No, not in our army," replied Hill calmly, "he is one of the enemy Generals. General Anderson met him when Zook was in command at Annapolis."

Anderson then spoke up, "He was also Pennsylvania Dutch, like you." "Deutsch," Jacob corrected.

"Pardon me?" answered General Anderson.

"It is pronounced, 'Deutsch,' meaning, 'German," advised Jacob, with not a note of resentment in his tone. "We are often called Dutch, but we are actually German in descent. Our forefathers came mainly from the province of Alsace. I speak English, German, and the local dialect of the people you called Pennsylvania Dutch."

"Well….," remarked Anderson, "I stand corrected…but is General Zook a relative of yours?"

"Probably not," answered Jacob. "The fact that he is in the military indications that he is not Amish, although he could be a Mennonite, or have that blood in his ancestry. Zook happens to be an extremely common last name for any of our people."

"This is a smart young man," observed Hill. "Perhaps we should commission him right here and now. We need some smart officers in this corps."

"Agreed, General," nodded Anderson.

Both men had sounded so serious in their conversation that Jacob felt obliged to answer. "I am sorry, sirs, but I cannot help you there. Amish may not fight for the country – either country."

"That is unfortunate, Jacob Zook," answered Hill, "but I was just joking, my boy." Then the General patted Jacob on the shoulder.

General Ambrose Powell Hill had been one of General Lee's most trustworthy Division Commanders, fighting tirelessly by the side of his immediate commanding officer, General Thomas Jackson. Even though the two were known to argue off the field, they were also a very battle-hardened team, and worked extremely effectively during a conflict. Hill tended to seem jittery, however, and was not a robust man. He was constantly ill, and many of his fellow officers considered that this was due to some form of socially transmitted disease, probably gonorrhea, which the General was said to have contracted while still a student at West Point. His beard looked straggly and mangy, at least it seemed that way from Jacob's viewpoint. The beard made the General look older than he actually was. He was still in his late thirties. He also wore a heavy mustache – a "soup strainer," as his folk liked to call it. No self-respecting Amish man would grow anything on his upper lip, even though Jacob secretly wished that he could do just that. Jacob remembered seeing a photograph of Abraham Lincoln after he grew his beard out, because, he said, a little girl wrote to him stating that a beard would make him look more distinguished. Jacob had observed, at the time, that Lincoln's facial hair made him appear…Amish. Hill was often referred to by only his initials, as in, General A.P. Hill, or, as some would have it, "Little Powell."

"You are going to remain with us until tomorrow, Mr. Zook," explained General Hill. "We are going to send some men into the town tomorrow to forage for supplies, and, if all goes well, we shall let you return home by tomorrow night." The General then turned back to the map table and addressed another senior officer who was studying the area. "General Heth?"

"Yes, sir?" answered the other officer.

"General…you are to stop by the Lutheran Seminary to confer with Jacob's parents, who are probably worried to death about him, to inform them that we have him in our possession and will return him at days end."

"Yes, sir," replied Heth.

"Either yourself, personally, General," Hill added, "or one of your immediate subordinates should do this. Do not forget this, sir."

"Yes, sir," acknowledged Heth.

"There…you see?" asked Hill. "Everything will be just fine. The Federal army is miles and miles from here, and you will be back home in just a day. In the interim, please…have the pleasure of our camp. The Captain here will see to it that you get a good meal, which, by the way, has been provided for you due to the courtesy and generosity of the people of the Great State of Pennsylvania."

*   *   *

The Federal Cavalry, under the command of Brigadier General John Buford, rode through the town of Gettysburg on the Chambersburg Pike, swinging around the property of the Lutheran Seminary, on the aptly named "Seminary Ridge." Buford and his men were on a scouting expedition – the lot in life for a cavalryman. In this case they were scouting for two things; the whereabouts of General Jeb Stuart's rebel cavalry, and the whereabouts of the entire Confederate Army. Buford already knew that Stuart's cavalry was far to the North of where they were positioned, and that he was not an immediate threat, but his information was such that he believed that at least one Corps of the Army of Northern Virginia – that of General A.P. Hill – was encamped about eight miles from Gettysburg, in the little hamlet of Cashtown. Arriving at the top of Seminary Ridge in the late afternoon of June 30, Buford was faced with a momentous decision: should he dig in and defend the higher ground that he was now standing upon, or should he allow Hill's Corp to march on through it in the morning – eventually running smack into pieces of the Federal Army, which was coming up slowly to Buford's rear.

Buford decided to stay put and to deploy his two brigades over the ridge, surrounding the Chambersburg Pike. He sent a courier to his immediate commanding officer, General John Reynolds, asking him if he should hold or fall back.

At the same time, General A.P. Hill was also gaining valuable information about the enemy army. He was under the impression that the main body of the Federal Army was considerably behind the advance of the Confederates; that any resistance along the way might be with cavalry, or possibly with the local militia. Either way, these organizations did not pose a serious threat to an entire Corps of infantry.

The Army of Northern Virginia was outnumbered – if numbers play a significant part of the battle. In the case of the battles of the American Civil War, which was still being waged under the same battlefield tactics and philosophies as the Napoleonic Wars of several decades earlier, the army with the greatest firepower would almost certainly be victorious. This was the common way of thinking, but General Robert E. Lee had proven this theory as incorrect time and time again. Lee's army had defeated the Federal army in almost every major battle of the war, and had not really suffered a single one-sided defeat. He had been the clear victor in both battles of Bull Run, as well as at Fredericksburg and at Chancellorsville. The Battle of Antietam was more of a draw that a victory for either side. In all of these cases, each of the battles were bloody, with terrible loss of life and limb.

Still, by the third summer of the war, Lee's army still totaled around 70,000 men. These men were divided into three large Corps, under the command of Generals Longstreet, Hill, and Ewell. The Federal army was divided into some ten Corps, but each of these Corps were smaller in number than their Confederate counterparts. Were all ten corps of the Army of the Potomac to show up on a given battlefield, then they would number in excess of 100,000 men. But even with this numerical advantage, Lee had outmaneuvered and out-fought the Union commanders. His army was well organized, and each commanding general knew his place within the chain of command. This was certainly not the case behind the Federal lines.

*   *   *

Georgia McClellan was in a great deal of pain. Her delivery had not been an easy one, although her new born son seemed to be in good health. Rebecca Tilden had spent the night at the McClellan home to assist with the baby and mother – along with Ginnie Wade. Ginnie sent her two younger brothers to spend the night at the Tilden home, just to get them from under foot.

*   *   *

Jacob wandered around the Confederate camp. The army was continuing to grow, with more units arriving hourly. His escort, Captain Richard Adams, was a friendly young man. Captain Adams was the signal corps officer, although he was not even twenty four years old. He was permanently assigned to General Hill's headquarters.

Not fearing any form of security issue, Captain Adams leisurely pointed out various points of interest as they casually walked through the large encampment. The captain was sure to point out the regimental colors of each of the brigades.

Jacob, too, had a barrage of questions. Even though he was able to recognize a General by the stars on his sleeve, he had no idea of how a large army was organized, so there were many terms which he did not understand, even though Captain Adams was rattling them of in such a matter-of-fact manner, as if anyone would know these things. Finally, showing his frustration, Jacob stopped in his tracks, and asked the captain if he might explain some of his terms.

"Well, Jacob," began the young captain, "an army is a very large group of soldiers. Our army – The Army of Northern Virginia – is almost one hundred thousand in number." This was a gross exaggeration, because Adams, despite his casual manner, had enough common sense to know that he should not give away the actual size of the army – even to an innocent looking farmboy.

"Golly!" replied Jacob, surveying the camp. "I can't believe I am looking at that number in this camp!"

"You aren't," answered the captain. "What you see…if you could actually see it all at once, would be able thirty thousand men. But more are arriving as we speak, which will soon double that number. Another Corps of the army will be stationed a bit further away."

"It still is far more many people than I have ever seen in my life," said Jacob. "If the entire town of Gettysburg were to turn out on the streets at one moment, there would only be a few thousand people, including the women and children."

"It is a very overwhelming sight, I'll give you that. Anyway, the army is divided into three corps. The corps are each commanded by a Lieutenant General – that's three stars, like General Hill. Each corps has at least two Divisions, which are commanded by Major Generals."

"Like Generals Anderson and Heth?"

"Exactly!" answered Adams. "Each Division then is broken into Brigades, which are usually commanded by a Brigadier General."

"And that would be one star?" asked Jacob.

"That's correct!" answered the captain, very impressed with his young pupil. "Each Brigade will have anywhere from three to six regiments, and each regiment will be under the command of a Colonel. The regiment is divided further into battalions, with a Lieutenant Colonel or a Major heading each of these. Each battalion is then divided into companies, which are led by the lower commissioned officers, such as captains and lieutenants. From there, we break down into squads, which are led by non-commissioned officers – mostly sergeants."

"Like the one I ran into earlier today."

"Exactly!" replied Adams. They stopped at a gathering of wagons that had grouped together to form the mobile cooking unit. The captain sauntered over to one of the cooks, and then returned with two plates of food. He handed one of the plates to Jacob. "I have no idea what this will taste like…or what it is made of…but it usually is good."

Jacob was so hungry that it really wasn't all that important to him how the food tasted. He filled his mouth with a scoopful of the stew-like concoction. "Um-um," soon started to sound from his closed lips.

"I'll assume that you like it," observed Adams. Jacob eagerly nodded. They resumed their tour of the constantly enlarging camp. The regimental flags had now changed in color; they were now entering a part of the camp belonging to a different corps.

"This here is II Corps," said the captain. "The man in charge of this corps is General Ewell. His corps is just beginning to arrive."

Jacob again nodded to indicate that he understood. He also understood that two corps represented about 60,000 soldiers, give or take. He wondered what could possible stand in the way of 60,000 soldiers…and what it must take to keep such an army of men supplied with food and other necessities.

Jacob and Captain Adams were passing by the tents belonging to the second Virginia Regiment, when Jacob heard his name called out. He spun himself around to see a very familiar face.

"Wesley Culp!" exclaimed an astonished Jacob. "Wesley! How good it is to see you." Jacob ran over to Private Culp and enthusiastically shook his hand.

Culp slapped Jacob on the back, obviously happy to see him again. "What are you doing here, Jacob? Are you enlisting with the rebs?"

Jacob stepped back a bit and took a good, long look at his acquaintance. Wesley was wearing the grey and butternut colored uniform of the Confederate States of America. He had known that Wesley had moved a year ago to Western Virginia, but he had little idea that he was a member of the Confederate army. He didn't want to call Wesley a traitor, but, then again, maybe he did. Jacob lowered his voice, speaking only so that Culp could hear him. "How does it feel, Wesley, to be so close to home?"

"Very strange, Jacob. Very strange, indeed!" Wesley answered, shaking his head. "We spent the last few months traipsing all over Virginia, and now here I am, only miles from the place I grew up."

"You must feel…confused," responded Jacob.

"Now there's a good word for it!" returned Culp. "Hey…so why are you here, Jacob?"

"I was picked up by a scouting party this morning. They thought I was spying on them, so they brought me here."

Private Culp couldn't believe his ears. "A spy?" He looked over at Captain Adams. "Sir? A spy? This boy is Amish. They don't care a bit about the war!"

"We know that, Private," the captain replied. "He will be free to return home after tomorrow."

Culp turned back to Jacob. "Uh-huh! There's something gonna happen tomorrow, then."

"Yep."

Culp nodded knowingly, then he grabbed Jacob by the arm and pulled him a few steps further away from the captain. "Jacob…a week or so ago…after a battle…I can't even remember which one anymore…I happened to be on duty by the medical tents…and there was this Federal corporal in there. He was pretty badly wounded, but…well…you know…we don't just let people die, you know?"

"Actually, Wesley…I think it is very odd. You purposely try to kill everyone on the other side, and then you try to prevent the wounded from dying. I think that is one part about war which I will never understand."

"We can debate that later, Jacob. Anyway….I look down at this corporal…and then I realize…that I know him!"

"You ran into someone else that you knew from Gettysburg?"

"I know…what are the chances of that happening? But there he was." "Well…who was it?" Jacob asked.

"No one you would know, I'm sure," Wesley answered. "You hardly ever get away from the farm."

"That's the truth," agreed Jacob. "That is…until yesterday."

Culp ignored the last statement his friend had made, continuing, "He is engaged to be married to one of the young ladies in Gettysburg."

"Bad timing, I'd say," said Jacob. "Who might that be?"

"Not that you would know that lady, Mr. Amish boy…but her name is…."

The captain cleared his throat. He non-verbally communicated to Jacob that it was time to move on. Jacob nodded quickly back to him, saying that he understood and would be there.

"What is the soldier's name, Wesley?"

"It's Corporal Jack Skelly, Jacob," Culp replied, slowly pulling a small scrap of paper out of his uniform blouse. "He gave me this note to give to his finance, as he was laid up. But seeing that you're here, and going back home tomorrow, maybe you can give it to her, instead of me."

"Sure, I guess I could do that," answered Jacob.

"Take my hand, like you're warmly wishing me well," said Culp.

Jacob reached out his right hand and grasped Culp's hand. He felt the scrap of paper in Culp's palm, and discreetly pulled it out and stuffed it in his pants.

"Who should I give this to, Wesley?"

"Her name is Virginia Wade, Jacob," he answered. "She lives over on Baltimore Street. All of her friends just call her 'Ginnie.' …Ginnie Wade.

Jacob didn't bother telling Wesley that he knew Ginnie, nor that he had just seen her the previous day, but it didn't matter because the captain was obviously anxious to get back to his own headquarters. Jacob dutifully followed him back through the camp. He was given the status of an honored guest of the Corps, and spent the night sleeping on the floor at the Cashtown Inn.

CHAPTER 9

July 1, 1863

Jacob was awakened by the noise of preparation. Two Brigades from General Heth's Division were mobilizing, preparing to march to Gettysburg. Jacob quickly moved to the upstairs window which faced out onto Cashtown Road. He witnessed the assembly of several thousand men, most of them in some form of uniform, although not always looking very similar – and many of them were barefoot.

He looked around the upstairs bedroom where he had stayed the night. He had shared the room with several other staff officers, but he was now alone. He could hear bugle calls and the sound of drums. The regimental colors were being unfurled. Had it not been such a terrible scene, he would have marveled at it.

But Jacob had their destination on his mind. He sat back down on the floor and began to pray, asking God to watch over his family – knowing that the brigades would march directly past the Lutheran Seminary before entering the town. He earnestly prayed that the day would be uneventful; that the rebel army would take whatever it needed and then go on its way; that no one would get hurt…or killed.

Jacob found a basin and washed his face and hands. He walked downstairs to see if the good Captain Adams was still present. He was not. As the chief signal officer, Adams was needed to convey communications with the advancing brigades.

General A.P. Hill was sipping a cup of coffee and leaning over the table with the map. He took notice of the boy standing at the doorway to the back room, but then went back to his thoughts, and the map. "Excuse me," came a voice from behind the young man. Jacob whirled around, and saw the face of a boy not much older than he was…perhaps eighteen or nineteen years old. Jacob stepped out of the way, allowing the young soldier to pass him by and enter the inner room. The young soldier, who happened to be wearing the insignia of a lieutenant on his uniform, stopped by the map table and saluted General Hill. He then offered Hill an envelope, saying, "With General Lee's compliments, sir." He then took a step back and waited where he was.

General Hill tore the envelope open. General Anderson moved around the table, as if to confer with Hill, as well as to read the enclosed document. "Gentlemen," General Hill announced, "General Lee would like to remind us that our scouts have discovered that there are some Federal troops in the area, and that we are advised not to engage the enemy at this time; We are to wait until the entire army has been brought up."

"Fine," said General Anderson, "we figured they were out there… somewhere. That message only pertains to Longstreet's Division. They are so far to our rear that they may be in the proximity of the enemy. I know the General wants us unified when we make our move on Harrisburg."

Jacob wanted to bolt out of the inn and head for home. All he had to do was follow the Chambersburg Road for eight miles. But he also figured that he would be shot along the way, and that wouldn't do his family any good, either. He didn't think that his father would do anything to provoke the rebels – his father would simply tell the family to stay inside the house. He was pretty sure that he would return home to find just about every animal in the barn taken, but that, too, remained to be seen. He wasn't really worried about the people in the Seminary; they would be respected as men of the cloth, but he did worry about the people of the town, particularly Ginnie and Georgia – and of course the new baby.

And then there was Rebecca Tilden....

Yes, Jacob Zook figured it was going to be a very long, hot day.

*   *   *

General Alfred Pleasonton had his cavalry brigades on the alert. He had gotten a great deal of information concerning the whereabouts of Jeb Stuart and the rebel cavalry, so he would dispatch his various brigades with the hope of intercepting and engaging the rebel General, and, as General Meade had put it, blind the eyes and ears of General Lee.

He had sent a cavalry brigade under the command of Brigadier General John Buford, to make a swing around to the west of the little town of Gettysburg. As luck would have it, just as Jacob Zook considered running away from the rebel army to warn his family of the coming attack, General Buford's Corps of horsemen was rounding the top of Seminary Ridge. Buford and his officers had noticed a cloud of dust rising in the distance, coming from the direction of Cashtown, along the Chambersburg Road. Buford and his staff officers mounted the stairs of the Lutheran Seminary building to gain access to the cupola, which gave them an excellent vantage point. Buford was aware, through Pleasonton, that Meade did not want a confrontation with the Confederate Army until his entire Army of the Potomac was in position; a feat that was still, on the morning of July 1, still days away from completion, especially in a spot as remote as Gettysburg. But Buford was quick to recognize the strategic position that he had been handed. Seminary Ridge was high ground, higher in fact than the lower lying MacPherson Ridge was lay just to the west. As the rebels were marching down the Chambersburg Pike in tight formation, as if on dress parade, Buford knew that their army would be unable to move quick enough to hide from any attack that he might bring. But he was also aware that a cavalry corps did not possess the manpower to keep up a successful barrage all day. He ordered his men to dismount and form rough defenses, feeling that he might confuse the rebels into thinking that they had come face to face with a Federal brigade. At the same time, he sent a courier to his immediate superior, General Reynolds, asking him to bring I Corps to assist him post haste. Both corps had been under orders not to engage the enemy until the remainder of the full army was in place, and yet both were about to engage. Heth would later complain that he couldn't hold his men back; that they were still looking to battle it out with the Federal troops, especially after the endless string of one-sided Confederate victories. Buford would explain later that he made a judgment based upon the terrain that he had found. He had remembered some of the painful losses; the embarrassment of Fredericksburg – especially the countless attempts to take the bridge over the Rappahannock River. General Burnside had doggedly sent regiment after regiment over the bridge, trying to take the town, but the entire Confederate army was situated on the heights above the other bank of the river, and rained down death throughout the day.

Only now…Buford had the advantage of the high ground…if he could keep it until reinforcements arrived.

Buford opened fire first, catching the first regiment in Heth's division completely surprised. The men in the front of the pack were simply mown down. Confusion reigned in the rebel ranks, which was not usual – it had usually gone the other way.

Heth quickly sent a courier back to Hill's headquarters at Cashtown, explaining that he had engaged the enemy. In fact, Robert E. Lee had heard some of the volleys some miles away and had asked his Aide de Camp to ascertain whether those were his guns.

*   *   *

Sarah Zook had been out behind the caretaker's house, hanging some wash on the line, when she heard the rumble of horses' hooves. To Sarah, the sound reminded her more of thunder than the sound of horses. A moment later she saw the double line of cavalry, the blue uniforms of the Federal army sitting astride. The long line of riders continued riding out to the overlook of the ridge. Abraham darted outside, running to his mother's side. He had never seen such a sight; for that matter, neither had Sarah.

Ishmael came running out of the barn, the milking stool still held in his hand. Some of the members of the faculty at the seminary also came outside to get a better look. The family was separated by the endless line of man and horse – Ishmael on one side, Sarah and Abraham on the other. If the noise wasn't bad enough, the

horses were carving great ruts in the dirt road, raising up a cloud of dust and pebbles. Ishmael waved to Sarah, giving her the signal to get Abraham back inside the house. A few minutes later, the line of cavalry finally passed, and Ishmael crossed through the dust to the house. He entered by the kitchen and checked on his family. They were frightened, but unharmed in any way.

Ishmael was visibly frustrated; first his son, Jacob, had disappeared, and now this. Ishmael had first believed that Jacob had run away; he felt that Jacob was well along the way to making that decision in any case, so this would not be much of a surprise. But the appearance of Federal troops meant that the war had arrived at their doorstep, which made him wonder again about Jacob. He wondered if Jacob had, in some way, become involved with the soldiers. For the first time in a day, Ishmael worried about his son. He knew that his son was good with 'the English,' but he also knew that their wars were quite a different story.

Sarah had already asked Ishmael to go looking for Jacob. She had done this when Jacob had not shown up for dinner …two nights ago. He had stubbornly refused, citing Bible verses concerning ungrateful children. She would have gone herself, but that would have been an act of disobedience to her husband, and the Amish Ordnung was very specific about this area of deportment. She also considered sending Abraham; she knew that Ishmael would forgive the child far quicker than he would forgive his own wife, but she decided against doing that, as well. And now she was even more relieved that she hadn't acted on that instinct; the town was being overrun with soldiers. It was no place for a fourteen year old Amish boy!

Ishmael went back into the barn and secured the animals. He cross-tied the horses and secure the cattle in pens. He shooed the chickens and geese into their coops, stopping to pick up one unfortunate hen that had been trampled by the cavalry. Ishmael found a padlock and put it on the barn door, but also realized that this attempt at security would probably not do him any good. He heard the distant sound of gunfire, so he returned to the house. A few minutes later there was a knock at the door. He answered the door, telling Sarah to stay put with Abraham. It was the staff of the Lutheran Seminary. They had been sent to the farmhouse to seek cover by the Federal officers, seeing as they had commandeered their building as a headquarters for the operation. Ishmael suggested that they all move to the basement of the house. He was well aware that a bullet could easily tear through the clapboard siding of the outer walls of the house, but he also knew that nothing in this world would stop a cannonball.

The Zook family, as well as the seminary staff, cowered in the basement as the noise of the battle continued to escalate. First there had only been rifle and musket fire, but eventually they heard the much louder explosions of mortar and cannon fire. It was easy to discern which side was firing; the Federal artillery was only a hundred yards from the house. The sound of the firing was immediate – and very loud, even inside the basement. As the Confederate army became more stabilized after the first initial attack, they also brought up the larger guns and began returning fire. Quite often, those in the basement could hear the effect of the cannon – that is to say, the damage; a breaking tree limb, the sound of siding being ripped asunder – before they heard the report from the mouth of the cannon. Sarah wondered what sights she would see when she, at last, emerged from the basement. She worried that the entire house would be destroyed above their heads. She wondered if the barn would be engulfed in flames.

She wondered if any of them would be hurt…or killed.

*   *   *

General Buford was extremely anxious of his position. He had chosen to defend the rise in Seminary Ridge, a slope that gradually increased some sixty feet in height, against two brigades of Confederate infantry. He knew that he could not hold this position indefinitely, and hoped that the reinforcements he had requested would arrive shortly. By around ten o'clock, those reinforcements did arrive, under the command of General John Reynolds, who successfully pushed the rebel brigades back to MacPherson's Ridge. General Howard's Corps also was arriving on the scene, which strengthened the Federal reserves. Unfortunately, a sniper's bullet hit General Reynolds in the neck as he was directing his troop placement, killing him instantly. One of his Division Commanders, General Abner Doubleday, assumed command at this point.

*   *   *

By the time Jacob had enough time to find his breakfast at the camp, he was rounded up by one of General Hill's orderlies. The orderly brought him back to the inn, where General Hill and several of his staff officers were waiting for him, already mounted on horses. A saddled horse was tied to the railing of the porch.

"Jacob," greeted the General, with a nervous twitch on his face, "I take it that you found something to eat this morning?"

"Yes, sir," replied the boy. "Your men have been quite hospitable to me." "Thank you, sir," answered the General. "We Southerners do pride ourselves on our hospitality. Now…Jacob…if you would do us the honor of accompanying us on a short ride." The General then nodded in the direction of the un-saddled horse. "You can ride…can't you?"

"Yes, sir," Jacob answered. "May I ask where we are going?"

This question seemed to trouble the General. His face twitched again. His removed his hat and wiped the perspiration from his forehead with his sleeve. "We are going to our other camp, to meet with General Lee."

"General Lee? General Robert E. Lee?" asked Jacob, his eyes wide open in amazement.

"You have heard of him, I see?"

"Everyone up here has, General." Jacob paused in his enthusiasm, his tone growing quieter. "Many people hate him; they call him a 'traitor,' but I think most still respect his ability."

Hill nodded. "And what do you think of him, Mr. Zook? Do you think that he is a traitor?" Then he gave a short, dry laugh. "For that matter…do you think that we are all traitors to the country?"

Jacob knew that the General was testing him…again. He realized that his position within the rebel camp was tenuous, at best, so he carefully chose his answer. "I am Amish, General. We don't care about the outcome of the war…unless it affects our trade with the English. We don't own slaves…we never would own slaves. Other than the fact that the war is killing a great many good men, I really have no stake in which side wins."

General Hill once again nodded to the boy. "So then you won't mind speaking with General Lee?"

"I would look forward to it, General," replied the boy.

But Jacob had lied to A.P. Hill, and he already was planning to lie to Robert E. Lee. He did care about the outcome of the war – even if his father, or any good member of the Amish community, took the posture that the war did not matter to him. Unlike his father, Jacob had made many more contacts within the 'English' community – people that he liked and cared about.

"Well, then, mount up, young man," the General said, once again smiling down at the boy. Jacob walked over to the porch of the inn and untied the horse, then, placing his boot into one of the stirrups, lifted himself expertly onto the back of the horse. He took the reins and pulled the horses head to one side, turning the horse in line with the rest of the party. "You sit well, Jacob."

"Thank you, sir," replied Jacob, with a smile on his face. "We Amish don't usually ride horses for pleasure, we usually hitch them to a wagon, or use them to help us in the fields. My father doesn't even know that I can saddle a horse. I learned how to ride from my neighbor, Wesley Culp, who is now serving in your army." The party set out for General Lee's encampment. One of the staff officers took the lead, while Jacob and General Hill were at the back of the pack.

"So…are you typical of a young Amish boy, Jacob?" asked the General.

"I don't know what you are asking me, General," replied Jacob.

"You have already spoken of several things that you have intimated to me that your father would not approve of…if he knew," said the General. "It seems to me that you are a young man who is not entirely enamored with his Amish ways."

Jacob realized that the General might be on to his little ruse. "My father and I sometimes disagree about some things, General. Didn't you ever disagree with your father?"

"All the time," replied Hill, smiling at the boy.

"Yes," Jacob said, "but Amish children are supposed to be obedient to their parents. I am not as obedient as I should be…but there are reasons for this, I believe." Jacob paused, wondering if he was talking too much.

"Go on, Jacob," the General quietly replied. "I am listening."

Jacob didn't think his family history was a breech in the security of the Federal army. Besides, he liked the General, so what did it really matter? "Well, for one thing…Amish usually live in big communities, where we support each other. I think that this helps everyone stick to the Ordnung."

"The Ordnung?" asked Hill.

"The Ordnung is translated from German as 'the Order' – the order of things….how we do things."

"I see," replied the General. "In the army we would call that living 'by the book.'"

"Exactly!" said Jacob. "But my father did something which the council felt was outside the Ordnung…he married my mother."

"There was a problem with him marrying your mother?"

"Yes," answered the boy. "My mother is not Amish. She is Mennonite. She is more like, as you English call it…Pennsylvania Dutch – but not really. She is not of our Ordnung, so the council did not approve of the marriage. They were able to marry because my grandfather was a member of the council…but he died a few years ago."

"So then your parents lost a strong ally on the council," observed Hill. "That is correct," replied Jacob. "What followed after that is very hard to understand…to anyone who is English."

"Hold on, there boy," demanded Hill. "I don't know why you keep calling us 'English.' I am American, even if I am now part of the Confederate States of America."

"I am sorry, General," Jacob answered, "but that is the term that we apply to anyone outside of the Amish community. We speak our language so much, that we refer to those who don't speak it as 'the English,' as a way of actually saying…'the outsiders.'

"That is preposterous!" said Hill, but not in an arrogant way. "Are you telling me that a small, religious sect, refers to the entire population of a large country….which, by the way…completely surrounds them… envelopes them, if you wish….that your people refer to us…as the outsiders?"

"I see your point, General Hill….but that is the way it has always been."

"I find that almost humorous, Jacob."

"I can see how you would see it that way, General," replied the young man, "and I take no offense at that. But there is more to explain about our ways, sir."

"Well, then…proceed."

"This is even more difficult to explain, sir," said Jacob. "After my grandfather died, the council decided that they could now punish my parents for what they had done. They…we….were shunned."

"Shunned?"

"We were sent out of the community…never to return." "You mean….as if excommunicated?" asked the General.

"I do not know the meaning of that word, General. I am sorry."
"Never mind," Hill answered. "Is that why you have come to live in Gettysburg?"

"It is," said Jacob. "My father hopes to return to Paradise someday, so he keeps very strictly to the Ordnung...but I don't care if we ever go back. I like it here among," and then he paused, "the English."

"And so that it why you have learned more of our customs and habits?" "Yes, sir." Jacob replied.

"Well, Jacob," began Hill, "you have spoken so candidly about your family, and the traditions of the Amish, that think that it is fair to tell you that I have had a similar circumstance in my life, as well."

"Sir?"

"A few years back I was engaged to be married to a young lady...Ellen Marcy. Her parents did not like me very much, but they did happen to like one of my friends from West Point. His name was George...actually, it still is." Hill seemed to laugh to himself at this little joke. "George is a very smart man, Jacob. Like you, he speaks several languages fluently. He was the top of the class at West Point. He cuts a dashing figure – not like me. On the other hand...I had a history of hanging around with the wrong people. I had many....lady friends."

"Lady friends?" Jacob said, interrupting.

"Yes, Jacob...and they were the kind of lady friends that a nice Amish boy should, or would not ever get to know," said the General. "Do you know what I mean?"

"No, sir...not really."

"That's just as well," answered the General. "So Ellen's parents start pressuring Ellen to break off our engagement. They tell her that old Georgie is a much better...more suitable match for her...and, being that she doesn't want to anger her parents," Hill said, looking straight at Jacob, "she did exactly that. She broke off our engagement and got herself married to George."

"Golly!" said Jacob.

"Yes…golly!" repeated Hill. Jacob could tell that the man still harbored a great deal of resentment for all involved with this deep seeded hurt.

"Do you ever hear from them?" Jacob asked.

Hill did one of his dry laughs again at this question. "Jacob…that is the strangest twist of fate. My dear Ellen married my best friend, George McClellan…the man who was leading the Federal Army against us."

"General McClellan?"

"The very same," Hill replied. "I have to tell you, Jacob…knowing the man…his keen intellect…I was a might worried when I heard that he had assumed command of the Army of the Potomac. I thought our days were numbered, for sure…but he was a terrible commander…. well, maybe not terrible…I hear his men loved him. "Little Mac" they called him. Lincoln must have thought highly of him, too – but George managed to convince everyone that he was really a good field general…. but he wasn't good enough for Lincoln."

Jacob knew this to be true. He was aware that the Federal army was losing the war, and that McClellan had been the commanding general for most of the action thus far.

"I would be married to Ellen right now," added Hill, "were it not for the fact that she felt obliged to do that which her parents wanted." Then Hill leaned over to Jacob. "Sometimes…Jacob…sometimes we all have to do what is best for us."

Jacob thought he saw Hill wink at him, although he wasn't quite sure that he winked….it could have been another facial twitch. The party reached General Lee's encampment around ten o'clock – about the same time that General Reynolds was taking a sniper's bullet in his neck. After the party dismounted, Jacob was kept back with the horses, while Hill and the rest of the party went on ahead. Jacob became concerned about his presence at Lee's camp. He had thought it odd, even right from the beginning that Hill had ordered him along. He was also sure that it wasn't so General Lee had the opportunity to meet a real, live Amish boy. He also noticed that he was being watched by two privates- albeit they were doing so in a very casual manner, as if to give the impression to Jacob that he wasn't being watched at all.

Jacob wondered why this was so? Why was it necessary to guard him? And then Jacob thought of a new possibility; he thought that they may want to interrogate him a little more forcefully – possibly using some torture to get the desired answers. Jacob had heard all about this from his father. His father had told him that this type of questioning was very common in Europe; that many of his ancestors had been persecuted in this manner. He wondered if General Lee would consider using these tactics on him.

Jacob worried that these southern gentlemen might simply be acting graciously toward him in order to lure him into a false sense of security. He wondered if it was all an act; all a ploy.

CHAPTER 10

General Lee

"General Hill, you are one of my most able officers; that is why I put you in command of General Jackson's Corps. Was there some part of my order to avoid, at any cost, an engagement with the enemy – until such time as our entire army was in place – that you did not understand, General?" Robert E. Lee was angrier than he usually tended to get, especially while in command in the field.

"No, sir," Hill replied. "I was unaware of the presence of Federal troops in this area, and I sent General Heth to the town to forage for shoes and other supplies."

"That is not quite correct, is it General?" asked Lee. "You sent out a scouting party for these shoes on 30 June, and they ran into a Federal advance. Did they not?"

"Yes, sir, they did."

"Then why did you risk exposing the entire Division…the entire army…for the sake of a few shoes?"

"I was under the impression, General, that we were facing a brigade of dismounted cavalry."

"Dismounted cavalry?" asked Lee.

"Yes, sir," answered Hill. "We knew that's what they were and figured we could push them right off that pretty ridge over there. I figured we might have some very good land under our feet well before the infantry could arrive to reinforce them."

"But General," Lee countered, "there is already a brigade, or two, of Federal infantry fortifying that ridge. How do you suppose the infantry arrived so quickly?"

"That, sir, I do not know," replied Hill, in a humbled voice.

"That is what I would like to know, as well, General Hill," soothed Lee. "I am at a loss for information, just as you were, because I have not heard one word from General Stuart. None of us can function wisely without his cavalry to give us guidance. He should have been able to advise us that a Federal Corps was right behind that cavalry brigade."

Hill nodded, but he knew that this was not a pardon for his actions. "General Lee…my scouts tell me that we are facing brigades from I Corps."

"I Corps?" asked Lee. "That is John Reynolds' Corps, is it not?" "It is, General," answered Hill.

"General Reynolds is, in my opinion, one of the best of the Federal Generals, Ambrose. I shudder to think what would be that fate of this army should Lincoln ever give him the command."

"We believe that we are facing Wordsworth and Doubleday's Divisions, sir." "I would think you are correct, Ambrose," Lee answered. Another General arrived on horseback. He dismounted and quickly joined the other officers, saluting his commanding general. "Good morning, General Longstreet."

"Good morning, sir," returned Longstreet. "Good morning, Ambrose." "Morning, Pete," answered Hill, saluting Longstreet.

James Longstreet, known to his friends as 'Pete,' was another of Lee's Corps Commanders, as well as second in command of the Army of Northern Virginia.

"You have something to report, General?" asked Lee.

"Indeed I do, General," replied Longstreet. My scouts inform me that there are at least three complete corps marching quickly down the Emmitsburg Pike – and that is in addition to Oliver Howard's corps, which is just about to take their position on the field."

"Once again, Gentlemen," observed Lee, "we are surprised by the quickness of our enemy. This is exactly the kind of information that we needed to hear from Jeb Stuart. General Hooker seems to be in a mighty hurry to re-engage us after we gave him such a whipping back in Maryland."

"Oh, and that is another thing, General," added Longstreet. "My spies have told me that Hooker is no longer in command of the army."

"What?" asked Hill.

"Evidently he was criticized by his own officers after Chancellorsville… some even complained to Lincoln. Hooker resigned in a grand gesture… but Lincoln accepted his resignation…and called his bluff."

Lee looked across the field. "General, do you know who the commanding general is now?"

Longstreet nodded. "It's George Meade, sir."

"George Meade?" questioned Lee. "Lincoln promoted George to command the army? That must have ruffled a few feathers, don't you think? George had just become a corps commander…and now he's in command."

"I am sure that it did, sir," answered Longstreet. "I don't know what Abe Lincoln is thinking, but, if I were him…I would have given the job to Reynolds."

"I agree, General…that's what I was just saying to Ambrose," said Lee. "Something is going on politically within that army, gentlemen… but whatever it is, don't be too quick to count Lincoln out of the picture. He is doing exactly what I would be doing, under the circumstances."

"What is that, General?" asked Hill.

Lee looked at his most recently appointed corps commander. He looked him straight in the eyes. "Lincoln is searching for the man who will be a successful leader with his army, and, after waiting on General McClellan for so long, he is expanding his search. Gentlemen, do not allow yourselves to slip into a false sense of accomplishment. Not all of the Federal Generals are incompetent; sooner or later Lincoln will find someone who will lead with great success. It is only a matter of time. The North has all of the advantages, gentlemen; money, manpower, railroads, telegraph system. They will be able to take us on, and they will outlast us."

"General?" questioned Hill, upset at Lee's negativism.

"You misunderstand me, General," calmed Lee. "This is why we are here in Pennsylvania. We must take the war to the North… to Washington. We must claim a victory in this war before our good fortune at last runs out."

A courier approached at a full gallop, jumping off of the horse before it came to a full stop. The courier handed Lee a dispatch, saluted the General, and then promptly departed. Lee hastily read the dispatch.

"Gentlemen…General Reynolds is dead. He was picked off by one of our snipers. Doubleday is now in command of the corps."

Longstreet shook his head. "Damn! How many more of my friends will I lose in this war?"

"General," said Lee, quietly, "there will be time to grieve. Now is the time for action. The Federal Corps will be in a state of confusion…that is what I am counting on. General Hill, you must reinforce your position. Send a dispatch to General Ewell telling him that we will prepare a flanking maneuver on the Federal left."

"Yes, sir, General," answered Hill, saluting his commander. He turned and relayed the orders to his staff, but also noticed the figure of a civilian youth standing with the horses.

"General?" asked Longstreet. "What do you think George Meade will do here?"

Lee thought for a moment, then said, "George Meade is a cautious man, Pete. He is a more than competent engineer. This I do know.... so I imagine he will choose to fight a defensive battle. He will select his terrain and defend it. He will create very imposing earthworks and lines, and then he will wait for us to come to him." "Then why don't we simply make him wait, or go around him?" asked Longstreet.

"Because he stands in our way, General," replied Lee. "We didn't pick this ground, but we are here, and the Federal army is there. Harrisburg and Washington lie beyond. We must attack."

Longstreet dutifully nodded, understanding that if allowed to come to full strength, the Federal army would vastly outnumber the rebel band.

One of Hill's staff officers joined the trio. With him was young Jacob Zook. "General Lee," interrupted Hill, "might I have the pleasure of introducing Master Jacob Zook."

Lee turned away from Longstreet and looked first at Hill, then to Jacob. Lee bowed to Jacob from the neck, and then smiled at the boy. "Jacob Zook...a pleasure," and then he looked quizzically at Hill.

"It is a pleasure to meet you, General Lee," replied Jacob.

"General Lee," advised Hill, "Jacob was captured by our scouting party on 29 June. He has been our guest since that time. He lives atop that ridge over there, by the building with the bell tower."

Lee's eyes widened. "Is that so?"

"Yes, sir," Jacob answered.

"General," continued Hill, "Jacob is something called Amish."

Lee's eyes narrowed again. Jacob could tell that the General was thinking; that he was processing a term. "Amish," he repeated. "Ah, yes....Amish. You are descendants of the Anabaptists, are you not?" Jacob nodded his agreement, and smiled at the general. "Your folk believe that adults should be baptized, and not children. Your biggest concentration of population is around the city of Lancaster."

"Yes, sir," replied Jacob, not comprehending if his happiness was based on the fact that Lee knew something of his people, or if it was just out of the honor of meeting the great general.

"How old are you, Jacob?" Lee asked.

"I just turned eighteen last month, sir."

"Eighteen?" questioned Lee. "You are remarkably fit for your age, son."

"Thank you, sir," answered Jacob. "That's from plenty of hard work."

"I don't doubt that, my boy."

Jacob was studying the general. Lee, in spite of the heat, was fully dressed in his field uniform. His beard was almost snow white, and was impeccably trimmed. He was, he thought, a very distinguished looking gentleman.

"Jacob" began the general, "as you are our guest, I was wondering if you might be able to be of some service to us."

Jacob realized that his time had come; Lee was about to ask him to reveal some key elements of the topography of the region – that he was supposed to unwittingly give the Confederate Army an advantage by offering them information.

He would have to be tortured to reveal these things. But still he answered, "What can I do for you, General?"

Lee looked deeply into the boy's eyes. "I know that your people have no use for war – this war, or any war. In a few hours this field will be littered with the bodies of the dead, the dying, and the wounded. As you are, as I said, our guest…I was wondering if you could assist us with transporting some of these poor wretches to safety to seek medical care?"

Jacob looked surprised at the request.

"You are surprised, my boy?" asked Lee.

"Surprised? Yes…I thought you were about to torture me."

"Torture you?" Lee laughed. "That went out in the Dark Ages, Jacob. You were worried that I would want information from you; is that it?" Jacob nodded.

"Don't worry, son. I have many, many scouts and spies whose job it is to find out everything we need to know about the land…and the position of the other army – which, by the way, you could not possibly know."

Jacob breathed a sigh of relief. "It would be an honor to help your men, General."

"Good," replied Lee. "General Hill? Jacob will be staying with us, for the present time. You and General Ewell will both be occupied with other matters. I suggest that you see to them."

General Hill saluted Lee. "Jacob Zook…it was a pleasure to have had you stay with our Corps. I hope to see you again, very soon, sir."

"Thank you, General Hill," nodded Jacob. "I, too, look forward to seeing you again…perhaps under different circumstances."

Hill smiled, and then walked back to his horse, mounted the beast, and then galloped away with his officers.

Jacob would never see the officer again.

CHAPTER 11

Pushing Back the Army

General A. P. Hill now had concrete orders from his commander to engage the opposing forces. He sent fresh divisions against the Union line, which was in a state of disorganization following the death of General Reynolds. General Doubleday, however, made an effective use of his new command and regrouped his forces in a defensive position.

New Confederate Divisions, under the leadership of Generals Rodes and Ewell, arrived on the battlefield. These new units made it impossible for the Federal troops to hold their secondary position on McPhearson's Ridge, so they were ordered to drop back to hold their original position by the Lutheran Seminary. This position was soon attacked by heavy Confederate forces, forcing the Federal troops to retreat through the town of Gettysburg.

General Winfield Scott Hancock and his II Corps arrived on the scene at around 11:30. Hancock had been directed by General Meade to assume command of the Federal forces, even though he was outranked by Howard, who promptly argued with Hancock over Meade's directive. Hancock prevailed, and immediately set to work re-organizing the defenses of the army, taking up a very favorable location on the outskirts of the town. The center of the Union line was positioned on Cemetery Ridge, and extended all the way to the Culp Farm to the right, and to the small hilltop on which Jacob Zook had spent the night several days prior.

But the Union troop withdrawal had now left the town of Gettysburg wide open to the Confederate army, not to mention allowing the town to be in the center of the crossfire between the two great armies.

*   *   *

The residents of Gettysburg were certainly alarmed by the events of July 1. Many had been awakened to the sound of gunfire, which had begun around the crack of dawn. By mid-morning, the sound of cannon and mortar was shaking their windows. Very few residents of the town ventured out onto the streets, except to flee to stronger, more stable buildings. This was certainly the case for the Tilden family. Mrs. Tilden had said goodbye to her husband, sending him off to his dry goods store, and then packed a few items for herself, her husband and Rebecca. She then quickly moved across the town to the house of Georgia McClellan, who had the good fortune to live in a house that was constructed primarily of brick. Mary Elizabeth also knew that the McClellan house had a sturdy basement which was large enough to house a good many people, in the case the battle escalated into a major fray.

When the Tilden women reached the McClellan house, they found that the house had already been receiving extra guests. Georgia's mother had already moved down the street in order to care for her newborn grandson, and had brought along her daughter, Mary Virginia, and a six year old named Isaac, who the mother had taken in as a boarder. The original pretext for the prolonged visit had been the care of mother and child, but now the extended family was there out of fear of for their lives. Mrs. Wade spent most of her time caring for Georgia, as she was still recovering from the breech birth of her son. The household chores were given over to Gennie, who happily moved around the McClellan house as surrogate housekeeper and cook.

With the advent of the Tilden women, these chores not only became lighter, they became more enjoyable, despite the chaos that was all around them.

The Tildens had arrived around eight o'clock in the morning, when the only military action was still confined to the area by Seminary and McPhearson's Ridges. By late morning, this condition was quickly dissolving. They could see the disorganized Federal troops retreating through the streets of the town, moving behind them to set up new defenses. They could then see, but just every once and a while, a Confederate uniform – mostly in the form of pickets, or skirmishers – who were being used to probe the new defenses of the Union Army.

Rebecca was most concerned for the safety of her father – John Tilden. Her parents had discussed the possibility of soldiers in the town, and, for business purposes, John decided to stay by the store. He knew that the Federal army would treat him fairly. He wasn't looking to make a windfall profit by the presence of a large force, but he didn't want to leave the shop available for wholesale plunder, either. He had considered the possibility that the Confederate army might also have need of some of the supplies within his shop, and he was pragmatic enough to know that they would simply 'take' whatever they needed, whether he was there, or not – but he didn't feel that he was in any real danger from the rebel soldiers, unless he was foolish enough to put up a resistance to their demands. John Tilden still earnestly believed that the southerners were still Americans; that they did not wish to inflict harm on the civilian population. But even though Rebecca Tilden was most concerned with her own small family and their safety, she also wondered what had become of the handsome young Amish youth she had met only a few days ago. He had seemed bound and determined to run far away from the town of Gettysburg, and had left the McClellan house to do so, directly after Georgia had her baby, but the events of the last day, or so, may have interrupted his plans. Rebecca wondered if Jacob had gone back to his parents on Seminary Ridge, or if he was behind enemy lines, or if he had long since left the area.

*   *   *

General Robert E. Lee reached the battlefield at about 2:30 in the afternoon. Up until that time, the General had been busy directing troop movements, and conferring over strategy with General Longstreet. As the fighting grew in intensity, Lee sought the frontline – knowing that he needed to see the battlefield himself, as he had yet to hear from his cavalry brigade, and General Stuart.

Even though the Federal army was constantly growing in strength, the Confederates were able to push their foe – almost at will, visiting terrible carnage on the Union brigades. The Union right was weakening by the minute, thanks to the efforts made by General Rodes and General Ewell, who were driving the Union forces off of Seminary Ridge.

*   *   *

Sarah Zook crouched in a corner of the basement, holding her fourteen year old son, Abraham, in her arms – as if he was still a small child. Her husband, Ishmael, stood in front of them, as if to block any intruder from reaching the rest of his family. Across the basement floor sat three of the Lutheran ministers, teachers at the seminary, who had been sent for cover by the Federal troops under General Buford. By mid-afternoon, Sarah had observed that the noise of battle had changed directions. She remembered the sounds of the attack from earlier that day, and how the sound of shelling and gunfire was all around their tiny home. But now it was a different matter. Sarah noticed that the gunfire was no longer being exchanged, rather it was coming toward them, with almost no reply from the men who had sent them below ground. That could only mean one thing…

…the Union Army was in retreat.

From above their heads came the sound of footsteps; the footfall of several men walking above them inside of their house. Ishmael heard the muffled and indistinct sound of a man's voice calling out, 'Is anyone in here?' Ishmael placed his index finger to his lips, silently telling the rest – particularly Abraham – that they should be quiet. Ishmael hoped the soldiers would see that the house was deserted, and then leave. They listened quietly as the footsteps seemed to walk all around the first floor of the cottage. They could also hear the men ascending to the second level to check the bedrooms – then they heard the footsteps exit the house. Sarah exhaled a breath of relief.

Ishmael had secured the outside entrance to the cellar – a wooden contraption that looked like a barn door. For the first time since they were sent to the cellar for safety, there was now a rapping on that door. Sarah once again tensed at the sound.

"Is anyone down there?" asked a voice.

Ishmael decided that it was futile to pretend that no one was in the cellar. It was obvious that the cellar door had been barred from the inside. "Wartet!" he yelled, walking toward the entrance. He lifted off the large beam that had secured both sides of the outer door, and then stepped back. The two doors were quickly thrown back, the sunlight of the hot July day pouring in.

"Now..y'all come on out of there…y'hear?" said a voice, dripping with a southern drawl.

One of the Lutheran Ministers, Reverend Meier, called out, "We are not soldiers. We are all civilians. There are three men of the cloth here, and my caretaker and his family."

"If you are armed, please throw your weapons outside," said the soldier.

"We have no weapons," answered Ishmael.

"That remains to be seen," said the voice. "Walk out of there…one at a time. If you are not a member of the enemy army, then you will have nothing to fear."

Ishmael nodded to his family. He would go first. If they were going to harm someone, let him be the first. He walked up the stone steps to the outside air, squinting his eyes because of the bright sunlight. He felt hands touching him all over as soon as he reached the last step. Several men pulled Ishmael away from the door, continuing to pat him all over, searching for concealed weapons. "Next!" ordered the soldier. Reverend Meier headed for the door. The soldiers gave the minister a bit more respect, as he was wearing his clerical collar. Sarah noticed this from the cellar below; that the men had a note of decency about them, so she decided to send Abraham out next. She watched closely as the soldiers didn't bother to touch her son at all. Abraham ran to the arms of his father for protection. Sarah decided to join the rest of her family, and she was afforded the same degree of respect. Finally, the other two ministers left the cellar.

They silently watched as several men in gray uniforms ran down the steps into the cellar to make sure that there were no other people below – especially any of the soldiers in the blue uniforms.

The man who had done all the talking now turned to Reverend Meier. "I am sorry for any inconvenience which we might have just put you all through. We had to be certain that there were no Yankees hiding in your cellar. I am Major Charles Lawson of the 55th Virginia

Regiment. We have taken this ridge and humbly request the use of that large building over there," meaning the Seminary, "to be used as a field hospital. We have many wounded men, Reverend, and we must see to them immediately. We will also be bringing along many of the Yankee wounded, as well. We are Christian, so we do not wish to leave a suffering man on the field, no matter his allegiance."

Reverend Maier nodded. "It makes no difference which flag they have fought under, Major – they are all God's children. You may certainly use our seminary as a hospital."

"Are there any women in the immediate area who might assist us as nurses?" asked the Major.

Sarah looked first at her husband, who shrugged his shoulders in defeat, then she turned to the officer. "I would like to help, if I may?"

"Thank you, M'am. We are grateful to have your assistance."

Sarah now began to look around, checking the damage that had been leveled at their home. She could see at least three large, gaping holes in the front of the house – probably the result of a cannon or mortar shell. The clapboard siding was riddled with small holes, of which she had no idea of their source – but she was actually looking at damage from minie balls and canister shot. She hadn't realized it before, but now she realized how fortunate it was that Ishmael had ordered them all into the cellar.

The squad of Confederate soldiers escorted their six captives – for that is what they truly were – toward the seminary building. All could see that the ground was strewn with bodies; some wearing blue, some wearing gray. Men were already being carried toward the seminary, the first in line to receive medical care. Sarah was quick to notice that, louder than the ever-present sound of gunfire, was the agonizing cries of the wounded and dying.

As they made their crossing of the property, another officer galloped up to them on horseback. He looked far more important to Sarah than the Major.

"Good afternoon," the officer greeted them. "I am General A.P. Hill of the Army of Northern Virginia. I wish to personally thank you for the use of this splendid building as our field hospital."

"You are welcome, General," answered Reverend Maier. "These are my fellow teachers of theology, and this is our caretaker and his family, Ishmael Zook."

"Zook?" asked General Hill.

"Ja," answered Ishmael.

"You are Ishmael Zook, and you are Sarah Zook," said the General, "which means…that this must be Abraham Zook, who is, unless I miss my guess…fourteen years old."

"I am fourteen, sir!"

"I knew it!"

"Yes," answered Ishmael, "you knew it…only…how did you know it?"

"I knew it because I have had the honor of spending the last few days with a young Amish gentleman named Jacob Zook," said Hill, smiling.

"Jacob?" asked Sarah. "Is he…?"

"Safe?" finished Hill. "Last time I spoke to him, he was just fine."

"But…?" asked Ishmael, now relieved to hear that his son was accounted for. "How did he end up with the Confederate Army?" Hill asked. The Zooks both nodded together. "He happened to be picked up a few days ago by one of our scouting parties. They mistook him for a spy and brought him to me. I was going to return him to you more than a day ago, but then all this fighting erupted, so he had to stay behind our lines. We couldn't let him go home, because he knew our positions, and now…with all the shooting…it would have been far too dangerous."

"Oh…thank God," gushed Sarah. "We hope he has not been too much trouble for you."

"Trouble? Jacob?" smiled Hill. "We all have found him to be a very courteous and intelligent young man, Mrs. Zook."

"You are speaking of our Jacob, Herr General?" asked Ishmael. "Courteous? Intelligent?"

"All that…and more, Mr. Zook," replied the General. "He was very informative about your people, the Amish. We in the South know nothing of your…culture, so Jacob was most enlightening. At the same time, Jacob protected his own people by avoiding any explanation of this terrain, the town, the whereabouts of the Federal Army…"

"Jacob doesn't know anything about the army," interrupted his mother. "That was clear to us, my dear lady," answered Hill. "I do believe, however, that he is now being put to work helping, as you seem to be, with our wounded. I am afraid this will make him grow up faster than you may wish."

"He is already too big for his own pants," said his father. The double entendre was not lost on Hill, who let out a short laugh.

CHAPTER 12

The end of the day

Jacob looked out from behind a tree onto the rolling Pennsylvania farmland in front of his eyes. The fields were filled with bodies; from his vantage point, most of the uniforms looked gray, but he could also see some blue. He had been advised that his turn to act would come under the cover of darkness. He, and some other younger men traveling with the army, would go out onto the field, using a white flag as a symbol of their intent, to find those poor wretches that were still alive, then remove those young men to safety and medical care.

Jacob had been assigned to a company of ragamuffin teenage boys. The term 'company' was very loosely applied, as they were not in the regular army, even though they thought they were. Jacob had first been introduced to the 'leader' of the band, a young man from Alabama named Bobby McLean. Bobby seemed to be a few years younger than Jacob, but they stood about the same height. Bobby's hair was matted and filthy, he was barefoot, and, as Jacob soon discovered, was totally illiterate. Bobby had been given the ceremonial title of Corporal, even though it was a title in name only. He received no pay for his service, but was content just to be in the company of the soldiers. Not only that – he could get three meals a day…most days.

In addition to Bobby, Jacob met two brothers from the backwoods of Virginia, Nate and Johnnie Hatfield. Like Bobby, the Hatfield's were neither literate nor dressed for the job that they had to perform. Nate Hatfield was just a little older than his brother, Abraham. Johnnie was almost fifteen. There were almost a dozen other boys of various ages in the company, but Jacob preferred not to learn their names. He didn't really plan to be in the company for much longer than this night.

The company worked in teams of two. It required at least two boys to move a wounded soldier. Each boy was issued a knife, which was their only weapon of defense, in case they happened upon a Yankee soldier who did not take kindly to the idea of a Confederate hospital.

Jacob was assigned to travel with Bobby that night. The Hatfield's always worked together. Jacob felt out of place within his new band of brothers. He was the only boy that wore boots – work boots. He still wore his black trousers and white shirt and black vest, and he still had his wide brimmed black hat. He felt like a fish out of water.

Bobby McLean approached Jacob from behind as he stood looking out on the battlefield from behind the tree. Bobby stepped on a downed twig, snapping it in two. Jacob turned at the sound and smiled at his new commander.

"Hey!" greeted Bobby.

Not really understanding the greeting, Jacob simply mimicked, "Hey!" "This your first sight of a battlefield?" asked Bobby.

Jacob sighed. "It sure is! And I have to say, it is a sight I will not be forgetting for a long time hence."

Bobby shook his head. "Boy…you sho' do talk funny! Yo' talks like you 'as gone to many a day o' school."

"I've never been to school a day in my life," answered Jacob. "My mother taught me everything I know."

"That a fact?" asked Bobby. "I ain't got no mother. She died when I was three."

"I'm sorry," replied Jacob.

"Smallpox," informed the other boy.

"Is that why you are with General Lee's army, Bobby? 'Cause you don't have anyone at home?"

"I suppose that might be one reason," said the boy from the Deep South. "My main reason to join up is 'cause I don't want to see ole Abe Lincoln free all the darkies."

"The slaves?" asked Jacob, his curiosity stirred by this unabashed confession of hostility toward an entire race.

"Yep," answered Bobby. "Now…the way I reckon it…if the Yankees get their way…them slaves will be free men…just like us white folks. Ceptin'….they will be po…and I wills be po…'cept they will have mo' rights 'en me."

Jacob really didn't see the logic in what McLean was saying. He wondered how his mind had been filled with such nonsense. "I don't understand what you are saying, Bobby. Are you saying that you don't want the negroes to be freed because then they will have about as much as you do?"

"Listen to me, Jacob," McLean answered, "Ah live in a place where there is a few rich folks…an' then the rest of the white folks is po'…dirt po'. Them rich whites have slaves…lots and lots o' slaves. If them slaves get freed, then they kin go git jobs and such, and dat about makes em as good as de' po' white folks…like me."

Jacob nodded to Bobby that he understood his explanation – but he only did it to change the subject of the discussion. "How many battles have you seen, Bobby?"

"Hoo, dat's a good question," McLean replied. "Ah joined up after Antietam, so Ah've bin to Fredericksburg and Chancellorsville, plus a few smaller battles."

"You must have seen quite a few dead soldiers," observed Jacob.

"That is a fact," agreed McLean, "but Ah've seen some people that wished they wus dead, Ah kin tell you that."

Now the conversation was getting more to the heart of the matter. Jacob was actually quite concerned about his ability to see the dead and, even more so, the wounded. "What is it like?" he asked his new friend.

"First time out," McLean confided, "Ah puked ma guts out." "You did?"

"Sho! First soldier I came upon was missing half his body," explained the boy. "Must uv bin hit wi' a cannonball....Ripped 'im almos in two."

"There must have been a lot of blood," said Jacob.

"Blood?" asked Bobby. "Nah, not much. By the time I got there, he done bled out into the groun.' His body wus pale as a ghost!"

Jacob wanted to know more about this soldier. "How old do you think he was?"

"Him? I dunno...young...probably jus a little older than you or me." McLean looked over and studied Jacob. "Why? You worried 'bout seein' 'em?"

"To be quite honest...yes, I am" replied Jacob.

"Don't worry none, Jake," McLean replied, using the familiar form of Jacob's name, "yuh gits usta it."

Jacob really didn't like being called, 'Jake.' He remembered that several of the shopkeepers in Gettysburg called him that, and he really didn't like it much. It didn't sound right to him. It didn't sound.... biblical. And that's when Jacob caught himself.

He was falling back into thinking like an Amish boy. He was an American citizen, too. He stopped himself from correcting Bobby

McLean, and simply smiled at him. "I don't think I want to get used to it, Bobby."

"Wha yo' mean?" asked McLean.

And with that question, Jacob realized just how simple-minded his new friend actually was; that, or maybe it was just plain ignorance. But Jacob decided that he wasn't about to change the Bobby McLeans of the world with a debate, but he did feel he was obliged to give him a bit of Amish wisdom – even though he was an emancipated American boy. "War is really not a good answer, Bobby. It's just a bunch of killing… that's all! There are people…people in important places…who decide where and when a war is going to happen…and then they send out the armies to do the fighting. And who are in these armies? Sure…there are officers, who are like the rich people of the country…but the army is mostly made up of poor people…innocent people…like you and me. These are the people that we will see tonight."

McLean nodded his head, seeming to understand, but then he observed, "We gonna see some officers out there, too." And with that, Jacob knew that it was futile to discuss the issue any further. He liked Bobby McLean a great deal, but there was just no getting through to him. "Lookie there!" cried Bobby, pointing out onto the field. It was mid-afternoon, and the Confederates were attempting another assault on the Federal positions.

From his vantage point near the Confederate line, Jacob could see most of the fields of McPhearson's farm. He could see the wheat field, which was just about ready for harvest. He could also see a sloping hill that held Mr. McPhearson's grove of Peach trees. And he could also see that crop of granite boulders; the same strange collection of rocks which Jacob had given a wide berth to the other morning. There was just something about those rocks that Jacob did not like; they spooked him.

Suddenly Jacob was startled. Bobby McLean had let out a blood-curdling scream, and was in the act of swinging his rebel cap over his head. Jacob would later find out that this was called the "Rebel Yell," and he noticed that many of the attacking rebels were doing much the same thing as they advanced. Jacob wasn't sure if the tactic was used to scare the enemy, or to get their own blood pumping. Whatever the case, Jacob was sure that there would be even more wounded, dying and dead on McPhearson's fields in just a few minutes.

In the distance, upon a ridge line, Jacob could see the erupting fire and smoke from the Union artillery. He saw the cannons belch smoke even before he heard the explosion of the shot. "Get down, Jake!" yelled McLean, who threw his entire body on top of the Amish boy, sending him sprawling to the ground. Something whizzed over their heads as they lay prone on the Pennsylvania soil, finally crashing into a tree and splintering it some yards to their rear.

McLean rolled off of Jacob, slightly giggling at the close call. "You better keep yo' head down if yo' wanna live to see the mo'ning, Jake!"

Jacob rolled over onto his side and faced his southern friend. "Thank you, Bobby. You saved my life!" A tear ran down Jacob's cheek.

"There's no need t' git all emoshunal, Jake," replied McLean, patting his northern friend on the shoulder. "Yo' woulda dun the same fer me."

Jacob was positive that he would have done so, but doubted he knew enough about warfare to know when such an event was about to take place. He thought back to his assessment of McLean – how he had been so quick to judge his intelligence. And yet, McLean knew just when to duck for cover. He smiled over at McLean and extended his right hand in friendship. "You know, Corporal McLean, I would be honored to know you as a friend after this war is all over."

"Ah would like tha' jus fine, too," answered McLean, with a wide toothless grin.

CHAPTER 13

The First Night

General Meade arrived at the Federal Headquarters on Cemetery Ridge just after 11:30 p.m. The General was unhappy that his directive had not been followed; the Confederates had been engaged. Meade considered this more of a personal affront to his command than anything else.

General Hancock was already present at Union Headquarters, having arrived there just minutes before his commanding general. He had spent most of the afternoon, and into the evening, arranging the various corps along the ridge line. He had the chief of engineers, Brigadier General Warren, draw a detailed map of the Federal defenses, which also included the perceived positions of the Confederate army. The Federal line now stretched along Cemetery Ridge for several miles, stopping at the hill on Culp's farm, and extending down to the larger, more formidable hill called 'Round Top." General Hancock did not see a need to fortify Round Top, as it was deemed unusable from an offense point of view. It was very steep and rocky, which prevented the easy placement of artillery. Hancock felt that the rebels would be wasting time and manpower trying to fortify that hill.

Knowing that Meade would want a full explanation of the events of the day, Hancock sent for General Buford. When the blustering Meade arrived, Hancock showed his Commander the detailed battle map. Meade, always a defensive general, was impressed with Hancock's troop placement, as well as his shrewd deployment of artillery. Meade, too, was very conscious of the fact that the Union Army now possessed very good terrain to defend themselves.

General Buford arrived at headquarters just a few minutes after Meade's arrival. Buford thoroughly expected to have Meade hand him his head, but Meade had, in the interim, seen the battle map. As enraged as he had been over the engagement of the enemy, he also recognized that the Federal troops had a strong entrenchment – something akin to what the rebels had enjoyed at Fredericksburg.

Buford entered and saluted Generals Meade and Hancock.

"General Buford," said Meade, "I understand that your cavalry brigade was first to confront the enemy."

"That is true, General," answered Buford. "My scouts had reports that Harry Heth was sending two brigades into Gettysburg to forage for supplies."

"Two brigades?" asked Meade, with a tone of skepticism.

"My feelings exactly, General," replied Meade. "Gettysburg is a small town. I can't imagine what supplies could be found there that couldn't be found with just a regiment. I think that they were knowledgeable of the position of I Corps…either that, or Lee was re-positioning his army to make a move on Harrisburg. I looked at the terrain…it was some beautiful terrain for defending…so I decided to slow Harry Heth up a bit. I didn't realize that the whole Confederate Army was right behind him."

"Almost the whole Confederate Army," corrected Hancock. "Longstreet's Corps is still on the way and should be here tomorrow."

"John," said Meade, "you may have defied my orders, but you did manage to get us the best defensive positioning of the entire war. Now we shall see what General Lee intends to do about it."

"He will either withdraw," observed Hancock, "or he will try to flank us. I expect the most logical place to do that is to try to take this little hill over on the right." Hancock had indicated the hill on Culp's farm.

"And what about our left, General?" asked Meade. "There is another hill on the left, which we do not occupy."

"That is true, George," replied Hancock, "but I have had General Warren survey this hill. It is so steep and rocky…not to mention exposed to our batteries, that it would be near to impossible for the rebels to arm that hill."

"The most important thing, General," added Meade, "is to keep the Federal line intact. Lee is a master at exploiting our smallest error. Let us not give him that opportunity. Let us let General Lee come to us… for a change."

*　　*　　*

Jacob had dozed off at around 10:00, too weary from the long, hot day to keep his eyes open any longer. He had become accepting of the intermittent bursts of gunfire; anything other than full-scale attack or retreat had become almost commonplace by the end of the day.

A hand gently, but firmly, gripped his shoulder and shook him. "Jake! Wake up!" Jacob quickly opened his eyes and tried to sit up, but the hand kept him down on the ground. "Not so fast, boy," the voice exclaimed. Jacob turned his head, still groggy from the rude awakening. He looked into Bobby McLean's face. "There ye' go, Jake, it's time t' git goin.'"

"What time is it?" asked Jacob.

"Jus' about midnight, I suppose," answered McLean. The Corporal sat down on the ground, his bare feet almost hitting Jacob in the face. Rather than stare at McLean's leather-hard soles, Jacob pulled himself up and sat next to his friend. "Here," said the corporal, handing Jacob a white piece of cotton cloth, "tie this aroun' yo' arm."

Jacob nodded and took the rag and then tied it around his right upper arm. He already knew that this white cloth was the only symbol they would be wearing on the dark battlefield that would distinguish them from actual soldiers.

McLean then handed the boy a satchel made of leather. The satchel had a shoulder strap, so that it could be slung around the neck. Jacob opened the pouch, and discovered that it was filled with many assorted scraps of cloth, none of which looked clean – some even had some dried blood caked on them. "That's in case we find a man that is bleeding somethin' bad, Jake. We gotta try t' stop the bleedin,' befo we kin try t' move 'em. Remember t' tie the bandage as tight as y' can," explained McLean.

McLean then handed Jacob a leather sheath, which contained a Bowie-style knife. They had already discussed the purpose of the weapon, but, as McLean had explained, more often than not, the knife was going to be used to cut away pieces of a man's uniform, so that they could wrap a wound.

Corporal McLean leaned into Jacob's face, whispering so that only he could hear. "It's a good thing that there is a moon out tonight, Jake; that way you can tell where you're goin' and who ye' are helpin.' But it's bad, too, 'cause now ye'll be able t' see some purty bad stuff." McLean nodded, seeking Jacob's approval. "Y'know?"

"I understand, Corporal."

A few minutes later, the entire company of a dozen or more youths had gathered by the clearing. Moments after the company was assembled, a young lieutenant stopped by to give McLean the order to begin the gruesome business of the night. The boys started to spread out over the field. McLean and Jacob went straight out, staying in the center of the operation in order to communicate with the others. McLean had warned Jacob that their work might continue until dawn.

McLean demonstrated to Jacob how to creep low to the ground, in order to avoid making himself into an easy target. They reached the first body about fifty yards out from the clearing. It had been a Confederate boy – a private. He was lying flat on his back, his eyes wide open to the moon and stars above, as if he was gazing at them. His musket had already been picked up, along with his supply of cartridges. Jacob couldn't see any large-scale wound on the boy's body, except for a small hole in his jacket, near his heart. He looked at McLean, his eyes asking the question, which the corporal understood. "That's where the bullet entered," he whispered. "It's small goin' in, Jake…but you don't wan' t' turn 'em over."

The minie ball, the most popular and widely used ammunition of the war, was a soft lead projectile. Once it hit its mark, the round would then flatten out, causing further internal damage. The exit wound was usually far more dramatic than the entry wound.

The team pushed on to the next victim of the battle. Most of those encountered were dead, but some were still alive. McLean and Jacob tended to several wounded soldiers – all of them privates, with the exception of one officer, who was a Captain. A few could speak, but others were either delirious, or unconscious. The night moved quickly, as they had so much to accomplish before the dawn.

As the night progressed, so did the company progress further out into the battlefield. They were now encountering some dead Federal troops, who were mixed in among the wounded and dead Confederates. The scene, as gruesome as it was, was a metaphor for the war itself.

Just a few yards ahead of them, lay a Federal man – his blue uniform reflecting in the moonlight. The man was lying on his stomach, and Jacob knew at once that the man was still alive; he could hear him coughing and gagging on his own sputum.

McLean silently gave him the signal to approach the man. When they were but several feet from the soldier, the corporal indicated that Jacob should say a prepared remark. "Sir…we are here to help you. You are in need of medical attention. Please allow us to examine you, and then allow us to transport you to our field hospital. Do you understand?" The soldier very clearly nodded his head.

The team advanced until they were each standing on either side of the man's waist. McLean pointed to the golden oak leaf on the man's jacket, but Jacob had no idea what that symbol meant, and gave his corporal a quizzical look. He could see McLean silently mouth the word, 'Major,' which, even though he recognized the rank, did not really know exactly what that term meant. McLean nodded to Jacob again.

"Sir…we will need to roll you over so that we can examine your wound," said Jacob, again addressing the man.

The boys knelt next to the man's body, gently placing their hands on the arm closest to McLean, then they rolling toward Jacob, they rolled the soldier onto his back. The movement and change of position caused obvious pain, as the man screamed in pain, clenching his eyes shut. The Major had a large wound in his chest, but away from his heart. "He's been hit in 'is lungs," observed McLean.

The Major opened his eyes, looking first at Jacob, who he smiled at. He then turned to face McLean. Bobby McLean was not wearing a Confederate uniform – he was only dressed in rags – but he was wearing a Confederate privates' cap. The Major's countenance immediately changed. Unbeknownst to the boys, he had been concealing his officer's pistol, which he was able to keep hidden from view when the boys rolled him over, as it had been on the side which had remained in contact with the earth. He now raised the weapon and pulled the trigger.

The sound of the handgun filled the emptiness of the battlefield. The bullet struck Corporal Bobby McLean squarely in his chest, sending him reeling backwards to the ground.

"No!" cried Jacob, as he watched his new friend sail away from him. He quickly rose from the Major's side to go to the aide of his company commander, but it was already too late. Bobby McLean, the same Bobby McLean whom Jacob had just gotten to know; had just spoken words of friendship to just hours before, was already dead. Jacob looked into his friend's face, weeping openly at the sight. Just like the young private they had come upon earlier that night, Bobby's eyes were wide open, his face formed in such a way that it, in a final moment, had nothing but a look of complete and utter surprise written upon it.

Jacob didn't know what to do. He knelt next to his friend and pulled his body up toward him, hugging him as if he could comfort him in his time of need. Jacob didn't notice that his shirt was getting wet; his white shirt soaking up the blood that was flowing freely out of McLean's chest. What did it matter? What did anything matter?

Jacob muttered his lost friend's name over and over, calling his name softly, as if he had it within his power to wake him from the most final sleep. Finally, as he felt the flush of anger welling up inside of him, he gently lay his company commander's body back down on the ground – another victim of the conflict. He turned back to the Major, who was now lying flat on his back, his pistol still gripped in his right hand.

"He was just here to help you," he said to the Major. "Why did you have to kill him?"

"He was the enemy," answered the Major. "He was going to take me prisoner."

"He was just a poor, ignorant boy," said Jacob, his voice rising with anger. "I should just leave you here to bleed to death! That's all you deserve!"

"Please!" hoarsely whispered the Major. "Help me."

Jacob looked around the field, searching for other members of the company. He couldn't see anyone. He looked back at McLean, lying broken and lifeless on the field. He thought of his brother, Abraham… and then he thought of his parents, wondering if they were out of harm's way; but he also thought of what his parents, particularly his mother, would have done at this moment in time.

He turned back to the Major. "I am not a Confederate, sir. I am a resident of Gettysburg, who has happened to have fallen into Confederate hands. I was helping with the wounded, so I will help you now."

Jacob watched as the Major dropped his right hand, along with the pistol, to his side. The boy approached the man again, still feeling angry at him for his actions, but sorry for him, as well – for he was in obvious pain from his wound. Jacob knelt back down by the Major's side. He reached for his satchel in order to retrieve some of the bandages.

Suddenly, the Major reached up with his left hand and grabbed Jacob by the collar, pulling the boy right up to his face. Jacob heard the familiar sound of a firearm being primed, and realized that the Major now had his pistol pressed against his head. "Now…boy…this is what you are going to do," the Major said, without much ease. "You are going to drag me…backward…toward the Federal line. Is that clear?"

"Sir," Jacob replied, "Your wound is very severe. I don't know if you will survive that distance."

"I will chance it, boy," said the Major. "You will grab me underneath my arms and pull. One false step and I will blow a hole in you…just like your friend."

"I will try, sir," answered Jacob.

"You had better do more than try, boy," threatened the soldier.

Jacob stepped around the soldier, placing his hands under his body and through his armpits. He lifted the Major. Even though Jacob was strong for his age due to his daily work on the farm, the Major was heavier than he expected. He began to drag the injured soldier backwards, as directed. He pulled the Major into McPhearson's wheat field, hoping that the tall grass would act as a cover so that they could advance undetected.

It was working.

Jacob had dragged the Major about thirty yards into the wheat field when he gently put the soldier's head back on the ground. "What's wrong?" asked the Major.

"Nothing," said Jacob, "except for the fact that you are bleeding to death. This dragging isn't going to increase your chances of surviving this war."

"I'll take that chance," returned the Major, gruffly. "How far across did we get?"

"We are almost halfway across the open field, sir," replied the boy. "After that, I couldn't tell you where your army is located."

"You get within the proper area," the Major advised, "and it won't really matter. They will find you!"

That really didn't seem very comforting to know. Jacob wondered if the rest of the Federal troops were as quick on the trigger as the Major. He wondered if they would shoot first, and ask questions later. Jacob lifted the Major by the shoulders and continued to drag him.

He dragged the officer for about twenty more yards. Jacob could hear approaching footsteps, so he pulled the Major out of the wide space between the rows, until they were both obscured by the tall wheat. Jacob could hear the sound of a patrol passing close by, but he didn't know whether the patrol was from the North, or from the South. He crouched close over the Major's body and drew his knife. "That for me, boy?" the soldier asked.

"Not unless you make me use it, sir," Jacob answered. "Besides… what good is a knife against a pistol?"

"Usually I would agree with you," said the Major, "but I don't even know if there is another bullet in the chamber. If you wanted to, you could probably kill me right here with that knife."

"I will not kill you, sir," replied the boy. "It is not within me to do such a thing."

The Major lay silent for a moment, obviously moved by what the boy had just spoken. "What is your name, son?"

"I am Jacob Zook."

"Jacob Zook….I am Major Robert Winslow of the 68th Pennsylvania Regiment."

"You are from Pennsylvania?" asked Jacob, astonished at the coincidence.

"From Philadelphia," he answered, and then grunted in pain.

"You must allow me to stop the bleeding," said Jacob. Major Winslow slowly nodded in agreement. Jacob gently unbuttoned his uniform blouse, revealing the lighter blue shirt below. The shirt was drenched in the Major's blood. With his Confederate issue Bowie knife, Jacob slowly cut the wet shirt away from the soldier's chest. This revealed the chest wound, which was remarkably small, just like the Confederate soldier he had come upon hours before…with McLean. Jacob reached into his bag and pulled out some rags. He found one that looked cleaner than the rest and used it to dress the wound, knowing that the minie ball was probably still in the Major's body.

The Major watched him work, his face saddening with each ministration by the youth. "Jacob," he said quietly, "please accept my apologies for shooting your friend back there."

Jacob did not want to hear the man apologize. "You were probably delirious from the loss of blood…or the heat…or both. You probably didn't mean to kill him."

Winslow looked up at the young man. He reminded him of his oldest son, Robbie. He had just killed another boy, a boy the same age as this; a boy the same age as his own son. How could he have done such an awful thing? "I did mean to kill him, Jacob?"

"What? Why?"

"I cannot tell you, son…but I will make this request." He looked into Jacob's eyes. "If I am captured by the rebels, you are to prevent this from happening by taking my pistol and shooting me."

"What?"

"I cannot be taken alive," he explained.

"I don't understand, Major," Jacob replied, "and even if you ask it…I will not do it!"

"Then I will do it myself," said Winslow. His manner was resolute and determined. "This is why I shot your friend…to avoid being captured."

"But we were here to help you, just as I am doing for you now," explained Jacob.

"Yes," agreed Winslow, "but eventually you would have taken me back behind the Confederate lines, and that was something which I could not allow."

"But why not?" asked Jacob.

"Never you mind," the soldier replied. "It would be best for both of us if you just get me to my lines."

Jacob nodded. He finished dressing the wound as best as he knew how, and then re-buttoned the Major's blouse in order to hold the bandage in place. Jacob really didn't put much stock in his ability as a doctor, but he prayed that he might be able to deliver this man to the Federal lines.

He grabbed Winslow under the arms again and started to drag him. It was a long, painful process. They did not make quick progress – advancing toward the Federal line in bursts of only twenty or thirty feet at a time. Jacob took the opportunity of a brief rest period to look up into the night sky. He could tell by the position of the moon that the night was quickly ending – it would be morning in an hour. He redoubled his efforts to get the officer to the safety of the Union line.

At long last, Jacob could see the end of the row of wheat. He knew that, once out of the rows, they would be very much in the open again. He worried that the fast approaching dawn would allow them to be discovered. More than that, Jacob was also on the verge of exhaustion. The Major weighed a great deal, and although Jacob wasn't sure exactly how much that was, he knew that the Major weighed more than he did.

Jacob continued to drag Winslow toward the opening in the wheat field, pulling him to within a few feet of the end of the row. Once again, and for the last time, he put the Major back on the ground, giving them both a rest. He stood up and slowly walked to the edge of the wheat, looking out toward what he hoped would be the Federal line. There, about fifty yards away, were picket lines. He could see hundreds of blue uniforms gathered for morning muster. But he also realized that if he was to walk out of the field toward them, he would probably be shot dead on the spot. He also knew that he would probably be shot if he were to drag the Major, as he had been doing for most of the night, because the pickets would not be able to see the officer, as Jacob was blocking him from view with his own body. He knew that there was only one way to get the Major over the final stretch of ground.

He had to carry him.

He walked back to Winslow. Jacob could tell that the Major was not doing very well. Even in the dim light of morning, he could see that the Major was looking very pale, as if all of his color had drained from his face. The boy knew that this was the time to act, if he was to save the Major – and that it already may have been too late, at that.

But Jacob also wondered if he had the physical strength to accomplish this task. He never carried another full grown man before, but he had carried his brother, if only in playing around with him on the farm. But Abraham was less than a hundred pounds, the Major was at least seventy five pounds heavier – and Jacob was exhausted, too. He thought about how to do this successfully.

And then Jacob remembered seeing his father bring in an injured calf from the field. The calf had hurt its front hoof, and his father didn't want the injured animal to put unnecessary weight on the hoof until he could wrap it. Ishmael Zook carried the calf all the way from the outermost field back to the barn – a distance of over two hundred yards. Jacob had assisted his father, but not by carrying the animal – that was a one person job. His father had wrapped the calf around his shoulders, carrying it like a woman would wear a shawl.

Jacob was confident that he could tolerate carrying the weight of the Major; what he couldn't fathom was how he was going to get the man up on his shoulders. His father had been able to get under the calf because it had been standing upright on the ground. The Major was semi-conscious and lying flat on his back. He also realized that the Major would not be able to assist in the process; he would be, for lack of a better term, 'dead weight.'

Jacob bent over the wounded soldier. "Major Winslow…can you hear me?" He thought he heard a slight groan come out of his mouth, but perhaps that was not in answer to his question. Considering the possibility that it was, Jacob decided to talk through the steps of the procedure. "Major…I have to take your pistol from your hand and put it back in your holster. Will you let me do that for you?" Jacob thought he heard another groan. He reached over to the Major's right hand and gently removed the pistol from his grip, which was surprisingly loose, he then returned the revolver to the leather holster on the Major's waist. He studied the Major's sword, which was still around his waist, the blade still sheathed in the scabbard. "Major…I am going to remove your sword from your waist. It will only get in the way. We can come back later to pick it up." Jacob didn't hear a groan, or any other noise, for that matter. He undid the catch which held the scabbard and pulled the chain from around the Major's body, then placed the sword to one side.

Jacob knew that he had just completed the easiest part of the whole sequence; now it would get appreciably tougher. "Major Winslow…I need to roll you onto your stomach. Do you understand?" Again, there was no sound from the officer. The boy reached over to the far side of the man's body, at his mid-section, and gently pulled the body toward him, backing up on his knees as the officer's body came closer to him. Raising his body off the ground was difficult, but once the body had reached its apogee, Jacob had an even more difficult time holding his body back, so that the Major wouldn't crash face-first into the soil of the wheat field. As the soldier's body started to pass the halfway point, Jacob changed the position of his hands to break the Major's return to the earth, but this put additional strain on his wound. Jacob heard the familiar groan of pain once again.

"Major? Can you hear me?" asked Jacob, but the officer was silent again. Jacob realized that he was about to face the most difficult part of the task – getting his own body positioned in a way that he would be able to lift the Major on his shoulders. He studied the silent man – thinking about the best way to accomplish this. He knew he had to get underneath him, and then lift him to his shoulders, straightening up to his knees; from there he simply had to stand up, one foot at a time. But he had absolutely no idea how to begin this feat.

Jacob rose from the ground. He had to find something, anything that would allow him to get the officer's body off of the ground. He walked down the rows of wheat, hoping that he would not encounter any other soldiers, living or dead. About fifty feet from the suffering Major, Jacob stumbled over something in the dirt. He discovered that he had tripped over a broken fence rail. He pulled the rotting timber out of the ground. It was only a about three feet long, but could possibly be of use, he thought. Jacob searched the adjacent area, looking for the rest of the rail. He found another piece a few feet away. It was even more rotten than the first piece, but Jacob felt that there was a chance that it would hold together. He grabbed both pieces and returned to Major Winslow.

He picked up his satchel and dumped the remaining bandage rags out of the bag. He took his Bowie knife and cut the wider strips lengthwise, creating two or three strips out of one. He now had several yards of cloth striping. Jacob placed the two timbers on either side of the Winslow's legs. He measured out some of the cotton strips, making sure that he had enough of them to create a makeshift splint – but he would splint both of the officer's legs together as one. Most importantly, the boy made sure that he had about five inches of the rail extended past the Winslow's boots. Jacob checked to see that the bonds were securely tied; they had to stay in place until he had Winslow on his shoulders. He then took the empty satchel and whatever scraps of cotton were left over and formed it into a pillow, placing it beneath Winslow's face.

It was now time to find out if his plan was going to work.

Jacob needed to get the Federal soldier to create an arch with his body; the splints would help do that work for him. The boy straddled the soldier and grabbed him around the midsection, lifting with all his might. He lifted the officer several inches off of the ground before pausing to see if his plan had worked.

It had – the twin splints were keeping the officers rump slightly off of the ground. Inspired by this success, Jacob lifted Winslow again, gaining another few inches of space beneath the man's stomach and the ground. The boy lifted again, straining with all of his might. There was now about eighteen inches of clearance under the officer's midsection. Moving quickly, Jacob stepped over Winslow's frame and positioned himself near the space he had just created.

It was now…or never.

Jacob bent his head down and pushed himself into the small space, lifting with his back and holding onto the Major with his arms. Using the strength of his back muscles, he again lifted the man, raising him even higher off the floor of the wheat field. Jacob knew that he had to be careful; he could not afford to lose his balance. He pushed up again, his shoulders digging into the man's stomach and intestinal areas. He pushed one more time and found that he had straightened his back.

The Major was now completely off of the ground.

Jacob knew that this next step was also going to be difficult, but he had to do it immediately, or he would tire himself out before he could complete the task. He slowly leaned his body to the left. He hoped that the extra weight he was carrying would not cause him to fall to the side. And just as that thought entered his mind, he felt resistance.

The splints had hit the dirt!

He had leaned over to the left in order to have the splints meet up with the ground again, allowing him to use this newly gained leverage to raise his right leg. This movement would almost bring the Major to an upright position. Once Jacob accomplished this, he quickly continued moving; leaning back to his right in order to take the weight off of his left knee, which he then straightened out.

The boy now had to get the added weight under control; he was swaying back and forth. He had to take that first step forward. He had to re-direct the weight forward, rather than side to side.

He took a step with his right foot…and then his left.

Then his right.

Then his left.

He was moving forward.

Jacob established a slow, careful step. He needed to be careful not to trip or stumble. He moved slowly in the direction of the edge of the wheat field.

He was aware of several thoughts, all at once. First, he was aware that he could not hear or feel Winslow breathing – nor had he heard a grunt or groan from the Major for quite some time. Second, because of how he was carrying Winslow, he was now aware that there was a musky odor floating around his nostrils. Probably when he was shot, the Major had emptied his bladder. Jacob was smelling the odor of the officer's urine. Third, he wondered how long he could keep carrying the man;

his weight was far greater than he ever had imagined it would be. Finally, about ten steps into his journey, he realized that his wide-brimmed black hat was lying on the ground, next to the officer's sword.

He approached the edge of the field. Jacob could see the Federal pickets again. He wanted to start yelling to them, but, after remembering the 'Rebel Yell' of his poor friend, Bobby McLean, dismissed this idea. He was afraid the pickets might confuse it for a Confederate attack.

He stepped out of the wheat field into the light of the dawn. He still had another fifty yards to walk, but he knew that he would never last that long.

Jacob heard the cries of the pickets. He couldn't see them, as his head was focused on the ground. His upper body was almost perpendicular to the ground, creating a platform to hold the Major.

He heard a voice yell, "It's an officer!"

He heard another say, "He's been wounded!"

He heard a third call, "Get a medic!"

And then he heard the sound of several men running toward him. To Jacob, time seemed to stand still for a while. He would later remember the strange sensation created when the Federal pickets lifted Major Winslow off of his back. He would also remember how difficult it had been to stand upright. He didn't remember the Federal Sergeant clapping him on the back, congratulating him for rescuing the Major – nor did he remember the cheers sent up all the picket line for the same act of compassion.

All Jacob Zook knew was that he had done what any other man should have done – and that he was now back on the other side of the battlefield for the first time in several days.

CHAPTER 14

A Chance Encounter

Mary Virgina Wade woke before dawn on the morning of 2 July, 1863. She quickly dressed and then proceeded up the stairs from the cellar, leaving Georgia and her infant son and the entire Tilden family sleeping in the lower level of home. Ginnie entered the kitchen and began preparations to mix some dough for bread. It was Ginnie's opinion, based on own anxiety over Jack Skelley – her finance, that she was bound by duty to make the lives of the Federal troops, of which Jack was a member, as comfortable and as welcome as possible. Ginnie Wade loved to bake bread; her loaves of bread were enjoyed by many of her friends and neighbors in Gettysburg. Now she would put that talent to good use.

She quickly moved about the kitchen, collecting the various ingredients needed for the first batch of dough. This was not going to be a short-lived project; she wasn't planning on baking a few loaves – she was planning on baking hundreds of loaves. She knew that she couldn't possibly bring enough bread to supply the entire Federal army, but she would do whatever part she could.

Most of the women in Gettysburg still baked their own bread, even if it was not baked fresh on a daily basis. They would bake a batch of wheat bread, or sour dough, or even rye – which might yield about two to three loaves out of the mix.

Ginnie had at her disposal a less common tool – a bread trough. Ginnie had moved her bread trough – a large rectangular shaped vessel on legs – over to the McClellan house as Georgia became closer to the time of her delivery. She could prepare almost a hundred loaves of bread at a time using the trough, which allowed her to knead a large quantity of dough, and then let it rise – all in the same container. Prior to the recent conflagration, she would give several loaves to her family to enjoy, and then she would sell the rest in order to earn a little more income for the family.

That, and the money which she made as a seamstress, along with her mother, was the primary source of income for the Wade family these days.

"What are you doing, Ginnie?" said a voice from within the shadows of the house.

"Rebecca? Is that you?"

"Yes," Rebecca answered. "Why are you up here? Don't you think it's dangerous?"

"Don't worry, Becky," she said, "if I hear just one gunshot I will hurry right back down to the cellar. Besides – the walls of the house are made of brick."

"Yes," agreed Rebecca, "but the windows are not." Rebecca Tilden walked further into the kitchen. "What are you doing?"

"Baking bread, silly. It's what I do."

"Yes…but why?"

"It's for the soldiers, Becky," Ginnie replied.

"The soldiers?"

Ginnie clapped her hands together, sending a cloud of flour dust into the air. "I keep thinking about poor Jack, Becky. I worry about him all the time. I know his brother, Daniel, is working for your father at the dry goods store, and he told me that the 87th Pennsylvania Regiment is now a part of something called the III Corps."

"The Third Corps?"

"No, III Corps, Becky,"Ginnie corrected. "I know that they saw a great deal of action down in Virginia, but I wonder if they are part of this battle, too."

"But that is the point, Ginnie," Rebecca replied. "I have seen the III Corps battle flags. They came into the area last night."

"Last night!" Ginnie said, in a shocked voice. "Becky! How do you know this to be so? We are in the middle of the Confederate line – there are gray uniforms running all around the town. How can you know this to be true?"

Rebecca looked down at the floor. "I know of a way to the Federal line, Ginnie. I was out there last night."

"What?"

"It was easy…really!" Rebecca said, smiling at her own audacity.

"Does your mother know you snuck out?"

"Of course not, Ginnie…and don't you tell her!"

"I should, you know," answered Ginnie, putting her hands back into the dough, beginning to knead it.

"Well," said Rebecca, "you can do that…but if you do you won't learn how to cross the lines, and then you won't be able to visit Jack."

Ginnie gasped. She wanted to see if her finance was still in one piece – not that it mattered, she thought, for even if he had lost an arm or an eye, she would still want to marry him after the war was over. "I would like to see Jack, but I would also go to deliver some of this bread to the men of his corps."

"That sounds like a perfect excuse to me, Ginnie," answered Rebecca, smiling at her friend.

Ginnie gave her younger friend a smirk. "But you never mentioned why it was that you ventured out behind the lines."

"Curiosity, mostly."

"Curiosity?" asked Ginnie. "That is no place for a sixteen year old girl!" "I'm seventeen!" she corrected.

"Fine!" Ginnie used both of her hands to rotate the large mound of dough in the dough trough. "Wait!" she said, stopping her kneading to look Rebecca in the eyes. "Did you go looking for that young man… what is his name?….Jacob Zook?"

Rebecca didn't answer the question.

"Becky! Have you lost your senses? What makes you think that boy has any interest in you? For that matter, what makes you so sure that he is even still anywhere near the town of Gettysburg? You risked your life for a stranger?"

"I didn't think I was risking my life, Ginnie…not really. There was no gunfire – and the Federal soldiers were real nice to me. I asked if they had seen a young, handsome Amish boy, but most didn't know what an Amish boy even was."

"But….?"

"But I have a feeling, that's all….a feeling that Jacob is still around here.

*   *   *

"Wake up! Wake up, boy!"

Jacob felt woozy. He felt as though he was walking in a fog.

"Wake up, boy!"

Jacob felt something cold and wet upon his forehead. He slowly opened his eyes.

"Are you alright, boy?" asked a Federal Sergeant.

"Where…am…I?" he asked.

"You are with the III Corps, Army of the Potomac, son," replied the sergeant.

"I made it?" Jacob asked, in disbelief.

"You certainly did," said the sergeant, "now we just have to see if the Major is going to pull through."

"Major Winslow?" asked Jacob.

"The very same. How is it that you happened to be out there on that field?" asked the sergeant.

Jacob closed his eyes. When he did, he felt the ground beneath him spinning.

"Never mind that, for now," smiled the Federal soldier, "you best git to see a doctor, too. Let me help you up." It was only then that Jacob realized that he was lying down on a cot. He looked around his new surroundings. He was in a field tent.

The sergeant extended his hand and grabbed Jacob's right arm, pulling him gently to an upright position. "How do you feel?"

"My head is spinning, sir," replied the boy. "Do you have any water?"

"I have some with me," answered the sergeant, hoisting up a military issue canteen. Jacob took a big gulp of the water, which tasted old and stale – not like the water he was accustomed to drinking, which came from the Seminary well. "Thank you, Sergeant."

"Mullins."

"Pardon me?" asked Jacob.

"Sergeant Mullins, at your service," smiled the soldier. "It looks like you got yourself caught in the middle of what is shaping up to be a pretty big battle, uh…."

"Jacob," the boy replied. "My name is Jacob Zook. I live over at the seminary." It was at this moment that Jacob realized that he wasn't wearing his white shirt or vest. He was wearing a blue shirt, the kind that was worn as an undergarment under a Federal uniform. He looked at the sergeant with questioning eyes.

"Oh…your clothes?" the sergeant said, understanding. "I took 'em off of you. You were covered with all matter of ….well…let me just tell you that you smelled something awful, Jacob." Jacob could hear the noise and activity of the Union camp. He could hear officers and sergeants barking orders, and he could also hear the sounds of horses and wagons…and even perhaps the movement of artillery. He tried to stand up, but his legs gave way beneath him. "I think you had best rest up for a while, Jacob. I will go git you somethin' to eat. If you can keep it down, that's a good sign."

"A good sign of what, Sergeant Mullins?"

"A good sign that your skull isn't cracked," answered Mullins, "but I don't think it is. I think you are just dehydrated."

"What is going to happen to me now, Sergeant?"

Mullins scratched his stubble, "I think that my commanding officer will want to know how you came to rescue Major Winslow, for starters. I'll see to that food." Jacob nodded. He knew what that meant; he was going to be asked about the Confederate Army. He was going to have the same questions asked of him that the Confederate Generals had asked only a few days before – only now….now he truly knew some of the answers. He had seen a great deal of Lee's army; he knew where a great many of the artillery pieces were placed.

For the second time in only a few days, Jacob felt that his neutrality was about to be questioned.

But he was also worried about his family. He quickly discovered that Seminary Ridge was now in the hands of the Confederates. He wondered whether or not his parents were being held as prisoners. He wondered if they were dead, or alive.

Mullins returned with a large plate of food; bacon, biscuits and something that reminded him of a wheatcake. The sergeant also carrying a container of a hot, dark brown liquid, which Jacob assumed was coffee. Also entering the tent but following Mullins was an officer.

"Sir," said Mullins, addressing the officer, "this is the young lad I was telling you about. This is a local boy…Jacob Zook. He is the boy…sorry, young man… who brought Major Winslow in from the field." Mullins handed Jacob the coffee and breakfast. Jacob looked up at the officer, waiting for his cue to begin eating.

"Please…Mr. Zook, do not let me stop you. Eat!" requested the officer. "I am Major General Birney; second in command of this corps. Do you have any idea what you have done, Jacob?"

Jacob stopped chewing, although his mouth was still full. "What I've done?" he asked, through the food.

"In saving Major Winslow's life," answered the General, "at least we believe he will live…thanks to you." The General looked down at the boy. He was ill at ease, a trait which Jacob quickly noticed. Jacob observed that, for a man who could wield the power of an army, the man seemed very uncomfortable speaking to him.

"Is there something else, General?" Jacob asked, sensing that the conversation was far from over. Is there wasn't anything else, he thought, why would there be an officer with the rank of Major General standing in the tent. Mere thanks could have been expressed by almost anyone.

"Why…ah…yes….young man," the officer quietly said. "Did Major Winslow speak to you while you were together out on the field of battle?"

"Yes, sir," Jacob answered, "the Major had a few things to say…but he said them mostly after he shot and killed my friend, Bobby McLean." Jacob decided to play this conversation out in a very careful manner. It was already obvious that the General had ulterior motives in making this visit.

The General was visibly shaken by the boy's last statement. "I'm sorry that he killed your friend. Any civilian casualty of war is regrettable, at best."

"Oh, no...General," Jacob answered, his eyes narrowing, "Bobby McLean was with the Confederate Army. He and I were on stretcher duty."

"I see," replied Birney. But the General didn't see, and Jacob knew it. "Are you saying that you have some allegiance to the rebel cause?"

Jacob shook his head. "No, sir...I have no allegiance to either cause – although, I must say, if I was actually given my choice in the matter, I think that I would side with President Lincoln."

"I don't follow you," said Birney, confused.

"The name 'Zook' is one of the most common names found in the Amish people of Lancaster County, sir." Jacob could tell that Birney was still confused. "I am Amish by birth – my father is Ishmael Zook. My mother, Sarah Zook, was born Sarah Loder – also a very common name among the people that you may know as the 'Pennsylvania Dutch.'"

"Ah," said Birney, as if a bell had struck inside of his brain. "Your people object to the war..." he began.

"...No, sir," Jacob interrupted, "we don't object to this war. We object to any war! We do not support any government, except the government set up by the elders of our own community." Birney seemed astonished at this statement. "For reasons I will not go into at this time, we were sent out of our Amish community in Paradise, Pennsylvania, over a year ago, and now we live at the Lutheran Seminary....on Seminary Ridge. I was taken prisoner, as a spy, by the Confederates...a few days ago...but they believed the same story which I am relating to you right now....that I only care about the value of human life...any human life...and that also included Major Winslow, who shot my new acquaintance, Bobby McLean, down like he was killing a crazed dog in the street. And why?"

Jacob paused, allowing his question to sink in. "Because he was wearing a rebel privates' cap. He shot a sixteen year old farm boy because he was wearing a Confederate cap."

"And still you chose to bring him in from the field?" asked the General.

Jacob slowly nodded. "I don't think I could have lived with myself if I had not done so, sir. Sure...at first, while he still had the strength in his body, he threatened me with his pistol...but there were many opportunities for me to just leave him there. But that wouldn't have been right."

Now it was Birney's turn to do the nodding. "You did an extraordinary thing, Mr. Zook."

"He made me promise to shoot him if I couldn't get him back," confided the boy, "so I had to do it, because there was no power on Earth that was going to get me to shoot a man."

Birney once again nodded. "Did he explain why he wanted you to shoot him?"

"Nah!" responded Jacob. "We were plenty angry at each other at the moment. He had just shot Bobby, so I was really, really angry at him – so I listened to him, but I didn't care about what he was saying to me. I just figured that he was out of his head."

"What did you find in his pockets?"

"In his pockets?" Jacob asked. "In his trousers?"

"No," answered the General. "In his jacket."

"The only thing I did was take off his sword – which is still in that wheat field, in case he needs it later – and I put his pistol back in the holster. I only opened his coat to bandage his wound."

"And what side was he wounded on?" asked Birney.

Jacob thought back for a moment. "His right side."

"So you didn't look in the left side of his jacket?"

"Not at all," answered the boy. "After I bandaged him, I buttoned his jacket to help keep the bandage in place." Birney looked away from the boy, satisfied in what he had heard him say. "Why?"

Birney looked back at the Amish boy. He knew that the boy wasn't a Confederate spy, and he really couldn't imagine him making a run for the rebel line. "Major Winslow was carrying some very sensitive documents in his jacket pocket, Jacob. Documents which would have proven very valuable to the rebels, had they fallen into their hands. Knowing this to be the case, was why the Major was so anxious to get back to his own line."

Jacob could now see the logic…and the necessity. "But why did he want me to shoot him?"

"That," answered the General, "was a matter of pride. If those documents had fallen into enemy hands, then the Major would have preferred to be dead rather than alive to witness the result."

"I don't quite understand," said the boy.

Birney studied the young man intensely. He didn't think that the boy was playing him; he actually had no idea about the documents, or their importance to the Union army. "Major Winslow was in the process of delivering some important information to General Meade from the army's chief engineer, Brigadier General Warren. If this information had been found on his body, whether alive or dead, it could have jeopardized our entire operation."

"Oh," was the only word Jacob could muster.

"Now you see the point, I'm afraid," said Birney. "Your friend's death, even though tragic – if he was only a stretcher bearer, instead of a soldier – was accidental, because the Major was trying to protect that information from falling into enemy hands. He probably chose not to shoot you because you didn't look at all like one of them." Jacob nodded. He was satisfied with the explanation, for the time being. He looked down at the plate of food sitting on his lap. He had only taken a few bites, and then he had been distracted by the General. "I will leave you to your breakfast, son. You are to be questioned by our staff officers later this morning, hopefully before the battle resumes in earnest. Please… do not try to leave this camp. It is dangerous away from here, even for a civilian." General Birney turned and exited the tent.

Jacob went back to eating his breakfast. He broke off a piece of the wheat cake and stuffed it in his mouth. Even though he was extremely hungry, he easily recognized that this pancake was not on the same par as those made by his own mother. He ate it, but it was only to fill the void in his stomach. He picked up a piece of the thickly sliced bacon, biting off a large piece. He put the plate down on the cot next to where he was sitting and then stood up. He suddenly felt very closed in, as if the tent had just become much smaller. He walked over to the tent flaps, pulling one back halfway to see what was going on outside. The boy could see plenty of activity, as soldiers were busy running around in just about every direction. There was also the ever-present sound of cannon and gunfire, but it seemed to be very distant, coming from either the far left or the far right of his position. He took in a deep breath of air. The odor of gunpowder was heavy in the morning air. Jacob could also tell that this was going to be another hot, humid July day – perhaps even hotter than the day before.

The young man walked back toward the cot, and his breakfast. He found one of the two upright tent poles and wrapped his arm around it – not for support, but just because it was there.

And then….he felt the tears begin to course down his cheeks. He didn't understand why that was happening…not now…not after going through the hell of the previous night and living to talk about it. Why would he start crying like a baby…now? But the longer he thought about it, the deeper he began to sob, until he was sobbing so deeply that he could hardly breathe. Suddenly, his stomach began to turn. Jacob ran again to the flap of the tent, getting his head through the flap just in time to vomit any food he had recently eaten.

CHAPTER 15

The Morning of 2 July

General Meade had worked throughout the night, making sure that the Army of the Potomac was suitably entrenched along Cemetery Ridge. The army had enjoyed the high ground on the first day of the battle, only to see that advantage squandered as the Confederate forces surged forward, pushing them back. But they had retreated back to even more advantageous ground, where the center of the army was now entrenched.

Meade was aware that he was facing two Generals of the highest caliber in Lee and Longstreet. Both were considered excellent battlefield strategists, and both were not afraid to use their forces to push the Union Corps – as they had demonstrated on many occasions already. Meade, too, was a cautious man. He did not want to waste his most valuable commodity, his manpower, so he chose to reinforce his defenses, choosing to wait for the enemy to come to him.

But he also recognized that there was a chink in the Union defenses, and that weak spot was on the Federal right flank, along the small hill that dominated the Culp farm and the other hill situated just to the left, Cemetery Hill. Meade had already entrenched General Howard's corps on Cemetery Hill, and had General Henry Slocum's corps stationed on Culp's Hill. Meade felt that the Union right was ready for Lee's attack.

But Meade had been advised by his chief engineer, General Warren, that the small hills at the Federal left were not occupied, and could allow that flank to be attacked at will, if those hills were occupied by the rebels. Part of this intelligence was sent to Meade in the early morning in the form of several pages of hand-drawn maps which had been sent by General Warren, based upon his observations atop one of those hills, and had been carried by a Major in General Sickles III Corps, by the name of Winslow. Winslow had almost been captured trying to deliver that information, but had been rescued by a local boy. Meade was now moving an additional corps to cover the smaller of the two hills, the one the locals referred to as "Sugar Loaf Hill." General Warren had also suggested that defending the larger hill – the one further out of the Union left, "Round Top," was not necessary, as the terrain would prove impossible to negotiate to make it a useful strategic location. Meade had quickly made a decision early in the morning on 2 July, to have the arriving V Corps, under the command of General George Sykes, to reinforce the left of the Union line by sending the earliest arriving brigades directly to Sugar Loaf Hill.

*   *   *

General Lee had also recognized the strategic importance of the hilly areas on either end of the Federal line. He instructed his second in command, General James Longstreet, to take two Divisions of his Corps and attack the Federal left, which he believed had been mistakenly left undefended. Longstreet sent two of his most able Division Commanders, Generals McLaws and Hood, to try to break the Union entrenchment by swinging around from the left. Once situated on top of the little rise of rock, known as Sugar Loaf Hill, the Federal troops would be at a definite disadvantage and would be forced to withdraw.

But at the same time, either to further distract the Federal forces away from the center, or to create the same flanking movement and acquisition of more high ground, Lee chose to send another Corp, under the command of General Richard Ewell, to attack Cemetery and Culp's Hills. Lee realized that the Union right was already well defended – that two Federal Corps already occupied those two outcroppings, so he gave Ewell a somewhat ambiguous order; to take the hills, if possible.

*　　*　　*

By 9:00, Mary Virginia Wade had about fifty loaves of bread out of the oven and cooling on the work table in the kitchen. Even though the front of the McClellan house was facing the Confederate occupied town, she discovered, through her close friend, Becky Tilden, that she could exit the rear of the house and easily reach the Federal line simply by walking up Baltimore Street. Never was this easier to do during the battle, than on the morning of 2 July.

Becky and Ginnie packed up the loaves, along with a few pints of the jam she had put up the previous month, and bundled it in several hampers. The two girls then set off for the Federal Line. As Baltimore Street was a constantly rising road, it was considered easily defensible by the Confederates, and they stayed away from the area. The two young women easily crossed over the Union picket lines and into the camp. They had just entered the encampment of General Howard's Corps, which was defending the area known as Cemetery Hill.

The picket line was manned by a group of Ohio volunteers; most of them were privates. The average age was between eighteen and nineteen years old. These young men were more than happy to see the two young ladies walking up Baltimore Street, their hampers swaying as they walked. Once past the defenses, Ginnie and Becky found themselves surrounded by battalions of young men…and a few older, crustier sergeants. They set to their task, passing out the bread to small groups of the men so that the fragrant meal could be shared within a company. Having some sense of what could be considered political acumen, the girls also held back a few loaves for the officers, knowing that their next journey through the line might be as easily accomplished if the right wheels were greased.

Ginnie asked a sergeant for the location of the officer's tents, and the gentleman was happy to point the way. Already warm from the hot sun on that July morning, they continued to climb Cemetery Hill. They ignored the cat calls from some of the members of a New York Regiment, although they smiled to each other after each occurrence. As they neared the tents, they were surprised to hear a familiar voice.

"Becky…Becky Tilden!"

Rebecca turned in the direction of the voice. A young man was walking toward her. He was wearing black trousers, and black boots, but a Federal blue undershirt. It was Jacob Zook. "Jacob? Jacob, is that really you?" Rebecca called.

"Becky?" Jacob asked, reaching the two young women, almost out of breath. "What are you two doing here?"

"We were going to ask you the same thing, Mr. Zook," said Ginnie.

"That is such an incredibly long, detailed story," informed the boy, "but I will be happy to tell it to you both when this battle is over. Right now, I have to be careful of what I say, or I may end up getting shot as a spy."

"You? A spy?" laughed Becky.

"That's precisely what I said," answered Jacob, "but they didn't seem to think it as funny as you do.…neither did the Confederates."

"Confederates?" asked Ginnie. "Were you over by the Confederate lines?" "That's another piece of that long story I will tell you about…one day soon.

Let me simply say that I have had a very busy beginning of the month." Then Jacob's face changed, as if the smile he was wearing had just melted off of his head. "Have you heard or seen anything of my family?"

The girls looked at each other. "No, Jacob," answered Ginnie, "we haven't heard any news about the area out by the seminary. We do know that it is behind the Confederate lines."

"Yes, I know that, too," responded Jacob. "I was just wondering if they were allowed to move into the town….or….well….if anyone had heard….anything."

"Jacob!" A voice called out from behind. It was Sergeant Mullins. He was trudging up the hill toward the boy, but moving slowly, as if he was scaling the highest mountain top. "You should take pity on me, boy! You can see that I can't scale these mountains as well as you."

"These are not mountains, Sergeant," Jacob explained good-naturedly.

"You just wait until you are my age, my boy," replied the sergeant, "then they will have grown into mountains." Mullins caught his breath and then observed the two young women. "And who are these heaven-sent creatures? Friends of yours, Jacob?"

"Yes, Sergeant," agreed Jacob. "Sergeant Mullins…may I present Mary Virginia Wade….and Rebecca Tilden."

"Charmed, ladies," smiled the sergeant. "What's that I smell? Bread?" "We have a loaf with your name on it, Sergeant Mullins," answered Ginnie, coyly.

The sergeant graciously accepted the bread. "Jacob…we must be on our way. Generals do not like to be kept waiting."

"Generals?" asked Rebecca.

"My popularity continues to grow, ladies," Jacob said. "They are all interested in seeing a real, live Amish boy."

"Yes, Jacob," said Rebecca, "you are quite a sight, but…Generals?"

"Not just any general, either," replied Jacob, "but General Meade, himself." "Jacob! What have you done?" asked Ginnie.

"Nothing!" said Jacob. "I saved one of his officers…that's all. He probably wants to thank me."

"You are telling tales, Jacob Zook!" exclaimed Rebecca.

"No, he is telling the truth, young lady," answered the Sergeant, "but, Jacob…we must truly be running along."

"Yes, Sergeant." Mullins turned away from the boy, and once again began trudging uphill. He took a few steps, stopped, and then turned around to see if Jacob

was following him. As Jacob had yet to start, Mullins cleared his throat. "I am coming, Sergeant Mullins..I will catch up." Jacob turned back to face the two girls.

Rebecca impulsively took two steps forward and threw her arms around the boy's neck, embracing him in a manner she had never experienced before this moment.

"Becky!" remarked Ginnie, shocked by her young friend's overly familiar attitude.

Jacob rolled his eyes at Ginnie, as if to say, 'What can I do?' But then his arms slowly wrapped around Rebecca's waist, drawing her closer to him. "I am sorry, Rebecca," he said.

Still holding on to him for dear life, she asked, "For what are you sorry?" "Rebecca…I know that I smell worse than if I had spent the night with the pigs."

"That is you, Jacob?" she asked. "I thought that was this camp."

"No," he replied, "I am in need of a bath something fierce." He let go of her waist, and she, in turn, released him from around his neck. For just a few moments, their eyes locked, both sets filling with tears. He quickly wiped his away, turning in the direction the sergeant had gone. He took two steps, and then turned back to the girl. "Rebecca…when this battle is over…may I call upon you?"

"That is for my father to decide, Jacob," she answered, smiling.

"That is true," he agreed, "but if it is alright with your father, may I call upon you?"

"We are awfully young to be courting, Jacob."

"I know," he said, "but will you allow me to call upon you?"

She smiled at him again. "There is, of course, a religious difference for us to overcome, Jacob."

He nodded. "I realize that, too, Becky, but…may I call upon you?"

She looked around the camp. She noticed the sights and sounds of war wherever she glanced, and then she looked beside her at Ginnie, who was smiling at her and nodding.

"Yes, Jacob," she said, "you may call upon me."

Jacob smiled at her and turned back to follow Mullins. He walked quickly and closed the distance between them in just a matter of moments. Mullins was huffing and puffing his way up the incline. "Nice girls," the sergeant observed. "One of them yours?"

"Mine?" asked Jacob, oblivious to the meaning of the question.

"Are you her beau?"

"Beau?" Jacob had no idea what the sergeant was asking, but he thought it had to do with marriage.

"Are you fond of one of the girls?" Mullins asked. "I would think it is Rebecca, as she seems about your age."

Finally Jacob understood the soldier's drift. "Yes, Sergeant Mullins, I am very fond of Rebecca." Then he grinned at the sergeant.

"Well, isn't that nice?" replied Mullins. His tone was genuine, not sarcastic at all. "It has been many a day since I last saw the beginnings of young love. I had thought that this damned war had just about killed that idea…but here it is…alive and well and living in you two."

"I hope her father will feel the same way, sir," Jacob mentioned.

"Of course he will," answered Mullins, "and how could he not?" Mullins thick Irish brogue now betrayed his ancestry. "Besides…if he says one word against you…he will have to answer to me!"

Jacob and Sergeant Mullins reached the Headquarters of the Army of the Potomac, a commandeered farmhouse on the back side of Cemetery Hill. Sergeant Mullins saluted an officer who was standing on the porch. "Sir, I have brought young Jacob Zook to see General Meade."

"Wait right there, Sergeant," the officer replied, and then he opened the door and went inside the house.

"Don't be nervous," Mullins told Jacob, "just because you're meeting the Commander of the entire army."

Jacob smiled at Mullins. He knew that he wasn't nervous; he hadn't really been anxious at all when he met Robert E. Lee a day before this, so now meeting Commanding Generals had become something like an old, worn hat. Still, Jacob wondered what General Meade would be like, as a man, compared to General Lee, who he admired and liked a great deal.

The door opened and a new face, another General appeared on the porch. "Mr. Zook, I presume?" asked the General, smiling at the boy. "I am General Hancock, Commander of II Corps. General Meade is ready to see you now. Please come in."

Sergeant Mullins patted Jacob on the back, as if to wish him 'good luck.' Jacob climbed the two stairs which led into the farmhouse, and walked to the door, which was being held open for him by Hancock. As the full vista of the farmhouse sitting room came into view, Jacob was astonished to see about a dozen generals standing around the room, talking. One of the men turned around to face him, and smiling broadly. "Ah…you must be Jacob Zook." The General extended his hand, which

Jacob took and shook vigorously. "I am General Meade. These men are my senior generals."

Jacob nodded to Meade and said, "I am proud to make your acquaintance, General."

Meade turned back to the men on his staff. "And he's well-mannered, too!" The other generals seemed to chortle at this remark. Jacob felt a little embarrassed. "Have they been treating you well over at III Corps, Jacob?"

"Yes, sir," the boy replied, "especially Sergeant Mullins. He's waiting for me right outside."

Meade laughed again…it was a nervous laugh. "You have become so famous around this army it seems, Jacob, that you now are in need of a bodyguard." Jacob didn't understand the humor in this observation; he had no idea what a bodyguard did. The General realized that the boy had not smiled at his little witticism, and changed his tact in order to get down to business. "Jacob…the reason you are here right now is because you spent the last two days behind enemy lines."

"Yes, sir," said Jacob, "I figured that's why you were bringing me up here."

"Son, the army is in great need of information. We need to know how to better fight General Lee's army."

And there is was! Jacob knew that he was going to be asked to divulge what he had seen when he was the guest of the Confederate Army. He looked around the room again. Every eye in the room was now trained on the eighteen year old.

"Jacob," said Meade, "come over to the table and look at this map of the area." Jacob walked to the center of the room where a large table was standing, in a very similar way to the one he had seen at the Cashtown Inn just a few days earlier. "Do you recognize anything on the map, Jacob?" Jacob didn't think that this was the proper moment to play dumb – he knew that he had to say something of what he knew…but he didn't want to hurt the people on the other side of the battlefield, either.

"I have seen a map such as this before," said the boy.

Meade seemed surprised. "You have? Where did you see the other one?"

"It was at the Cashtown Inn, just two days ago," replied Jacob. "I was there as the guest of General Ambrose Hill." The officers found this statement very amusing. Jacob looked up from the table and into their faces. "You don't believe me?"

A General stepped forward. "Let us say that it must be clear in our minds that which is fact, and that which is…imagination."

"I see," said Jacob, his pride stinging at the General's barb. "What else can I tell you about the Cashtown Inn?" Jacob straightened up, and said, "Let me see…If I remember correctly, General Harry Heth was there…I believe that he is the Commanding General of one of Hill's Divisions, and General Pender was also there…poor man…I understand he didn't survive the first day of the battle. I also met the other Division Commander, General Anderson. They were all extra-ordinary gentlemen, and each, in turn took the time to greet me and see to my needs. So, having said this," Jacob paused, looking at the strange General, "I might observe that I still do not know who I am speaking to…sir."

There was a deadly silence in the room for a palpable amount of time. Jacob was sure that he had gone too far; that he was about to be run through by one of the officer's ceremonial swords. But then…he heard guffaws and laughter. Generals Hancock and Meade were laughing harder than the rest.

"How do you like that, Dan?" Meade asked the inquiring General. "I think you had better mind your manners. This boy might one day be the President, and then you'd have your hands full."

The other General smirked, but offered his hand to the boy. "I am Major General Daniel Sickles, Mr. Zook. I am at your service." The General bowed from his waist to the youth.

"I am pleased to meet you, General Sickles," returned Jacob, repeating the bow."

"So now that we have all the pleasantries out of the way," continued Sickles, "can you tell us if you recognize any of the features on this map?"

Jacob returned to the map. He knew exactly what he was viewing, especially after seeing a similar map at the Cashtown Inn. He looked up from the table and into the faces of the Generals. "You are going to ask me if I remember where the Confederate forces are placed – are you not? You are going to ask me about their cannon, and their cavalry."

Meade placed his hand on Jacob's shoulder. "Don't you wish to be a service to your country, Jacob?"

And just like that, Meade had asked the question that had been bothering him for the last year, or so – probably from about the time that his family was forced to leave Paradise. Was he Amish, or was he an American? For that matter, was he Amish or Union; Amish or Confederate? He had made friends on both sides of the conflict. He had made friends in the town of Gettysburg. He had family on Seminary Ridge.

Why was there any issue at all? He was just plain old Jacob Zook – an eighteen year old boy. A boy who now desperately wanted to see his brother, mother, and yes…his father…again.

Jacob stepped back from the map table. "I know what you want me to tell you," he began, "but this is not something that I can bring myself to do." Jacob witnessed some of the Generals reacting to his opening statement. "My upbringing does not permit me to become a part of the English community, nor does it allow me to service in the army. We live apart from your society. The moment I give you this information, I become a part of your way of thinking, and I become an active participant in your war. The moment I speak to you of the Confederate artillery placement is the precise moment that I condemn those men across the field to death – just as if I had actually pulled the trigger of a gun. I cannot do this…I will not do this!"

General Meade cleared his throat. "Jacob…there are some who might call what you have described as…traitorous!"

"And there are some," countered General Hancock, "who might call what you have described as committed…a sign of personal integrity." The two Generals locked eyes for a moment, but this disagreement was suddenly shattered by a courier bursting into the room.

"Beg pardon, General," the courier said, almost totally out of breath, "but the rebs are attacking the Federal left, just as General Warren had predicted. Colonel Strong Vincent of General Sykes Corps is defending the flank with a few regiments – mostly militia – but they need reinforcement soon. They are under attack by two Divisions of rebels."

"We need to get reinforcements out to the left flank immediately," said Meade. "Where is the attack concentrated?" he asked the courier.

"It is on a small hill, sir," replied the courier. "The hill is known as 'Sugar Hill."

"Sugar Loaf Hill," corrected Jacob.

"You know this hill?" asked Meade.

"I slept there only two days ago," answered the boy.

CHAPTER 16

Redefining the Orders of the Day

The Union line was now shaped like a fish hook. There was a Corps under General Slocum stationed at Culp's Hill on the extreme right end of the line – the entrenchments following the curve of the hilltop. This position connected to Cemetery Hill, which was manned by Howard's Corps. The Union center was fortified with the remnants of General Reynolds Corps, Hancock's Corps and Sickles Corps. The Federal left was rushing to fortify the small hill known as Sugar Loaf Hill. It was being defended by a brigade from General Sykes' Corps under the command of Colonel Strong Vincent, with the end of the Union line being held in place by a regiment from Maine, under the command of a college professor, now regimental commander, Colonel Joshua Chamberlain.

Lee's strategy was based upon classical flanking maneuvers; he would sweep around the end of the Union line, attempting to break or turn the line. This would force the center of the line to pull back to gain a better defensive position, that, or withdraw entirely. After Lee was made aware of the tactical importance of Sugar Loaf Hill, he decided to send an overwhelming force to sweep the Union left. His I Corps, commanded by General Longstreet, was given the task of accomplishing this flanking move. At the same time, he ordered General Ewell to begin to position his men for an attack on the Union right. Lee realized that the Federal Army had much stronger defenses on this side, and securely held the high ground on both Culp's Hill and Cemetery Hill, so he decided to give Ewell the option to attack the two hillsides, or not. Figuring also into Lee's plan was the idea that any flanking maneuver would draw reinforcements from the Union center, which would ultimately weaken those defenses should he decide to push up the center.

Meade now quickly sent reinforcements to the aid of Colonel Strong Vincent and his brigade holding down the Union left. Longstreet ordered Confederate Divisions, commanded by General John Bell Hood and Layfayette McLaws, with additional support from a Division from General A.P. Hill's Corps, to attack the Union left. They were repelled several times, and, after their supply of ammunition ran out, were completely taken by surprise when the 20th Maine Regiment, commanded by Colonel Joshua Chamberlain, initiated a bayonet charge down the hill. The charge, which simulated a swinging gate, had the effect of both attacking and flanking the rebels in one fluid motion. The Federal troops were able to capture over one hundred Confederate soldiers with this daring move.

General Meade, ever the engineer, had painstakingly arranged his corps to form a cohesive defensive line. As was the case for hundreds, if not thousands of years prior to this particular conflict, the choice of where to fight a battle was greatly dependent upon the topography of the landscape. It was not considered an advantage to have to attack going uphill, but it was considered a definite advantage to have a higher terrain to defend.

Jacob Zook, now safely ensconced with the Army of the Potomac, could view the action of the second day of the battle from his promontory on Cemetery Ridge. He was allowed to wander freely, but was compelled by the officers to remain in the rear of the line – back by the reserve units and the artillery. For the first time since encountering either army, Jacob's curiosity turned to the big guns. He wandered over to a gun crew, which was assigned to a six gun battery near the rear of the fortifications. This battery, which consisted of four six pound guns and two twelve pound howitzers, was placed at this position in the event the forward line was breeched. Jacob walked over to one of the large howitzers, inspecting the weapon, trying to answer the innumerable questions he had in his mind concerning warfare.

"What are you doing there?" asked a young corporal in the gun crew. Jacob quickly withdrew his hand, startled by the question. "Nothing… just looking."

"Sometimes it's even dangerous to look at a weapon such as this," the corporal replied. "It's loaded, you know."

Jacob shook his head. "I don't know anything about these things. They are fearsome pieces of invention, though."

"That they are," agreed the corporal. "You don't want to be on the receiving end when this piece fires."

Jacob nodded to the soldier. He completely understood that fact. "I am sorry, sir. My name is Jacob Zook." He extended his hand in friendship toward the corporal, who firmly grasped his hand.

"You are the one who saved Major Winslow," replied the soldier. "I am happy to make your acquaintance. My name is Davey Anderson."

"Like the Confederate General?" Jacob asked.

"Actually…the man is my uncle," answered the corporal.

"Your uncle?" asked an astonished Zook. "I do not understand this war. How can you be fighting against your uncle?" Anderson just shrugged off the question. "I know a young man from this area…he used to live over there, near the end of the Federal line…but he is now fighting for the Confederates."

"It happens," replied Anderson. "My family is split over this war."

Jacob could understand and relate to family rifts; he felt he was on the verge of causing one, himself – and his father had certainly caused one when he married outside of the Ordnung – but he certainly couldn't pick up a weapon and kill his father over a difference in opinion. Maybe, he thought, the wiser thing to do was to shun someone – to send them away – at least they got the message loud and clear, and no blood was shed in the process.

Jacob looked back at Corporal Anderson. "Where are you from?" Anderson grinned back at Jacob. "I'm from a little town in New Jersey. It's called Newton."

"New Town?" asked Jacob.

"No," corrected Anderson, "Newton; as in Sir Isaac Newton." "I have no idea who you are speaking of," answered Jacob.

Anderson shook his head in amazement. "Didn't you ever go to school?" "There are a great many things that I have not done, which you probably have already experienced in your life," replied Jacob, "and school…as you know it…is one of them." Anderson looked at the strange, new boy – the one old enough to be in uniform, but wasn't. "Can you tell me about these guns?"

Anderson smiled back at this new acquaintance. "Sure, I can. I know all kinds of things about them. What did you want to know?"

"I have never really studied up close something so designed that it's only purpose is the taking of human life," said Jacob. "I see that there are different types of shot to be fired from this gun. Let's start with that."

"Good!" answered the corporal. "This Howitzer is capable of projecting a twelve pound shell for over a mile."

"Over a mile?"

"You bet!" said the corporal. "This piece can fire solid projectiles, or canister."

"I understand what a solid projectile is," said Jacob, "but what is canister?" The corporal walked over to a pile of ammunition, and placed his hand on the top of the ordinance. "These are canisters. They are meant to explode during their flight, and release the iron shot contained inside. One projectile can take out many men in a single shot. It is…devastating!"

"It is…unimaginable!" answered Jacob. He turned to a different pile of ordinance, and then asked his next question, "And these?"

The corporal walked behind the field piece to the other pile of ammunition. "These are concussion shells. These are meant to explode upon impact, either with a wall, a tree, a building…or the ground. These are better for long distances."

Jacob shook his head in dismay. "I can't believe that men actually study how to build a better way to kill each other!" He looked away, noticing the other field pieces in the battery. "Those cannon are smaller. It looks like they shoot cannon balls."

"They do," replied the corporal. "They fire solid shot…six pound balls. They can pass right through several men lined up in a column – but the piece itself is harder to aim."

Behind the battery stood a single, oddly shaped piece, which Jacob observed and pointed to, "What is that back there?"

"That," answered Anderson, "is a mortar. The projectile from a mortar is sent in a high arc. We can project the heaviest shot with a mortar, but they aren't very accurate."

"Thank God," muttered Jacob. "So…Corporal…you look about as old as me. How old are you?"

"I just turned seventeen last month," replied the soldier, evidently proud of the fact that he was in command of a big gun at such a young age. "That's nothing. We've got a Major in this Corps who is only nineteen years old – and I hear there's a Colonel in the cavalry – Colonel Custer – who is still in his early twenties."

"I see," observed Jacob, "but most of the big decisions are still made by much older men than you; men who are agreeable to send young boys, like you, into the fray."

"That's true," said the corporal.

Jacob looked out onto the battlefield below. There was a great deal of activity going on at the Union lines. Something major was underway, although Jacob certainly had no idea what it was all about. An officer ran over to the artillery battery and began shouting orders. They were to fire long range ordinance beyond the advancing troops.

"You had better back up a bit, Jacob," yelled Anderson. "Go back up near the encampment, for your own safety. The area around these guns is definitely not for spectators."

Jacob nodded, patting his new comrade on the shoulder as he left. He ran about a hundred feet up Cemetery Ridge and then turned around to see the battlefield again. From this spot, he could see Sugar Loaf Hill, the peach orchard, the wheat field, and even that outcropping of granite boulders that always gave him the shivers. He was standing above the exact place where he had carried Major Winslow off the field of battle just the previous evening.

Several brigades were advancing onto the battlefield, leaving their fortifications behind them, and leaving the rest of the Army of the Potomac behind, as well. Jacob could see that arrogant man, General Sickles; the man who had questioned his truthfulness earlier that morning. The General was mounted on his horse and giving orders from the saddle. He was commanding his troops – and Jacob assumed that this was his entire Corps of thousands of men – forward, and away from their positions.

The artillery batteries now began to erupt with fire and smoke as they hurled their lethal projectiles across the field toward the Confederates. Within minutes, the entire slope of Cemetery Ridge was covered with a cloud of dust and smoke, which hung low to the rise of the hillside, like an early morning fog. To the left was Sugar Loaf Hill, where the Federal troops had successfully repulsed the Confederate onslaught, but even to a set of eyes as uneducated in military tactics as Jacob Zook's, it was apparent that there was now a sizeable break in the line of defenses which General Meade had worked on through the night to put in place.

Jacob decided to move his position, finding a rock abutment jutting out from the face of the ridge. He climbed onto the rock and held the palm of his hand over his eyes in order to shield his face from the hot, July sun. As he stood on that rock, perhaps half a body taller than anyone else in the area, General Meade galloped up to his side on horseback, his staff officers in his retinue.

"What in God's name does Sickles think he is doing?" screamed Meade. "General," a staff officer replied, "the III Corps is attacking the enemy." Meade turned on the officer, in obvious disgust. "I know that he is attacking, Major. The question is: Why? He is defying a direct order given by me to keep this army in a defensive posture. He has now caused a breech in the Federal line."

"Yes, sir," replied the admonished Major. "Shall I ride down to the General and encourage him to return to his breastworks?"

"That man will only shoo you away, Major, like some annoying insect," replied Meade. "I will ride down there to personally deliver him the message…if it is not too late, already."

"Sir, you must take care," cautioned the Major. "Remember, sir…we have already lost General Reynolds in this battle. We cannot afford to lose you, as well."

"Thank you for your concern, Major," Meade answered, "but I need to assert my command. If Sickles disobeyed Joe Hooker, then he certainly feels no obligation to answer to me. This must change…today! Please have General Sedgewick and General Sykes bring forward reserves to plug this hole in our defenses." Meade gave his horse the spurs and galloped away, with several officers following. The Major turned his horse and rode to the rear to give the order for reinforcements.

Jacob watched from his promontory, as Meade and his company galloped onto the battlefield. Sickles Corps had splintered into divisions, by brigade and by regiment. The heaviest fighting was in the peach orchard, and in the wheat field – the same wheat field where Jacob had encountered Major Winslow the night before.

General Sickles had observed that the peach orchard had a slightly better elevation than his breastworks on Cemetery Ridge, so without orders from Meade to do so, he decided to take his two Divisions and marched out a little more than half a mile to occupy this piece of high ground. Sickles was still smarting from the army's defeat at Chancellorsville, when they did not seize the same opportunity. Unfortunately, he had put his two Divisions, under General Humphreys and General Birney, into a salient, a triangular shaped formation that could be attacked from multiple sides at once. He also had his troops spread out over a great distance, covering far more ground than he could efficiently defend.

But this offensive move by Sickles had the positive effect of confusing the Confederate attack. Longstreet, in his desire to carry out General Lee's battle plan to the letter, had his Corps march very wide of the battlefield, taking a much longer route than planned, partly to remain out of the view of the Federal signal corps. Longstreet had planned to capture the strategic Sugar Loaf Hill, which was completely unguarded when they had set out. Thanks to General Warren's insight on the matter, the hill was now in Federal control, albeit lightly defended by only a few regiments. But Longstreet had been totally surprised to find elements of Sickles Corps in that part of the field, which forced his hand in several ways. Longstreet refused to part with General Lee's battle plan, against the judgment of his Division Generals, McLaws and Hood. Instead of hitting Sugar Loaf Hill with all of his massed forces, Longstreet was now forced to deal with III Corps. The fighting was fierce.

General Meade had ridden down to argue with Sickles about his insubordination, but he realized that this point was already moot. Meade had no choice but to reinforce Sickles wherever he could. III Corps was overrun in the wheat field – now named "the bloody wheat field," and in the peach orchard. There wasn't a monster to be found within the outcropping of granite boulders, which was to be renamed 'Devil's Den,' nevertheless the casualties were high for both sides.

*   *   *

General Meade rode back up Cemetery Ridge to his command post. He was still fuming over General Sickles obvious insubordination – an act he was bound and determined to write up after the battle was concluded. Meade picked up his field glasses and surveyed the battle. III Corps was dissolving on the field in front of his eyes. Meade recognized that the casualties in that particular corps would be unfathomable – but there was nothing more he could do to stop the carnage. He turned his body to look down the line at the right flank. He could see General Ewell's Corps positioned to begin an assault on Cemetery Hill and Culp's Hill, but at the present time he could only see minimal contact from the enemy. He swung his body around even more, and then stopped, startled by the image that entered the field glasses.

It was young Jacob Zook, perched on a rock outcropping. He, too, was watching the battle.

Jacob had also been watching Meade return from the front. He waved to the General as soon as he noticed that Meade had him in his sights. Meade put his field glasses down and gestured back to the boy. "Hello, Mr. Zook."

"Hello, General Meade," the boy replied, "It doesn't look as if it is going well for General Sickles."

"You have a keen eye for the obvious," said the General. Meade hadn't meant the comment to come off the way that it did, so instantly added, "I mean to say, you have a good sense of taking in the entire vantage of the battle."

Jacob was sitting on the rock, his legs hanging over the edge. He pulled himself up and addressed the General. "Is there anything that I can do to help, General Meade?"

"Do you want to go shoot some rebels for me, son?"

"I won't shoot anyone, mind you," answered Jacob. "Can I be of assistance with the medical corps? I helped the Confederates last night… tonight I could help the Federal army."

"I appreciate your offer, Jacob," said Meade. "We're going to need a great deal of help."

"I would much rather preserve life, than take it, sir," Jacob added, hoping to make the General understand that his comments earlier in the farmhouse were based on his personal and religious beliefs, and not a matter of treachery.

"I know that, Jacob," Meade answered. "I think you will be assigned to the surgical tent in the rear of the encampment. I think you will be a big help to us there."

"Thank you, sir," Jacob replied. He was happy that he was not going to be sent down onto the battlefield as he had done the previous night.

Jacob looked back toward the field. He spotted a group of soldiers assisting a wounded officer, who was still on horseback, heading back up Cemetery Ridge. As the detail got closer, Jacob could see that the officer was, in fact, a General. Meade dismounted his horse and ran down the slope to meet the party. Jacob watched silently as the Commanding General said a few words to the other General, who was partially slumped over in his saddle. Meade moved out of the way, allowing the detail to continue toward the back of the fortifications – to the hospital tents. As the little unit approached the spot where Jacob stood, Meade waved to the boy, indicating that he, too, should accompany the soldiers to the rear of the camp.

Jacob saluted the General and hopped down from the rock. A young lieutenant was riding his horse on the right side of the wounded general. He spotted Jacob as he approached them to assist. "You look like a local boy," said the lieutenant.

"I am, sir," replied the boy. "General Meade has asked me to help out in the hospital tent. I am to follow you there."

"That's good!" answered the officer. "I have always been of the opinion that there are two kinds of bravery exhibited in a battle; that on the field, and that off the field – especially by those who must witness the horrors visited upon us by our own hands."

"I agree with you, sir," said Jacob. "I have spent the last night helping with the Confederate wounded, and I will spend this night with the Federal wounded. It is a terrible business!"

The General, who had been drifting in and out of consciousness, straightened up a bit. He could not see the boy walking beside his aide-de-camp, but he could clearly see the young officer who had been like a son to him. He reached over and grabbed the lieutenant's arm and said, "It's all up for me, Lieutenant Favill." Jacob could see that the young lieutenant had tears in his eyes. Nothing more was spoken until the detail reached the hospital tents.

Jacob assisted the soldiers as they carefully lowered the General down from his horse. It was in doing this that Jacob observed the General's wound; he had been shot squarely in the stomach. It was a mortal wound, but it was also a wound that would not allow the victim to drift painlessly into oblivion; this was a wound that would cause the body to painfully linger – perhaps a day…perhaps even more, but eventually the result would be the same.

The General was carried into the tent, which was already filled with countless Union wounded, many of them crying out in agonizing screams. Whereas Jacob had witnessed many of the battlefield dead on the previous evening, he was now privy to the battlefield wounded. Many of these soldiers were casualties of the battle on the first day of the campaign; the wounded from this day's hostilities were yet to be accounted for. There were not enough doctors to do the work – there was certainly not enough medicine to quell the agony.

But rank has privilege, and before too long a doctor appeared by the General's bedside. The doctor looked at Jacob, and asked the boy whether or not he had any experience tending to the wounded.

"Yes, doctor," answered the boy, "I helped out on the battlefield last night." "The only reason I ask this," continued the doctor, "is because I need people who will not blanch at the sight of blood and guts."

"I can help you, then," said Jacob, with confidence.

"Good!" replied the doctor, opening up the General's tunic. "We must try to stop the bleeding," he added, observing the wound, "but this may not be possible. I will see if I can find the minie ball." The doctor uncorked a brown bottle and poured some of the liquid that it contained onto a white cloth. He placed the cloth over the General's nose. "Hold this rag, boy, so that the General breathes in the Chloroform. This should put him out for a few minutes."

Jacob held the white cloth in place. The doctor produced a small, sharp knife and cut back the General's shirt, exposing his stomach… and the wound. The doctor took his finger and put it into the entry wound. Jacob watched, totally engrossed as the doctor felt around the man's insides, searching for the projectile. "I cannot feel it," said the doctor. "This is not a good sign."

The doctor withdrew his finger. He produced a bottle of alcohol and poured some directly onto the wound, he then dressed the wound with a clean, white bandage. "We can only pray for General Zook now."

"Pardon me?" asked Jacob.

"What is wrong, boy?" asked the doctor.

"General Zook," said Jacob. "I am not General Zook."

The doctor looked at him as if he had grown a second head. "Have you lost your senses, son? Of course you are not General Zook! This… is General Zook!"

Jacob looked down at the wounded man on the cot. "This man is General Zook?" asked Jacob. The doctor nodded. "My name is Jacob Zook."

"Well…that is certainly a coincidence," exclaimed the doctor. "It is, or General Meade has a very unusual sense of humor." Jacob considered that this was a possibility, but dismissed it quickly. The tent was again starting to fill with new wounded soldiers. One of the new wounded men was making a great deal of noise. He wasn't screaming or moaning; he was laughing and cursing at the top of his lungs.

It was General Sickles!

CHAPTER 17

The Second Day Continues

Mary Virginia Wade and Rebecca Tilden returned to the McClellan house around 11:00 in the morning. They had distributed ninety six loaves of bread to the Federal troops that morning, and Ginnie had already decided that she would accomplish the same feat on 3 July. Rebecca, of course, would be her stalwart assistant – not only because she was indebted to the older girl, who along with her mother and sister had taken the Tilden family into their home in this time of need, but also because the two young ladies were kindred spirits.

Ginnie and Becky entered the McClellan house via the rear door, the same way as they had left the home earlier that morning. Both were in high spirits, but for different reasons.

Ginnie was happy to have made a contribution to the war effort. Up until that morning, she had no idea that she could feel good about a thing as horrific as this war. She never felt that she had any opinion on the question of slavery; she couldn't imagine owning another person, but, then again, she did not live in a society that put any kind of stock in that kind of thing. Moreover, the economy of Pennsylvania was not built upon agrarian output based upon the use of slaves. Pennsylvanians were industrious and hard-working – descendants of German, Quaker, Amish and English immigrants.

Becky had a different viewpoint on the events of that morning. She also was happy to lend a hand to the war effort, but she was also in the middle of her first infatuation with a young man – albeit a young man that came from a different social circle than she. As far-fetched as it would seem for her to take up with one of the soon-to-be-freed black African slaves, it was equally foolish to think that she had any kind of chance courting an Amish boy, even if he was as polite and kind as Jacob Zook. Becky knew that her parents would have a problem with any kind of relationship, and she also knew that Jacob's parents, particularly his father, would be adamantly opposed. His solution would entail shunning from his family, and that would not be the way to begin a life together.

But Becky had given the matter a great deal of thought, even midst the clamor and chaos of cannon fire. Becky was a grounded, sensible young lady. Her father would sometimes go on to the neighbors, proudly bragging to them that his daughter, Becky, was 'five times smarter than any girl ought to be.' Becky was well-read, even though she hadn't spent much time in formal education. Her mother had spent long hours with her as a child, teaching her how to read and write, and, truth be told, she was a better scholar than most of the young men in the town – including some of those boys who were now in attendance at Gettysburg College.

So Becky wondered, in a very intellectual manner, the effect that this war might have on her own future. She considered the fate of the nation if the Confederacy won the war. She had a difficult time at first, trying to imagine how the country would change – if this dreadful event came to pass. Gettysburg was situated very close to the Border State of Maryland. Maryland had been divided over the issue of slavery, and almost separated from the Union. If the Confederacy won the war, how long would it take before the Border States, including Maryland, pulled out of the Union? And if this was true, how would that affect their tiny town?

But Becky also looked at her own situation. How would the emancipation of slaves affect the role that women play in the American Society? For that matter, how would the same emancipation affect the way young women and young men behaved toward each other? She had read the newspaper concerning the casualty reports from the front. Every battle fought cost the country thousands of lives – and she was including the Confederates in this thought, because to Becky's way of thinking, the Southern States were still part of the country. Becky felt sure that something was going to come out of this time period, and that she wanted to have a stake in what was going to happen.

She had been considering Jacob Zook a great deal. She really liked the boy. He was gentle, polite, and very intelligent. He was a hard worker… and he had all of his teeth. She felt a little flutter in her stomach when she thought about Jacob, especially how handsome he was. But she also wondered if she was taking advantage of him; using him like a puppet in order to prove a point with her family. True, that issue had yet to be argued…but it may come to a head once the fighting moves on to a new location.

Becky entered the house, following her good friend, Ginnie Wade. She removed her bonnet and shawl and hung them by the door. Her mother was sitting in the sitting room, knitting a blanket for the baby. Her euphoria instantly disappeared.

"Where have you been, young lady?" her mother demanded.

Becky knew that it was no use to lie about it. "We were out visiting the troops, Mama. We brought them some bread and jam to help lift their spirits."

"You could have been killed, Rebecca Tilden! Don't you realize how dangerous it is out on the street? There are bullets and shrapnel flying around everywhere! A minie ball does not have a mind, Rebecca! It does not say to itself, 'there goes Rebecca Tilden. I think I will look for someone else to kill."

"Mama!"

"Don't dismiss me like that, Becky! You know that what I say is true!" "But, Mama, Ginnie and I..."

"Ginnie has her own reasons for doing what she is doing, Rebecca. I am sure that she feels a sense of obligation, because Jack is a part of the army....but you are a different story. You are just seventeen..."

"Seventeen, mother!" replied Rebecca, raising her voice...slightly. "Mother...do you realize that Juliet was younger than I when she swallowed poison so that she could be with her Romeo? Do you realize that many of the soldiers in the Continental Army were younger than I am? That many of the soldiers out there right now are younger than I am? That Mary, the Mother of our Lord, Jesus Christ, was younger than I am when she gave birth to the Messiah?"

"Lower your voice, Rebecca Tilden," replied her mother. "Not only are you speaking in a rude tone to your mother, but you are liable to wake the baby."

"I am sorry, Mother."

"Sometimes I wonder why I ever taught you to read and write," Mary Elizabeth said, "as you constantly are quoting what you have learned as a means of defying me."

"I am not defying you, Mama," Becky retorted, "I am simply stretching my wings a bit."

Mary Elizabeth did not respond to Becky's answer. She simply went back to her knitting. Rebecca stared at her mother, waiting for the reply that never came. Finally, frustrated with the icy silence, Rebecca stormed out of the sitting room and went downstairs to the cellar. Mary Elizabeth continued to knit, but addressed the older girl as she put the hampers away. "Ginnie…she is not to go with you, if you are planning to go back to visit the troops tomorrow."

Ginnie stopped cleaning up and turned to face Rebecca's mother. "Then I would suggest that you take this opportunity to bar the windows in this house, Mrs. Tilden, because that is the only way that you are going to keep her here."

*   *   *

Two medical orderlies carried General Daniel Sickles into the hospital tent on a stretcher. He was smoking a cigar and making jokes with some of the wounded men that were already confined to the hospital.

Jacob stayed right where he had been, sitting on a chair next to General Zook, watching after him as if he were some long, lost relative. Jacob felt a tinge of shame welling up inside of his soul. He looked over at that braggart Sickles, wishing that he hadn't been wounded just so that he wouldn't be in this hospital tent this evening.

There was something about the man that irked the boy.

Sickles was brought to an examining table in the center of the tent. The doctor quickly moved to that location so that he could examine the blustery general. The doctor used the same knife that he had used to cut away General Zook's uniform to cut away General Sickles uniform pants leg. Throughout this process, Sickles continually joked with the men around him, telling vulgar jokes, cursing the Confederates, belittling the Southern cause. As he did this he puffed vigorously on his cigar, blowing large belches of smoke in the doctor's face.

"General…must you smoke that cigar in here?" asked the tired, exasperated doctor.

Sickles reached up with his right hand and grabbed the doctor by his collar, pulling him up to his face. "Listen, Doc…the alternative to this is that I lay here screaming from the pain. I don't want the men to see me like that. Do you?"

"No! You are correct, General," replied the doctor. "It is bad for morale." Sickles let the doctor go, "Now do what you have to do."

But Doctor Thomas Sim, the III Corps surgeon, already knew what he had to do. A cannonball had caught Sickles just below the knee of his right leg, shattering the bone so badly that the leg was almost removed from his body. There was no hope of repairing such a horrible wound and still save the leg. The General's leg had to be amputated – immediately.

Doctor Sim quickly glanced around the tent, looking for his assistant. His surgical assistant was busy tending to a young private who had taken a minie ball to the head. The wound had not killed him straight off, but the boy had suffered a great deal of damage, especially to one of his eyes. He was bleeding profusely, and was terrified, as well.

The doctor then spotted Jacob, who was still sitting beside his namesake, General Zook. The surgeon gestured for Jacob to join him at the table. Jacob reluctantly shook his head.

"Come over here, son," Doctor Sim gently urged. "General Zook is unconscious and you cannot possibly help him – but you may be able to assist me with General Sickles." Jacob patted the hand of the oblivious General Zook and then left his bedside to assist the doctor.

As the boy walked towards the center of the tent, he was amazed to see the amount of blood, tissue, bone and internal organs that were littered around the operating table. Most grotesque of all was a large pile of amputated limbs which sat heaped on the floor in mute testimony of the horrors that the battle had produced. The hospital tent had been pitched on a reasonably flat piece of land, which had at one point been a pasture, so it had originally been a bucolic meadow, covered with grasses. These lush, green growths were now slick with blood and other bodily fluids. The ground upon which the boy trod was slippery and covered with debris. He felt thankful that he had eaten his breakfast so long ago that his nausea at the sight and smell of the place could go no further than the back of his throat. Even still more amazing to the boy was the fact that Jacob had never really been fond of the sight of blood; he was, as his mother would call it, 'squeamish.' Now, walking across the hospital tent to the operating table, and seeing all of the gore laid out before him like some grotesque banquet, Jacob was surprised that the sight and smell of the place hadn't sent him running out with his hand clamped firmly over his mouth. It took him all of three seconds – part of the length of time needed to make the journey across the tent – to realize that this was a different situation; he needed to focus on the terrible work that lay ahead of him. Vomiting was definitely not an option! He swallowed back the bile in his throat and continued onward. He had work to do.

"I need you on the opposite side of the table from me," said Doctor Sim, as the boy approached the table. Jacob nodded and dutifully took his place. "If you wish it, son, I can get you a drink of whiskey to steady your nerves a bit."

Jacob considered the offer. He never had a drink of spirits in his life, but the offer did seem tempting. "If he isn't going to take the drink," said Sickles, "then give it to me."

"Don't worry, General," replied Sim, "you will be completely out."

Sickles turned his head away from the doctor and looked at his new assistant. His eyes widened as his memory from earlier that day kicked in. "Wait a moment!" he exclaimed. "You're that Amish kid!" – Except for the fact that he pronounced Amish as "A-mish."

Jacob weakly smiled down at the General. "Yes, sir, General Sickles… Jacob Zook."

"Zook," answered Sickles. "Just like poor Sam, over there." "Yes, sir," agreed the boy.

"We have no time for small talk," said Sim. "Jacob…you have experience now with the Chloroform, so after I put it on the cloth, please put the General out."

Jacob nodded in agreement with the doctor. Sim produced a clean rag and poured some of the chemical into the middle, then he handed it to Jacob.

Sickles grabbed Jacob by the arm, stopping him from using the drug. "Boy…I want my leg! Make sure the Doctor doesn't toss my leg on that pile of bones over there. I want my leg!"

Jacob thought the General was delirious, but nodded to his demand. The boy placed the rag over Sickles nose. "Breathe deeply," he instructed the General.

Moments later, Sickles was quiet. His cigar had fallen out of his hand and was now just another casualty of the war – it was being extinguished in the mud, blood and intestines on the ground.

"Jacob…do exactly as I tell you," said Sim. "There is going to be a great deal of blood during this procedure. Are you ready?"

"I am feeling a little nauseous, Doctor. Could I have that whiskey? I don't know if it will help…but maybe it couldn't hurt."

Sim turned back to his instrument table. He reached for a bottle, which he had stowed away on the lower shelf. He uncorked the bottle and handed to the youth. "Here…take a really good swig. Swallow it fast!" Jacob did as he was told. He took in a mouthful of the liquid, swallowing it as quickly as he could. The whiskey burned his throat, and he immediately had the sensation that he was warming all over. But it did seem to steady him. He gave the bottle back to the Doctor.

For the first time since arriving at the table, Jacob allowed himself to look down at Sickles wounded leg. As Sim had already cut away his trouser leg, the injury was now exposed. Jacob found that he was not disgusted by the sight, but rather found it similar to events he had actually witnessed on the farm. Now braced by the whiskey, Jacob looked at Sim and nodded.

He was ready!

"I need you most of all to keep pressure on the leg, in a downward direction – toward the tabletop. Do you understand?"

"Yes," answered Jacob, nodding nervously at the same time.

"Good," replied Sim. "The first thing I need to do is remove the tourniquet that was applied on the field so that the General wouldn't bleed right out before getting any help. He will probably start to bleed heavily when I do this, but if you keep good, strong pressure on the spot the bleeding may come under control."

Jacob once again nodded. He reached over the table and over Sickles' body. He watched as Sim showed him how to grab the General's leg with both of his hands, strongly clenching his upper leg, as if choking it. He placed his hands just a little above the tourniquet. The doctor then untied the knot. As predicted, the General began to bleed. Jacob squeezed harder, his hands soon covered with the man's blood.

The doctor worked quickly. He cut away the part of the trouser that had been under the tourniquet, exposing the part of the upper leg not injured by the cannonball. Jacob was now fascinated by the operation. Sim quickly washed out the wound in a vain attempt to get a better view of the sight of the injury. There was absolutely no question; Sickles would have to have his right leg amputated.

Sim cut two incisions into Sickles thigh, creating a 'flap' of skin on one side of his leg. He took a sharp surgical knife, one with a longer blade, and used it to cut through the dense muscle until he reached the General's thigh bone. Jacob watched Sim return to his table of tools. He turned back to the operating table holding a bonesaw, which to Jacob's untrained eyes looked just like any other saw that he might encounter in a barn or toolshed.

"This is where you have to hold his leg still, Jacob. It won't take me very long to cut through the bone, but it helps if his leg doesn't rock back and forth." Jacob understood the concept; it was exactly the same as cutting through a board of wood. Sim placed the saw into the deep cut he had made with the knife and began to saw. Jacob was immediately repulsed by the sound of the sawing. He could taste a bitter substance in the back of his throat, but he swallowed back, wincing at the flavor. Within a few minutes, the Doctor had severed the bone. He went back to his long knife and cut through the remaining muscle on the underside of the leg. Sickles' leg was now in two very separate pieces.

Sim now needed to address the new wound he had just created. He picked up the amputated leg, and lifted it from the table. "Wait!" yelled Jacob, seeing what Sim was about to do. "He wants to keep his leg!"

"What?"

"He told me so, just before I put him under," explained Jacob. "He wants to save his leg!"

"That is absolutely ridiculous!" answered the Doctor. "But...he is a Major General...not to mention the fact that he is highly connected in Washington...so...I will put it to the side, and we can ask him about it again...after he comes to....if he comes to!"

"You mean he still may die?" asked the boy.

"Of course!" answered the Doctor. "Especially if we keep talking, instead of closing this wound."

Sim now began the closing procedure. He found a fine needle and cotton thread and tied off the severed veins and arteries. Returning again to his tool table, Sim selected a file – an ordinary workbench file – and used it to scrape down the roughly cut thigh bone, removing any of the rough edges. Finally, Sim pulled the flap of skin that he had created and sewed around the bottom of the leg, leaving a hole on one side to allow for drainage. He then bandaged the leg in several layers of cotton. "We will give the General a more permanent covering a little later, Jacob," the Doctor explained, "when we have a bit more time. I will have many more amputations to administer before this day is over." Sim smiled at the boy, grateful for his help. "You fared very well, son. Would you be available to help me with other poor souls?"

Jacob nodded to the Doctor. "Yes…I would like to be of assistance."

"Good! General Sickles will be out for a while, but I am sure that he will wake up quite cantankerous. I will allow you to minister to the two Generals, when the time is appropriate. We will need to watch General Sickles for signs of gangrene, or other post-operative maladies."

"I don't know what that means, Doctor"

"I will show you," said Sim, "but first we have to get these wounded boys taken care of."

CHAPTER 18

The evening of 2 July

General Robert E. Lee was furious – angrier than the normally placid General usually allowed himself to be. The main focus of his anger was one of his Corps Commanders, General Richard Ewell. Lee had given Ewell the ambiguous command to take the high ground on Cemetery and Culp's Hills, inserting the words, 'if practical,' as part of the orders.

For whatever reason, Ewell chose not to act on this command. Whether the two hills were, in his mind, considered 'impractical to take,' or he had, in some way, developed a field strategy closer to that of Union Generals Burnside and McClellan, is not clear. Ewell did observe that the two hills were well fortified, but mistook the amount of fortification during the daylight of the second day of battle.

Lee's battle plan had called for flanking maneuvers on both sides of the Federal line. He had marginal success on the Union left flank. Unfortunately, General Longstreet had taken so long to get his Corps in position that the Army of the Potomac was able to send brigades in time to hold onto the strategic terrain of Sugar Loaf Hill. In later years, this hill would be renamed to match its larger neighbor as "Little Round Top." But Longstreet was able to capitalize on the mistake in judgment by General Sickles, and his Corps was able to smash the Union III Corps very badly – rendering it useless for the rest of the battle. Longstreet's Corps had taken heavy casualties, though, especially trying to take Sugar Loaf Hill.

Lee had been hoping to drawn Federal reserve away from the center of the line, softening it up for another blow. He did not calculate Ewell's reticence in attacking the Federal right – and this was the subject of the General's ire at the moment.

The battle was eventually joined, but only in the evening. It seemed for a while that the Confederates would succeed in taking the hilly section, but then the Federal units were reinforced, and the rebels were repulsed from the hillside, with the exception of a toehold retained at the base of Culp's Hill. The Confederates had suffered heavy casualties during this attack. Had it come earlier in the day, the Confederates might have won the day – and the battle.

*   *   *

In a scene very reminiscent of that which Jacob Zook had just witnessed, a similar ordeal was being played out at the Lutheran Seminary on Seminary Ridge. From the time that the ridge had been overrun with Confederates, the seminary had served as a field hospital. By the evening of 2 July, the building was filled to overflowing with the wounded.

The Confederate Army did not enjoy the same degree of medical expertise or medical supplies that their enemy had. Where the Union Army had over 11,000 doctors in the field, the Confederacy had only about 3,000. Moreover, the term 'doctor' was also ambiguous, and often a misnomer. Most of the physicians – on either side – had never performed the type of surgery required of them on a battlefield. This was particularly the case with amputation. Just as the cannonball and minie ball did not respect rank or station, neither did the preferred cure.

Confederate General Thomas "Stonewall" Jackson had his arm amputated, as did Union General Oliver Howard. The problems realized in the battlefield hospitals of this conflict surrounded the use of the minie ball, a soft lead projectile which, when fired, hurtled through the air at a slow speed than the older, smooth bore shot. The result: the minie ball would flatten out upon impact – tearing through bone, muscle, and anything else that stood in its way. The damage was devastating.

Medical science had lagged far behind that of military armament in the Nineteenth Century. A wound to the head or the abdomen was considered a 'mortal wound,' and those having wounds of that nature were often left to the side, as they were considered 'hopeless.' Wounds to the extremities were considered 'treatable,' especially with amputation – however, many died in the days that followed the procedure due to infection.

It was in this reality that the Zook family now existed. Abraham was engaged as an errand boy, running to and fro around the building – fetching whatever medical supplies could be found for the surgeons, and occasionally helping the orderlies to carry the wounded to the operating table. It would be an experience that he, like his older brother, Jacob, would never forget – but in the case of Abraham, it would leave scars that would last through the rest of his life. Abraham would re-live the horrific events of the second day of the battle in the form of nightmares; dreams that would prevent him from getting a restful, sound sleep until the day that he died.

Sarah Zook had taken on the role of nurse, although, in many cases, she was actually performing the tasks normally assigned to a physician. Living on a farm had given her many different life skills, and tending to sick or injured animals, as well as to her growing family in their time of illness, had given her the tools to do almost anything required of her in the field hospital – including amputations.

Ishmael was not suited to this work. His place was that of a laborer, and he was happy to do it. He worked at keeping the floors free from the spattering blood and guts. Unlike the Federal field hospital, which had been set up in a tent, and therefore a floor of dirt and grass, the seminary building was decorated with hardwood floors. These floors were finished with varnish, so the blood made them slippery…and dangerous, especially with sharp surgical tools in hand. Ishmael spent hour after hour mopping the floors, emptying the bloody water, refilling the buckets, and repeating the entire procedure – over and over.

They had just about caught up with the casualties of the day when the attack was resumed, this time much closer to home on the two neighboring hills. The casualties from the Confederate attack started arriving near midnight. The only soldiers to be brought in were wearing gray, due to the fact that the battle was being fought against entrenched Federal forces, and not in an open field.

Sarah refused to take a break, having worked either by the side of a surgeon, or independently for the previous twelve hours. Her work had been continuous, and she had not eaten since rising at six that morning. Now, almost midnight, the sounds of wagons arriving with the wounded filled the air. Orderlies delivered soldier after soldier, each with a significant wound; the soldiers that had only minor wounds, including bayonet wounds, were treated on the field and returned to duty.

Even though there was a shortage of cots, empty places to lay the wounded kept appearing, as the mortally wounded passed on.

Around 12:30 am Sarah bent over a new patient. The young man was writhing in pain, and on his side, rolled away from her. Like General Zook, the boy had taken a minie ball to the stomach.

Sarah put her hand on the boy's shoulder. She spoke gently to comfort him, and at the same time exerted a slight bit of pressure, trying to get him to roll onto his back so that she could treat him. But the young man was hysterical – he was well aware that his wound was mortal. He was frightened at the prospect of dying.

"You must not give up hope," she said to the soldier. "I know, M'am," he wheezed, "but I know I'm done for." "Let me take a look…please," she gently asked.

At last, the young man rolled onto his back. He had closed his eyes, wincing from unspeakable pain. She looked immediately to the wound, taking her shears to cut away part of his uniform. The minie ball had struck the soldier just below the rib cage on his right side. Sarah quickly moved to the other side of the cot. "I want to roll you the other way for just a moment," she said to the young man. "Can you help me do this?"

"Yes, M'am," he replied. With a great deal of effort, she pushed him up, lifting up the blouse of his uniform as his weight shifted. She wanted to see if there was an exit wound.

There was. Larger than the entry wound by almost three times, the exit wound was enlarged due to the flattening of the minie ball. The minie ball had gone straight through the soft tissue of the young man's insides, missing the ribs and the spine. It had then exited out of his back and through his uniform. Unfortunately, she had no idea how much damage had been done to any of his internal organs; his stomach, lungs, liver, or kidneys. She gently returned the soldier to his back.

The young man opened his eyes. He thought that he was seeing a vision.

"Mrs. Zook?" the soldier said, coughing.

Sarah turned back to look at the soldier, now looking at his face for the very first time. She had made it a habit not to connect with any of these men, knowing that it would make accomplishing her job more difficult than it already was. But this soldier….she knew him.

"Wesley Culp?" she asked. "Is that you, poor boy?"

"It is, Mrs. Zook," he answered. "Am I going to die, Mrs. Zook?" "Shh, Wesley," she comforted, "you must not use up your energy by speaking."

But Wesley wouldn't hear of this. "Did Jacob make it home, M'am?" "Jacob?" she asked, using her more Germanic pronunciation of her son's name. "My Jacob?"

"The very same," he said, forcing a slight smile. "I saw him just the other day down by Cashtown."

Sarah took a bowl of clean water and a cloth and began to wash out Wesley's entry wound. Her instincts were telling her that the boy was bleeding internally, but she would not bring herself to believe it. Of all the soldiers she had worked on over the past day, this was the first time she was working on someone that she knew.

Sarah noticed that her husband was once again making his rounds with the bucket and mop, and gestured for him to come over to the boy's bed side.

"Look, Ishmael," she said, "Look who is here? Wesley Culp! You remember him, don't you?"

Ishmael looked down at the boy, intent on ignoring him. What did it matter to him, he thought? But he did look down; he looked down right into Wesley's eyes. Only he didn't see Wesley's eye…he saw Jacob's eyes. He put his hand on Wesley's head, giving it a tender pat, but all the while he was sinking slowly to his knees, coming to a kneeling position next to the wounded boy's cot. He reached out and took Wesley's hand in his own, raising his head to the heavens and praying silently to the God he still believed in.

"Why did you run away, boy?" Ishmael asked. "Why did you go?"

"I had to go, sir," explained Wesley. "There was nothing here for me anymore."

"Nothing here?" said Ishmael, astonished at the boy's bluntness. "Your entire family is here."

Wesley shook his head. "But they have never understood me, sir… any more than you've understood me."

Ishmael began to weep. "I do understand you. I do. You want to strike out on your own…to visit other places in the English world…but this is your home. This is your home!"

Sarah was also in tears. She had never seen her husband weep so openly before.

Wesley reached over with his other hand and patted the top of Ishmael's hand. "You know…it is a strange twist of fate….isn't it?"

"Isn't what?" asked Sarah.

"That I live my life in Gettysburg, always wanting to leave, to be free of this place…so I run away…then join the Confederacy…only to be shot on the exact same hill that I played on so often as a boy. That…is what the poet….would ..call…irony."

"What?" said Ishmael, confused by his son's statement. He looked over at the boy, and now recognized him as Wesley Culp – his former neighbor. He stood quickly, confused by what he had just experienced. "Where is…Jacob?"

"Wesley thinks that Jacob is fine, Ishmael," soothed Sarah. "He saw him in Cashtown, just like the officer told us yesterday."

Ishmael nodded, shaking his head. "A great deal has happened in these last few days, Sarah."

Sarah nodded, but her eyes were fixed on Wesley, who was growing visibly weaker with each passing moment. "Is there a message you would like me to send to your family, Wesley?"

"A…message?"

"Yes," she continued, "something you would like them to know."

A calm, serene look came over the young man's face. He was aware that his moment was at hand, and yet he remained perfectly calm. "Tell the Culp family…the Culp family…my mother…and brother…that…I am sorry for leaving…them."

"I am sure that they know that, Wesley," said Sarah.

"Will you tell them…for…me?"

"You will tell them yourself, when this is all over," she said, "Isn't that correct, Ishmael?"

Ishmael, too, had been deeply affected by what he was witnessing, but he was startled when his wife addressed him. "What? Yes…you will tell them."

"I…will…tell…"

And with those words on his lips, Wesley Culp, late of Gettysburg, Pennsylvania, died. He became another of the more than 9,000 estimated Confederate casualties of the second day of the battle. The Federal forces also lost an estimated 9,000 men – and the battle wasn't yet over.

*   *   *

Ginnie Wade and Rebecca Tilden were lying next to each other on blankets which they had spread out on the cellar floor. Some of the family members, along with the Tilden family, had decided to sleep on the main floor of the house, as all seemed very quiet on that second night. Rebecca did not want to be near her mother – not right now, at least. She knew she was under house arrest, so to speak. She was doing the only girlish thing she knew how to do at this point…she was pouting.

"Don't make so much of this, Becky," cautioned Ginnie, "you will still be able to help me bake the bread, so you are still contributing to the war effort – even if you can't leave the house to deliver it."

"That's not the same thing, Ginnie."

"Becky," the older girl said, with an older, wiser tone in her voice, "you know that the reason you are so angry is because you have hopes of seeing Jacob Zook again in your travels."

"Yes….but…"

"I am not saying that you do not care about our soldiers," Ginnie continued. She wasn't scolding Rebecca, nor was her voice condescending in any way, "I just think you have an ulterior motive for going up there."

Rebecca wanted to answer her friend in a way that would remove the doubt that she had just expressed, but she knew that she could not – Ginnie had spoken the truth.

"If you happen to see Jacob in the morning, would you ask him how he is?" Rebecca asked her friend.

"Of course I will, Becky!"

"Would you tell him that I was asking about him?"

"Of course!" answered Ginnie. "Don't you think I know what it's like? I miss Jack something awful!"

Becky nodded at her honesty. "You tell Jacob to keep his head down!"

"I will, Becky. I promise."

CHAPTER 19

The Early Morning

Doctor Sim sent Jacob out of the hospital tent at midnight so that he could get a little sleep. Jacob had worked with Sim throughout the evening of 2 July, and now, with the passing of the midnight hour, it was already the next day. Jacob walked a little further up Cemetery Ridge and found a large Elm tree to use as his resting place. He was almost beyond the army encampment.

General Sickles was still out from the Chloroform, and General Zook was going in and out of consciousness. Jacob couldn't help either General in any way, and he had reached the point in his own exhaustion where he had not become very useful to Doctor Sim. Fortunately for the Doctor, and for the field hospital on Cemetery Ridge, most of the casualties from the action that evening on Cemetery Hill and Culp's Hill had been taken to a different field hospital – one behind the Union right flank. For the first time in almost two days, there were very few new soldiers entering the hospital tent in need of care.

Jacob felt the heavy hand of sleep falling over him. He positioned his back upright against the trunk of the tree and looked up at the stars in the night sky. He wondered if God, in all His majesty, took any stock in the events unfolding in the United States of American – and in the Pennsylvania countryside. He drifted off into a sound sleep.

As if only an instant had gone by, Jacob felt a hand on his shoulder, shaking him gently. "Jacob? Jacob? Wake up!"

Jacob's eyes snapped open. He looked up to see one of the orderlies from the hospital tent. "Yes?" he answered.

"General Sickles is awake – God help us! – and he is asking for you!" the aide nervously answered.

"For me?" asked the boy. "Of all the people on God's green Earth – Why me?" "Sometimes it is better not to ask," replied the orderly. "Please come, quickly!"

The orderly turned and ran back toward the hospital tent. Jacob slowly stood up, feeling as though he hadn't slept at all. In reality, he had no idea of the time, or that he had only cat-napped for a little over an hour. But he also became quickly aware of a new instinct – a new feeling. In his activities of the past evening, he had never had the urge to relieve himself of his bodily fluids – but that urge was very strong at the moment, and could not wait. Jacob stepped behind the large elm tree and undid the small hook and eye system that held his trouser fly together. His fingers fumbled with the tiny hooks, and with each fumble he need to urinate seemed to become stronger. Here, he thought, was something that really didn't need to be so 'plain.' What was so 'fancy' about the button fly that most men had on their trousers? Some men, mostly the well-to-do, were even wearing a new gadget, which had been invented in 1851 by Elias Howe – inventor of the sewing machine – the zipper. Not only did the Amish consider the zipper to be a creation of man's vanity, they also considered the sewing machine very much in the same broad category.

Finally, after much worry over the outcome, Jacob was able to relieve himself. Having re-fastened all of the tiny hooks on his fly, his next anxiety evolved when he realized that he had to find some water to rinse off his hands. Unlike many of the 'English,' he had been raised that a good rinse, or even a washing, was a good thing to do after a visit to the necessary. His mother had been adamant about that behavior; these were, after all, the same two hands which he would use to eat his food. Jacob decided to make use of the supply of fresh water at the medical tent to take care of this chore – even if no one else there understood the procedure. He walked back down the hill toward the hospital tent. On his way back down, he came upon a cistern of water that was there for the horses. Jacob dipped his two hands in the trough and rubbed them together, then wiped the excess water off on his blood-encrusted shirt. He paled at the thought of rubbing his hands in the blood of other unknown men, but, he rationalized, at least he had rid himself of any excess urine.

Reaching the field hospital, Jacob drew back the flap and entered the large tent. Doctor Sim was still busy performing amputations; he would work non-stop on this one procedure until the end of 4 July. His eyes met the gaze of the orderly, who simply nodded in the direction of the cantankerous General. Jacob wasted no time walking over to Sickles bedside. The General was already puffing on a fresh cigar, but Jacob could also see that he was not smoking the cigar as much as chewing on it. As the boy drew closer he could also see that Sickles was wincing before each puff, or chew, that he took. He was chomping on the cigar in order to mask the pain he was now feeling in the stump of his leg.

"A-mish boy!" yelled the General, as soon as he caught sight of Jacob. "Come here!"

"I am coming there directly, sir," answered Jacob, although he really didn't know why he felt the need to be as respectful to such a man as Sickles. Jacob grabbed a small stool and brought it next to Sickles' cot. "How are you feeling, General?"

"That, sir…is a ridiculous question! Don't you agree?"

Jacob nodded; it had been ridiculous, and he knew it. "I am sorry, General. I was only trying to be pleasant…for your sake."

"Damn!" yelled Sickles.

"Sir?"

Sickles shook his head. "Sorry, son…I didn't aim that insult at you. I was having…a spasm."

"I can't imagine what that must feel like, General," observed the boy.

"It doesn't feel very good…I can tell you that." Sickles felt another spasm come on and smacked the cot with both of his hands. The sudden movement startled the boy.

Jacob waited patiently while the General regained his composure. "Is there something I can do for you, General Sickles?"

Sickles drew in a deep breath of air, then leaned his upper body toward the boy. "Did you remember to keep my leg, A-mish boy?"

"With all due respect, sir," Jacob answered, "Ah-mish." "What the hell?"

"Ah-mish, sir! It is pronounced Ah-mish."

Sickles raised his eyebrows, his face becoming red. "You dare to correct a Major General in the United States Army over his pronunciation?"

"Why not?" answered the boy. "I'm not in your army, nor will I ever be. I don't have to take orders from you, but I was one who helped you at your most dire time of need. The way I figure it…my people have earned your respect…so you could at least pronounce the name of the sect correctly."

Sickles relaxed back on the cot. A smile formed on his lips, gradually broadening out until he was grinning. "Well, I'll be a son of a bitch! You are quite something, you know that, boy? I wish the rest of the Corps Commanders had the stones that you have."

"Stones, sir?"

"Never mind," dismissed the General. "So…did you remember the leg?" Jacob looked him in the eyes. He started to shake his head, but then said, "Yes, I did."

"You should run for Congress, son. You're a natural politician."

Jacob smiled at this remark, but also knew that was never going to happen – not in his lifetime. He stood up and looked toward the operating table. The large pile of amputated arms and legs was now gone. In his absence, someone must have cleaned up the pile, probably because it was taking up too much precious room in the operating space. A new, smaller pile was already beginning to accumulate.

But Jacob felt a slight, sinking feeling in his stomach. "I need to check on it, General." He quickly walked over to where Sim was operating on a wounded Captain. "Doctor Sim?"

"Ah, good," he replied, seeing the boy. "I am happy to have you back, Jacob. As you can see, we still have many amputations to perform."

"Yes, sir," the boy agreed, "but first I am with General Sickles. He is awake." "Oh, Damn!" muttered the surgeon.

"Doctor? Did you happen to put his shattered leg to the side, or did you throw it out with the rest of the pieces of limbs?"

Sim never stopped working throughout this conversation; he barely even looked up from the table to look at Jacob. "Son…you will learn many things in this life, but one of the most important things you will ever learn is….do not…under any circumstances…ever argue logic… with a crazy person."

"Doctor?"

"Of course I kept the leg, Jacob," the Doctor said. "It's over by the supply bin." "Thank you, Doctor Sim."

"It's not for you to thank me, son. That's for him to do…but he never will. I have no idea why he wants such a ghastly prize…but…like I said…" "…never argue with a crazy person."

"That's correct!" assured the Doctor.

Jacob returned to Sickles side. "We still have the leg, sir!" "Good!"

Jacob paused to think for a moment, but the question he really wanted to ask just wouldn't wait. "What are you going to do with it, sir?"

"With what?" asked Sickles, obviously distracted by his pain.

"With your leg," answered the young man. "Don't you think it's a bit odd to want to keep it?"

"It probably is," agreed Sickles. "You are right, Jacob. I must find a purpose for it. Problem is – I just don't know what that purpose is, quite yet." Sickles looked to his other side. General Zook was laying there, still unconscious. "Look at him, Jacob."

"General Zook?"

"That's right…General Zook," replied Sickles. "He was one of my best officers, you know. He was a man after my own heart…except that he really wasn't much of a drinker…not like me."

"You speak as if the General had already passed on, sir," observed the boy.

"He practically has done so," remarked Sickles. "He has been gut shot, boy. There isn't any coming back from that! But he was a good man. I once saw him stand toe-to-toe with old stiff-britches Hancock over a disagreement in deployment strategy. Hancock swore at Zook and cussed him out something fierce. I never heard Hancock swear like that in my life…why he almost sounded like….me! But…then…do you know what happened?"

"What?"

"Sam Zook gave it right back to him…cussing and swearing and all! It was poetry to my ears, boy!"

"I don't follow you, General," Jacob mentioned.

"No? Well let me tell you this, young man…General Sam Zook had integrity…that's what! Do you know what he said when I gave the order to attack yesterday?"

"What, sir?"

"If you will give me the order, General Sickles, I will obey it. That's what he said," responded Sickles, who dropped his head to his chest, shaking it back and forth. "He knew that we were going to get whipped, and yet he followed my orders anyway."

"Wouldn't you say that he did his duty, General?" asked the boy.

"Yes, he did do his duty, Jacob," answered the soldier. "But he is going to die soon, and I am going to live. Is that justice? Is that God's mercy?"

"I can never answer for God, General," Jacob replied.

"No, neither can I," said Sickles, "even though we Generals sometimes act as though we were gods. I need a drink, Jacob. I am very, very thirsty, son."

"The Doctor said you would be just that when you woke up, sir," said Jacob. "I will get you some water."

"Water? I need something stronger than water!" thundered the General.

"I can't give you that, sir…sorry… Doctor Sim's orders."

"Sim's orders?" he bellowed, loud enough for the Doctor to hear him. "He is only a Major…I am a General!"

"A General who is a God, isn't that right, sir?" asked Jacob, slyly.

The General smiled again at Jacob, nodding his head slowly. "You really should consider politics, Jacob Zook. The people of New York City would love you!"

Jacob shook his head. "My people don't believe in politics, General. That is something that the 'English' do – not us."

"English?"

"Anyone who is not Amish, sir," taught Jacob. "We don't have that kind of social order."

"Then you might not fit into New York politics after all, boy. Nothing in that city happens unless ten to twenty people have a say in it, and their hands in the deep pockets of the city."

"That doesn't sound right," observed the boy.

"No, it doesn't, does it? And yet that's exactly how things get done, Jacob. This country has two classes of people, son; those who are rich… and those who would like to be rich…if only they had a way to do it. I worked for Boss Tweed up in New York City – the champion of the poor – especially the poor Irish. We fight for everything that is due us… even for things that are not due us. And why? Because the real, rich folks want to keep us under their thumbs - that's why!"

"I don't understand what you are talking about, sir," Jacob said.

"I can imagine you don't," said the General, shaking his head. "I will give you an example. Do you see that poor sucker over there?"

"The corporal?"

"That's right!" nodded Sickles. "Not many know this…but I do. That man is a 'substitute.'"

"A substitute for what?" Jacob asked.

"A substitute for someone who was drafted into the army, but chose to pay the sum of three hundred dollars so that he wouldn't have to serve."

"Is that a right thing to do?" asked Jacob, his curiosity being peaked.

"That's what we asked at Tammany Hall, Jacob! The poor people in the South had a phrase for it…they called it a "rich man's war but a poor man's fight."

"So…if I had the money…I could sit out the war?" asked Jacob.

Sickles shrugged. "You don't have the money, and yet you did just that, didn't you?"

Jacob was taken back by the General's question. That wasn't fair, and he knew it – especially in light of the past few days, and how Jacob came to the assistance of whomever was in need.

"I am sorry, Jacob," said Sickles, "I spoke out of line. The point is – that man over there will die simply because some other man chose to buy his way out of service in the army. We have many of these rich men in New York, Jacob. I know, for example, there is this rich banker, who has paid for a substitute for his son. I also know that his son's substitute was killed last year at Antietam." The General winced again with pain. He took another bite out of his cigar, chewing on the tobacco. "I guess I could really use that water, Jacob."

Jacob nodded and quickly retrieved a cupful of water. Sickles gulped it down, and Jacob fetched a second cupful, which Sickles slowly sipped. Jacob studied the arrogant officer; a man who he had instantly disliked upon their first encounter. He now was modifying his opinion of the man – even if just slightly. "General? What is your opinion of slavery?"

"Slavery?" asked Sickles, surprised at the question.

"Why do you seem surprised?" asked Jacob. "Isn't that what this war is all about?"

"Ha!" Sickles laughed, loudly. "Is that what you have been told, boy? That this war is about freeing the slaves?" Dan Sickles eyed his young pupil as if he was giving him a school examination.

"That is what I have come to believe, sir," answered Jacob.

"Well…that may be part of it," explained Sickles, "but it may be just a small part of it."

"Then what is the biggest part of it?" asked the boy.

"States' Rights," answered the General.

"States' Rights?" asked Jacob. "Now there's a term I have never heard in my life. General Sickles, I know that you think I am some bumpkin who has spent his entire life living on a farm in Southern Pennsylvania, with a bunch of people who don't care for education, or America, or the army….or pretty much anything else that you can think of…but you would be wrong. I can read, and I can write…very well, as a matter of fact! I may not have gone to school, but I have kept up on everything I can find out about this war."

"Calm down, Jacob! I am not meaning to insult your intelligence. This is exactly what I have been talking about, boy! The poor people think it's about one thing, but the rich people…and many of them are the politicians…they think a totally different way. The war is over the fact that we in the North want those in the South to behave a particular way. The issue for now is over slavery, which has been a big issue since before we were a country – way back in '76. Thomas Jefferson wanted to write that into the Declaration of Independence, but those words were crossed out by the Southern members of the Continental Congress. He agreed to do it, because if he hadn't, they wouldn't have approved it… and we would all still be part of England…and then we would all truly be… 'English.'" Sickles laughed, thinking himself very witty.

"So…it's about power?" asked Jacob.

"Something like that," said the General, wincing with pain. He took another sip of the water. "Politics is very strange, Jacob. Politicians get themselves elected to office in order to benefit the people who they represent…so they say….but, there's more to it than that. I know… because I am also a politician." "But you are a General in the army?"

"And I only received this rank because I helped Abe Lincoln raise this here Corps," answered Sickles. "I used my political power to get this military power; that's what makes the likes of Hancock and Meade so angry at me sometimes. They know I don't have the West Point training that they have, so they don't have much respect for my ability on the battlefield. After yesterday, I may have to admit they are correct…but I will never do it to their faces. Never!"

"But the slaves….?"

"Slavery is tied into the economy of the South, Jacob. Look at the typical farm in Pennsylvania or New Jersey. You farm fifty to a hundred acres, if you are lucky.

You work the land with the rest of your family. If you do well, you can afford to hire someone to help you with the work."

Jacob nodded in agreement with most of this discussion. "We Amish don't hire workers, sir. We work together as a family. We believe in big families…and, when we marry, we build another house on the family farm."

"That's perfect!" exclaimed Sickles. "You Amish have created your own economy. But, Jacob…that's not how it is in the South. When this country was first settled, large parcels of land were doled out to some very wealthy Englishmen. These farms still exist today – they are called Plantations. Whatever is grown on these plantations, be it cotton, or tobacco, or sugar…they cannot make a good profit on these crops if they don't have really cheap labor…and nothing is cheaper…than free! This is why the rich, southern farmers want slavery to continue…so that they continue. The vast majority of the people in the south are not rich…in fact…most of them are very poor."

"Then why do they fight to support slavery? They should want to see it go?" asked Jacob.

"They fight because they don't want to see their way of life change… and they get especially angry when they realize that it is us Yankees who are the ones who are telling them that they have to change their way of life."

"States' Rights?"

"Now you have it!" answered the General.

Sickles twitched a bit, and rotated his weight on the cot, trying desperately to make himself more comfortable. "Jacob…you said you can read? Well, I mean?"

"Yes, General…I can read very well."

"Have you ever read any books by an English author by the name of Charles Dickens?

"I have heard of his name, but I have not read anything by him," replied the boy.

"I know for a fact, that the English – the real English, Jacob, not your 'English,' – the English do not like our practice of slavery. They abolished it long ago. Mr. Dickens is a very outspoken critic of the practice."

"Then I should like to read what he has written," answered the boy. Sickles smiled, like a fisherman who has just landed a large catch. "As it

happens, I have a copy of a very unusual fable by Mr. Dickens in my footlocker. When you accompany me back to my tent, I shall give it to you to read."

"That is very gracious of you, sir," answered Jacob, "but how do you know I will be accompanying you back to your tent? Isn't that a bit…. pardon the word, sir…presumptuous?"

"It's the correct word, Jacob," said the General, smiling at the boy. "It is presumptuous, of course, but I think that it would be better for me, and for you, as well – if we were friends, rather than adversaries. There is much I can do for you, after this damn war is over."

"Such as…?

Sickles drained the rest of his water. Taking the cup away from his lips, he looked Jacob straight in his eyes, and asked, "Have you ever considered attending a university, Jacob?"

CHAPTER 20

The Beginning of the End

Early in the morning of 3 July, just before dawn, Mary Virginia Wade arose from her bedding that lay scattered on the cellar floor of the McClellan house in order to begin the process of baking another hundred loaves of bread for the Federal troops. She rose from her prone position, giving consideration not to disturb her friend, Rebecca Tilden, who was still sleeping deeply. Ginnie wrapped her long shawl around her housedress and climbed the stairs to the main floor of the house. As she had done previously, she immediately set about to secure the ingredients needed for the task ahead. She had an abundance of whole wheat flour, so even though that was the bread she had baked on the previous day, it would be the bread of choice for this new day, as well.

By six thirty, Ginnie had mixed the dough – a huge mass that would later be cut down and formed into loaves. But first, she had to wait – wait until the dough raised enough to be knocked down, only to be allowed to rise again.

Ginnie sat down in the sitting room, content that the work was progressing well. She let her mind wander as she sat in a rocker. She thought of her finance, Jack Skelly. She wondered when she would see him again. She wondered how the war would alter their plans to marry. She prayed that he would be kept out of harm's way.

Her thoughts of Jack finished, she turned her mind onto her memory of her father. Her father, though still very much alive, was in a mental hospital; put there for attempting to kill himself several years before. His attempt at suicide had created a dark cloud which still hung over the Wade/McClellan family – the conventional wisdom of the day stating that mental illness was often passed down from generation to generation.

Ginnie often wondered about her future mental health. She recognized the fact that, quite often, she would feel herself slipping into a very dark place; a place that seemed to dampen her spirits and give her feelings of loneliness and melancholy. That is, unless she was in the company of Rebecca Tilden.

Ginnie liked Becky a great deal, but she also used the girl as a kind of tonic for her soul – especially when she felt a dark period begin to overtake her. It was on those occasions that Ginnie would send for Becky, or go to the Tilden house to retrieve her. It was in those long days and nights that Ginnie would make the most of their friendship, especially now that the war was in progress, and certainly over the last few days, when the war had actually settled in Gettysburg.

By the time Ginnie had run all of these thoughts through her mind, an hour had passed. It was now seven thirty, and time to knock the massive block of dough down. She would start off by punching the dough with her fists, but after only a few minutes she would resort to hitting the clump with the rolling pin – her fists hurting from the incessant beating. Having accomplished this task, Ginnie covered the dough with some cloths, and let the dough rise again.

Ginnie used the second hour to make some breakfast in the kitchen for the rest of the family and guests now in residence. She lit the oven, knowing that she would need it for baking the bread. It would first be used, however, to bake some biscuits for breakfast. She put a tea kettle on for some tea, and started to brew some coffee for her mother and Mrs. Tilden. By 7:45, the rest of the household began to make its way through the living area of the house. By 8:00, the only person Ginnie had yet to see was Becky Tilden.

The dough was still in the process of rising, so Ginnie decided to go back downstairs to the cellar to check on Rebecca. When she reached the spot where they had slept, side by side onto of several blankets laid out on the dirt floor, she discovered that Becky was no longer there. The McClellan cellar was divided into two large sections, bisecting the house in half. Ginnie walked through the door which served as the pass-through to the other side of the cellar, in the hope that her friend might be on that side.

She was not there, either.

Ginnie instantly became worried. If she wasn't in the cellar, and she wasn't upstairs – then she must have left the house undetected, which meant there was only one place that she was going...

...she was going to search for Jacob.

Ginnie now faced a quandary. If she kept Becky's secret to herself, she would risk alienating herself from the rest of Becky's family, particularly her mother. She also was aware of the other side of the coin. If she told her mother that Becky was missing, her mother might go looking for her, which could also play out in several possible scenarios. The first, and most likely scenario had Becky blaming Ginnie for her indiscretion; which meant that there was a possibility that there friendship might be in jeopardy. The second scenario was worse; in this drama, Becky's mother gets hurt or killed during the search for her daughter, but it would also relieve Ginnie of the guilt she was feeling at the moment.

Ginnie decided that the truth was the best policy, and returned to the upper level to confront Mary Elizabeth Tilden. She decided not to give her mother any specifics, like the actual spot where they had seen Jacob the other day, but rather would keep it simple – they had gone to distribute bread to the troops at the top of Cemetery Ridge, and that was probably where Becky went this morning.

And Ginnie Wade did just that, although Mary Elizabeth's reaction was not one that she was figuring on. Mrs. Tilden enlisted the rest of the household to search for her missing daughter. Ginnie's Mother would search the shops along the Emmitsburg Pike, along with Ginnie's younger brother, and Mary Elizabeth would take the young boarder, Isaac, and head up toward the Union entrenchment on the top of Cemetery Ridge. Ginnie was to stay at home to assist Georgia with the baby, or in case Becky returned to the house while the others were out scouring the area. Ginnie considered this a lucky stroke on her part, because her dough was just about ready for the final preparation before baking.

The search party left the McClellan house at around 8:15. As had been the case for the last two days, there was the ever-present sound of gunfire in the air, but the sound seemed to be coming from the area around Cemetery Hill and Culp's Hill.

*   *   *

"University?" Jacob asked Sickles. That was a notion which had never entered his mind. He had always resigned himself to a life as an Amish farmer, working on the same tract of land that had been owned by his family for generations. Of course, in order for this to occur, there first had to be a reconciliation between the Elders and his parents.

"What's wrong with that?" replied Sickles, with a rhetorical question. "Amish boys don't go to college?"

"As a rule – no!" answered Jacob. But the idea was very attractive to him, and it renewed some of those inner feelings that he had squelched over the past few days. He wondered, as he had in the days before the battle, if this war would change any of the ways the Amish lived their lives.

"There are many fine schools of advanced learning in and around this state, and its neighbors," said Sickles. "There's the College of New Jersey, which is over in Princeton, New Jersey…and then there's Columbia in New York City, Dartmouth in New Hampshire, and…"

"…don't forget the University of Pennsylvania," said a weak voice from the cot next to Sickles. Jacob whirled around on his stool to see the man who had spoken those words. It was General Zook; he was conscious.

"General Zook!" exclaimed Jacob. "How are you feeling, sir?"

"I have felt much better, I can tell you that!" replied the General. "I see they also got you, Dan!"

"Cannonball, Sam," Sickles mentioned, as if it didn't matter. "Nearly took my right leg off, and what it didn't do…Sawbones Sim did."

"And who is this bright young lad?" asked Zook, looking over at Jacob. "You haven't met Jacob, yet?" answered Sickles. "Well…this should be a real treat for you. Samuel Zook….meet Jacob Zook."

General Zook's eyes lit up. "Zook? Bist du Deutsch?"

"Ja, Herr General," replied Jacob. "Ich bin Jacob Zook von Paradise." "Gott in Himmel!" exclaimed the General. "Another Zook!"

"Quite a coincidence, isn't it, Sam?" observed Sickles. "I was just trying to convince our friend here to get some formal education – you know, make a name for himself in the 'English' world."

"You finally understand the term, Dan. It took a long time," laughed Zook. "You should listen to what the General is telling you, Jacob." Jacob was listening, but the conversation did nothing more than confuse him all the more. "Is he smart, Dan?"

"I should say so!" answered Sickles. "He's been assisting Sim with the amputations – he actually helped with mine. Oh…he helped with you when they brought you in last night."

"Is that so?"

"Yes, General," admitted the boy, "I have been very happy to have been some help."

"Then perhaps you might want to study medicine?" asked General Zook. "No…I don't think so," responded Jacob. "I think I have seen enough suffering to last me a lifetime already."

Zook nodded, understanding the boy's words. "Ach! It doesn't matter, does it? You have plenty of time to decide…but, Jacob…leave this place…go out and see the rest of the world. You will not regret it!"

But Jacob quickly turned the General's own words back on him. "Don't you regret it, General? Look at you! If you had stayed on the farm, you might not be lying here right now."

"That is true, Jacob," the General admitted, "but I would not have had the honor to die for my country."

"This is an idea which I cannot understand, General," Jacob professed. "And the reason you cannot understand it, my boy, is because you have not left the isolation of your own community," said Zook.

Jacob once again nodded in agreement with what the older man said. General Zook smiled at the boy, but as he was doing this, he began to cough, his upper body trembling with spasms. He raised his hand to his mouth, as if to stop the coughing, but to no avail. The coughing would eventually subside on its own schedule. When the General pulled his hand away from his mouth, his hand was covered with blood, which was also smeared onto his face. Seeing this, Jacob quickly ran to get a wet rag, and proceeded to clean up General Zook. The General, who had been overjoyed at the conversation of the previous minutes, was now somber and quiet.

"Jacob.." he whispered, "would you be so kind to send for my aide, Lieutenant Favill?"

Jacob quickly left the General and sought out military assistance. By the time he returned to his original place, the General had rolled onto his side, away from Sickles. Jacob brought his stool close to Sickles head and sat down. "What is happening?" he whispered.

"Coughing up blood is never a good sign," answered Sickles, also in a whisper. "He knows that he is going to…you know."

"No!"

"Jacob..please remain calm…for his sake," answered Sickles.

Jacob lowered his head. "How long?"

"It's hard to tell," Sickles observed, "but he thinks it may be soon."

*   *   *

General Robert E. Lee began the morning of 3 July by trying one more time to dislodge the Federal forces on Culp's Hill, sending General Ewell's Corps against the Union Corps entrenched there. At the same time, General Meade shared the same vision, realizing that the rebel army still maintained a toe-hold at the base of the hill. The morning fighting was fierce, but the Federals were able to blast the Confederates back using their artillery. This second failure to capture the strategic mound only underscored the disappointment Lee felt over Ewell's inability to take the hill when first instructed.

At the same time, Lee instructed General Longstreet to once again attack the Federal left flank – the area around Sugar Loaf Hill. These attacks were to commence at the same time, once again pulling the strongest part of the Federal line, the center, away from their positions. Unfortunately, the Federal cannons began firing on Ewell's Corps before Longstreet was in position, whereupon he was told to call off his attack.

General Lee was under the impression, however, that the Union center was not as heavily fortified as he was led to believe. Lee believed, and he may have been the only Confederate officer who was of this opinion, that he had sent so many of his forces against the two Union flanks over the past two days, that an attack on the center of the line would be unexpected.

He unveiled his plan to Longstreet even before Ewell pulled back from Culp's Hill. He would have Longstreet send his Corps, along with a part of General Hill's Corps, up the center for a final attack. The attack would be led by General George Pickett, one of Longstreet's Division Commanders, who had just arrived on the scene with his fresh soldiers. Also in command would be General Trimble and General Pettigrew of Hill's Corps.

A significant part of Lee's plan for the third day of the campaign hinged on General Jeb Stuart's cavalry, which was to hamper the Union flank. Stuart had just returned from fighting skirmishes with the Federal cavalry, and was now put to use trying to turn the course of the battle.

At midday of 3 July, General Robert E. Lee was convinced that he could still win the battle.

CHAPTER 21

Bread for the Soldiers

At 8:15, Ginnie Wade was alone in the McClellan home, with the exception of her sister, Georgia, and Georgia's newborn son. The rest of the household, plus visitors, had gone off in search of Rebecca Tilden – who had also gone off in search of Jacob Zook.

Ginnie walked to Georgia's room to check on her sister and the baby before tending to the big job of baking her bread. Georgia smiled at her sister when she poked her head in the door, but said nothing. She was busy nursing the baby, who had refused to nurse for the past several days because of the cannon fire that had been so close to the house. Even now, the cannon fire was intense, but the baby had finally accepted the noise as the status quo, and had given in to his hunger. Ginnie smiled at her sister and closed the door, returning to the kitchen.

* * *

At 8:00 am, Corporal Jess Riley and Private Lewis McMultry were on the roof of one of the taller commercial buildings on the Emmitsburg Pike. Their position was very close to the intersection of the Pike and

Baltimore Street, which they both new led up to the Federal entrenchment on Cemetery Ridge.

Both were members of General Pettigrew's Division of General A.P. Hill's Corps.

They were both from the hills of Tennessee – the home of Davey Crockett.

They were both crack shots with a rifle – their skills honed while hunting game for their dinner tables. Now they were putting those skills to good use in the Army of Northern Virginia.

They were both Confederate snipers.

From their vantage point they could see clear to the Federal pickets. The height of the roof had negated some of the natural height of Cemetery Ridge. They had been given specific orders not to fire on any citizen of the town of Gettysburg. There was to be no collateral damage. But they had also been cautioned that the Federal couriers might try sneaking through the lines in disguise; that they might try to get through dressed as ordinary citizens. They might even dress in women's clothing in order to fool their Confederate counterparts.

Private McMultry was first to notice two citizens emerging from the house near the intersection of Emmitsburg and Baltimore. One definitely was wearing a dress, or skirt – covered by a long shawl and bonnet. The other was most definitely a child. Perhaps it was a mother and child heading out to the market, thought McMultry, and he lowered his weapon. Still continuing to watch the pair with caution, he noticed that they were continuing along the Pike toward the center of the town.

Within a minute, two more figures exited the house. Once again, McMultry noticed that one was dressed like a woman, and the other seemed to be a small boy. The private signaled his friend and partner, Corporal Riley, to crawl over to his position to take a look.

"It looks like a Yankee lady and her kid," observed the Corporal.

"That it does," agreed the Private, "but I ain't seen her face. She left the house with her back to me…and look…she's headin' up the hill toward the Blue Bellies."

"She's got a child with her, Lewis," Riley mentioned.

"So what? Maybe it's a trick! Maybe it's a Yankee spy, and he's using the kid as a kind of…

"…human shield?"

"Yep," nodded McMultry. "That's what it could be, alright."

"I think the sun has gotten to you, Lewis," observed Riley. "There are any number of shops along Baltimore Street that they could be headed off to. I don't think they are headed for the Union line."

"Wanna bet?" asked McMultry.

"What?"

"Wanna bet? I will bet you…a dollar…that they head straight for the camp." "A dollar?" asked the Corporal. "You are that sure of yourself?"

The Private gave a quick nod. Even though the bet was unusually large, the two had learned to spend the time in such a way, hatching all sorts of foolish wagers to help break the monotony of baking in the hot July sun.

"What d'ya say, Jess?"

"When do we know who wins?" the Corporal asked. "Do we wait until she's past the pickets, or is there a designated spot?"

"I'm not trying to rob you, Jess," answered the Private, "let's make it when she, or he, crosses the line. That should be proof enough!"

"Done," said the Corporal, and he rolled over slightly to shake his friend's hand and seal the bet. "I hate taking your money like this!"

"We shall see," assured the Private.

They turned back to watch the woman and child walk up the incline of Baltimore Street. They were now about a hundred feet from their house, progressing slowly because of the child. He seemed to be bogging the woman down. It looked like she was dragging him.

"What makes you so sure about this, Lewis?"

"I just thought it was odd that a woman and a child come outta that house, and headed off that way…and then, less than a minute later, here comes another woman and child, and they are headin' up the hill. They all came out of the same house, Jess."

The Corporal nodded his head slowly. "You do have a point there, Private, it is mighty odd, I will give you that…but it still don't mean that they are Yankee spies…or couriers."

"You callin' off the bet, Jess?"

"Me?" asked the Corporal. "Nah! I like takin' yer money, Lewis!"

"We will see! Look! They're still walkin' up the hill." The woman and child were now several hundred feet past the starting point. They were now halfway to the Union line.

"Have you ever considered, Lewis," asked the Corporal, "that maybe…just maybe…that they happen to be the family of someone in the enemy army? We are in Yankee territory, you know – it is possible that a Pennsylvania Brigade is right at the top of that hill."

"That is true, Jess," answered the Private, "and I never considered that possibility." The Private then rolled over on his side so that he could face his friend. "But if that is true, and they are going up there to visit the husband, who is probably also the boy's father…and they cross over that line….then I still win the bet!"

"What? Never! You made this bet on account you thought they was spies," argued the Corporal.

"That was maybe true in the beginning, Corporal," said McMultry, "but the terms of the bet clearly stated that I win if they cross over the Federal line."

The Corporal accepted the terms with dignity. It now was beginning to look as though the woman and child were actually going to make it to the Federal pickets.

"Look at that!" shouted McMultry. "They are opening the line for her!" The two Confederates could easily see that someone, indeed, was pushing back the barricade to let the woman and child inside. The woman and her charge were still almost a hundred feet away from the line, but the line was opening to let them in.

Even before this was completed, several Union soldiers began to charge through the breech in the line. They were running toward the woman and child, in a most anxious way.

"Private," said Corporal Riley, "we are not going to fire on innocent woman and children…but no one says we can't take shots at Blue Bellies."

"I agree," said McMultry, "and…if I get me one…well then…the bet is off. I'll take a Yankee over a dollar any day of the week!"

"I like the way you think, Private. You will go far in this army!"

The two snipers quickly picked their targets. There were about four blue figures running downhill from the breastworks. In order to remain concealed from the enemy, the snipers had been lying prone on the rear side of the roof, the peak of the roofline rising up in front of their faces. Now, in order to get a better shot, they needed to crawl up a bit higher on the roof, which would enable them to steady their rifles on the peak of the roof. They had to move quickly, though; the Federal soldiers had almost reached the woman and child.

At this range, both men were dead shots. They were both skilled in hunting small game from far greater distances than this, and their long, rifled gun barrels spun a projectile that was far more accurate than most of the weapons used in field combat.

"I am going for one of them on the left, and you go for one on the right," instructed the Corporal.

"Gotcha, Corporal." They both took careful aim, each lining an unsuspecting Union soldier in their sights.

Private McMultry inched forward again, trying to get a more secure position for his shot. He reached down with his hand, putting it over the peak of the roof, and then pulled himself up. He felt something give way under his left hand.

He had removed a shingle off of the roof. It was falling down the roofline toward the façade of the building facing the Emmitsburg Pike. The tumbling shingle startled a group of pigeon-like birds called Mourning Doves. The doves, skittish as

they tend to be, quickly took off from their resting place, quickly flapping their wings in fright. The flock of doves headed straight for the shooters.

Lewis McMultry tried to catch the falling shingle, but could not grab it in time. But by doing this, more than half of his body length was bent over the top of the roof, and his rifle with him. Moreover, his right hand, and in particular, his right index finger, was still on the trigger of the rifle. In the blink of an eye, he had lost the shingle, startled the birds, and found that he was awkwardly positioned over the roofline.

He discharged his rifle.

"Lewis!" exclaimed the Corporal. "Get back!"

But it was too late. The rifle had already gone off, giving away their position. In just a moment, the Federals would try to pick them off using their own snipers and sharpshooters. They had no choice but to let themselves back down the roof on the back side of the building.

Before leaving his position, the last thing that Corporal Jess Riley noticed was the woman and child safely walking inside of the Federal breastworks.

He owed his friend, Lewis, a dollar. They had made it, and they hadn't bagged any Yankee soldiers.

It was now 8:30 am.

*   *   *

Ginnie wade looked at the mantel clock in the sitting room. It was now 8:25 am. Her bread would now be finished proofing. She walked back to the bread trough and uncovered the large mass of dough. She dug her fingers into the clump of sticky dough, kneading it one final time before sectioning off small pieces that would be baked into individual loaves of bread.

Ginnie started to hum a song – a song of her own invention. She liked to sing, but she dare not open her mouth while Georgia was still nursing the baby. She lightly hummed her little tune, tossing aside any worries of Jack Skelly, or Becky Tilden, or even the war.

She never knew what happened next.

A bullet crashed into the side door of the McClellan house, passing cleanly through the wood without shattering the board. Not deflected in its trajectory, the bullet continued in a straight line, hitting Mary Virginia Wade in her back, and lodging in her spine.

She died instantly, falling to the floor next to her bread trough.

It was now 8:30 am.

*   *   *

Mary Elizabeth Tilden, along with the Wade's young boarder, Isaac, were climbing up Baltimore Street in search of Mary Elizabeth's errant daughter, Rebecca. Mary Elizabeth made the assessment that the Union camp was the only logical destination for her head-strong daughter to go, but she had sent out Mrs. Wade and her son to search the other side of the town – just in case.

Now, with less than a hundred feet to go, she noticed that soldiers behind the breastworks were moving some of their defenses. It looked like they were making ready to let them enter the fortification. She was only slightly alarmed when she saw four uniformed soldiers dash out of the same fortifications, running toward them with all good speed.

The soldiers closed the distance in only a few seconds.

"Beg your pardon, M'am," said a Private, "but we don't know why you have come up here, but you are certainly in great danger. There are rebel snipers everywhere."

"We are here to escort you behind our lines," said another young Private.

"Take my arm, M'am."

The young Private offered Mary Elizabeth his arm, which she gratefully accepted. At the same time, another Private scooped up young Isaac into his arms, and proceeded to carry him the rest of the way uphill. Isaac, never one to cooperate fully, kicked and screamed at the handling he was receiving at the hands of the Union Private. The fact was that Isaac screamed and yelled so loudly...and continuously...that Mary Elizabeth never noticed the sound of a single gunshot being fired down the hill.

It was now 8:30 am.

Mary Elizabeth entered the breastworks. She thanked the soldiers for their kindness, and particularly thanked the young Private for his rough, but necessary handling of Isaac.

"Begging your pardon again, M'am," asked the soldier who had escorted her to safety, "but why have you risked your life to come up here?"

"My daughter has run away this morning," Mary Elizabeth replied, "and it is my suspicion that she has also crossed this line. Have you seen her? Her name is Rebecca Tilden. She sometimes goes by 'Becky."

"Becky?" asked another Private.

"Rebecca?" asked another.

Other soldiers paid no attention to the conversation, instead they worked on re-closing the break in the breastworks.

"Perhaps we should let you speak to one of our officers, M'am," the first Private said. Then, as an afterthought, he asked, "Do you know of anyone up here that your daughter would be coming to see? A young soldier, perhaps?"

Mary Elizabeth looked down at the ground. The question embarrassed her, and yet, it was the source of all of her anxiousness. "Yes, she may have come up here looking for someone…but I don't think that it is a soldier."

The Private laughed a bit. "Pardon me, M'am, but there's only two things up in this neck of the woods right now…soldiers….and horses. If she didn't come to see a soldier, then she must have come about a horse!" The soldiers in the adjacent area to the conversation, at least those who could hear it, began to laugh at this joke.

Mary Elizabeth kept a strong hold on her patience. "Please…try to understand," she said. "I think that there is a boy that she is looking for…but he is not a soldier…but she believes that he is up on this hill."

The soldiers had puzzled and perplexed looks on their faces.

"Is this a riddle, M'am?" asked the Private.

"No, young man…ah….Private," answered Mary Elizabeth, "this boy is…Amish!"

"Amish?" asked another Private.

"Are you speaking of Jacob Zook?" asked another.

"Jacob? Yes…" replied Mary Elizabeth, surprised to hear the recognition in their voices. "You know him?"

"Almost everyone in III Corps knows Jacob, M'am," said another. "He rescued Major Winslow from certain death in the wheat field."

"I heard he helped amputate General Sickles leg," chimed in another.

"Are we speaking of the same Jacob Zook?" Mary Elizabeth asked, not believing her ears. Were they, after all, speaking of an eighteen year old farm boy? "Did he fight in the battle, as well?"

"Oh, no M'am," said the original speaker. "The Amish...they's agin' fightin.' He only helps out around the camp."

Mary Elizabeth was still skeptical that this was the same boy; the boy that she had discovered in the McClellan house just a day before, almost ready to help deliver Georgia's baby. He looked at that time as if he would vomit from the intensity of childbirth. How could this be the same boy? "Describe him to me, if you would."

"Well..." said one of the soldiers, "he's pretty tall...maybe almost six foot. He's got fairly light blonde hair – and a lot of it."

"He's very gangly," said another, "you know...like most teenage boys get at that age."

"But he's a good looking young man," added another.

"And he was wearing black and white...," added yet another.

"...ceptin' his white shirt was all covered in blood, so somebody gave him a uniform shirt to wear," said the first.

"And he has these black boots," said another Private. "We all wish we had boots like them."

"This is unbelievable!" exclaimed Mary Elizabeth. She had been under the impression that the Amish boy was a dead end for her daughter, Rebecca. What prospects did her offer her anyway, especially if he clung to his own religious traditions. The only life that she would know would be on the family farm, having lots and lots of babies. She could not ever imagine a boy of that background making something of himself in the real world – even if he was a gentleman and naturally intelligent. "So... do you know where Jacob is right now?"

"Probably in the hospital tent, helping out our surgeon, Doctor Sim," answered one of the Privates. "We hope he stays there, too, because we don't want to see him get shot up by coming down here."

"And have you seen my daughter, Rebecca Tilden?"

"We can't say for sure, M'am," another replied. "We only came on post about a half hour ago, so if she came through before that, we weren't on duty yet."

"Well then….can one of you show me to the hospital tent?" asked Mary Elizabeth.

"We can't leave our post, Mrs. Tilden," answered the boy who had walked her through the picket, "but we can get someone to take you up there."

The young soldier was true to his word. In just a few minutes, Mary Elizabeth was being escorted to the hospital tent, with little Isaac once again in tow. Her escort opened the flap of the tent and pulled it back, allowing enough of an opening for the woman to enter. The escort then stopped Isaac from following her, giving the child the premise that he would take him to see the horses and wagons. Isaac gleefully went with the soldier.

The soldier had, of course, acted wisely and sensitively. The hospital tent was no place for a six year old – but, then again, neither was the encampment. Mary Elizabeth walked past the first few cots containing the wounded from the battle. She immediately was filled with compassion at the sight, and momentarily forgot her purpose in being there. The tent was now once again noisy; filled with the sounds of terror and agony – of men wounded or dying. Toward the middle of the large tent she spied a Doctor bent over an operating table, a hacksaw in his hand, performing an amputation. She also noticed that standing directly next to the Doctor was a young man with blonde hair.

It was Jacob Zook!

"Mother! What are you doing here?"

Mary Elizabeth turned on her heel. There, sitting next to a wounded sergeant, was her daughter, Rebecca. She was holding the soldier's hand with one hand, and mopping his brow with a wet cloth with the other hand. She was wearing an apron, but it was completely covered with blood, and she had blood smeared on her face.

"Rebecca!" her mother cried, instantly alarmed at the sight of the blood.

"I have been working here for the last three hours, Mother. I hope you do not wish me to return with you down the hill – for I will not go!" Rebecca turned away from her mother, and returned to caring for the Sergeant.

Mary Elizabeth considered giving her daughter an argument, but that thought was short-lived. She knew that she would be hard-pressed to think of a better reason for her to leave, than for the one to stay. Mary Elizabeth removed her bonnet and gloves and placed them on a nearby cabinet. She took off her shawl and placed it over the back of a chair.

"What are you doing, Mother?" Rebecca asked.

"Since you will not leave this place, I have decided to stay with you," Mary Elizabeth replied. "I think I can be of great assistance to some of these men."

Rebecca looked over at her mother and smiled. "Jacob is over by Doctor Sim. He is assisting with an amputation right now. Doctor Sim thinks that Jacob has all the makings of a fine physician, Mother."

"Is that a fact, Becky?" Mary Elizabeth asked. "Does Doctor Sim realize that the boy is Amish?"

"Yes," Rebecca replied. "Yes, he does," which was the extent of her answer. Rebecca immediately turned back to help the Sergeant, turning her back on her mother.

Mary Elizabeth crossed to the other side of the hospital tent, where she found a young physician dressing the wound of another soldier. She quickly became involved in the treatment of several soldiers.

CHAPTER 22

A Fateful Choice

Georgia McClellan had not heard the sound of the bullet passing through her side door. She had not heard her sister, Mary Virginia, cry out in pain when the bullet struck her in the back. The only sound Georgia was aware of was the sound of breaking dishes; as if there was a fist fight going on in the adjacent rooms.

As no one else was in the McClellan home at the moment, Georgia need to find out if everything was alright.

"Ginnie?" she called out, still allowing her infant son to stay at her breast.

She waited, but there wasn't any answer.

"Ginnie? Is everything alright?"

Again…silence.

Georgia broke the suction that the baby had created in nursing, then pulled her son away. She lay the baby on her legs, leaning forward in the direction of the bedroom door. "Ginnie," she called, again. Not getting any answer, she called all the more louder. "Ginnie!"

Still there was no answer.

Georgia picked up the baby again, and then swung her legs to the right so that they were off of the mattress. She knew that she was not really supposed to leave the confinement of her bed, but she also felt that there was something definitely wrong. She let her feet drop to the floor. "Ginnie?" she called out again, still hoping to hear an answer.

Then she stood up. Her legs seemed a bit wobbly, and they threatened to collapse beneath her. She really couldn't check her balance with her arms, as she was using them to hold her son.

Georgia used a waddle-like step to head toward the baby's cradle, which was about five steps from the bed. She laid the baby in the cradle, and then grabbed her shawl, which was lying on the end of the footboard of the bed. She took a step toward the door and immediately felt a cramping feeling coming over her, especially in her abdominal area. She grasped her mid-section with her right hand and continued to slowly walk toward the bedroom door.

The baby started to cry.

Georgia continued to walk toward the door – one step at a time. She felt something wet running down the inside of her left leg. It was more than a trickle – it felt thicker and more dense than urine. She finished taking another step and then looked down. A thin line of blood was curling its way across her foot.

She was hemorrhaging. Georgia realized that she had made a very foolish decision – there was probably nothing wrong. Her sister, Ginnie, was probably on the other end of the house and couldn't hear her through the closed bedroom door.

But then again…

She placed her hand on the door knob and turned the knob. The door gave way under the slight pressure that Georgia exerted. Georgia slowly stepped out into the narrow hallway, slowly inching her way toward the living area of the house. For added support, she put both of her hands against the wall of the hallway, keeping her palms at a little lower than face height.

"Ginnie?" she called out again, but there was still no answer.

Georgia slowly and painfully edged her way toward the kitchen. It was normally a short walk of some fifteen feet, but the trip taken on this day was accomplished in spent inches, not in feet.

The baby continued to cry.

Georgia needed to take about one or two normal size steps before she would be able to see the kitchen. She now turned her entire body into the hallway wall, as if the wall itself would be able to support her frame. She took a side-step with her left foot. She was almost immediately greeted by a sharp cramp in her lower abdomen. Her uterus was still contracting, and her body was still in the process of rejecting the materials used in the birthing process. To Georgia, it felt as though her insides were falling out of her and onto the floor.

Nevertheless, she lifted her right leg and brought it together with her left.

She had closed the distance to the kitchen in half, in just one step.

She did it again, and again she was met with a horrific cramping sensation – one so severe that she thought she might fall to the hallway floor.

But she didn't.

Once again, she lifted her right leg and brought it into her left.

Now it was simply a matter of turning her head.

But it wasn't a simple matter, at all.

Georgia's face was virtually plastered to the wall. She was feeling light-headed, and could hardly breathe. Her head was turned to the right, and away from her destination – she was looking back up the hallway from where she had come.

With whatever strength she had left in her upper body, she pushed her chest out from the wall, allowing her head to turn all the way to the left.

She could now see the kitchen…and she could see her sister, Ginnie, laying on the floor.

"Ginnie!" she cried, but her entreaty was useless. Ginnie still lay motionless on the floor. Georgia was not able to see her sister entire frame – the bread trough was blocking most of her view.

Suddenly, the front door to the house burst open. Mrs. Wade entered, along with her son – back from the search for Rebecca Tilden.

"Georgia!" Mrs. Wade exclaimed, seeing her daughter out of bed and holding on to the wall for dear life.

"Mother!" It's Ginnie!" Georgia gasped.

Mrs. Wade moved quickly to Ginnie's side. She could now see the tear in her dress where the bullet had pierced her back. Rolling her gently over, she saw the pool of blood that her daughter had been lying in. "She isn't breathing, Georgia!"

"Mother!"

"She's been shot, Georgia! I think that she's dead!" "Dead?" Georgia asked. "How?"

"I don't know, dear," said her mother, still holding Ginnie's body in her arms, but looking around the room for shattered glass. "Harry…. please see to your sister, Georgia. Help her back to her bed."

Harry Wade nodded and walked to Georgia's side. "Mama," he said, "there's all sorts of blood and….I don't know what else…all over the floor back here. I think Georgia's is not well."

"Help her to bed, Harry. She shouldn't be out of her bed!"

"Mother, you need my help!" screamed Georgia, now near hysterics.

"One thing I do not need is another dead daughter, Georgia Wade McClellan," her mother answered firmly. "Now get back to bed before you bleed to death! Harry, after you get Georgia back to bed, go get a pail and mop."

"Yes, mum!" answered the boy.

"I wonder where Mary Elizabeth is …and Isaac? I hope that she found Rebecca – we could really use their help right now."

"Mother?" Georgia asked. "What are you going to do with Ginnie?"

"I have no idea, dear," replied her mother. "You must worry about yourself, for now…and your son."

Mrs. Wade was playing the part of the pillar of strength. She had already been through a difficult time with her husband. In 1855, when Harry was still just an infant, her husband, named James Wade, suffered a mental collapse and tried to kill himself by hanging himself in the tool shed. Luckily, Ginnie happened to be playing outside at the time and heard the commotion in the shed, as Harry thrashed and kicked as the oxygen was being choked out of his system. Ginnie, just barely in her teens, screamed for her mother, while lifting her father's weight by supporting him by his legs. Help arrived in the form of their neighbor, Ben Croft, who cut James down and carried him into the house. The doctor was called, and a decision was made to commit Harry to a sanatorium in Harrisburg.

This was only one of several incidents that had discredited the Wade family during their stay in Gettysburg. James Wade had also had several encounters with law enforcement, mainly stemming, by all accounts, from petty theft.

From that point on, life for the Wade family had not been particularly easy – especially as far as the family finances were concerned. The children suffered for wanting certain creature comforts, but other than that, carried on nobly. Martha Wade was a different story. She became sullen and almost despondent – shutting herself away from all social engagements; blaming their poverty on Harry, and his condition, and complaining on a daily basis about their sad lot in life.

The war seemed to change her attitude somewhat. The Wade family was able to get sewing work – even if it was 'by the piece.' The slowly maturing ages of daughters, Georgia and Virginia, helped with the income a great deal, for Martha had instructed her daughters very well in the fine art of the sewing needle. To augment their income even more, Martha took in young Isaac Barnes, a child of a local girl, who had given birth to a child who suffered with 'handicaps.' Considered a liability to the family, the boy's grandparents were prominent citizens in Gettysburg, and this arrangement was conceived to cover up the birth and rearing of the child, to avoid possible embarrassment to the family.

The family finances were certainly not great, but they were better than they had been prior to James's attempted suicide. The Wade family was moving forward, not sideways. Georgia became engaged to John Louis McClellan, who was by trade, a carpenter. "Lou," as her husband would be known, was away from home, serving the Union as a part of the Pennsylvania cavalry. The Wade's had also had another son, Samuel, who was also away, fighting the war.

Now completely overwhelmed by the death of Ginnie, her mother sat alone and shrouded in grief – unable to make a decision regarding her body, and unable to move from her position on the kitchen floor. When her youngest child, Harry, finished mopping the floor and assisting Georgia, his mother sent him to their nearest neighbor, asking for assistance. Together they would carry Ginnie to the cellar, awaiting that time when the hostilities were over so that they could properly see to the girl's funeral and burial. For now, the cellar would have to do. The cooler temperatures would keep the body for a day or two, especially considering the heat of early July.

*   *   *

Brigadier General Lewis Armistead was one of General Pickett's most trustworthy Brigade Commanders. A veteran of the Mexican War, Armistead had been close friends with Winfield Scott Hancock while stationed in California. Now he was a General in the Army of Northern Virginia, and Hancock was the Commander of II Corps for the Union.

Ironically, Armistead's uncle, George Armistead, had been the Commander of Fort McHenry in Baltimore Harbor during the War of 1812. It had been his uncle who had run up the immense garrison flag that flew over the fort the morning after the bombardment by the British navy -the same sight that had inspired Francis Scott Key to pen the immortal words to "The Star-spangled Banner." The war that was now in progress was a war that contained many interlocking pieces. As one set of pieces was the relationship between the Armistead's – uncle and nephew, so was the relationship between the Keys – Francis Scott and Phillip Barton Key, who Daniel Sickles had shot down in cold blood just a few years prior to the war.

Armistead's personal life had been anything but pleasant. He had married Cecelia Lee Love, a distant cousin of Robert E. Lee. The couple was married in 1844 and had two children together. His wife died in 1850 of an unknown cause. In 1852, Armistead received news that the family home in Virginia had burned to the ground. He received a leave from the Army and returned home to assist his family. While there, he married his second wife, Cornelia Jamison. He returned to the West, and to active duty, shortly after that. The Armistead's had one child together, a son – Lewis B., who died in infancy. Cornelia Armistead died the following year, during an outbreak of cholera. He was now a Brigadier General in Pickett's Division, a part of Longstreet's Corps, in the Army of Northern Virginia.

As noon arrived on 3 July, the plan for the final attack of the battle was being put into place. Lee's plan called for a massive artillery cannonade, beginning at 1:00 pm. The purpose of this shelling was to soften up the Federal center of the line, with the ultimate hope of knocking out the Union artillery that was stationed there. It was still Lee's contention that the Federal fortifications and armament were not as strong as they appeared. He also put a great deal of stock in the fact that the Confederate Army now had a history of being able to move the Federal troops without much difficulty. Lee would send about 12,000 men across the field that afternoon.

*   *   *

At the same time, somewhere behind the Union line, on a farm belonging to the Spangler family, another drama was about to play out in the field hospital. General Samuel Zook's lungs had been filling up with blood throughout the night and into the morning of 3 July. Now, in the afternoon of the same day, the General knew that his time on this Earth was extremely limited, and so he sent for his trusted aide, Lieutenant Favill.

Favill, who was more like a son to the General than an aide de camp, arrived at a little past the noontime hour. He came, knowing that the General had been mortally wounded, and expected the worse possible news. He was, in fact, surprised to see the General still alive and conscious.

"Ah, Favill," Zook exclaimed, seeing his loyal aide, "I see you have come to see me die."

"General Zook," the younger man protested, "you mustn't speak this way. You must not give up hope."

"There is no hope, Lieutenant," replied the General. "I have been a soldier far too long to misread the nature of my wound. It is inevitable, and that is that."

"Then you will pardon me, General, if I continue to pray for your eventual recovery?"

"You may," acquiesced Zook. "How goes the battle?"

"We are expecting a rather large attack on the center of the line, General," answered Favill, "so you can be sure that you will hear the noise from it. We already know that there are many brigades of rebels congregating behind the wood line on the other side of the field."

"Let them come," encouraged Zook. "Hancock has the center protected quite well."

"Yes, sir, I believe that is the case."

"Then, Lieutenant, you should go there and do your duty. But please remember to come back to see me after the battle is over. I should like to know the result."

"I will, sir," answered Favill. "You can count on it!" And with that said, Lieutenant Favill turned on his heel and exited the tent.

General Zook turned to his Commander, General Sickles, with a forlorn look on his face. "I do hope I am still around at the end of the battle, Dan. I do care for that boy, and it would be a shame if those represented our last words together."

"Then I would suggest, Sam – you stubborn German – that you hang in there until he returns."

*   *   *   *

As ordered, the Confederate cannonade began promptly at 1:00 pm. The volleys of solid shell lasted for about forty five minutes, during which time the Federal forces spent much of that under cover. General

Hancock did not allow his batteries to return fire, hoping to tempt the Confederate forces into thinking that their cannon had successfully neutralized the Union big guns.

In truth, they had done nothing of the kind.

The Confederate infantry stepped off as the last of the salvos were being fired. Lee planned to trick the Federal commanders into believing that the Confederate force, which spanned more than a mile in width, was going to attack the entire center of the Union line – which also spanned more than a mile. This ruse was employed by having all of the brigades used in the attack lined up as they exited the tree line, as if on dress parade. To close the distance between the tree line and the Union line required a march of more than three quarters of a mile across an open field – with no place for shelter. But Lee had a much more compact objective – a low stone wall that was built at a right angle to the field, which formed the direct center of the Union line. In order to accomplish this, his men had to start spread out across the field, but they would negotiate an oblique turn every hundred yards, or so, which would serve to compress their numbers toward the center of the field. Lee's biggest fear was the Union artillery, particularly if those guns were filled with canister shot, which would easily rip through each regiment. By creating the diversion, allowing the Union leadership to believe that Lee was attacking the entire line, the big guns would have to remain where they were placed, and would be rendered useless.

Lee's plan also had a second prong. Cavalry General Jeb Stuart was to ride out with his corps and swing wide around the Union defenses, attacking the Union center from the rear at the precise moment that the infantry was reaching the Union center at the low stone wall. The desired effect was to cut the Union army into two confused sections.

General Longstreet was opposed to this plan. It was his belief that the Federal cannon were still in place and were capable of delivering a mortal blow to his division. When General Pickett asked the General if he could begin the attack, Longstreet reluctantly gave the command to start the march across the field, gesturing only with a nod.

General Pickett's Division consisted of brigades under the command of Generals Armistead, Kemper, and Garnett. General Garnett had been wounded and had to be strapped to the saddle of his horse in order to make the charge. In doing so, he was an instant target for the Yankee sharpshooters.

The Confederates marched slowly and deliberately toward the Union line. They encountered a wooden fence around the time they reached the Emmitsburg Road. Even though it was neither a large or strongly constructed fence, the fence did prove to be an obstacle for the rebel force, and many were cut down trying to scale it. Up until this point, the Confederates were being hit by cannon fire from the flanks of the Union Line – from Cemetery Hill and Round Top – but as the rebel army reached the Emmitsburg Road, General Hancock had his cannon open fire – the cannons that General Lee had believed had been taken out. The effect was devastating! Whole brigades were destroyed in a matter of moments. Of the 12,500 men that marched out of the woods on 3 July, more than half never made it back to the Confederate line.

All three of Pickett's Brigadier Generals were shot. Garnett was shot off of his horse – although it was not clear if he was struck by canister or solid shot. Kemper also received a wound and was captured.

General Armistead reached the stone wall at "the angle" with about three hundred men in his brigade. He inspired his men by removing his hat, then putting it on the end of his sword, waving his faltering men onward. It had a positive effect on his soldiers, who broke through the Union center and started capturing some of the Federal cannon. They were in the process of turning these cannon to fire upon their own owners, when Hancock sent in fresh reinforcements, who drove the

Confederates back. Lewis Armistead was shot three times during this final push, but none of the wounds were considered life threatening. Armistead, a loyal member of the Masons, gave a Masonic signal that he was in need of assistance when he was wounded, and he was immediately attended to by Captain Henry Bingham – a fellow Mason, but an officer for the Federal army.

"General," asked Bingham, "how may I be of assistance to you?" Armistead reached into his jacket pocket and produced his watch.

"Please..give this watch to my good friend, General Hancock," the General replied. "Is he in this proximity?"

The Captain nodded. "This part of the line is manned by II Corps, General Hancock's Corps, however the General has also just been wounded in the fray."

General Armistead immediately began to weep. Throughout the war, he had feared that this moment might arrive; the moment when he would have to face Hancock on the field of battle. Armistead had taken a solemn oath stating that he wished the "God would strike him down dead" if he ever did anything to harm his friend, Hancock.

Bingham would see to the General's wounds, but Armistead, now full of regret, would impart one more piece of Gettysburg lore, "Tell General Hancock for me that I have done him and done you all an injury which I shall regret the longest day I live."

Armistead was then removed to the field hospital at Spangler's woods. Although Hancock's wound was not a mortal one, the two men did not see each other on that day, or any other.

General Stuart did, in fact, sweep his cavalry around the rear of the Union defenses, but his move to the rear was met by a brigade of Union cavalry, commanded by one of the youngest Brigadier Generals in that army, General George Armstrong Custer. Fierce fighting broke out between the two brigades, the result of which was a draw – but Stuart's attack was, as a result, called off. This prong of Lee's plan completely dissolved.

As Federal reinforcements were brought up from the rear, the Confederate Army turned and fled back down the hill toward the open field and the safety of the woods from whence they had appeared.

General Lee, fearing a Federal counter-offensive, was quick in his attempt to rally the retreating Confederates as they approached the tree line. He admonished his foot soldiers to make ready their defenses, as the Union soldiers would undoubtedly attempt to finish them off that day. To General Pickett, Lee said, "General…please kindly see to your Division, so that they may prepare our defenses."

"Division?" replied Pickett. "General Lee, I have no Division!"

This was an accurate assessment of the damages. Of the participating Confederate Divisions, all took heavy casualties, but Pickett's Division was almost wiped off of the map. Hundreds of soldiers were captured, but thousands were killed or wounded in this final major act of the battle.

*   *   *

At 3:30 pm, Lieutenant Favill returned to the field hospital at Spangler's farm. He was relieved to see that his friend and mentor, General Samuel Zook, was still alive.

"So, Lieutenant Favill," greeted Zook, still in good spirits, "how goes the fighting at the front?"

"General, sir, " reported Favill, "the bands have been ordered to the front, the flags are flying, and the enemy is in retreat."

"Then I am perfectly satisfied," responded Zook, "and ready to die."

*   *   *

General Judson Kilpatrick, commanding General of a Union Cavalry Division, was ordered by General George Meade and Cavalry Commanding Officer, General Alfred Pleasonton, to attack General Longstreet's right flank with a cavalry charge. Kilpatrick had already loaned out one of his cavalry brigades to General Gregg – that being the brigade under General Custer, so he had but one brigade remaining to mount this attack.

This remaining brigade was under the command of Brigadier General Elon Farnsworth, who remarked to Kilpatrick that the maneuver was ill-conceived, at best. Kilpatrick burst into a rage.

"You are a coward, Farnsworth! The enemy is on the run! This is the time for glory!"

General Farnsworth continued to protest. "The right flank of Longstreet's Corps is firmly entrenched. They are not on the run, but are dug in, protecting the retreat of the army."

"If you are too cowardly to lead this attack," countered Kilpatrick, "then I shall be forced to do it myself."

Shamed by Kilpatrick's words, Farnsworth obeyed his orders and led the attack. The cavalry attacked remnants of John Bell Hood's Division, which was now under the command of General Evander Law – Hood having been wounded the previous day. Farnsworth was shot five times in the chest and died immediately. His brigade suffered heavy losses.

CHAPTER 23

The Aftermath of the Battle

General Lee ordered his army to dig in, preparing themselves for the counterattack by the Union forces.

The attack never came.

Despite the urging by his subordinate Generals, George Meade refused to allow his army to budge from the safety offered by the high ground. The armies sat in battle-ready position for the rest of 3 July, and then spent the anniversary of the founding of the nation, 4 July, in the exact same positions. By the evening of the 4th, Lee had ordered the retreat of his army, falling back across the State line in Maryland, and then, soon after, into Virginia.

The Army of Northern Virginia would never fight another battle on Northern soil.

General Lee took the defeat at Gettysburg very personally, admitting over and over to his officers, as well as to his enlisted men, that the finale to the battle was "all my fault." This reference was to the assault labeled "Pickett's Charge," for up until that point in time, the Confederates had fought at least to a draw – and it could also be argued that they had, in fact, won the battle. In a time where superior numbers were used as a barometer for success in battle, the Union army suffered far more casualties than the Confederates, although the three day battle was arguably the most deadly conflict in the history of the United States – that is, if both sides in the battle were still considered Americans.

*   *   *

In the late afternoon of 3 July, in the field hospital tent on Spangler's Farm, General Samuel Zook took his last breath. It was almost 5:00 pm.

Near his bed side stood Lieutenant Favill, his trusted aide de camp. He had in his possession most of the General's personal effects, ready to return them to the officer's relatives. Also in attendance were Mary Elizabeth Tilden, Rebecca Tilden, and Jacob Zook. General Daniel Sickles observed the passing of his friend and fellow senior officer from the cot to the left, still puffing on a cigar.

"He was a good man," said Sickles, "a good soldier, and a great friend. He was the only man I ever saw stand up to that stuck up Winfield Scott Hancock. Maybe because they were both from Pennsylvania – right around here, I believe."

"The General was never one to keep his thoughts bottled up," attested Favill, bending over to close General Zook's eyes. "Good luck to you, General Sickles," he added, shaking the General's hand. Favill then saluted the officer, turned, and left the tent.

Mary Elizabeth used the military issue blanket to cover General Zook's face, then turned back to her daughter. "Rebecca, I think that we should head back down the hill now."

"There are still many wounded men to take care of, Mother."

"Yes," replied Mary Elizabeth, "but the Wades must be worried sick about us. They probably think something happened to us…perhaps that we were killed during the battle."

"Or that we are simply hiding out until the conflict ends," offered Rebecca. Jacob had been sitting on a stool next to the other Zook. He now stood up, and began walking back to the operating table, ready to assist Doctor Sim. There was no possible way that he was going to allow himself to become embroiled in a family squabble.

But General Sickles had other thoughts in his mind. "Jacob? Where are you going, boy?"

"Back to work, General," he answered. "We still have many more wounded to attend."

"I realize that, son," remarked Sickles, "but I was wondering if you have given any consideration to my offer." Sickles said this, but said it looking not at Jacob, but rather over at Mary Elizabeth. Daniel Sickles was a master politician; he knew exactly what was at stake here.

Jacob slowly returned to the General's side. "I really haven't had the time to give it much thought, General – although I must say, it is a very generous offer."

Jacob's response garnered a facial response from Mary Elizabeth. She pretended to fuss with General Zook's final positioning, but was listening intensely to the conversation. Sickles was well aware that he had caught Mary Elizabeth's ear.

"Come, come," urged Sickles, "when this war is over, the government is going to be in need of smart, educated men to help pick up the pieces of this country and put them back together again. A young man of your overwhelming intelligence could really make his mark in the world, you know."

Mary Elizabeth turned suddenly and looked straight at General Sickles. "Pardon me, General," she interrupted, "might I inquire about the generous offer that you made Mr. Zook, here?"

"Pardon me, M'am," Sickles replied, "but at the risk of sounding impertinent, may I ask you what possible business that would be of yours?"

Mary Elizabeth looked over at Jacob, who blandly returned her stare. "Might I ask if we could discuss this in private, General?" she asked.

"In private?" Sickles questioned. "Doesn't that seem a bit…odd? You wish to discuss an offer I made to young Zook without him being present?" Sickles smiled up at Mary Elizabeth and then took another puff on his cigar.

Mary Elizabeth looked across the tent. Rebecca had already started to tend to the wounds of a Confederate officer who had been brought into the tent. "Well…yes…you see…," she said, "it also concerns my daughter."

Sickles nodded slowly. "Your daughter? You are referring to Becky?"

"Yes, that is correct."

"Well then," the General replied, "if it concerns Becky, then she ought to be a part of the discussion, as well! Don't you think?"

"Well…yes…No!...."

"Becky!" the General bellowed. "I need you, as soon as you are finished attending to that reb officer!"

"I'll be over as soon as I can, General," the girl answered.

"There!" said Sickles, "We just need to wait a bit….unless, of course, there are things that can't wait…things that have to be said right now."

Mary Elizabeth sat quickly on the stool that had just been occupied by Jacob Zook. "Yes…I suppose there are," she said. She looked up at the boy. "Jacob…I have no doubt that you are a remarkable young man. I also know that my daughter, Rebecca, likes you a great deal."

"She does?" asked Jacob.

"Surely you realized that?" responded her mother. "I…I…hoped that she did," replied the boy. "It's just that…"

"Go on, Jacob," coaxed Sickles, his voice actually gentle. "Take your time, boy."

"Our backgrounds are different," said Jacob. "I know enough to realize that there is no hope for a union between an Amish boy and an 'English' girl."

"Great Thunder!" shouted Sickles. "What is this with the 'English' again, boy? We are all Americans here!"

"I have explained all this to you, General," stated Jacob, firmly. "You know of my heritage…my culture."

"Aye," admitted Sickles. "You are a complicated young man, indeed – but that shouldn't stop you from having dreams…plans…ambitions."

"Dreams, plans and ambitions are not part of the Ordnung, General," Jacob explained. "They are a part of man's vanity. We are to follow the way…the path that the Maker has set out for us. Anything else….is pure vanity!"

"And you truly believe this?" questioned Sickles, grabbing Jacob by the arm. "Answer me that, Jacob Zook!" The boy was silent for a moment, but it was a moment too long for Sickles. "You can't say it, can you? There is something brewing inside of you, Jacob…and you know it….you feel it! You have a desire to be

someone…to do something greater than live a life on an Amish farm." "Don't say that, General," rebutted Jacob.

"Why not, Jacob?" thundered Sickles. "Because it's the truth?"

Using his free hand, Jacob gently pried Sickles' hand off of his arm. The boy turned away from the officer. He didn't want the General to see the tears of frustration that were brimming in his eyes. In turning, Jacob was again able to see Becky, who was still working on the Confederate officer across the way. "Mrs. Tilden," he said, softly, "would you accept me as a suitor for Becky if I was not…Amish?" His nose began to run, so he wiped it on his sleeve.

Mary Elizabeth knew the answer to his question immediately. "Why…yes…of course, Jacob."

"But that is the wrong answer, Mrs. Tilden," Jacob replied, obviously disappointed at the answer. "Asking an Amish man to change his perspective on the world is very much the same as asking one of the dark-skinned slaves to become white – just because the government has freed them from oppression. It cannot be done!"

"But…."

Jacob turned back to face the woman. "I am to be judged for who and what I am," he said, with tears rolling down his cheeks, "or I am not to be judged at all – and I say this knowing that I am jeopardizing my future with your daughter in doing so."

"Here! Here!" agreed Sickles.

"The General has offered to bring me back to Washington with him. He has further offered to pay for my education…at any university that will accept me. He thinks I show great promise…so does Doctor Sim."

"I had no idea, Jacob," replied Mary Elizabeth.

"Does this make a difference to you, M'am?" asked Sickles.

Mary Elizabeth felt trapped. If she said that it didn't make a difference – in which case she would be lying – she would be making a conscious decision that would affect Rebecca's happiness – perhaps for the rest of her life. If she replied that it did make a difference, she knew that she would appear hypocritical and unenlightened. "I don't know what to say," she responded, taking an easier path.

Mary Elizabeth walked across the hospital tent, putting her arm around Rebecca and helping her tend to the wounded Confederate officer.

"That was a good speech, Jacob," remarked Sickles.

"Hmm," Jacob mused.

"So let me ask you this…and remember, Jacob," said the General, "I like you!" Jacob wiped his eyes and looked down at Sickles.

"Was that the speech that was intended for Becky's mother….or was it intended for someone…closer to you?" Jacob looked at the General with a question on his lips. "Much closer to you?"

Jacob nodded. "My father?" The General also nodded. "That's why I ran away in the first place, General. That's why I can't give you an answer about my education! What good will it do to become successful in the – pardon the expression, sir – 'English' world, if I can't ever go back to visit my parents…because they have shunned me?"

"I didn't think your mother would shun you, Jacob!"

"She won't…really," he answered, "but it won't make any difference. I will still be shunned! It is as it says in the Book of Matthew: 'For what is a man profited, if he shall gain the whole world, and lose his own soul?' I will be gaining education, wealth, social position…even the girl that I wish to spend my life with – but I will be giving up my family!"

Sickles, surprisingly enough…fell silent.

A Federal Corporal entered the tent. "Pardon me," the young man said, "I have a young boy outside…a Harry Wade. He is looking for a Mrs. Tilden, or anyone else that he may know."

Mary Elizabeth, Rebecca, and Jacob all turned quickly to speak to the Corporal, all three acknowledging at the same instant that they knew Harry Wade. The Corporal then nodded and left the tent. A moment later, Harry Wade entered. He quickly saw Mary Elizabeth and ran to her, embracing her.

"What is it?" asked Mary Elizabeth. "Is something wrong with the baby?" "It's Ginnie!" the boy cried, still holding Mary Elizabeth around her waist.

"She's been shot!" He pulled back so that he could look up in her face. "She's dead!" "Dead?" cried a shocked Rebecca. "How can she be dead?"

"She was shot clear through the side door to the house," said the boy. "She was kneading her bread. She was shot in the back. We put her in the cellar!"

"Oh, your poor, poor mother!" sobbed Mary Elizabeth. Rebecca wept bitterly.

"How did you manage to get here, Harry?" asked Jacob.

"The rebel army is in full retreat," answered the boy. "The snipers are long gone."

CHAPTER 24

Sad Revelations

Mary Virginia Wade was brought up from the cellar of the McClellan house on the morning of 4 July. As was the custom, she was dressed in her best dress, one which she herself had sewn – one that she would have worn that evening to the annual July 4th Celebration Ball - and laid out on a bed in the McClellan home. Toward the evening of that day, Mrs. Wade received visitors, who paid their respects to both Ginnie and the Wade/McClellan family. Visitors who looked closely enough could see dried pieces of dough on the dead girl's hands and fingers.

As far as anyone could tell, Ginnie was the only civilian casualty of the battle of Gettysburg.

Harry Wade had made a grisly discovery on the afternoon of 4 July. He, and a few of his friends, were busy exploring some of the entrenchments and other areas that had been employed by the Confederate Army, and happened to come across a coffin. As luck would have it, the coffin was empty. The casket was lined with expensive material, and seemed to indicate, upon examination by some of the elders of the community, that it had been manufactured specifically for use by a Confederate officer.

The officer, evidently, had planned for the worst, and had bothered to secure and transport his own means of burial – should the event arise.

On the afternoon of 4 July, Harry Wade thought this was more fitting to hold his sister than any rebel officer, so he and his friends dragged the heavy wooden box home with them to Baltimore Street. She was to be buried in a coffin that had been meant for a Confederate officer.

The eighty-seventh anniversary of the founding of the country was not a particularly pleasant experience in Gettysburg. Most of the Confederates had either left the area, or were in the process of doing so, but a summer rain had done nothing to abate the humid temperatures that had plagued the locale for the past few days. Now, lying out on open fields, and under the heat of July, and the damp of the rain, the countless number of bodies, both Federal and Confederate, began to rot. The stench from rotting corpses, both human and equine, was unimaginable. Adding to that smell was the foul smell of spent ammunition, which still hung in the air like a sulfur-laden cloud that would not dissipate.

The good people of Gettysburg were slowly returning to their homes. Many of them found their possessions damaged or completely destroyed. Most that enjoyed the boon of livestock, found that their animals were missing, and most probably slaughtered or, in the case of horses, stolen. Large holes were discovered in buildings all around the town, and many spent rounds were found stuck into the brick or mortar of the town homes and places of business.

Worst of all for an agrarian society, whose very existence was dependent upon the harvest of crops grown during the summer months, many of the fields and orchards were either leveled in the fray of battle, or picked clean by the 170,000 soldiers who had made the area their home for the past three days.

The Federal Army was still encamped on Cemetery Ridge. Most of the activity in the camp centered around two distinct areas: the care of the wounded and burial of the dead, and the preparation for another Confederate attack – one that would never come.

*   *   *

On the morning of 4 July, Ishmael Zook noticed that the Confederate soldiers were pulling out of their position on Seminary Ridge. The field hospital that had been set up in the Seminary building was being abandoned, and all the wounded, with the exception of the most seriously injured, were readied for transportation. The most seriously wounded – the ones the doctors felt would never survive the long journey back to Virginia – were left to the care and sympathy of the Army of the Potomac. Sarah Zook, along with the staff of the seminary, were still very much involved with the care of theses soldiers – many of whom were double amputees, or were deemed mortally wounded.

At 8:00 am, Ishmael Zook decided that it was high time to begin to look for his son, Jacob. He decided to take his younger son, Abraham, along with him. He felt that his son had witnessed so much suffering and pain, that he didn't want the boy to become overwhelmed with it for another moment. Together, they left the seminary building.

They walked across a small wooded area until they reached the farmhouse and barn that had been their home for the past two years. The farmhouse was nothing more than a charred frame. It had been burned to the ground. As far as Ishmael was concerned, it really didn't matter what, or who, had done this. They would have to re-build the house. Unfortunately, he realized that almost all of this would have to be done by him alone. If they had been a part of the Amish community in Paradise, such a disaster would have found instant support within the members of the community. A new home would have been raised in a matter of days. This would require hard work, and patience.

The barn was in better condition than the house. There were holes in the roof, probably the result of artillery. These matched the holes in the walls of the building. All of the animals were gone, including his favorite rooster, "Ol Jehosophat," which Ishmael reckoned had been caught and eaten. The wagon had been commandeered, along with his draft horse. The cows were nowhere to be seen.

"Come," he quietly said to Abraham. They slowly walked toward the town.

"What is that smell, Fati?" asked the boy.

"That is the smell of foolishness," replied Ishmael. "That is what happens when men argue with each other, and do not allow Divine Providence to take its course."

"I do not understand," said the boy.

"I know, Abraham," replied Ishmael, "and I hope that you never will."

All around them were visions of the destruction left in the wake of the battle. There were overturned carts and wagons scattered on the road, and there were dead animals everywhere – especially horses. Occasionally, they would come upon a horse lying dead in the road which was still saddled – the complete set of tack still on the horse, including the bridle in its mouth. The rider was gone, but the animal remained as a testament to the conflict of the past three days. But Ishmael and Abraham also passed other dead animals – mostly livestock which had been butchered there on the spot. Very often, especially in the case of the chickens and roosters, only the heads, feet, and feathers remained behind to tell the tale. Just as often, they came upon a dead soldier. Ishmael did not prevent his son from looking at the poor unfortunate soul, but did shield his eyes with his hands, if he felt that the scene was too graphic to be viewed by his son.

They walked off of the seminary property and headed east on Spring Street. Now they were headed toward the center of the town, where very little fighting had taken place. There were fewer bodies and dead horses, but the buildings showed many signs of the battle, especially with the number of rounds which were stuck into the outer walls of many of the homes.

Ishmael had instinctively wanted to head toward Cashtown, and the Cashtown Inn, for that was the place he had heard several times as the last known location of his son, Jacob. But something else, perhaps Divine guidance, had instructed him to head toward the 'English' town, itself. Ishmael felt certain that he would find his son holed up somewhere – perhaps in the arms of some English woman.

But then Ishmael would think to himself…attempt to correct his way of thinking….ask himself if it really mattered. His mind started to replay the biblical story of "The Prodigal Son," and Ishmael began to see great similarities between that story, and the story which had been played out before his own eyes.

As Ishmael and Abraham drew closer to the center of the little town, he encountered a phenomenon. This happened several times to the man in just a few minutes time, which made the man wonder even more.

As Ishmael guided his younger son down the street, a man – a complete unknown – stopped him along the way.

"Excuse me, sir," the man began, "I would hate to sound rude, but you look as though you are one of those Amish men. Is that so?"

Normally, Ishmael would simply grunt and ignore the man. This time, he stopped in his tracks and gave the gentleman a curious look.

"I am sorry," continued the man, "but I am taken by your style of dress; your black pants and boots, your white shirt, your black, wide-brimmed hat, and especially by your beard - your long, blonde beard."

"What have you to do with me?" asked Ishmael. He remembered that this was a common occurrence back in Paradise, but especially in the larger town of Lancaster, where non-Amish would often accost the members of the community for the very differences that this man just recounted.

But there was something different about this man.

This man wasn't accosting him – it was as if he…recognized him.

"I am sorry," said the man. "I didn't mean to embarrass you, sir. It's just that…considering all that happened here these last three days…"

"Yes?" asked Ishmael.

"…the battle, you know…"

"Yes? Yes?"

"Well," the man continued, "we really don't have that many of you Amish folks around these parts, and…well…your beard…"

"What about my beard?" demanded Ishmael, now becoming a little more impatient with the man.

"Nothing, sir," replied the man. "You are Amish…and your beard is…blonde." "So…what?" asked Ishmael.

"So…you wouldn't happen to be the father of Jacob Zook, would you?" Ishmael took a step back. "Jacob?" he asked, reaching out a holding the man by his shoulders. "You know my Jacob?"

The man was intimidated by the Amish man. "Well…not personally….no. In fact…I've never met him."

"Oh," replied Ishmael, visibly disappointed.

"But most people in this town know of him, Mr. Zook."

"And how would that come to be?" asked Ishmael, a note of doubt in his voice.

"Because he is a hero, Mr. Zook!" The man beamed a great smile at Ishmael.

"I do not understand this term…'hero,'" replied Ishmael.

"A hero is a man who goes above and beyond the call of duty for the sake of his fellow man," instructed the man.

"And my son, Jacob, has done this?" asked Ishmael.

"Indeed, he has. Jacob has saved the life of a Federal Major, and has been a valuable assistant in the hospital tent for the last two days. The entire town is very proud that he is one of our own, Mr. Zook."

Ishmael had mixed emotions when the man said the words 'one of our own.' He wasn't one of their own – he couldn't possibly be. He was Amish, and that was that! On the other hand, Ishmael did feel a funny warm spot in his heart when the man beamed with pride for the accomplishments Jacob had visited upon the town of Gettysburg. Ishmael certainly understood what is felt like to be proud of his own children. He was having difficulty understanding how the entire populace of the town could feel the same way. How could an entire town embrace his son, Jacob, as their son?

"Do you know where my son is, sir?" Ishmael asked.

"Humbolt…Andrew Humbolt," replied the man.

"Mr. Humbolt," repeated Ishmael, shaking the man's hand, "do you know where Jacob is at?"

"I would think he is still at the military field hospital, Mr. Zook."

"And where is that, Mr…Humbolt? I am sorry, but my wife and I have been guests of the men in the gray coats for the last two days."

"You don't say? That must have been quite an ordeal!"

"No," replied Zook, "they treated us with a great deal of respect. What was terrible was the blood and the poor men dying."

"That is a fact, Mr. Zook!" Humbolt agreed.

"Now, tell me," Ishmael asked again, anxiously, "where is this field hospital?" "Sure thing, Mr. Zook! Do you know Spangler's Farm?" "Up on top of Cemetery Ridge?" asked Ishmael.

"That's correct, sir," Humbolt answered. "The hospital is up there." "Thank you, Mr. Humbolt," Ishmael said, shaking his hand again. "Andrew!"

"Thank you…Andrew," Ishmael corrected himself. For the first time in his four decades of life, he had made an 'English' friend. "Come along, Abraham."

"Abraham?" repeated Humbolt. "Isn't that something? Your boy has the same name as the President of the United States!"

"Does he?" asked Ishmael, as the two started off. "We named him after the first Patriarch of the Hebrew people."

"As in the book of Genesis!" added Andrew Humbolt.

Ishmael stopped dead in his tracks, totally amazed. "Yes, Andrew… just as in the Book of Genesis!" Ishmael was even more surprised at this revelation. All of the 'English' were not the heathens which he had come to believe.

Ishmael and his son, Abraham had now reached the intersection of the Emmitsburg Pike; the section of that main road which passed through the center of the town of Gettysburg. People were now out on the streets. Some were working on mending broken windows, or patching up the places that had been struck by ordinance or minie ball. Ishmael now instinctively grabbed Abraham's hand, although the boy didn't appreciate this sign of protection.

Ishmael had become accustomed to feeling the townspeople stare at him, or at his family, as if they were from a civilization far removed from that of the United States of America. Ishmael now noticed that many of the people had stopped along the way to greet them, or simply to smile a smile of recognition. Ishmael harkened back to his recent conversation with Andrew Humbolt, remembering what he had said about his son's fame throughout the town. Could this be the reason that he was now being treated so differently? Occasionally, Ishmael was even bid 'good morning' with his name attached to that salutation. It was never, "good morning, Ishmael," – that would have been far too familiar – besides, very few would have even known his given name – but he was simply greeted with a friendly, "good morning, Mr. Zook." And even though it was not in his nature to do so, especially with the 'English," Ishmael found himself responding back with a friendly 'good morning' himself.

Ishmael and Abraham walked along the city streets of Gettysburg, as if this was the very first time they had ever done so. Up ahead, a small crowd had convened. They were surrounding something lying in the street. As Ishmael neared, he could tell that it was a dead Confederate soldier. He stopped to listen to what the people in the group were saying about the soldier.

One man kicked the young soldier's leg. "Rebel dog! Look what your kind did to our town!"

"Have some respect for the dead, Claude!" cautioned a woman. "This boy didn't do anything wrong by you. It isn't his fault!"

"What's the matter with you, Sadie?" the first man asked. "All of them rebels are nothing but traitors to the country. If this boy hadn't fallen off this building and broken his neck, we should have hung him by a rope."

Ishmael looked down at the young soldier again, noticing the bulge in his neck. The boy had indeed broken his neck. He hadn't been shot!

"This boy was a sniper, I'll wager," said another man. "I'll wager he was perched on top of one of these buildings, ready to pick one of our boys off."

A woman in the crowd gasped. "I wonder if this was the one who shot poor Mary Virginia Wade?"

Most of the heads in the crowd turned, looking across the Emmitsburg Pike, to a house that stood near the intersection of the Pike with Baltimore Street.

It was the McClellan house.

"There is no way to tell that," observed another man. "It could have been this boy what did it, but it is just as likely that he was aiming up Baltimore Street toward our boys in blue. He must have slipped and fell."

"And remember," added another woman, "somewhere, somewhere miles from here, a mother is going to weep for the loss of this boy."

"Amen," said a man in the crowd. "Did anyone check the boy to see if he was carrying any papers on him. Maybe we can find out who he was."

"I already did that," replied the first man. "I didn't find a blessed thing, 'cept this picture." The man held up a small, well-bent photograph of a young lady of perhaps twenty years. "Must have been his girl," he noted.

"Pretty young thing!" another woman commented.

Ishmael patted Abraham on the shoulder, urging him to move on. They moved away from the little pack of Gettysburg citizenry, leaving the crumpled body of the soldier lying in the road. They had left the crowd to the speculations, observations, and opinions about the young soldier and his purpose leading up to the moment of his death.

But they were correct about several of their theories. He had been a sniper, and he had been on post atop the building which faced up Baltimore Street.

The soldier's name was Private Lewis McMultry. He had accidentally shot Ginnie Wade in the back. He never even realized that he had done so. He had fallen to his death moments after discharging his rifle.

Ishmael and his younger son crossed the Emmitsburg Pike over to the base of Baltimore Street. They started to walk up the incline, toward Cemetery Ridge. Ishmael could see four figures walking down the hills towards them. It was immediately obviously to the man that one of them was no more than a child. As they drew closer, he could see that two were females, and that the other two were boys – one about the age of Abraham, and the other much younger.

Ishmael noticed that one of the women had broken away from the rest of the company, and was walking – almost running – down the hill toward them, as if she recognized him. That – was impossible! He had no idea who this young woman was. He had formed no bonds with the 'English,' especially not with a young lady! She stopped running about fifteen feet ahead of them, catching her breath.

"Mr. Zook?" she asked. Ishmael slowly nodded. "I am Rebecca Tilden." Ishmael looked at the girl, obviously confused. "Did Jacob ever speak of me to you?" Ishmael shook his head. "We are … friends."

"My son," Ishmael replied, with a slight smile on his face, "is full of surprises." Mary Elizabeth and the two boys now caught up to Becky, and joined in the conversation.

"Mr. Zook," greeted Mary Elizabeth, "I am Rebecca's mother, Mary Elizabeth Tilden. This is my youngest son, Harry, and our boarder…Isaac."

Still amazed that everyone seemed to know exactly who he was, even though he knew absolutely no one, Ishmael did manage a response. "This is my son, Abraham….Jacob's brother. We have come looking for Jacob."

"He is fine," answered Rebecca. "We have just left him, only minutes ago, at the army hospital."

"Yes," responded Zook, "that is what the people on the street have told me; that Jacob is working at the hospital."

"Not just working," corrected Mary Elizabeth. "He is performing the work of a doctor, and sometimes that of a surgeon. He is an amazing young man!" Rebecca smiled at her mother. It was the first time that she had heard her mother say something positive about Jacob. "Don't look at me like that, Rebecca. You know that I think that Jacob's contribution is nothing short of amazing!"

"We are pleased to make your acquaintance, Mr. Zook," said Rebecca, "and also yours, Abraham. I can see that Jacob looks a great deal like you."

"Yes," agreed his father, "but that is where the similarities stop. He has a very independent mind."

"I do believe that may be part of being that age," explained Mary Elizabeth, casting an eye in Rebecca's direction. "Do you know the way to the hospital?"

"It is on the Spangler farm, is it not?"

"Yes," replied Rebecca. "If you have any difficulty finding it, just ask one of the Federal soldiers."

"In the gray uniforms?" asked Ishmael.

"No!" corrected Harry. "Those are the rebels. The ones in blue!"

"Harry!" reprimanded his mother. "I am sorry for my son's rudeness, Mr. Zook. We are on our way down to the house near the bottom of the hill. One of our friends was killed yesterday while she was standing in her house - the apparent victim of a Confederate sniper – although no one really knows for sure."

Ishmael whirled around. He could still see the small crowd of people standing on the Emmitsburg Pike, surrounding the body of the young Confederate soldier. He wondered if Mary Elizabeth had been speaking of the same event.

Ishmael tipped his hat to the women and smiled at them. They hurried along their way, continuing down the hill. Ishmael then took Abraham by the shoulder and restarted their climb toward Cemetery Ridge. He felt the first few drops of rain hit his face. The rain started as little more than a drizzle, but continued to increase in its intensity, becoming a steady rain by the time they had reached the top of the ridge.

Ishmael quickened his steps as the rain began to fall harder. They crossed the Union lines a few minutes after leaving the Tilden party, but they still had a considerable way to go before reaching the Spangler farm. As before, Ishmael was surprised to see how friendly the Union pickets greeted him when he approached the line. He thought that he heard one of the young soldiers mentioned his name as they passed through the line, but he quickly dismissed it as his imagination. They crossed over Hunt Street, a major intersection, but one of the last roads they would cross as they left the town of Gettysburg proper. They were now on the Baltimore Pike, which would eventually lead them to the city in Maryland of that same name. The Spangler farm would come up on the right hand side of the road in less than a mile, but it would be difficult going in the heavy rain, which had now turned all of the ruts made by the army wagons and caissons, into mud.

Finally, about a half hour after leaving the Tilden party, Ishmael and Abraham reached the dirt road that led into the Spangler farm. Ishmael had done some business with Abraham Spangler, who owned the farm – along with his son, Henry, who actually occupied the house there. Ishmael had built a few pieces of wooden furniture for their kitchen, including a large trestle table and chairs, and a sideboard. He had delivered the pieces to the Spangler farmhouse in June of the previous summer, using the same wagon which was now missing from his own home at the Lutheran Seminary.

The Spangler farm was two hundred and thirty acres, divided into a number of fields and pastures. The terrain was mostly level, having reached a plateau at the top of Cemetery Ridge. A modest stone and clapboard farmhouse stood next to the access road, with some outer buildings, including a large barn, standing just beyond. The barn was also being used as part of the hospital, and in a flat field, adjacent to the barn, stood the hospital tent. Ishmael directed his younger son in the direction of the field tent.

"Ishmael!" heralded a call from the porch of the farmhouse.

"Ach," Ishmael yelled back, "Henry Spangler! How good to see you again!" "I was wondering when I would see you around these parts,

Ishmael," said Henry, stepping down off his porch and into the rain. "I figured you'd be up here to fetch Jacob."

"You have seen my son?" asked Ishmael.

"Sure have!" confessed Henry. "I could never forget a handsome young lad such as him. I remembered him from when you delivered my table. He's probably still in the tent, helping with the wounded. My wife and I have been supplying food and coffee up there for the last few days. I've seen Jacob in there quite a bit."

Ishmael, usually a man of very few words, could only mumble a few now. "Thank you for keeping an eye on him for me, Henry."

"Our pleasure, Ishmael," Henry replied. "This must be your other boy. He doesn't look as much like you, like Jacob does."

"This is Abraham," Ishmael said, looking proudly down at his fourteen year old. "He takes after his mother."

"Abraham, eh?"

"Yes," Ishmael said, nodding his head, "I know. Just like the President of the United States."

"I suppose that is correct, sir," replied Spangler, "but I was first going to remark that his name was just like my father's."

And then Ishmael did something which was very out of character for him – He laughed.

It was so unlike him that Abraham looked up at his father with great surprise – as though the world had just turned an extra rotation.

"Go right ahead to that big tent over there," directed Henry. "If he's not there, then he must be in the barn – but be sure to stop by the house on your way back. We can have something to eat."

"That is very welcoming of you, Henry," Ishmael answered. "Thank you." Ishmael reached out and embraced Spangler. He had no idea what prompted him to do so, it was done on an impulse.

Father and son headed in the direction of the tent. It was now about 8:45 am.

A guard at the tent stopped them from entering, and inquired about their business.

"I have come to see my son, Jacob Zook," replied Ishmael.

"Well, why didn't you just say so in the first place," said the sentry, with a broad smile. The soldier pulled back the flap of the tent, allowing them admittance.

Ishmael was not shocked by what he could see inside the large tent; he, as well as Abraham, had been privy to a very similar scene for the previous two days at the Lutheran Seminary. He quickly surveyed the tent, which was now dark and unlit, as if night had once again fallen, due to the cloud cover and rain. Only the momentarily light from the open tent flap had illumined his face.

"Hello, there," called a voice from the dark. "Are you Ishmael Zook?" "I am," answered Zook. "Where are you?"

"Just give your eyes a minute to adjust," said the voice, "then step further in. I am to your left, about twelve cots in."

"You stay put right here," admonished Ishmael, speaking to his son. He feared that Abraham had already witnessed far too much for a boy his age. He waited a few moments more, and then started down the center aisle of the tent, counting the cots as he proceeded.

"I'm right here," said the voice, as Ishmael approached. Ishmael turned to face the left side of the tent. His eyes now focused, he could see that he was looking at an officer in a blue uniform. The man had brown hair and a brown drooping mustache. He was missing most of his right leg. "I am Major General Daniel Sickles of the III Corps of the Army of the Potomac, sir. I would stand to greet you, but, as you can plainly see, I am in no condition to do so at this time."

"Do you know where my boy is, General?" asked Zook.

"He is not in this tent, I can tell you that," answered Sickles. "If he was in here, I'd be spending much of his time, talking to him."

"Then where else can he be?" asked his father.

"He could be in the barn. That is also being used as a hospital," replied Sickles. "But there are wounded in just about every one of the buildings on this property."

"Thank you," answered Ishmael, and turned to leave.

"Wait!" said Sickles. "You had best leave your other son here…with me. If you are going to the barn, I should warn you that part of the barn is being used to hold some of the Confederate prisoners of war. That might not be an experience that you want your younger son to have."

Ishmael gave it a moment of thought, and after a brief moment said, "I will let him stay here with you, General. His name is…"

"…Abraham. Like the father of the Hebrew nation."

Ishmael smiled at the General, and then called his son over to his bed side. "You visit with the General here, Abraham," his father instructed. "Please…be mindful of your manners."

"Yes, Fati," answered the boy. Ishmael exited the tent.

"By asking you to be mindful of your manners," Sickles asked, "does that include asking me how my one leg came to be shorter than the other?"

"I suppose it does," the boy answered glumly.

"But it is something that you would like to hear about, isn't it?"

The boy happily nodded. "Yes, if you will tell me how it came to pass." Sickles smiled at the boy's phrasing of the sentence, thinking how archaic it sounded. "Abraham…it just so happens that I am going to be telling many people how I came to lose most of my right leg, so you have the honor to be one of the first to hear the story. I am going to practice my tale…on you. What do you think of that?"

"That will be fine, sir," answered the boy, smiling at the prospect.

Sickles then began to launch into his account of the battle in the wheat field and peach orchard, leading up to him being hit in his leg by a cannonball. He painted a picture of glory and valor – mostly his own – but kept the details remarkably free of gore and pain – as if the wound had not caused him to suffer at all. The final detail of the story included the fact that it was Abraham's own brother, Jacob, who had rescued his shattered, amputated right leg from the bone pile.

Ishmael walked over to Spangler's barn. The barn was built as a bank barn. There was a large embankment, or ramp of earth, that went from ground level to the second level on the outside of one side of the barn, enabling wagons and cattle to be housed on either level, if need be. This was a very typical style of barn building in Pennsylvania. Both levels of the barn were now being used as the Federal Army Hospital, with a shed, meant to house the wagons, being used at the moment to hold over a hundred Confederate prisoners.

Ishmael walked through both levels of the barn, looking for his son, Jacob – but the boy was nowhere to be found. He decided to check some of the outbuildings on the farm, as General Sickles had mentioned that they, too, were being used as appendages of the hospital.

Ishmael walked back toward the farmhouse. Adjacent to the farmhouse was a small wooden building that was used as a cook house during the summer months. A Federal private stood as a sentry at the door to the cook house, giving Ishmael ample information that the building was also being used as a hospital.

The sentry blocked Ishmael's entrance to the cook house. "Pardon me, sir," he said, "but you cannot enter this building. We have a high-ranking wounded prisoner in there."

"I see," replied Ishmael. "Might I ask…is the prisoner alone, or is he being attended to by a boy….a boy with blonde hair?"

The sentry suddenly understood to whom he was speaking. His face lit up, and he seemed very excited to meet Ishmael. "You are inquiring about young Jacob Zook, are you not? You are his father, I imagine."

The soldier knocked on the door to the cook house, then opened the door. Ishmael heard the Private say, "Jacob, there is someone here to see you."

Ishmael heard a voice within the hut ask, "Who is it, Private?"

"Come out here and see for yourself," the Private replied, pulling himself out of the building. The soldier turned and smiled at Ishmael, a tear running down his cheek. He resumed his position, guarding the small outbuilding, as if nothing had just transpired.

The door to the cook house opened, and within a moment Ishmael could clearly see his son, Jacob, being framed by the doorway.

"Papa?" Jacob asked, a note of disbelief in his voice.

"Jakob," his father answered, speaking his name in its Germanic form. But Ishmael was still anxious; he was anxious that his son was still angry at him.

"Papa! Fati!" Jacob shouted, and then ran out of the cook house and up to where his father was standing. Jacob threw his arms around his father and embraced him tightly. Ishmael responded to this overt sign of affection by doing the same, holding his son in his arms for the first time since he was a baby. After holding onto his son for over a minute, Ishmael pushed the boy away from him, and then, reaching up with both hands, grabbed the boy on both sides of his face, pulled his head toward his, and then kissed him on both cheeks.

Jacob was now openly weeping. "Fati! I have sinned against you! I have behaved shamefully in your sight! I only wish to be your loving son once again!"

But Ishmael would have none of this. "Jakob, it is I who must apologize. You are a credit to your mother and I – and a blessing on our household. We must never let anything – not even war – come between us again." Ishmael let his son go and stepped back. "Let me look at you."

His son was covered from head to toe with all manner of gore. His golden blonde hair was matted with a mixture of blood, sweat, mud, and rainwater. His clothes were tattered and filthy – but Ishmael didn't notice any of these things. "You seem….older to me, Jakob."

"I feel older, Papa," answered the boy. "I feel as though I have been away from home for over a year."

"Your mother and I have felt the same way. That's how much we have missed you."

"But, Papa," the boy exclaimed, his voice filling with excitement, "there is much I wish to show you…to tell you about. In this small hut lies…" Jacob turned, ready to lead Ishmael into the cook house, but stopped upon seeing the sentry. "What is wrong, Private?" Jacob asked.

The young Private was also in tears. "I was overcome at the sight of your reunion, Jacob. I was thinking about how much I miss my parents… and the rest of my family. I am wondering if I will ever see them again."

Jacob walked over to the young soldier and placed his hand firmly on his shoulder. "You must have faith, Private. Even in this dark time, you must have faith."

The Private nodded, wiping the tears from his face. Ishmael could only stand off and watch with amazement as his son comforted a boy much older than his own age.

"Come, Papa," Jacob called, "I want you to meet someone." Ishmael hesitated, not knowing if it was prudent for his son to make such a decision – not with an armed guard standing at the threshold. "It is alright, Papa. They trust me a great deal up here." The young Private nodded his head in agreement with Jacob's observation.

Ishmael followed his son into the cook house.

Inside the hut only one cot was set up, holding a Confederate General. "Papa…I would like you to meet Brigadier General Lewis Armistead. General Armistead, this is my father, Ishmael Zook."

"A pleasure, Mr. Zook," replied the General. Ishmael bowed deferentially with his head to the officer. "I cannot tell you how warmly your son has treated me, sir. I am the enemy, and yet he treats me as well as one of the Federal Generals."

"My son knows no difference between the two sides in the conflict, General," said Ishmael. "He is wise to stay impartial; he weighs the worth of each man on his own merits…as do I."

"Well, then…" expanded Armistead, broadly, "I can see where he gets his philosophic viewpoint from." Armistead wriggled a little on his cot, trying to find a more comfortable way of spending his time. As it was, he was half sitting up, and half lying down.

To the Union physicians and surgeons, General Armistead's two wounds did not appear to be life-threatening. He had a wound on his arm, and another in a leg. Neither of the minie balls used had managed to hit bone or major artery. Yet, in spite of this outward appearance, the General was worn down, and, even though he was putting up a very good front for the sake of Jacob at this moment – talking with his father and passing the time – he was mentally exhausted. In addition to this, he was wrought with guilt and deep in the clutches of a melancholy that would not let him be.

The guilt was due to his own involvement in this war. It was true that General Armistead was an ardent supporter of the troops from his adopted state of Virginia – he had fought valiantly and led bravely throughout the war thus far. But his heart, truth be told, was not in 'the cause' as much as it was for other Confederate soldiers, particularly the officers. His position, as a servant of the Old Dominion, was, in many respects, very similar to that of Robert E. Lee. Armistead vowed to fight for the right to allow his state to express itself politically, but he personally did not own a slave, nor was he a successful plantation owner. He was also, like Lee, pragmatic enough to know that the war could not go on forever, and that the longer it did, the worse it would fare for the Confederacy. He also knew that victory in battle had to be immediate and swift; that the northern states needed to have a very bad taste in their mouths from the effects of the conflict.

But that was only part of the guilt that General Armistead was dealing with. The other part concerned his very good friend, General Winfield Scott Hancock, the Commander of II Corps, and the man directly responsible for holding the Federal line during the final Confederate attack of the battle. Armistead feared that the day would come when he would have to lead men against a position held by his closest of friends, Win Hancock. He had vowed to do himself bodily harm, should he ever directly cause harm to come to his friend – and now, mainly because of his leadership in the final moments of the charge up Cemetery Ridge, his good friend was also in a military hospital – and his wound was far more serious than his own – or so he had learned.

At the highest point of the charge, General Hancock had been giving orders from horseback – a very easy target for any sniper or sharpshooter. He had watched as a brigade of Confederates managed to reach the stone wall angle, which had formed the very center of the Union line. He, too, was aware that his old friend from his days in California, Lewis Armistead, was leading a brigade of troops. He also remembered how tenacious Armistead could be. Hancock clearly remembered that Armistead had been expelled from West Point for breaking a dish over the head of a classmate, Jubal Early. Ironically, both of these men were leading troops at Gettysburg for the Confederacy; Armistead with a brigade, and Early commanding a division of A.P. Hill's Corps Hancock observed the Federal line falter, and then be overrun with gray uniforms.

He ordered several brigades to fill the hole that had been created, and that was when he was hit. A minie ball, perhaps from a sniper, but possibly just a stray shot, hit his saddle. The ball penetrated his saddle and tore into his groin, creating a wound about eight inches in length. Hancock was helped down from his horse, badly wounded. A tourniquet was applied to staunch the bleeding. Hancock insisted that he remain on the field, directing operations until the outcome was well in hand. During this time, he reached down and removed an object from his leg; a nail which had been used in the construction of his saddle. He had jokingly remarked to an aide that he was surprised at the kind of thing that the rebels were putting in their canister shot. He hadn't realized, at that time, that he had been wounded, in part, by a piece of his own saddle.

Back in the summer cook house, General Armistead had wished that he could visit with his dear friend, Win, but this was not going to happen. Hancock had been taken to a different field hospital, and the perceived severity of his wound made his condition during those first hours after the battle very guarded. Moreover, Armistead was a high-ranking prisoner of war; one who was expected to make a full recovery. Other Confederate Generals had fallen during the battle of Gettysburg, but Armistead was the highest ranking officer to have been captured alive.

But there was still the aspect of mental exhaustion. In spite of Lewis Armistead's exceptional military record, that is, once past the embarrassment of the West Point incident, his personal life had been something of a shambles. He had already buried two wives, and a son. His daughters were well, but still living far away from the corn fields of Pennsylvania. Even though he was still, as Generals go, a very young senior officer – he was also deficient of the morale needed to continually command. He was ready to give up.

"I assume, sir," he said to Ishmael, "that you are here to take Jacob back to his home – safe and sound?"

"No," replied Ishmael, shaking his head. "I have come to see if my son is healthy and sound – that is all."

"Papa?" questioned Jacob, not believing his own ears. "You do not wish me to return home with you?"

"Of course I do, Jakob," answered Ishmael. "So does your mother, but I have come to understand how you must feel; how you want to be independent of our way of life."

"But I am no longer sure that I wish to be independent of the Ordnung, Papa," said Jacob. "I have been witness to many things over these past few days, and, having seen them, I am not sure that I am meant to be anywhere but on the farm with you and mother."

Ishmael placed his hand on the boy's shoulder and then spoke gently to him. "And I have been witness to many things of these past few days, as well, and, having seen them, I am not sure that it is fair to you to ordain that you spend the rest of your very promising life cooped up on a little farm in Pennsylvania."

"Papa…?"

"Many people have explained, in great detail, how much they think of you, Jakob," continued his father. "We do not belong to an Amish Community, so perhaps there is no harm in allowing you to find out for yourself what is available to you with the 'English.'"

Jacob could not believe his own ears. "Are you sure, Papa?"

"No," Ishmael replied. "Of course I am not sure…any more than you are sure." General Armistead cleared his throat.

"I am sorry, General," apologized Jacob, "we were so busy talking to each other that we forgot about you."

"Never you mind," said Armistead. "If you would not mind however, I would like to offer my opinion on your discussion, which you have now had in front of me."

Jacob nodded his assent, soon followed by that of his father. "This war won't be ending tomorrow, or any time too soon, but eventually it will end, and this country is going to have to pick up the pieces and put itself back together again. When it does, there will be ample opportunities for smart young men, such as you, Jacob. If I am right about this…and I think I am…your father is saying that, no matter what it is that you decide to do, he – and your mother – will always be proud of you."

"That is true," smiled Ishmael. "It has taken me experiencing war to understand this fully, but it is true. Your mother and I love you very much….so does Abraham." Jacob nodded, and then gave his father an embrace. "Zounds!" cried Ishmael, suddenly remembering. "I have forgotten about Abraham.

"Abraham is here, too?" asked Jacob. "Where is he?"

"I left him in the big hospital tent," said Ishmael. "I left him talking to that other General…the one dressed in blue…the one without one of his legs."

"With General Sickles?" asked Jacob.

"Dan Sickles?" asked Armistead, with a wry laugh. "Your son is getting an education now, I'll bet."

"What does that mean?" asked Ishmael.

"I am joking, Mr. Zook," replied Armistead, "although I wish I could say that Sickles is more bark than bite. He is a very complicated man!"

"He is a little rough on the edges, Papa," informed Jacob. "But I have gotten to know him very well, and, well, he's not that bad…once you know him. I actually assisted Doctor Sim in removing his leg after it was hit with a cannonball."

"You did?" asked Ishmael. "The boy I used to know went weak in the knees at the sight of blood."

"Papa!"

"That is strange," observed the General. "Jacob has been tending to my dressings since I was moved over to this little hut."

But Jacob had other items on his agenda, especially since his father had mentioned General Sickles. "Papa…I would like you to talk with General Sickles. He has offered to assist me to get an education at a university."

"In what way does he mean to 'assist'?" asked Ishmael.

"He would like to help me in two ways," answered the boy. "First, he would help me select and gain acceptance to a university, and second, he would help pay the expenses."

"Dan Sickles offered to do that?" exclaimed Armistead, his voice rising with shock.

"Why, sir?" asked Jacob. "You seem surprised."

"Surprised, and flabbergasted!" expressed Armistead. "Not that I know the General particularly well, but the man is infamous. You have heard of his brush with the law?"

"Actually, yes," responded Jacob, "yes, I have. Some of the other officers filled me in on the General's past while he was knocked out from the chloroform."

"What?" asked his father. "What about him, Jacob?"

"I will tell you later, Papa," Jacob answered. "I am not entirely sure that it means anything."

"You are correct, Jacob," replied Armistead. "A man can hope for redemption. I know I am hoping for a little of the same."

"Then, may I ask, sir," asked Ishmael, "how it is that you know the General?" Armistead gave his answer a little thought before replying. "General Sickles….was the Confederacies secret weapon, Mr. Zook."

Even Ishmael knew that they had fought on opposing sides. "I don't understand, sir," he said.

"He is a General we could almost always count on to act of his own accord – to strike out without orders, always looking for glory in battle; to garner a name for himself – but in doing so, he would put his brigade or corps in harm's way – as he did yesterday in the peach orchard. But he is a fighter…and he is more aggressive than almost any other Federal General."

"You almost sound like you admire him, General," observed Jacob.

"In a way, I do, Jacob," the General said.

"What do you think he is talking about with Abraham?" asked Ishmael. "If I understand that man over there," noted Armistead, "he is probably entrancing your son, Abraham, with a most picturesque narrative of the events leading up to the removal of his leg by amputation." "What?" Ishmael exclaimed.

Jacob could only laugh a bit at his father's reaction. "Papa, we had better go rescue Abraham, otherwise General Sickles will have him smoking cigars and drinking whiskey."

"And this is a man you like, Jakob?" asked his father.

"Yes," Jacob admitted, "I do. I actually enjoy his company a great deal, Papa. General Sickles is a very colorful man."

Jacob and Ishmael returned to the hospital tent in order to pick up Abraham Zook. Jacob bade General Sickles farewell, but promised to return to see him the following day. He had already made a commitment with Doctor Sim to further assist with any operations that he might need to perform on 5 July. He also wanted to check in on General Armistead.

They began the long walk back down Cemetery Ridge.

CHAPTER 25

Burying the Dead

The three days of battle, on the first three days of July, 1863, had been so fierce that there had been no time available to bury the dead. Now, on the anniversary day of the reading of the Declaration of Independence, this task was obvious.

The dead needed to be buried – or the town, as well as the army, would be faced with the smell of rotting flesh, as well as the threat of pestilence.

General Lee had yet to withdraw from the field of battle, but there were already thousands of dead to be put in the ground. The citizens of Gettysburg were quick to help with the task, and many of the fallen soldiers were, simply, buried on the spot where they fell. Some, as in the case on the Spangler Farm, were arranged in neat rows, in a similar manner to a graveyard. One member of the burial detail was made responsible to make a drawing that gave the position of each grave. The detail also buried some of the Confederate dead, especially those who had died while in the Federal hospital. Some of these men were also buried on the Spangler Farm, however they were buried in their own little section – away from the area designated for the Federal troops.

Most of the dead were left out on the open field of battle, where they would lie for the next few months, rotting in the same position in which they had fallen. New York photographer Matthew Brady, already famous for his portraits of President Abraham Lincoln, would take many pictures of this gruesome sight, developing the images and then displaying them in the front window of his New York photographic studio. No longer were the masses insulated from the reality of battle; Brady's images were sold to the public, and he profited greatly from their sale. But even this windfall profiteering had its own limitations, and, before too long had passed, newpapers were beginning to publish some of Brady's ghastly prints. Brady was outraged. He would eventually petition Congress that photographic work should be included under the United States Copyright Law, and that photographers should be afforded the same rights under that law as fine artists, writers, and composers. The law was changed to included rights extending to photography when the law was re-vamped shortly after the Civil War.

*   *   *

The men of the Zook household walked back down Baltimore Street, and toward the center of Gettysburg. The rain had slowed a bit, from a downpour to a steady drizzle, but the rain had not dissipated the humidity in the air – if anything, it had made the dampness even worse.

Ishmael walked with his one arm around Abraham, as if shielding him from any mishap they might encounter along their descent. "I happened to meet a group of English on my way up this hill, Jakob," Ishmael said, initiating small talk. "They seemed to know you very well."

"Oh?" asked Jacob.

Ishmael deliberately turned to his older son and gave him a slight smile. "Yes…their name was…Tilden."

"Tilden?" Jacob asked. "Rebecca Tilden?"

"I believe that was one of the young women amongst them," answered Ishmael. "Yes…yes…that was her name."

"Papa?"

"Yes, Jakob?"

"Never mind," the boy reluctantly answered. Abraham opened his mouth, as if to say something, but Jacob shot him a warning glance, his eyes narrowing to slits.

"There was a young boy with them," continued Ishmael. "I think he was just a little younger than Abraham. And there was also the mother. Her name was…um…."

"Mary Elizabeth," finished Jacob.

"Yes," said Ishmael, "that was the name, Jacob. So…you do know them?" "Yes, I know them," replied Jacob. "They are…my friends." "Your English friends, Jacob?"

"Yes, Papa," agreed Jacob. "They are Outlanders…but they are very good people."

"I never said they weren't good people, Jakob."

"I know, Papa," Jacob said quickly. "I am sorry."

The trio walked a few more paces. They moved slowly and carefully, the rain having made Baltimore Street a rutty, slippery mess.

"A very attractive girl, that Rebecca Tilden," slyly observed Ishmael. "Don't you agree, Jakob?"

"What, Papa?" asked Jacob, with astonishment clearly in his voice.

"She is an attractive young lady," repeated Ishmael. "I was asking you if you agree with my opinion."

Jacob closed his eyes momentarily. He took a big breath, and then exhaled with an even larger sigh. "Yes, Papa…I am bound to agree with your opinion."

Ishmael stopped walking, his arm still tightly wound around Abraham's shoulder. "Well," he said, "now it is all out in the open, Jakob!" Jacob instinctively knew that this was not the time for him to speak. Even Abraham knew that this was the case, and he looked at his big brother with eyes that could only express his abject pity for him. "I suppose the only thing that I can add now…is that we will have to wait to see if your Mother shares the same opinion."

And then Ishmael smiled at his son.

"I….don't understand, Papa," Jacob answered.

"What is there to not understand, Jakob?" asked his father. "I was a fool trying to cling to the old ways – the same Ordnung that sent me away in the first place – and in the process I almost lost my son."

"Papa, I…."

"Don't say any more about it, Jakob," soothed his father. "All we need now…is time."

The Zook men had almost reached the bottom of the hill on Baltimore Street. The McClellan house was approaching them on the right. "Papa…this is the house where the Tildens had been staying throughout the battle," Jacob pointed out. "They were staying here with…." Jacob stopped dead in his tracks. He could clearly see into the yard of the McClellan house. Something was going on in the yard; something that looked like…a burial. "Someone has died here, Papa!"

The boy ran the rest of the distance down the hill, his father and brother continuing down behind him. Jacob ran around the back of the McClellan house to see if he could confirm his observations.

He could.

A group of townsmen were digging a grave in the yard. A small company of friends and neighbors had assembled by the rear of the house – many of them were in tears. As his father and brother joined him in the yard, Jacob spotted a wooden coffin. The box had the letters

"C.S.A." carved on the top, along with a very intricately carved emblem of the "Stars and Bars" – the Confederate Flag. Jacob breathed a sigh of relief. A Confederate soldier, perhaps even an officer, must have fallen in the yard of the McClellan house, he thought. The McClellans, and their neighbors, were giving the man a proper Christian burial. The only thing Jacob couldn't understand was how they happened to find such an elaborate coffin – especially one that so fit the occasion?

"Jacob!"

Jacob quickly turned in the direction of the voice. It was Becky Tilden. She ran to his side and embraced him. Jacob happily accepted her affection, even though he was aware that his clothes were still covered with all manner of blood and gore. He held his arms tightly around her body; a part of him relieved to see that she was not the poor soul about to be placed in the ground.

But then, he thought…who was it?

He let go of Becky, allowing her to let him go, as well. He noticed that she had been crying; that she was upset – which told him immediately that the person in the coffin was not, in fact, a Confederate soldier.

"Becky….?"

"Jacob," she answered, horsely, "it's poor Ginnie." "Ginnie?" he asked. "Ginnie Wade?"

"She was shot through clear through her door while she was baking bread for the Federal troops," Becky explained. "Georgia found her lying on the floor next to the bread trough. She was already dead."

Jacob turned away from Rebecca Tilden. He noticed his father and brother standing in the yard. He walked over to his father.

"They are about to bury a friend of mine, Papa," Jacob said, the tears beginning to course down the sides of his face. He buried his face into his father's chest and wept bitterly. "She was a good woman, Papa! She was going to be married!"

Ishmael put his arm around his son. "Jakob, mein Sohn," he said, quietly, continuing in German, "this is what happens in war. Sometimes the innocent also are hurt."

Mary Elizabeth approached, along with her husband, John. Mary Elizabeth placed her hand on Jacob's shoulder. "Jacob," she began, but immediately broke into sobs. She took the boy in her arms, and held him as if he was her own. "Forgive me, Jacob."

"Forgive you, Mrs. Tilden?" he asked.

"Forgive me, Jacob," she replied, "for being so blind. These past few days have taught me the value of human life…and that human life is far too brief to worry about things that are…well….unimportant."

Mary Elizabeth kissed Jacob on the forehead and then turned to Ishmael. "You should be very proud of your son, Mr. Zook! He is a remarkable young man!"

Ishmael nodded slowly. "Thank you, Mrs. Tilden," he answered. "I am just beginning to realize how truly blessed I am." John Tilden then stepped forward and introduced himself to the Zook men, shaking hands with each one of them.

The Wade/McClellan family now began to exit the home, heading for the gentle sloping yard. Ginnie's mother was dressed in black, but she was the only member of the immediate family to have done so. It was a hastily prepared funeral, amid other burials around the Gettysburg area too numerous to count. There were several men already in the yard, in addition to John Tilden and the three Zooks. The three men had been busy digging the grave. They were covered with mud and grass as they emerged from the hole, which was about four feet deep. The family had been anxious to get Ginnie into the earth as quickly as possible, realizing that she would be moved at some point in the future, when a more fitting funeral would be possible.

The three Zook men now stepped forward to assist the gravediggers, as they prepared to lower the coffin into the grave. Three large straps lay on the ground beneath the coffin – one under the center, and then the other two placed about a foot in from either end. It would take six to lift and lower the casket into the hole in the ground. Harry Wade, along with John Tilden, was the only other male present, over the age of twelve. Abraham Zook, although only fourteen, had worked enough for his father on the farm to be able to lift heavy loads, and Ishmael was confident that Abraham was up to the task before him. Even so, Ishmael positioned Abraham in the center of the casket, and then stood to his right on the same side of the coffin, should Abraham falter. Jacob stood on the other side of the casket, across from his father.

One of the men from the neighborhood, a man named Tom, quietly gave the command to lift the coffin. The combined weight of Ginnie and the wooden casket was just a little over two hundred pounds, so the lifting was very controlled and easy. Under the quiet orders of Tom, the four men and two boys side-stepped to the right as smoothly as could be managed, considering that they were also walking up a slight incline. The process of side-stepping to the right was repeated some twenty times, until the casket hovered directly above the newly excavated gravesite. Tom gave a nod, and the pallbearers slowly and gently lowered the box and its contents into the hole. Jacob did his part, but his tears burned his eyes as he lowered the body of his friend into her temporary resting place. He was very aware of the fact that the others mourners were audibly sobbing as the casket entered its dark abode. He was certain that he could pick out Becky Tilden's voice among the bereaved, and he knew that she had every right to be disconsolate. Finally, the coffin came to rest on the bottom of the hole. Ishmael, Abraham and another neighbor were instructed to drop their straps, while Jacob, Tom, and the other neighbor pulled their ends through to the other side.

The neighbor, Tom, said a few words over the gravesite. There were no flowers to be scattered over the grave. There was no preacher available to console the bereaved, or to say a prayer at the grave. Tom finished up his brief homily with the words of the 23rd Psalm.

"The Lord is my Shepherd I shall not want…"

Jacob could hear his father reciting the psalm in German. Abraham was simply crying, which Jacob found surprising, considering that he hadn't known Ginnie at all – but, then again, perhaps it was the solemnity of the occasion, or the fact that there had been just too much tension building up over the last few days. Maybe it was now time to let it all go.

And then, as he was observing his brother, Jacob did just that – he let it all go. He broke down and sobbed deeper than he had for the past four days, and that included the time out in the middle of the field on the night of 1 July, right after Major Winslow had shot his southern friend, Bobby McLean. But maybe that was part of it…or maybe that was all of it. He wasn't sure.

All he knew was that the entire world…his entire world…had turned upside down over the course of three…four…maybe five days. And he had no idea if this was the end of this topsy-turvy existence he had come to know. He understood that the Confederates could be planning to attack again; that more death could be visited upon them at any moment's notice. Who would be the next to die? Would it be his father, or mother, or brother? Would it be Rebecca?

Or would it be…himself?

Jacob buried his head into his two hands and wept. His chest rose and sank with every sob, and his sobs were so heavy and labored that he felt as if he could not catch his next breathe without much difficulty. He felt a calming hand placed on his shoulder, and then another hand placed on his other shoulder. He looked to the right, and looked into the eyes of his father, Ishmael. He looked to the left, and down a bit, and looked into the eyes of his brother, Abraham.

And then…quietly…he muttered, "Oh, when will this end, O Lord?" As if an answer to his murmured prayer, he heard his father whisper,

"Amen."

And…as if to complete the cycle, he heard his brother, Abraham, say, "Amen." Tom, the fellow who had taken charge of the burial detail in the McClellan yard, bent down and picked up a shovel. This action was quickly mimicked by the other two men from the town. Ishmael took notice of a fourth shovel, which was leaning against a shed. He walked over to the shed and grabbed the shovel, ready to join the other men in covering the coffin. As he turned to return to the grave, he felt a hand on top of his own.

"I will do it, Papa," Jacob said, looking into his eyes. "Ginnie was also a friend of mine." Ishmael nodded in silence and handed the shovel to his firstborn. The grave was covered with the wet dirt in only a few minutes. The only action remaining was the formality of paying their final respects to the Wade/McClellan family.

Ginnie's mother decided that it would be best if she addressed the company as a whole. "My dear friends…Thank you for all of your help and sincerest condolences at our time of bereavement. This has been a shock for all of us, and I am sure that it will be several days before these events entirely sink into our minds and hearts. For my part, I will honor my daughter by returning to the kitchen that she loved so much, in order to bake the dough that she was preparing for the Federal troops. She felt a calling to do this for the men…what with her own beau, Jack Skelly, away somewhere with the army…so, if that was her wish, even if it was her last wish, then I am obliged to see that it is carried out."

The small assembly of friends lined up to greet the family. The Tilden family and the Zook men were almost the last to pay their respects to

Ginnie's family before heading for their homes. For the first time in almost a week, Rebecca Tilden was going to spend the night in her own house, and in her own bed. For Jacob Zook, that reality was going to take a little longer to settle into his mind.

After bidding good-bye to Rebecca, Jacob caught up with his father and brother as they walked through the town on their way back to Seminary Ridge. Jacob had a great deal on his mind; things that he wanted to say to his father, realizing that this was an opportunity which he hadn't expected. But he couldn't bring himself to do so; there was still a pall about the area, and Jacob didn't find it appropriate to discuss anything that didn't pertain to the immense sorrow that all were feeling at the moment. Ishmael, too, had been greatly affected by the events of the last few days, but no day had affected him more than the day after the fighting had ceased – 4 July. It had been a day of revelations…and of new beginnings.

CHAPTER 25

Planning for the Future

The Zook men were still almost a hundred yards from the farmhouse, talking about the futility of life and other such things, when Jacob looked up, hoping to see the happy sight that was his home. His father had done nothing to prepare him for the sight that would meet his eyes. His home for the past two years, or so, was now a charred pile of rubble. The only part of the home that was still standing on its own was the chimney.

"Papa! Abraham! Why didn't you tell me that our house was burned?"

"I am not very sure of the answer, Jakob," his father replied. "When we left here earlier today, I can assure you, it was heavy on my mind. But as the day unfolded, it mattered less and less."

"It doesn't matter to you?" asked Jacob, shocked at his father's lack of interest in the house.

"Jakob," his father answered calmly, "it is only a house!"

Jacob looked over at his father after he said this. He couldn't believe those words had just escaped his lips. 'It is only a house,' he thought to himself. To an Amish man, his house was his world. But, more than that…he wondered where they would live and how they would now survive. "But Papa, what will we do?"

"We will do what we have done for centuries, mein Sohn," he father replied. "We will re-build."

But Jacob shook his head. This was not that easy a task to accomplish, especially here in Gettysburg. "Papa…we are not in Lancaster County anymore. If our house or barn was to burn to the ground while we were living in Paradise, we could expect all of our neighbors to turn out with just a few days' notice, and by the end of that one day we would see the framework of a house…or a barn. I don't think that will happen out here in Gettysburg among all of these 'English.' I don't think it will happen because we are different…and I also don't think it will happen because all of the people in the town will have their own repairs to worry about."

"You may be correct, Jakob," his father answered.

"So…then…what are we going to do?"

Ishmael gave his son's question a bit of thought and then replied, "Then we will have to do it ourselves."

"Ourselves?" asked Jacob, incredulously. "With just you and I and a little help from Abraham, it will still take years to rebuild the house."

Ishmael gently placed his hand on his son's head. "God will provide, Jakob." Jacob knew that there was nothing he could possibly say to refute or challenge the last words of his father. Had the boy received an education in comparative religions, he would have been quick to recognize the oblivious Calvinist leanings in his father's faith-filled statement. As it was, the Amish were believers in the old adage that "God helps he who helps himself;" that predestination had very little to do with their ordered, daily lives. A good life was based upon good works, and plenty of hard work. Certainly God's Will played a part in the grand design of things, but the Amish were not disposed to leave anything to chance.

So as much as Jacob would have loved to debate his father endlessly on his final, somewhat whimsical statement, Jacob knew that this was not the time to react to what his father had said. It had been, after all, a very long, trying week. Survival had been the first chore; rebuilding their community would be the second.

"In any case," his father said, "I was under the impression that you were making plans to leave this area…perhaps tag along with that General friend of yours?"

"General Sickles?" Jacob asked.

"Yes…I believe that is his name," his father quipped. "The man who lost his leg to the cannonball." Ishmael knew very well what the General's name was; it was all a big test that he had concocted.

"I do not have to let him know today…or tomorrow, Papa," Jacob replied. "Anyway…it's not like he is going to go anywhere too fast."

"Jakob!" his father scolded. "That is a terrible thing to say!"

"You are right, Papa. I don't know what possessed me to say such a thing." "Look, Jacob," cried Abraham, "there is Mama!" Jacob's brother ran ahead and threw his arms around Sarah Zook. Sarah waved happily at her husband and oldest son, overjoyed to see them returning to her safe and sound.

"Ishmael," she counseled, "the Lutheran preacher wishes us to stay in the seminary building until such time as we have rebuilt our house."

"Really?" Ishmael asked. "This is quite a surprise, woman. What brought this about?"

"Nothing, really," she answered. "He knows that we are now without a house, and has offered us shelter out of Christian goodness."

"Is that so?" questioned Ishmael, a bit shocked at the news. He knew that they had proven themselves to be invaluable to the running of the seminary over the past few years, but he also knew that the Lutherans regarded the Zook family as strangers within their midst. As shunned as they had been by their own Amish community, they were also outside of the bounds of community in Gettysburg.

Jacob put his arm around his brother, Abraham, and together they walked over to the burned-out shell that once had served as their home. The fire had been extinguished, but some of the heavier timbers that had been used to support the structure were still smoldering – smoke was still rising from the wood frame even throughout the light drizzle.

"What shall we do now, Jacob?" Abraham asked.

"Papa will decide what is best for the family, Abraham. We will probably rebuild the house, but the land is owned by the Lutherans, so it is really up to them, I suppose."

"And if they say 'no,' Jacob?" the younger boy queried. "Where are we to go?" "Perhaps we will return to Lancaster County," answered Jacob. "Perhaps we will go live with our family in Paradise." But Jacob knew that this was definitely not an option. He was tired of being 'shunned.' He would certainly assist his father and mother rebuild their home here in Gettysburg, but he would not allow himself to crawl and grovel back to the elders in Paradise – even if his father was not above doing so. Once again, he felt the same feelings of resentment beginning to well up within him, as he recalled General Sickles offer of education and a different way of life. But then, he asked himself, what would he do about his brother?

The Lutheran minister and several seminarians were crossing from the main building of the seminary toward his parents. Jacob gently pulled Abraham from viewing the charred rubble of the house in order to hear what the man had to say. The boys rejoined their parents just as the men from the seminary greeted them.

The Reverend Meier, the administrator of the seminary, did all of the talking, and, as they had always done in the past, their conversation was in German. "Ishmael, I am happy to see that you have found your son, Jacob."

"Yes, Reverend. He was amongst the Federal army."

"Well…welcome home, Jacob," said the minister, smiling at Jacob. "Ishmael…I suppose Sarah has mentioned to you that we would like you to stay on here at the seminary. We can set your family up in a grouping of rooms on the lower level."

"That is very kind of you, Reverend," Ishmael replied, "but our house…."

"Your house will be re-built, Ishmael," quickly added the minister.

"We will see to that. We don't want to see you leave, Ishmael."

"But….?

"Not another word, Ishmael," continued the minister. "I will have some of the seminarians out here working to clear the debris as soon as the embers cool down. I think this rain will help speed things along a bit; don't you think? We have some damage to the seminary buildings, too – from all manner of things hurled in this direction over the past three days. I will be in need of your unique abilities, Ishmael. I cannot have you spending your energies pulled out burned planking, when they can be better spent repairing the seminary. The students can work on your house – if you will work on mine. What do you say?"

Ishmael was surprised and pleased with the minister's candor. "I would say that this is a very good arrangement, Reverend." But another thought was still gnawing at his mind. "But, may I ask, if it is not to forward of me, to ask you why you are doing this for us?"

"Why?"

"Why are you helping my family, when there are so many other families in the town – other 'English' families – who are equally as needy as we?"

The older man rubbed his chin while he thought of his answer to Ishmael's question. "Ishmael…you may not realize this, but you are also a member of this community – much to your chagrin and disappointment. We do not withdraw our Christian charity simply because you worship God in another manner than we do, anymore than we believe that those raised with European backgrounds hold dominion over those with backgrounds from Africa. I witnessed, first-hand, as you cared for the wounded of this terrible battle – and you made no distinction between those from the South as from the North. I realize that to your way of thinking – your Amish heritage – that you did not hold a particular stake in the outcome of the battle, but still…you, and your family, performed a service to mankind, regardless of who these poor unfortunates represented. I especially noticed this as you cared for the hapless Culp boy."

Jacob was startled to hear the mention of the name 'Culp.' "Pardon me, Reverend," he interrupted, "but did you say, 'Culp?' As in….Wesley Culp?"

"The very same, Jacob. You were friends with the young man, were you not?"

Jacob's mother put her arm around her son's shoulders, confirming what had not yet been clearly stated. "Are you saying that Wesley was killed in the battle?"

Ishmael looked over at his wife, hoping that she would say something to her son about the Culp boy's death, but it was the minister who provided the explanation. "Jacob…Wesley died on the second night of the battle. Your mother and father were both there to ease him through his passing."

"But how? Why?"

"That I cannot answer you, Jacob," the minister continued, "but I can tell you this much. Wesley Culp was shot while he was attempting to capture the hill that bears his own family name. He was killed on that very same hillside that he had played upon as a boy."

"I had just seen him the day before," answered Jacob. "I ran into him at the Confederate encampment over at Cashtown. He seemed so…

happy. He was happy to be fighting for the Confederacy – as if his many years in Gettysburg didn't matter a bit."

"Wesley was a confused young man," consoled the minister. "He was one who never exactly knew what he wanted out of life. That was why he ran away to Western Virginia – but, when all was said and done, it was still here in Gettysburg where his fate was decided."

Jacob nodded, but he had hardly heard the voice of the preacher. Now, with the death of Wesley Culp, he had lost two friends during this battle. He realized that he had only known the hapless Bobby McLean a very brief span of time – but they had become friends, nevertheless. And wasn't it Bobby who had pulled him to the ground to protect him from the Federal shelling of their position? He had helped to bury Ginnie Wade, and now he was among the mourners for Wesley. He wondered how many more of his friends and neighbors he would also have to mourn before the war came to an end. "Where is Wesley's body?" he asked.

"I had it sent to his family over on the Culp Farm," replied the minister. "They will bury him somewhere on the farm. Naturally, they were devastated."

Jacob once again slowly nodded, his eyes filling with tears. "Reverend…how can God allow this killing to continue? How can He allow this war to take the lives of so many innocent victims?"

"Jacob!" cautioned his mother.

"It is alright, Sarah," said the minister. "Jacob has every right to question his faith…under the circumstances. I would be worried about him if he didn't do exactly that." The man of the cloth turned back to the boy. "Jacob…I know what you are asking. You think that God has abandoned us; that he has, in some strange way, condoned this war. There are many leaders on both sides who feel that God is on their side in this war. There are many who would evoke the power and majesty of our Maker in order to justify all the meaningless killing. There are those who truly believe that their opinion carries with it the approval of the Almighty."

"And does it?" asked Jacob.

"Of course not!" replied the minister. "The Commandment does not read, "Thou Shalt Not Kill…except in time of war." We have been given the right of 'free will,' and it is that very same free will which allows us to do terrible things…sometimes in the name of God. Just look at what happened centuries ago when the Roman church decided to wage a Holy War on the children of Islam."

"You are speaking of the Crusades?" asked Jacob.

"Exactly," confirmed Meier. "Thousands of innocent souls were lost – on both sides – simply because a few powerful men decided that this would be an action that would be supported by God. Believe me, my boy, there would be a lot less cruelty in the world if everyone were to follow the precepts of your Amish brethren." The minister let out a very large sigh. "On the other hand, it is also important for people to stand up to the gross injustice that is slavery. This is an institution which is, for us in the country, the mark of Cain. It is a curse, and a blasphemy against the human soul!"

"Amen," added Ishmael.

"Come," said Sarah Zook. "The day is quickly waning. Let me see what stores of food are still available to us in the seminary kitchen, and I will prepare dinner for all of us."

"I fear that there may not be any meat to be found," answered Meier, "but there may still be some vegetables in the root cellar, and my students may be able to forage for some more out in the fields."

The evening of 4 July, 1863, was spent without the customary illuminations to celebrate the anniversary of the birth of the nation. It had been John Adams who had predicted accurately that the day would be spent hereafter in celebration, including the use of incendiary devices, such as fireworks, to cap off the festivities.

There would be no such fireworks on the night of 4 July, 1863, in and around Gettysburg, Pennsylvania. Those fireworks had already taken place over the past three days and nights. And the Annual Fourth of July Ball – the event many in the town most looked forward to each year – was indefinitely postponed.

The town had spent the last three evenings witnessing a far more spectacular display of gunpowder and rockets. This Fourth of July was a time for reflection, repair and burying the dead.

The celebration would have to wait.

CHAPTER 26

More Losses

Jacob and Abraham Zook spent the night of 4 July in a small inner room on the ground floor of the main building of the Lutheran Seminary. Their parents had spent the night in a similar room directly across the hall from their boys.

Jacob arose early on the morning of 5 July. Even though the bed provided to him by Reverend Meier had been comfortable – the most comfort, in fact, that he had experienced in quite a few days – the fact was that Jacob had not had a very restful sleep. His mind was still full of images of the battle; his time in the field hospital, the burial of Ginnie Wade, the killing of Bobby McLean by Major Winslow, and his last memories of Wesley Culp. His mind was racing so quickly that Jacob had found it nearly impossible to get any sleep at all, and it was only sheer exhaustion that had provided him with the occasional cat nap. His brother, Abraham, on the other hand, had fallen to sleep almost immediately upon entering his bed.

But Abraham would not sleep comfortably through the night, either. About an hour into Jacob's own bout with insomnia, he noticed that his brother began to toss in his bed. Jacob had dozed off at last, but the guttural sounds being emitted from Abraham's mouth had caused him to wake from the light sleep that had overtaken him. As the boys were sharing the bed, Jacob had moved as far to the extreme outside of the mattress during the restless part of his night. He couldn't make out what the boy was trying to say, but realized that he was being tormented by some dream – perhaps a nightmare. Jacob rolled over in order to face his brother. "Abraham?" he quietly said, but his brother continued to writhe and toss as if possessed. Jacob put his hand gently on Abraham's shoulder to quiet him, but was shocked when his brother instinctively reached up and threw his hand off – even though he was still quite asleep.

Jacob tried again – this time placing his hand on the side of Abraham's face. "Shh, Abraham," he said in a whisper. The action seemed to do the trick, for his brother settled down into a more restful sleep, but the episode had done nothing to ease or lull Jacob into a more relaxed state.

Now fully awake, his recurring thoughts raced back and through his mind. He quickly rose from the bed, finding the basin for washing that had been set out for him by the seminarians when they had prepared the room for their guests. Jacob poured some water from a large pitcher into the basin and splashed some on his face. He turned back to his bed, finding his undergarments and trousers lying near the foot of the bed. He quickly pulled on his trousers, lifting his nightshirt high enough to get it out of his way. He removed his nightshirt, which had been loaned to him by a first year seminarian, and returned to the basin. He found a washrag on the bureau and wet it in the basin so that he could wash the dirt off of his upper body. This completed, he found a clean white shirt and put it on. His dressing however, was not complete until he pulled on his high, black boots.

Jacob knew that he had responsibilities to his family, especially to his father. But he also knew that there was no need for his usual schedule of morning chores; most of the livestock was either gone or eaten. There were no cows to be milked, and no eggs to be gathered.

But Jacob first wanted to check in with some of his newest acquaintances. He felt a need to return to Cemetery Ridge – to the field hospital there. He wanted to check in on General Lewis Armistead; he was uncertain about the General's well-being, even though the physicians had said that he would make a full recovery. Jacob also wanted to see General Sickles. He wanted to make sure that Sickles was past the ever-present danger of infection, which was more likely to be the cause of death of an amputation patient than any other cause.

He also thought about stopping by to see Rebecca Tilden, but wisely counseled himself that this should only be allowed to happen if their meeting was completely by chance. The Tilden family, and especially Rebecca, would still be deep in mourning over the death of Ginnie Wade, and Jacob did not want to force himself into that scenario. But he did want to be Rebecca's friend, so he would avail himself to her, should she decide that she needed him to be present.

Still, he thought, this was not to be a clandestine operation. He quietly opened the door to the room and walked out into the hall. He could still hear the sounds of sobbing and of agony, as the building was still filled with many soldiers, from both sides of the conflict, who were still billeted in the seminary building for hospitalization. Jacob did not bother to knock on his parent's room. He knew that they would not be inside. He guessed that his mother would either be attending to the wounded, or she would be busy in the kitchen. His father would probably be starting to do some repairs.

Jacob found his mother in the kitchen.

"Jakob…you are up very early today," she observed, as she worked over the worktable preparing a great deal of food.

"Yes, Muti," he answered. "I did not sleep very well, so I decided to get up." "And…?"

"And….?" He returned.

"And what are you going to do this morning, Jakob?" she asked.

"I am planning on helping Fati with the repairs to the seminary," he said, "but first I need to run over to Cemetery Ridge to check on my patients."

"Your patients?" she asked. "You speak as though you are a doctor."

"I did sound like that, didn't I?"

"You did."

"I should only be gone a little more than a few hours, Muti," he answered. "I will be back around noon to help Fati with the repairs."

"And you expect that I am going to explain all of this to your father, Jakob?" "Well…."

"Never you mind," she said. "Your father and I have already had this discussion. He knows that you have certain responsibilities to those army men. He has told me that you should go to see them this morning, but be back by the afternoon."

"He did?" Jacob could not believe his ears. Was this the same man who he had known all of his life as his father?

"He did. Now take a few biscuits and get along on your way."

Jacob grabbed three biscuits off of the worktable. They had just come out of the oven and were still warm to the touch. He kissed his mother on her cheek and head out of the kitchen, taking a bite out of the biscuit while he walked.

The boy decided to take a shortcut up to the top of Cemetery Ridge; crossing behind the town, instead of walking along the main roads and turning left on the Baltimore Pike. Even though the terrain was rough, and the undergrowth was still quite wet, this route cut off several minutes of walking. He also knew that he was far less likely to run into a passerby, and so less likely to be engaged in conversation – which would slow down his progress.

He reached the Federal picket line in less than ten minutes.

*   *   *

Robert E. Lee disengaged his army late in the early morning of 5 July. By the time Jacob Zook was climbing up Cemetery Ridge, the Army of Northern Virginia was already crossing back into Maryland. The train of infantry, cavalry and supply wagons stretched between fifteen and twenty miles during the retreat.

General Meade had not taken advantage of the disorganized condition of the Confederate Army following the disastrous final attack which had been commanded by General Pickett of Longstreet's Corps, with detachments from General Hill's Corps. Such was the disorganization of the rebel army following the repulsion from Cemetery Ridge that Meade could have easily swept the rebel army from the field, thus taking a large step toward ending the war. Instead, Meade's cautiousness allowed Lee and his subordinates to regroup and prepare their defenses, which they worked on during the late afternoon and evening of 3 July, as well as into the early morning of 4 July. But it had been immediately apparent to General Longstreet that they were not to expect a massed counter-offensive; that Meade was content to sit upon the high ground in a strong, defensive position.

It would take almost two weeks for the Army of Northern Virginia to cross the Potomac River into Virginia. During this period, the army would be attacked in smaller skirmishes and minor battles, hindering and hampering their movements, but Meade had chosen to allow Lee's army to slip back into the mother state, and out of his grasp.

*　　　*　　　*

Jacob had reached the Spangler Farm – site of the Federal army field hospital. The day was going to be hot and humid, just as the past few days had been, but it would be free of rain.

Jacob looked carefully for Henry Spangler, son of the owner of the farm. He stopped by the farmhouse on his way to the barn, but Henry was not to be seen anywhere. Jacob now turned his attention to his most recent patient, Confederate General Lewis Armistead.

The boy walked around the farmhouse to the cookhouse; the small hut which had been converted into a small field hospital, specifically used to hold the General. Jacob noticed that the Federal sentry was gone. No one was guarding a Confederate

officer of the highest military rank. Jacob walked to the door of the hut and gently knocked.

"Yes," called a voice from inside.

"Hello," Jacob called back. "It's Jacob Zook."

"Jacob?" returned a voice. "Come in, Jacob."

Jacob gave the door a shove. He discovered a Federal physician leaning over Armistead, changing the dressing on his wounds. Armistead's facial color had turned a sallow gray; he did not look very good. The General seemed to be asleep.

"He is not in very good shape, I'm afraid," said the doctor.

"I was under the impression that his wounds were not mortal, doctor," recalled Jacob.

"That is what we all thought," answered the doctor. "Something has gone terribly wrong, I'm afraid."

"What?" asked Jacob. "What could have happened?"

"I am not sure. I don't think his wounds are turning infected."

"Then what is it?" asked a concerned Jacob Zook. The doctor gestured to Jacob that he should leave the hut and join him outside to confer.

"I don't know why this may be the case," said the doctor, "but my theory is that the General has lost the desire to live…that he has given up."

"Given up?" asked Jacob. "That doesn't sound like a good trait in a General!" "Indeed not," answered the doctor, "but that is exactly what I am observing.

He was awake and lucid last evening after you left, but his words were full of doubt and held tremendous sorrow. He had hoped to see General Hancock, but the General is also severely wounded, and there is great fear that he may not live to see tomorrow. General Armistead is also aware of this, although I do not know how, and I think this fact has greatly contributed to his current state. I think he blames himself for Hancock's wound."

Jacob took all of the words that the physician used in his assessment to heart. "What may I do, Doctor, to help the man recover?"

"I am not sure, Jacob," answered the doctor. "You can try speaking to him, but he has already slipped into unconsciousness, so I do not know if it will have any effect on him."

Jacob nodded and headed back into the hut. He dragged a small stool that had been set to one side of the kitchen so that it was near the side of the bed. The boy thought that the General looked serene and peaceful; like he had finished fighting the war and had gone home to his family. But Jacob was also aware that the General's face had turned an ashen shade of gray since he last saw him not twenty four hours prior.

He placed his hand on the General's forearm, patting it gently. Suddenly, General Armistead reached across his body with his right arm, crossing his midsection until his right hand was directly above Jacob's hand. His right hand clenched, as if he was grabbing something;

something that required strength. His right arm then rose on a diagonal away from his body, his hand twisting when it approached the apogee of the ascent. Jacob recognized that it was a pantomime action of one drawing a sword.

"Charge men!" the General cried, his eyes still shut. "Give them the cold, hard steel!"

"General Armistead!" Jacob called, but he dared not shake or disturb him.

"Forward men of Virginia! Don't let that fence slow you down!" "Sir!" cried Jacob. "It's Jacob Zook! Can you hear me?" "Push them back," yelled the General. "What's that you say?"

The General's eyes popped wide open. He had a maniacal look upon his face, as if he was one possessed.

"I said that it is Jacob Zook, General."

"Win? What did you say? He is shot?"

"Who, General?"

"General Hancock?" Armistead asked. "Will he recover?"

"Yes," replied Jacob to the General's question. "I know that for a fact. General Hancock will recover."

"You say that it's mortal?" Armistead asked.

"Mortal?" asked Jacob, wondering why the General could not hear a word that he said to him. "General Armistead...I know for a fact that General Hancock will live."

Armistead turned his face and looked directly into Jacob's eyes. He reached up with his left hand and grabbed the boy by the collar, in a way similar to the way Major Winslow had done several nights earlier. "Listen to me," the General whispered, hoarsely. He reached across his chest, the sword now gone, and pulled an imaginary object out of his imaginary breast pocket. "You must take this token of my affection to Mrs. Hancock. General Longstreet has my Bible. He will see that she gets it."

"But General Armistead," the boy pleaded, "you are not mortally wounded. You will make a full recovery."

"I go to join those who have gone before me," the General seemed to answer.

"No," said Jacob. "You cannot say things like this! You cannot think things like this!"

"I wear the mark of Cain upon my head," answered the General. "I have been branded as one who has taken up the sword in order to kill my brother." Armistead tightened his grip on Jacob's collar. He was beginning to choke the boy. "You didn't, General," Jacob gasped. "General Hancock still lives."

"I swore an oath, that I did," growled Armistead, "that God should strike me down dead if I was ever to raise my hand up against my brother."

"General...?" Armistead began to loosen his grip on Jacob's neck. "Strike me down...dead!" Armistead said, his voice growing softer. "General...?"

"...against my brother." Armistead fell back onto the bed.

"General Armistead?"

"Win!" Armistead said at a whisper, and then closed his eyes.

"General Armistead?" Jacob leaned over the officer and shook him. **"General Armistead?"** All movement and breathing on the part of the General had completely stopped. Jacob was stunned at the sudden and unexpected departure from this world on the part of Armistead. "No!" he cried, and threw himself over the man's body.

"Is he dead, son?" asked a voice.

Jacob pushed himself up quickly, wiping away the tears in his eyes and sitting up in one fluid movement. He turned toward the door to the summer cook house. It was the doctor. "He became like a wild man, doctor," Jacob explained, " and then…he just…died."

"I feared that this might happen, Jacob," said the doctor.

"But why?" Jacob asked. "Why did he have to die, especially since his wounds were not that grave?"

The doctor merely shook his head. "I can't answer you precisely, Jacob. For all of my medical education, every once and a while I see a case which I cannot explain. General Armistead was one such case. I think that the poor man did not want to go on living anymore."

"I don't understand," Jacob replied.

"I know…it does sound odd," answered the doctor, "but we doctors can only do so much. We can cut off badly damaged limbs, and patch up holes made by minie balls – but a man must really want to recover… to survive. General Armistead gave up."

"He gave up?" asked Jacob. "You mean….he surrendered?"

"In a very real way?" asked the doctor. "Yes! He stopped wanting to make a full recovery. The man was so racked with guilt that he had no inclination to face anyone after the war was over…so he gave up. He surrendered."

"Then I am sorry for him," said Jacob. "He was a gentleman, for a soldier. I am sorry to see that this battle took even those who did not receive mortal wounds – but died nevertheless."

"You are correct, Jacob," the doctor agreed, "he was a southern gentleman – but I must correct you about what the war will take and not take. More will die of their wounds…or infection….or disease… than those who are right out killed on the

battlefield by musket or cannon fire. This death….the General's death…was another kind of death…that's all…just another kind of death."

Jacob nodded; he didn't understand what the doctor was trying to tell him, but he nodded anyway.

"What will happen to him now, doctor?"

"We will have him buried – probably somewhere here on this farm," answered the doctor. "And then…after this cursed war is over, maybe his family will come and claim him, and cart him back to Virginia, for re-burial with the rest of his family."

"I feel…" Jacob stopped. He didn't know how to express his sorrow over the death of the kindly General.

"Would you like me to give you a few moments alone in here, Jacob?" asked the doctor.

Jacob looked back at the physician, who was still standing at the doorway to the hut. "Thank you, Doctor. That would be most kind of you."

The doctor nodded and took a step backwards, closing the door. Jacob dropped down on his knees, kneeling on the rough-hewn floor of the cook house.

He clasped his hands together and looked into the face of General Lewis Armistead; a face that was once again peaceful and serene…then he gazed up at the ceiling, and beyond it…to the heavens.

"Dear God," he prayed, "please accept the soul of my friend, General Armistead. He was a good and kind man…and I don't think that his life went exactly as he had planned it to go for him…but I think he was a just and righteous man. Please forgive him for all of his shortcomings… and for all of his sins. Amen."

Jacob wiped the tears from his eyes … again. He slowly stood up, never taking his eyes off of the face of the departed General. He didn't think that saluting the man was proper; he was not, after all, in the military – so he simply bowed to him by tilting his head forward at his neck. Having accomplished this, he swiftly turned on one heel and headed for the door. He opened the latch and exited the cook house, never looking back.

The boy exhaled a deep and emotion-filled sigh. He could see the large field hospital tent looming in the distance, the large Pennsylvania styled barn standing behind the tent. He was confident that General Sickles would not be the kind of man to 'give up' the way that General Armistead had done, but he also recognized that General Armistead was, perhaps, a better man than Sickles in the first place. Jacob wasn't quite sure whether or not he felt up to facing the abrasive General at this point in time. He certainly did not wish to tell him of the passing of General Armistead, in fact, he feared what the man might say about it when he found out. It might not be something that Jacob would like to hear said. Jacob felt that the dead should be respected, and Sickles might not think along the same lines, especially since Armistead was in rebellion.

Better to just not say a word, Jacob thought.

The boy started trudging through the deep and muddy ruts that had been carved by many heavy wagons, pulled by many large draft horses. His black boots were once again caked with the brownish-red mud. Jacob didn't think that his spirits could get much lower than they were at the moment, and he was positive that a conversation with Sickles wasn't going to make them any higher.

Jacob reached the hospital tent. He raised the flap and walked in. He was immediately greeted by a familiar voice. "Jacob Zook! Where have you been?"

It was General Sickles.

He was sitting up in his bed, his back propped up by an amalgam of blankets, bedrolls, and gunny sacks. His right leg, or rather the stump from where his right leg had been, had been freshly wrapped. If he was in any pain, he certainly didn't look the part. Jacob wondered, in fact, if he was drunk.

"General Sickles," he said, in a stage whisper, "I will be right over." The boy wandered through the morass of cots, which had now taken up virtually every spare inch of space in the tent. There were more than double the amount of wounded men in the tent than when Jacob had first set eyes on it several days earlier, but now there were Confederate wounded present, as well as the Federal soldiers. The only man to have any extra room at all – was General Sickles.

Jacob found that the General still had a stool positioned next to his bed, as if he was the only soldier within the tent who was eligible to receive visitors. Jacob sat on the stool, smiling weakly at the General. "How are you feeling today, General?"

"Feeling?" Sickles asked. "The only thing that I can do is feel, my boy. Do you have any idea what it feels like to have something hurt you that isn't even there?"

"Pardon me, General?"

"My leg, dammit!" the General shouted. Many of those lying on the cots jumped a bit as the General roared, and, surprisingly, Sickles took notice of this. "Sorry, Jacob…I really didn't mean to yell at you."

"It is alright, General," said Jacob. "You were saying?"

"Saying?" asked the General. Jacob pointed to his stump. "Oh, yes… the leg. The thing is, Jacob…the pain is so great, that I could swear that I still have the rest of my leg still attached to me. It sounds crazy, I know… but I could swear that it is still there."

"I suppose that it will take some getting used to, General," said the boy. "And that is exactly what I mean to do, you can bet on that," answered the General. Then, just as quickly as he had shouted before, Sickles became quiet. "How are things at home, Jacob?"

Jacob wasn't exactly sure if the General was referring to his relationship with his family – particularly his father – or with his abode; his home – so he thought that he would cover the building first. "Our home was burned to the ground, General." "What?" said the General, his voice rising with anger. "Rebel scum!"

"General…we don't know what caused the fire. It could have been fire from your army."

The sneer washed away from Sickles' face. "That is true, I suppose." There was a palpable silence between the boy and the General. "What will your father do about it?"

"Are you asking if he will re-build the house?"

"If that is an option," answered Sickles, "otherwise, I would think that your parents might move away from Gettysburg."

"Now that is oddly put, General," said the boy, "because those were the two options that my father actually discussed."

"Really?" asked the General.

"Yes," replied Jacob. "It almost worries me how similar you two think." Sickles let out a short, gruff laugh, but then his face immediately fell again as a new thought entered his mind. "So…I suppose you feel obligated to assist him with the rebuilding of the house?"

"Yes…," the boy answered, slowly, "and….no." Jacob peered over at Sickles' face, trying to judge his reaction to his negative answer.

"What do you mean, Jacob?"

"Well, General…I do feel obligated to help him…but only because he is my father, and I would have helped him anyway. If you had asked me that a few days ago, I would not have answered quite the same way, but I am looking at life a little differently as of late."

Jacob paused. He had given Sickles his affirmative answer – the one that Sickles had expected in the first place. "Well…go on," prompted the General.

"I am getting to that, General," replied the boy. "Please don't rush me." "Rush you? Why would I rush you? I'm not about to get up and leave! Jacob rolled his eyes. "The reason for me not helping is because the house is not our own. It belongs to the Lutheran Seminary – the one out on Seminary Ridge." Sickles nodded to the boy. He knew about the institution of sacred learning. "Anyway…the Lutherans are already set to help my father to rebuild the house. They are going to start tomorrow by clearing away all the charred debris. I think that they can salvage some of the stonework – particularly the chimney and the foundation."

"I see," muttered Sickles.

"Yes, but in our tradition…in the Amish tradition…when member of the community is in need of a new barn, or a new house…the entire community turns out to help. The barn…or house…is raised up from nothing in just one day."

"One day?" asked the General, astounded at the speed mentioned. "As the Bible says," quoted Jacob, "Many hands make light work." "You have witnessed this?"

"Many times, General," responded the boy. "But that was back in Lancaster County. There are a great many more Amish in Lancaster County than here."

"How many more?" asked the General.

"A great many more, sir," Jacob said. "We are the only Amish family in Gettysburg."

"I see," Sickles muttered again. "So your father will have help…so you said. You said that he will get help from the Lutherans."

"Yes," Jacob continued, "but even with their help – which will be appreciated a great deal – the going will take a very long time. I am sure that the seminarians are not skilled carpenters or masons. They are men of God – what do they know about building a house? So, even though he will have some help, my father will eventually get frustrated – which brings me back to why I should be around to help him."

"You have just argued yourself full circle, boy," Sickles observed.

"I know my father, General. He is a proud, but very stubborn German." "Don't give it a thought, Jacob," replied Sickles. "I know how fathers can be." "Yes…but that isn't all!" added Jacob. "My father will insist that the house be 'plain.' That it is built in a manner that follows the Ordnung. It cannot have any modern conveniences in the kitchen, and it cannot have Victorian-style ornamentation on it, because that would be 'fancy.'"

"Lord!" exclaimed the General. "But was the old house…the burned out house…built to be 'plain?'"

"No, not really," answered Jacob. "But my parents were desperate, so they looked the other way on a few points. The Lutherans are not always very plain."

"And what about you, son?" asked the General. "Are you 'plain?'" "What do you mean, sir?"

"Do you follow your tradition to the letter of the law?" asked Sickles.

"I try to, sir," answered the boy. "Whenever possible, that is."

"A-ha!" proclaimed Sickles. "Are you good with your hands, Jacob?" "In what way, General?"

"Woodworking, boy!" answered the General. "Can you do woodworking? I hear the Amish have a real talent for the craft."

"My father has taught me the trade, sir," Jacob said. "This is a primary source of income for our family."

"Very good….very good," said the General. Jacob eyed the officer carefully. It was obvious to the boy that the man was leading him down a particular path. "If I asked you to build me something, Jacob…would you do it?"

And there it was! Jacob narrowed his eyes, squinting through smaller apertures at this strange, yet driven man. "What would you like me to build you, General?"

"I won't tell you quite yet, Jacob," answered Sickles with a sly grin. "I want to know if you will build it for me… if I ask it of you, that is?"

"How can I answer that question, General, if I do not know what you are going to ask me to build for you? I have certain carpentry skills, but I do not claim to be a master craftsman like my father."

"I understand that, foolish boy! I want to know if I can trust you!"

"Trust me?" asked Jacob. "What has trust got to do with woodworking?"

"Bah!" shouted the General. "Your trouble is that you are too clever, Jacob!

Why can't you just humor a wounded soldier and say that you would build anything that I commanded you to build me?"

Jacob slowly nodded his head. He knew that the General was testing him; that he was baiting him. He was not about to deliver the wrong answer.

"You will remember, General," he answered slowly and calmly, without a hint of abrasiveness, "that I am not one of your soldiers. Anything that I do for you, I do not do because you have commanded me to do it."

Sickles pulled himself a little higher in his bed. "Then why would you do it, if I did not command you so?"

Jacob lowered his head toward the ground and softly spoke. "I would only do this for you because you are my friend."

Jacob felt his mind suddenly flood with many different memories – but the sharpest images were the most recent – the death of the other General…General Armistead. He had been through a great deal over the last few days, but with each passing new day there was also something new; something terrible; something totally unexpected that kept him wondering if his life would ever return to the way it was before July.

He felt the tears begin to well up in his eyes, which he had not counted on. He didn't wish to show this kind of emotion to General Sickles. But he couldn't help it; no matter how much he tried, he could not keep the tears from brimming over and running down his cheeks.

Sickles reached over with his hand and lifted the boy's head up by the chin. "Why are you so emotional, Jacob? Have you not gotten to understand my personality by now? You know that I am more bark than bite."

"I know, General," the boy answered. "I couldn't help but think of some things that happened lately…and that caused me to….weep. I'm sorry."

"There's nothing to feel sorry about, Jacob," the General said. "If you promise me on everything that is Amish in this here world that you will never tell another soul for as long as you live, I will let you in on a little secret."

Jacob wasn't sure that he wanted to agree to this challenge. It still smacked of General Sickles trickery. "I guess so, I suppose."

"I'll take it at that, Jacob," said the General, quickly. "I don't want you ever to tell another living soul that General Dan Sickles – the man who had his leg shot off by a rebel cannonball – the man who shot a man dead in the streets of Washington – the man who was carried off the field of battle cursing and smoking a cigar…that Dan Sickles… when nighttime falls, and the tent is filled with nothing but the sounds of agony – the sounds of the poor, hapless men of my Corps, and others – that the brave General Sickles can take solace in the fact that so much blubbering is the most useful disguise for the sobbing that he makes, as he laments over and over again the loss of his right leg."

"General?"

"You heard me, Jacob," Sickles said. "I weep nightly over my lot in life. Oh sure, it's great to act like it doesn't matter! What's a leg? But at night….at night the reality sinks in, Jacob. I will never be the same again. I will be disfigured for the rest of my life!"

There was another long period of silence between the boy and the General.

"What is it that you would like me to build for you, General Sickles?" Jacob asked.

Sickles smiled at the boy. He was, perhaps, the most unique and special young man he had ever met in his entire career. He could be great, Sickles thought. He could be destined for greatness…if only….if only he could attain his true potential.

"I want you to build me a coffin, Jacob"

Jacob's eyes widened. "What?"

"A coffin, Jacob. It's actually very simple carpentry."

"I know that, sir," Jacob answered. "I don't think that you are going to die, sir."

"Everyone dies…sooner or later, Jacob."

"You're too on'ry to die, sir," Jacob observed.

"Thank you….I think. But anyway…the coffin is not for my body, Jacob."

Jacob looked at the General as if he had grown another head. "I don't understand, sir."

"Listen to me, boy," the General said, calmly. "I want you to build me a small coffin – about a yard in total length, give or take a few inches."

Jacob still did not understand the General's meaning.

"Jacob….I want you to build it for my leg."

"Your leg?"

"You remember, Jacob," the General said, giving him a wink, "that you pulled my amputated leg out of the limb pile after Doc Sawbones cut it off?"

Jacob nodded. He was trying to forget that he had to do that task.

"Well…I am thinking that leg might make a really good exhibit, or something." "What?" asked the boy.

"Yes," continued the General. "I think the folks in Washington would just love to see it. Don't you think? They're a pretty cold-blooded lot, they are! They would just love to see an amputated leg. Let them see what they all missed out here on the battlefield."

"Oh, General!" the boy exclaimed in an amazed voice.

"So…can you do that for me, Jacob?" Sickles asked.

Jacob looked at the soldier as if he had lost his mind, but he also felt a bit of pity for him, as well. "Yes…I will make it for you, sir," he relented.

"Good!" said Sickles. "Now you may have to work quickly, Jacob. I don't know how long I am going to stay here in this hospital. I may only have a few more days, so work fast."

"Don't worry, General," the boy replied, "a coffin is pretty simple carpentry." "Yes…but I am particular about this piece, Jacob," the General answered, his mouth drawn up in a wry smile. "I want the traditional shape, but I want it lined with black velvet."

"Black velvet, sir?"

"I know…I know…it does sound a bit macabre, but I think it will make a better statement that way. I was examining the leg just yesterday. I think that there are still pieces of shrapnel imbedded in the bone."

"How can you tell that?" asked the boy.

"Well…you do have to poke around a bit. I was using my dinner fork to do it. I swear that I hit metal. So I am going to have all the tissue removed; all the skin, muscle, tendon and sinew. I just want the skeletal parts."

Jacob gave a shudder at the thought of the whole procedure.

"Now, Jacob…your father is probably is dire need of your help. Don't you think that you've spent enough time talking to me for this day? Go home and help your family. Give some thought to my coffin idea, and then come back to visit me sometime tomorrow."

"I will sir," replied the boy.

"And Jacob?"

"Yes sir, General."

"Would you be so kind as to find General Humphries of my Corps? If you can't find him immediately upon crossing through the lines on the Ridge, then ask one of his subordinates to send him to me."

"I will do that, sir," answered Jacob, standing to leave.

"Thank you, Jacob," responded the General. "Tell Humphries that I have need of his services."

CHAPTER 27

A New Beginning

Jacob had a difficult time finding General Humphries, who was a Division Commander in Sickles' III Corps, and one of his immediate subordinates. Humphries had taken command on the field, along with the other Division Commander, General Birney, when Sickles had been wounded in the battle on the second day. Jacob, however, was able to find an officer on III Corps, and entrusted the General's message to him to give to Humphries. That business out of the way, Jacob headed home to Seminary Ridge.

He walked quickly down the Baltimore Pike, heading for the intersection with the Chambersburg Pike – which meant he would pass directly by the McClellan house. He wondered if Rebecca Tilden was still living with the McClellan/Wade family, or if she and her family had found it safe enough to return to their own home. He had left the Seminary before seven in the morning that day, and had not even considered knocking on the door of the house on Baltimore Street. He knew that there were rules concerning bereavement that needed to be observed. But now it was close to noon, and so he once again weighed the pros and cons of an impromptu visit to the residents of the house.

He weighed these points as he walked downhill, and having made no clear decision on the matter by the time he reached the house itself, he decided that the best course of action for that particular day was to keep right on walking.

The town of Gettysburg was still looking very like the thing that it had become – a battle zone. But at midday of 5 July, the streets of the town were far more occupied than they had been over the past forty-eight hours. Many of the citizens were busy discussing the battle, but most were engaged in the fine art of repair – many of them patching up the holes in brick and mortar left behind by the shelling and minie ball fire.

Jacob was also surprised to find how many of the townpeople – people that he barely knew – were calling out to him and wishing him a pleasant day. He could not place even the most recognizable face by name, and most of the passersby were completely unknown to him – and yet they seemed to know him quite well. Jacob smiled at the strangers, or gave a slight nod of his head. He knew that he dared not speak, for that might betray the fact that he really did not know his own neighbors – such had been his families' seclusion as members of an Amish community of a single family.

He arrived back at Seminary Ridge at almost one in the afternoon. He noticed that there was a group of about six seminarians working on the farmhouse, pulling out the charred wood and other materials left over from the fire. He could see that there was a figure up in the copula of the bell tower of the main seminary building. He recognized immediately that the person above him was his father, and that he was busy with a repair to the copula.

Jacob walked through the entrance of the main building of the seminary and headed for the staircase. He climbed up to the second floor landing, and then proceeded up to the third floor. When he reached the third floor, he located a small wooden ladder that seemed to climb straight up through the ceiling. He placed his right foot on the first rung of the ladder, and then climbed up hand-over-hand, until his head poked out into the humid Pennsylvania daylight.

He expected to receive a gruff greeting from his father, but was proven wrong on this account.

"Jakob!" his father said, his voice almost joyful. "How are your friends this morning?"

The boy was confused. Did his father actually sound as if he cared about the welfare of the 'English?' Because…if that was the case, then his father must certainly have contracted some rare disease…or possibly he was suffering a complete mental breakdown…which the boy had heard was common in times of war.

"They seem to be doing fine, for the most part, Papa," he replied. "That is good. That is good." His father returned to his work. He was patching the roof of the copula. "Would you like to help me here?"

"Yes, sir," answered the boy. Even this question surprised Jacob. He was used to being ordered around by his father, not asked if he would like to help.

"Good! I need to replace a few of the shingles on the peak, so I will need you to hand me the materials." Ishmael Zook threaded his upper body through one of the openings in the cupola, which were situated directly below the domed roof. "So there are no changes at the hospital, Jacob?"

"Well…you remember General Armistead…the Confederate General…the one who was kept in the cook house?"

"Yes," his father said, taking a new shingle from Jacob's hand, "I remember him. He is a nice 'English' gentleman. He thinks a great deal of you…I can tell."

Jacob shook his head, a movement that was unseen by his father, who had already started to nail the replacement shingle onto the copula roof. "He died this morning."

The hammering ceased. "What did you say, Jakob?"

"I said that he died this morning."

"Who…Jacob?" His father began hammering again.

"General Armistead."

The hammering stopped. "Who, Jacob?"

"**General Armistead**," Jacob answered, raising his voice to almost a shout. "He died this morning."

Ishmael Zook stopped what he was doing and re-entered the small area within the copula. He looked squarely in his son's eyes. "I'm sorry to hear this, Jakob. I think he was a good man. Ja?"

"Yes," replied Jacob, "I believe that he was." And just like that, he started to weep.

Ishmael put his hammer and tacks down on the floor, and then did the unexpected – he stepped forward and embraced his son.

"Why does this happen, Papa?" Jacob asked. "Why is it that so many good people must die in these wars? What does it prove? When will it end?"

"I don't have an answer for you, Jakob," Ishmael said, stroking his son's hair. "Men have fought wars for thousands of years, and what does it ever prove? Nothing! It proves nothing!" Jacob shook his head, but still kept it buried against his father's chest. "But I have a feeling that you have more on you mind than just the death of the General."

"I have been a terrible son, Papa! I have given serious thought to leaving you and Mama here to tend to this farm by yourselves. I have thought only of myself – which I now realize was nothing but pure selfishness." Jacob paused to heave a deep sob.

But Ishmael knew that there was still more for his first-born to say; there was still another point that he had to address. "Is that all, Jakob?"

"No, Papa," Jacob answered, letting his father go. He walked to the other side of the tower and gazed out on the battlefield, which was still littered with dead horses, abandoned equipment, and many, many dead soldiers. "I have come to realize that I was ready to sacrifice my own family for my own desires. I would have chosen to leave home and never see any of you again… and if this battle had gone in a different direction, I might not have seen any of you again. If there was one thing that I learned over the last three or four days, it was that I should be more thankful for the home and family that I have. My heart was broken as I lowered poor Ginnie Wade into the ground – but I know how much worse I would have felt if it had been you, or Mama…or Abraham." Jacob sniffed back the mucus that was running out of his nose, and the wiped his eyes with his shirt sleeve.

"Jakob," his father said softly. "I, too, have come to a realization."

Jacob understood very well what was about to happen; his father was about to reinforce the strong Amish traditions that had been so absent from Jacob over the past days and weeks. It seemed the perfect time – he had already confessed how worthless he was. Jacob lowered his head and looked down at the ground below.

"Jakob," his father said, "would you please turn around so that I can speak to you … face-to-face – like two men talk to each other."

The boy was surprised to hear his father refer to him as a 'man.' He had never done this before. He had always called him, 'boy.' Very often, he never would even address him by his name.

Jacob turned around and faced his father.

"I know that you want to leave, Jakob. I know that your General Sickles has made you an offer of education out among the 'English.' I know that this offer is very tempting for you."

"It is alright, Papa," Jacob answered. "My place is here with you."

"That would have been the perfect answer," Ishmael said, "if you were speaking with my father, Isaac. That might have also been the perfect answer if you were speaking to me about a month ago. But it is no longer the perfect answer, Jakob."

Jacob swallowed deeply. He wondered what horrible punishment his father was about the meet out on him.

"I have come to realize, Jakob, that I, too, have been selfish. I have forced my family to cling to the ways of the people who have rejected us – as if one day they would welcome us back if we remained righteous in our faith. I have come to understand that you are a very smart young man. I have met many an 'English' over the last few days who tell me that you should go further than the family farm; that you should be given the chance to get a good education."

"But, Papa…."

"Shh, Jakob," his father said, bringing his finger to his mouth, "do not interrupt your father." And then he smiled at his son. "I think I would agree to let you attend a university of the English, like your General wants you to do."

"What?"

"Did you not hear me?"

"I am sorry, Papa," stammered Jacob. "I did hear you…I just can't believe what I am hearing."

"But here is the thing, my boy," Ishmael continued. "It is only under the condition that our house is rebuilt first. I need you to help build our house – there is no other way around that. You may have to put off your plans for a year, or so – especially with the war still going on."

"Thank you, Papa," Jacob said quietly.

"I am thinking that you might like to become a doctor, especially after all of your experience in the hospital tent. You used to get sick at the sight of blood, but I think that the battle has changed that in your makeup. I think you have a stronger stomach."

Jacob laughed a bit at his father's candid observation. "That is true…I really did not like the sight of blood – even animal blood. I would like to study medicine, Papa," he said, smiling, "but I don't think I would like to be a surgeon. Too much hacking away! I might as well just stay a carpenter! I think I would like to work to find out why so many of the soldiers get worse….after the surgery has been performed. Why they get gangrene, or infection. I want to discover the reason, and then find a way to prevent this. I think that would cut down on the number of men that die from these wounds."

"That sounds like a very noble thing to do, Jakob," said his father. Ishmael began to collect his tools. "You know, Jakob, your mother and I"… and then he faltered for a moment…"are very proud of you."

"Vielen Danke, Fati," replied Jacob, using the term of affection that his father preferred.

CHAPTER 28

Sunrise at Seminary Ridge

Jacob woke from a very deep sleep at around six thirty on the morning of 6, July. He hadn't slept as deeply or soundly as he had for more than a week, and even though he wasn't sleeping in his own bed, he had found the nighttime accommodations at the seminary to be clean and comfortable. He sat upright on his bed. The morning sunlight was already beginning to stream into the room. He looked over to see his brother, Abraham, still fast asleep in the bed next to his.

It was now Monday morning. The battle had taken such a toll on the town of Gettysburg, and in particular, the Zook family, that the Sabbath had been all but overlooked. Sunday services had been observed within the seminary building, but many of the other residents of the town had too many repairs that needed immediate attention to attend. Moreover, the many burial details, which had been organized by some of the community leaders, still had an inordinate amount of work to accomplish.

Jacob hopped out of his bed and walked over to the window, which looked out on Seminary Ridge. The sun was just about to creep over the distant hills and light the entire area. Jacob considered that, even if he disregarded the carnage that lay strewn on the valley below, the sunrise gave him hope to think that God had allowed a new day to dawn – and with that dawning, a new hope for mankind. Jacob crossed the room to a bureau that stood against the opposite wall. Just as he had down more than a week before, he poured a generous amount of water from a pitcher into a basin that was standing on the bureau. He scooped up some of the water from the basin, using the palms of both his hands and proceeded to wash his face. Finding a washing cloth, he first stripped off his nightshirt – the one which had been borrowed from one of the seminarians – and began to wash his body. He wet the cloth and raised his left arm and started to wash, beginning with his left shoulder. As he brought the cloth beneath his shoulder in order to wash his armpit, he turned his head to the left. It was then that he made a discovery.

Perhaps because it had already been dark in the room on the previous two nights when he had gone there to sleep, and perhaps because Abraham was also sound asleep – or maybe even because the sky had been so overcast that the moonlight could not enter his window – Jacob had failed to notice the one singular non-Amish object that had been placed in the bedroom.

It was a mirror.

The Lutherans had placed large mirrors on the back of each of the dormitory room doors, so that the seminarians, when dressing in their vestments for worship services, could see if the various trappings of their religious order were applied squarely and neatly.

The mirror was virtually full-length.

This was the first time that Jacob had ever seen himself in a mirror, with the possible exception of being able to see his reflection in a pool of water, or in a store front window on the Emmitsburg Pike. And that had just been his face; he was now totally naked.

He felt instantly ashamed; not because of his nakedness, but because of the way that he looked. He knew that his mother, if they had still been back in their own farmhouse, would never have allowed him to get into his bed in the condition he was in. She would have made him take a bath first.

Jacob stopped washing himself and took a step toward the mirror. There were dark blotches of caked on mud and dirt all over his arms, legs, and chest. He noticed several large bruises, now turned black and blue that stood out prominently on his right thigh and left upper arm. There was still a fair amount of caked blood on his arms and legs – but especially so in his blonde hair, which lay matted and in total disarray. There were obvious scratches on his face and on his stomach area.

He took another step closer to the mirror. Even in the pale morning light, he could discern that he was beginning to show signs of his inevitable beard, which was beginning to appear as light blonde hairs, both on his chin and above his upper lip.

He went back to the bureau and moved the basin closer to the edge of the table top, rewetting and wringing out the cloth. Using the mirror as a guide, he began to clean off his body, starting with his face, and then moving lower to his chest and extremities, rinsing the rag as he went, turning the basin water filthy with mud and dried blood. Seeing the basin filled with brown water, he emptied it into the chamber pot, and then refilled it with clean water from the pitcher. He used this clean water to clean the clots of blood and dirt out of his hair – using a hair brush, which he found on the dresser, to further remove any of the sticking debris.

Finally finished with his informal bath, he stood in front of the mirror and surveyed his work. He decided that it was a vast improvement over what he had first seen.

"You missed a few places," said a voice in the room.

Jacob turned quickly in the direction of the voice. It was his brother, Abraham.

"How long have you been awake?" asked Jacob.

"Long enough, Jacob," his brother replied. Gesturing to the mirror, he said, "You know that thing is a symbol of man's vanity!"

"I know that, Abraham," Jacob answered. "It is a useful tool, though." "Yes," laughed his brother, "but it is only good for looking at yourself from one side. You should see what your other side looks like!" "What?"

Abraham giggled again. "You're clean on the front and dirty on the back." Jacob shook his head in disgust. "This is why I need a bath. The dirt needs to soak off, not be rubbed off." Jacob returned to the bureau, rinsing the cloth again.

He then tried to reach behind his back to wipe off the remaining dirt.

"Here," said his brother, "let me help you." Abraham jumped out of his bed and crossed over to his brother. He took the rag from Jacob's hand. "Turn around," he commanded. He cleaned off a patch of blood that was stuck to Jacob's right shoulder blade, and some caked dirt that was in the small of his back. "Jacob," the boy observed, "you've got a very large bruise back here. It's the size of an apple!"

"Where?" asked Jacob.

"Right here," answered his brother, taking his index finger and poking him in the left buttock. He then laughed again.

"Very funny, Abraham! Do I have a bruise, or not?"

"You do," the younger boy replied, "but it is actually on the other cheek."

"Am I dirty…you know…down there?" asked Jacob.

"Probably…but I'm not cleaning that. You will just have to wait for a bath!" Abraham placed the wash cloth back on the rim of the basin. Jacob opened the top drawer of the bureau, where he found some of the other borrowed pieces of clothing. He selected some undergarments and stockings. He pulled on his undergarments and turned to his brother.

"Thank you, Abraham."

"You are very welcome, Jacob," the boy replied. "I knew you would want to look better than you did, especially if you are going to see Rebecca Tilden today."

"What? You know how I feel about Rebecca?"

"You talk in your sleep, Jacob!" answered his brother, who then gave Jacob a large grin.

Jacob opened the second drawer of the bureau and found a clean white shirt and put it on. He also found a pair of trousers which he donned. They were a little loose, but he managed to adjust the suspenders to keep them in place. He sat down on his bed and pulled on the stockings, and then found his dirty black boots. He used his soiled and blood-covered blue shirt – the same shirt he had worn since the second day of the battle, to wipe some of the heavy dirt from his boots.

As he pulled on the second boot, Abraham walked over to where he was sitting and sat down next to him on the bed. Jacob noticed that Abraham's borrowed nightshirt was touching the floor – it was obviously too large for the boy.

The younger boy sat quietly for a few moments, but Jacob knew that Abraham had something more to say, so he patiently waited. Jacob decided to put his arm around his brother's shoulder. "Jacob?"

"Yes?"

"I was worried that I would never see you again."

It was at that moment that Jacob considered telling his brother about the nightmares that he had been witness to over the past few nights, but he couldn't bring himself to heap another worry on top of his brother, so he merely replied, "I felt the same way about you."

"You did?"

"Certainly!" Jacob affirmed. "You are the only brother I have. What would I do without you?"

"I was worried that you had been killed out there," said Abraham.

Jacob nodded. "Trust me, Abraham…you would not believe the things that I saw and what I went through over the past few days."

"I know…I saw some of those same things up here on the ridge."

"But all the long, I kept thinking that I had made a big mistake," said Jacob.

"A mistake?"

"You know…running away like I did," answered Jacob. "If I hadn't done that, I would have been here, with the rest of the family."

"Yes," agreed Abraham, "but you know what Papa always says, don't you? 'God's Will!'"

Jacob knew exactly what his brother was telling him; that God had a purpose for him – a mission that needed to be accomplished, and to do that he had to send him away from his home and family – just like he had sent Jonah to Nineveh. When Jonah decided not to obey God's Will, he tried to run away to sea, and was cast overboard and then swallowed by the whale. If Jacob had stayed put at home, many of the events that had transpired in the last few days may never have come to pass, including the thing which was foremost in Abraham's mind.

"Papa is…different," said Abraham quietly.

Jacob already knew that to be the case, but he was also interested in hearing his brother's observations. "In what way?"

"He is…more friendly," stated Abraham. "I don't think he is so eager to follow the Ordnung as he used to be."

"I have noticed that, too," replied Jacob. "Is that a good thing?"

Abraham pushed himself away from Jacob's grasp and punched him lightly on the arm. "Don't you realize that if you hadn't done the things that you have done, that you would be stuck here on this farm for the rest of your life?"

Jacob hadn't thought about it in that way – not exactly, but he was surprised to hear his fourteen year old brother elucidate that theory in such a manner.

Not hearing a response from his brother, Abraham continued. "Don't you realize, that as the first-born, if nothing had changed for you…that certainly nothing was about to change…for me?"

Jacob never considered his brother's question before this moment. He was eighteen years old, and had spent far more time growing up within the Ordnung and the Amish traditions. He had been pretty well established as an Amish youth when his family moved to Gettysburg. Abraham had been a little more than a child when they had moved. They had both spent the last two years fighting off the temptations of being assimilated into the 'English' community. If it had been a difficult time for Jacob, who was already well on the way to becoming an Amish young man, then it must have been even more challenging for Abraham.

"I am truly sorry, my brother," Jacob said, "but I never realized that you also had conflicts with our traditions."

"All the time, Jacob," answered his brother. "All the time. If Papa lets you go out of here to the 'English' university, then it will be far less difficult when it comes to me. Don't you see?"

"I do see," answered Jacob.

"So you must do well, Jacob," added his brother, "because if you do not, Papa could very well change his mind back again."

Jacob nodded. He knew that his father feared the outside world.

Abraham grabbed Jacob by both of his shoulders and turned him. "You must do well prove to Papa that we can still be righteous and live among the 'English, Jacob!"

"I will try my best, Abraham."

And then, Abraham threw his arms around his brother and hugged him, squeezing his upper body with all of his strength. He held on to his older brother for some time, his face buried deeply into Jacob's chest. But through the nice, clean white shirt that Jacob had borrowed from an unknown seminarian, he could still manage to feel the dampness that had been created by his brother's tears.

"And Jacob…?" Abraham added, speaking to his brother in muffled tones through the material of his shirt.

"Yes, Abraham?"

The fourteen year old pulled his head away from his older brother's chest, and looked up into his face. Jacob could see the lines on his brother's cheeks where the tears had run down, but other than that, Abraham now had a slight grin on his face. "English girls, such as Rebecca, appreciate it when their men are clean-shaven, so I would advise you to do something about your whiskers."

CHAPTER 29

A Big Surprise

Jacob patted his brother on his head, and rose from the bed. "I will see you at breakfast, Abraham."

"I'll be there in just a few minutes," answered his brother. "Unlike you, I took a bath last night before going to bed."

Jacob playfully punched his brother and then left the room. He hurried down the hall to the dormitory kitchen, where his mother and father were already eating their breakfast. The seminary cook, Mrs. Davies, was already preparing a large breakfast for her seminarians and instructors, but was also making additional food for the Zook family, as well as for some of the doctors and nurses who were still in residence.

"Guten morgen," Jacob said, as he entered the kitchen. He walked over to his mother and gave her a kiss on the cheek, and then did the same to his father.

"Well," exclaimed his astonished mother, "someone is in a very good mood this morning, Ishmael. I wonder what has brought this on?"

"Sarah, my darling wife," answered Ishmael, "it is nothing more than the anticipation of a hard day's work ahead that has brightened Jakob's outlook on life. Isn't that so, Jakob?"

Jacob smiled at his father. "That must be it, Fati. So what is on the schedule for today?"

"Well…" said his father, "we have no cows to milk, and no crops to weed or harvest…so I suppose our time can be best spent in starting to re-build our house."

"We are starting so soon?" asked the boy.

"We might as well. This is the first day in two that it isn't raining. The skies are clear and it is not as humid. The rain has put out the remaining hot embers, so we can spend most of the day getting rid of the debris. We will need to be careful, though…some of the embers below the surface may still be hot, and there even may be some big timber that we will be able to salvage for the new house." Jacob nodded, while he poured himself a cup of coffee, which did not go unnoticed by his mother.

"Since when did you start drinking coffee, Jakob?" she asked.

Jacob smiled, as if he had been caught cheating. "I had a great deal of the drink when I was in the Confederate and Federal camps, Muti. But, I must say, this coffee tastes far superior to what I had in either of those two places." Jacob's assessment was enough to make Mrs. Davies turn and give him a broad smile. She handed Jacob a bowl of oatmeal. This staple was among the few available for consumption that morning. There were no eggs to be found, and most of the chickens had either stopped laying because of the cannon fire, or had themselves been, in fact, eaten by the foraging armies.

"Is your brother awake yet?" asked Ishmael.

"Yes, Fati," answered Jacob. "I have already spoken to him this morning. He should be here any minute."

"Good!" replied Ishmael. "We will make good use of him today." Ishmael stared across the table at his son. "Jakob…we Amish only grown our beards out after we marry. You are still not married, I presume?"

Jacob smiled sheepishly at his father. "No, Fati…not yet."

"Then I will try to find you a razor so that you may look like a proper young man…Amish or English. But I am sure that my old razor was destroyed in the fire…so we will just have to venture into the town to buy you one of your own."

"Thank you, Fati," said Jacob, eating a mouthful of oatmeal to help conceal his embarrassment.

Within a few minutes, Abraham also joined the family breakfast. In many respects, Abraham was far more personable than his older brother, Jacob. Of the two, Abraham had a more effervescent personality. Where Jacob was more reserved, a bit more on the shy side, and softer spoken, Abraham was an engaging conversationalist. He loved to talk, and he could talk easily with almost anyone. Jacob was the spitting image of Ishmael; they shared the same hair color, and their personalities seemed very similar – except, of course, they had always failed to notice this one trait. Abraham, on the other hand, strongly resembled his mother, Sarah. His hair was a medium brown color, like hers. It was almost chestnut in tone. His facial features were also very similar to his mother's, in fact, the two boys looked so dissimilar that it was often difficult to see any family resemblance at all.

In the recent past, Ishmael might ask Abraham to join with Jacob and him on a project, only to receive more than a fair share of complaining on the part of the boy. Abraham was not disrespectful – he simply had other ideas on how he would spend his waking hours. At times, this had been a source of consternation for Jacob, who was always the first go-to man on any job. Jacob had always been slightly jealous of his brother's ability to offer up even the slightest resistance to his father's former iron will; it was something that he wished he had been able to do as a child, and was only able to do more recently – which, of course, had caused quite a rift between his father and he.

But, this morning, Abraham happily agreed to the work. There was no discussion or argument of any kind, which surprised the rest of the family.

Breakfast concluded, the Zook males left for their old property, ready to begin the salvage work that needed to be finished before any new construction could begin. The seminarians had already cleared a great deal of the burned out house, and the only remaining piece of salvage remaining centered around the foundation of the house. Ishmael began giving instructions to his boys on what kind of materials he would like salvaged, and had even gone as far as to explain that he would be the only one among them who would venture into the cellar. But this explanation was overshadowed by the sound of an army unit marching in their direction, along with a small caravan of wagons and horses.

Jacob looked toward the road. The unit had left the main road and was now marching in their direction across seminary ridge. An officer on horseback rode around from the rear of the detachment and approached the Zook men. Jacob instantly recognized the man. It was General Humphries – General Sickle's immediate subordinate in III Corps. General Humphries, along with General Birney, had been responsible for picking up the pieces of III Corps after Sickles was wounded. The Corps had taken heavy casualties, but managed to withdraw back to the safety of Cemetery Ridge by the end of the second day of the battle. Unfortunately for Sickles, he could only get reports sent to him in the hospital tent, as he was busy having his leg removed from his body. Jacob had seen General Humphries on a number of occasions in the tent, checking in with Sickles. As far as General Meade was concerned, Sickles was no longer in command of III Corps. As far as Generals Humphries and Birney were concerned, that was not even subject for discussion. No one had the nerve to countermand any order given by Sickles – even if he had been on his deathbed.

General Humphries dismounted his horse and walked over to Ishmael Zook. "Mr. Zook," Humphries said, "General Sickles sends his compliments to you, to Jacob, and to the rest of your family."

Ishmael simply nodded as a reply to this salutation. Jacob and Abraham walked over by their father.

"The General sent out a call early this morning for volunteers, sir. Volunteers who had knowledge in carpentry, masonry, woodworking, and so on, who could be of assistance to you and your family in the rebuilding of your house. I have here over one hundred and fifty men who volunteered for this task."

"One hundred and fifty?" asked Jacob.

"Over one hundred and fifty, Jacob," corrected the General.

"I don't understand," said Ishmael.

"The General realizes that in your tradition, when an Amish family is in need of a new barn, that a barn-raising is arranged, and, within a single day's work, a new barn of immense proportions is raised and virtually completed by all of the community. General Sickles is also aware that you are not living within your Amish community, so there is no hope of such a thing happening here for you, unless, of course, you get some outside help. So, Mr. Zook, here is your outside help. Some of my officers studied engineering at West Point, and many of these men had worked in skilled trades prior to the war. The rest are strong backs… they will supply the muscle."

"But…?" interjected Ishmael.

"We are confident that we can raise a house on this spot within this day, sir…and if we cannot, then we will be back in the morning tomorrow to finish what we have started. We have also brought several wagons of supplies, courtesy of the Army of the Potomac."

"Fati!" exclaimed Jacob. "This is…unbelievable!"

"It is not that I am ungrateful to the General," said Ishmael, "but…"

"I also realize," interrupted Humphries, "that your tradition calls for strict limitations on what is placed in and on the house. We therefore request that you act as our supervisor throughout the day. We want you to be happy in your new home. Feel free to enlarge the home to suit your needs."

"General, how is General Sickles this morning?" asked Jacob.

"Jacob, General Sickles is his usual cantankerous self," replied Humphries, "and he is even more cantankerous over this building project." The General turned to Ishmael. "Mr. Zook...I hope that you will accept this offer from General Sickles...for all of our sakes, sir."

Ishmael was confused. He was not accustomed to receiving this kind of gift from the 'English.' "Did you have something to do with this, Jakob?"

Jacob was taken aback by his father's question. "Upon my soul, Fati...no I did not! I had no idea that the General would do such a thing!"

"The lad is telling the truth, Mr. Zook," General Humphries explained. "This is something that the General thought up completely on his own. But, to tell you the truth, sir... we wouldn't be here if it wasn't for the fact that we are all in total agreement with the General's idea...and for that, you can thank your son, Jacob."

Ishmael turned and smiled at his son. "Thank you, General. I am very proud of him, too."

"Then it is all settled," answered the General. "We will get these men to work straight away." Humphries turned and went back to consult his officers on the first steps of the construction.

"Well, jungen," Ishmael said, with a laugh, "it looks as if you have managed to get yourselves out of work today, after all. Jakob, you take Abraham with you, and go back up to the hospital to thank the General before he is moved to another place. You tell him that he is welcome at our house any time he wishes to come. You tell him that, Jakob."

"I will, Fati. I will!"

"And Abraham..." Ishmael continued.

"Yes, Fati."

"You make sure that Jacob goes directly to that hospital tent, boy. I don't want him wasting precious daylight over at Rebecca Tilden's house. Do you understand, Abraham?"

"Yes, sir," replied the boy. "I do." Abraham looked at his brother with a sly smile. "Jacob is not to stop to flirt with Becky. You are sending me to spy on him."

"Not entirely, but this may keep both of you out of trouble," answered his father. "Now be back sometime in the afternoon. I may still need your help here."

"Yes, Fati," answered Jacob, as he grabbed Abraham and pulled him along in tow. "What was that all about?" asked Jacob of his brother.

"I was only fooling with you, Jacob," answered his brother. "You know that, don't you?"

"Just be careful what you say around Papa. I am still not sure what he considers a joke, and what he considers to be serious."

"Jacob…have you forgotten what I told you before?" Abraham asked. "I need whatever you are doing now to work, otherwise it won't work for me later on."

Jacob reluctantly agreed. "Yes, but be careful of your wording." The two boys quickly walked into the town of Gettysburg, along the Emmittsburg Pike. Jacob had to drag his brother past some of the store fronts, as Abraham had spent very little time away from the farm. Now, on Monday morning, the Monday morning after the big battle, many of the stores were once again opening for business, and many of them offered sights for the eyes of a twelve year old to feast upon. But as distracted as Abraham was at the sight of the bustling little town, Jacob was battling his own distractions – particularly the fact that they were quickly approaching the intersection with the Baltimore Pike – the intersection that would not only take them up to the Federal camp, but would also take them past the Wade/McClellan house.

The two boys crossed the Emmittsburg Pike and headed toward Cemetery Ridge. "Isn't there another way up to the camp?" asked Abraham.

"Why?"

"I don't know, Jacob. I thought that you might not want to pass that house again."

"Checking up on me already, are you?"

"No!" said Abraham defiantly. "It's not that at all! I think that house holds too many bad memories for my taste, Jacob."

"I know exactly what you mean, but this is the shortest way to the Spangler Farm."

"Then let's cross the Pike and head up on the other side of the street," suggested Abraham.

Jacob nodded in agreement. He was not aware that Becky Tilden had gone back to her own house to live, and there was very little chance that she would be at the McClellan house this early on Monday morning – especially now that Ginnie was dead and gone. They crossed the Baltimore Pike to the side of the street opposite the house.

"I don't like that place, Jacob," admitted his brother.

"The house?" asked Jacob. "It's just a house."

"I couldn't sleep at all after the funeral in the yard." Jacob was well aware that his brother had been suffering from nightmares, which, he had already concluded, were the direct result of the past few days and nights. He remembered how his brother tossed and turned on that first night in the seminary bed, but he didn't want to immediately let on that he had observed this behavior.

Still, he continued the conversation, hoping to learn more about what was bothering his brother. "You were sound asleep when I came into the room last night," observed Jacob.

"Not last night, Jacob…the night before that."

"Really? You seemed pretty out that night, as well," he lied. Jacob wondered if his brother would tell his about his dreams – that was, of course, if he actually remembered them. But Abraham wasn't even on the same train of thought.

"No…not all the time," answered Abraham. "I was awake when you came in, Jacob. I closed my eyes so that you would see me awake, but when you turned away to get undressed I opened them again."

"Sure you did."

"I did," protested his brother. "I swear to you I was awake…..I…." He paused, debating whether or not he should tell his brother what he had witnessed. "I…"

"Yes…what?" asked Jacob.

"You got undressed and then got into your bed," said the younger boy, "and then…I heard you."

"What?" asked Jacob. "Now you are going to tell me what I said in my sleep, I suppose?"

"No, Jacob," his brother replied. "You started to cry. I heard you crying." Jacob stopped walking. His brother took a few more paces and then stopped, turning around. "I couldn't help it, Abraham. I just couldn't keep it in anymore. I was so grateful to be home again, with you, and with Muti and Fati, that I lost control of my emotions."

"I know, Jacob. I started to cry, too – but you were sobbing, so you didn't hear me. I kept thinking about poor Ginnie being lowered into the ground. I kept thinking that how I would feel if it was you…"

"And I kept thinking how I would feel if it was you, Abraham," added Jacob. "I guess that's what set me off in the first place. It could have just as easily have been our family that was suffering."

"I know," agreed his brother.

"And that's why you don't want to pass near the house?" asked Jacob.

Abraham nodded. "Too many bad memories." He paused. "Sometimes…sometimes, Jacob…there are times that I am actually afraid to go to sleep at night. I get worried that I might have another dream about that day. I don't want to think about it, Jacob."

"I agree," said Jacob, "but they are still my friends."

"I know that they are," replied his brother, "but I still need more time." They continued to climb the incline that led to the top of Cemetery Ridge.

Much of the Federal army had already broken camp and had moved out; the order had been given to pursue Lee's army back to Virginia with the hope of crushing it. Unfortunately for General Meade, he had given this order about a day too late to effectively do something about it. The ridge evened out and they continued on a bit more level ground, reaching the Spangler Farm in just a few more minutes.

Jacob was still surprised to see how many soldiers – soldiers he didn't know from sight – were stopping there daily business to either wave or shout a greeting to him. This, of course, impressed Abraham, as well. They continued on their way, passing the farmhouse belonging to the Spangler family, and the small outdoor cooking hut, where General Armistead had died the day before. Jacob, too, had some bad memories of this particular little house, but he kept them to himself and did not bother to share any of his thoughts with his brother.

They pushed on toward the hospital tent.

Upon entering the tent, they found General Sickles sitting up in his bed and enjoying his breakfast.

"Well, my stars! If it isn't the Zook brothers…come to pay a visit to their favorite General."

Jacob would never have wanted to correct Sickles, even if he had already met several Generals who he had more affection for than he, including General Armistead, and General Zook. Then again, he thought,

Sickles was responsible for having their house rebuilt. Jacob wondered if his gesture to the Zook family came with a price tag attached to it. He wondered if he was going to be like some form of an indentured servant to the man for the services rendered.

"General," Jacob said, "my family and I would like to thank you for your kind wishes and best intentions for sending the detachment of workers to rebuild our home."

"My pleasure, Jacob," answered the General. "I was happy to arrange the project, and the men were happy to oblige."

"Yes, sir…I understand that," responded Jacob.

"Do I detect a certain tone in your voice, boy?" asked the General. "Perhaps you do, General, although I am trying my best to suppress it." "Jacob..what are you doing?" asked Abraham. "Shh, Abraham!"

"What is on your mind, my boy?" asked Sickles calmly. "General… it isn't that I don't appreciate what you are doing for my

family…because I do appreciate it, sir…from the bottom of my heart." "Yes…?" asked the General.

"It just seems like a very extravagant gift to give in return for me building you a coffin for your leg."

"I see," said the General. "You doubt my intentions."

"No, not in that many words, sir," answered the boy. "I have come to know you quite well, General, and I have come to know that you are no person to be trifled with."

"Which means?"

Jacob cleared his throat. He knew what he wanted to say; what he wanted to ask. "I think you want me to do something for you, General."

Sickles stared at the boy for a very long time before answering. "You are correct, Jacob. I do want something in return. I want you!"

"What?" asked the boy.

"I want you to accompany me back to Washington, Jacob. I will be leaving in a few days' time. I want you to come with me."

Jacob had no idea that the General would be asking him to leave so soon. "I heard your father say that the first priority was to re-build the family home, so I saw to it that your house would be built…and built well. When that is complete, I am hoping that your father will see his way to letting you start your education."

"This is unbelievable!" answered Jacob, the anger starting to build within him.

"I don't understand," said the General. "I thought you would be happy that I helped arrange your passage out of here."

"My passage out of here?" asked Jacob. "You make it sound like I want to escape from rural Pennsylvania; like I don't have any ties to home or family!"

"And I thought," thundered Sickles, "that, based upon some of our previous conversations, that this was exactly the case!"

Jacob stopped for a moment; he had to think back – he had to remember what it was that he had actually said to the General. Could he have possibly hinted that he was less than happy at home? Did he give the General the impression that he had been living a life of captivity within his own home? He looked over at his brother, who had a very nervous look on his face. Jacob knew that his brother was prone to outbursts of emotion; that he might simply start talking and offering his opinion. He knew that it couldn't come to that.

"General Sickles, sir," responded Jacob, with a cooler, calmer voice, "I appreciate everything that you are doing for my family. I appreciate everything that you have offered to do for me. But General…in spite of what I may have led you to believe – especially when we first made our acquaintance – I still do have very strong ties with my family. Yes, my father was very strongly set in his traditional ways – that part was true – but this battle, and the recent series of events surrounding it, have softened his heart. I would prefer if he recognized the opportunity to send me away to school on his own timetable. I think he is smart enough to know that he is…pardon the expression…being manipulated."

"Manipulated?" Sickles asked. "Is that what you think I am doing?"

Jacob closed his eyes and slowly nodded his head. "I know that you will work to get what you want, General."

Sickles stared at the boy, then he turned his glance and stared at the boy's younger brother, then he turned back and stared at the boy again. "The problem with you, Jacob Zook, is that you are too damn smart." Then the General let out a great laugh, which helped to break the palpable tension by his bedside. "You know, boy…if you were twenty years older, or so…had gone to West Point…and had the right connections in Washington…you would probably be the Commander of this whole damn army…and I can tell you something else…Bobby Lee would be in fear of you! Yes, he would!"

Jacob let out a sigh, which was closely followed by another sigh from his brother. "You aren't angry at me, sir?" he asked.

"Angry? No! I am actually happy to see that I am backing not only a very smart young man, but also one with a great deal of personal integrity."

"What's integrity?" asked Abraham.

Sickles laughed. "Abraham, don't feel bad about not knowing what that word means. Most of the Federal officers don't have a clue as to its definition. Integrity is a way of deporting yourself, so that, even under the most dire circumstances, when all common sense is telling you to do something that might not turn out well for everyone, but would actually make your own life easier or better – instead of doing that, you see – you choose to do what you believe in your heart is the right thing to do. That is your brother, Jacob! Sometimes it is a very difficult thing to stand up for what you believe in!"

"I thought that he was just plain stubborn," replied Abraham.

Sickles laughed. "Another smart one! Jacob…I'll bet your brother is very smart, too."

"At least as smart as I am, sir," answered Jacob, "and possibly even smarter. Just ask him."

Sickles laughed again. "Fine…fine. We will play this thing your way, Jacob. We will let you decide when you will ask for your father's leave. I think that they will be moving me to a hospital in the Capitol later this week, so I suppose I will be here until then. If you can make that item for me before I go, I would appreciate it a great deal."

"What item?" asked Abraham.

"Never you mind," said Jacob.

"If you don't convince your father until after I leave, then I will make sure that you find out how to contact me. There are a few very powerful men in the Capitol that I would like you to meet, so I would like to begin there. After that, we will spend some time together picking out the right school for you. My time in this war is over, lad, so I will have plenty of time on my hands for pet projects…like your future."

"I don't know what to say, General," replied the boy.

"How about you don't say anything then," said Sickles, "until everything is official. At that point, you can thank me from the bottom of your heart."

Jacob smiled at the man, cantankerous as he was.

Abraham stepped up to the General and extended his hand. The General smiled and took the boy's hand and shook it vigorously. "General, sir," said the younger boy, "I do hope you will do us the honor of coming to our house for dinner…when this war is all over…and after you get…you know…your new wooden leg."

"Abraham!" Jacob corrected.

"Don't worry, Jacob," Sickles said, "the boy is absolutely correct. Until I get fitted with my replacement limb, I can't do much of anything. But yes, Abraham, I would be happy to accept your invitation to dinner."

"Really?" asked the astounded boy.

"Really," answered the General. "Even if Jacob is away at the university, what is there to stop me from coming back to Gettysburg to visit the place where I lost my leg, and to spend some time with the other Zook boy?"

"Come on, Abraham," urged Jacob, "it's time to get on home. Fati might need us at the new house. Good-bye General. I should have that project finished within a day, or two, so I hope to deliver it to you before you leave."

"Good-bye, Jacob. Good-bye, Abraham. Say hello to your folks for me, will you?"

The Zook boys left the hospital tent. Sickles went back to his breakfast, content that he was still backing the right horse.

Jacob and his brother began the long walk home. It was still only about nine thirty in the morning.

"Jacob…I cannot believe that you spoke to him like that!" Abraham commented. "You were taking a really big chance with your future!"

"I know," he answered. "But I had to stand up to him, Abraham. In many ways, General Sickles is like a bully. He likes to push people around."

"But you didn't let him push you around, Jacob."

"No…that is my point," he answered. "As I said, the General likes to push people around, and if he can do that…if he can push them, either because they fear him, or because they want something from him…then he won't respect them, because he knows that they are easily pushed. That's exactly what a bully does, Abraham."

"And you held your ground, didn't you? It sure sounded like you did."

"I think I did," said Jacob. "He tried getting angry at me, but when that didn't work he seemed to let up."

"I think you did great, Jacob!"

"Thank you, Abraham…but, remember…not a word of any of this to Fati!"

CHAPTER 30

In the Amish Tradition

The boys continued down the hill toward the Emmittsburg Pike, walking down Baltimore Street, heading toward the center of the small town. As they had done when ascending the street, both boys were walking on the side of the street that was opposite that of the Wade/McClellan house – and the gravesite of Ginnie Wade. At the intersection of the two pikes, they crossed to the far side of the Emmittsburg Pike and turned to the right, heading once again toward home. Once past the cursed residence, Abraham became his old self again; his spirits were much higher than they had been earlier in the morning, and he playfully teased his older brother as the two walked by the store fronts and markets.

"Jacob!" a voice called from their rear. It was a female voice. Both boys, particularly Jacob, recognized the voice at once. It was Rebecca Tilden.

Jacob whirled around on one heel, his face brightening into a wide smile. He waved to the girl that was walked quickly, trying to gain on their position. "Hello, Becky!"

"Wait there for me," she called again, once again hastening her pace.

He turned to look at his brother, a moon-faced smile on his face, just to see Abraham scowl at him. "Fati told us not to stop to talk to her, Jacob," the younger boy said.

"That's not really what he said, Abraham," Jacob replied. "At least… that's not what he really meant!"

"Is that so?" asked his brother. "I have always found that it is sometimes dangerous to interpret what Fati says, and what he really, truly means by it."

"Very humorous," observed Jacob. "I hope you are going to be polite!" "Certainly," the boy answered. "I have no reason to be rude."

Jacob shook his head, but he had no reason to feel that his brother would embarrass or betray him to his father. He had no intention of running off with the girl and getting married at eighteen years old. He was only planning to speak to her for a few minutes. Jacob placed his hand on Abraham's shoulder.

"Don't worry, Jacob," said Abraham, smiling up at his brother. "I'm not going to tell."

"Thanks," acknowledged Jacob. "Listen…how would you like to get something to eat and drink?"

"What?"

"I'll bet you are hungry…correct?"

"We only had breakfast a few hours ago, Jacob."

"I know…but you're already hungry…aren't you?" Jacob cocked his head to the side, raising his eyebrows to punctuate his question.

"You are trying to get rid of me, aren't you?" asked the boy.

"In a word…yes," answered his big brother. "I know that Mr. Reilly, over at the pharmacy…over there," he pointed in the direction ahead , "makes a really good cherry phosphate, and they have terrific cookies."

"Better than Muti's cookies?" asked Abraham.

"Well…no," answered his brother. "Nobody makes better cookies than Muti." And he wasn't lying about that fact. His mother was very proud of the traditional Amish cookie known as the 'snickerdoodle.'

"And what am I going to use to purchase these things, Jacob? Hm?"

"I was getting to that," answered Jacob, plunging his hand into his trousers pocket. He pulled out a small silver piece and handed it to his brother.

"Jacob!" his brother said in amazement. "You are giving me all of this money to spend?"

"Absolutely!"

"Just to keep me quiet?"

"No," said Jacob. "Just to get you out of the way for a few minutes!" Abraham extended the palm of his hand to accept the coin. The money aside, this was the first time that the boy had been able to enjoy the offerings of the main thoroughfare of Gettysburg, either on his own, or in the company of his parents. This had become far more than the chance to spy on his older brother; this had become an adventure – an experience. Jacob deposited the silver coin in his brother's hand. The boy turned quickly and headed off in the direction of the pharmacy.

"Abraham!" he called after his brother. "Stay put! Do you understand? Stay at Reilly's!"

"Stay at Reilly's!" the boy answered back. "I will, Jacob. You just take your good-old time."

Jacob rolled his eyes.

"Jacob!" he heard Becky say, as she walked up from behind him.

He turned around to face her. "Becky! It is good to see you again!" Jacob noticed that, in spite of the fact that she was not a member of the immediate Wade/McClellan family, that Becky was wearing black. She was dressed in mourning clothes.

"How have you been, Jacob?"

Jacob nodded. "Good, Becky…I mean…except for all that has gone on over the past week…all things considered, I mean…I think I am better than I was a week ago."

"You seem…relaxed," she observed.

"Maybe that's it," he agreed.

Rebecca looked down the pike a bit. "Wasn't your brother, Abraham, just standing with you? Where did he go?"

"I sent him to Reilly's for refreshment," he answered.

"Why did you do that?"

Jacob felt all of the blood in his upper body rush to his face. "I did it so that I could have the opportunity to talk with you…alone."

"Really?"

"Yes," he replied. "May I walk with you for a bit?"

"Certainly, Jacob," she said demurely. "But you will pardon me if I do not behave like some love-sick schoolgirl, Mr. Zook. I am, after all, still in mourning for my dear friend, Ginnie."

Jacob's face fell. "I know that, Becky." He offered the girl his arm, which she quickly took with her hand. They walk slowly down the main street of town, but turned to the left when they reached the first side street. "Becky…what would you say if I told you that I had a chance to go to a university?"

"Which university?" she asked.

"Does it really matter, Becky?"

"Well…I suppose not," she answered. "Isn't that a bit odd? I mean, I don't want to appear rude, but I didn't think that the Amish went to university."

"We don't…as a rule," said Jacob."

"My goodness!" she answered, thinking deeply about what he was telling her. "How can this be possible, Jacob? Surely your father must be against this!"

Jacob laughed a bit at her observation. "I would have said the same thing about a week ago…but the battle changed him a great deal. I think he might be in support of the idea now!"

They had now entered a more residential part of the town. The narrow side street was lined with large trees. There had been only slight damage inflicted on this part of town by the two armies. Becky's mind flooded with a myriad of thoughts – all of them reflecting in some way upon the possibilities that might, in some way, govern the rest of her life. She looked over at the young man whose arm she was holding. She knew that she favored the boy a great deal, but she also knew that, even considering his newly improved status within the community, her parents would not take kindly to any kind of romantic relationship between their daughter and a young man who was destined to spend the entire balance of his life living on a farm.

They had higher hopes for her.

But she really liked this young man.

She liked him a great deal.

Her hand slipped off of his arm, but she quickly reached out with the same hand and caught him by the hand.

"Did you trip, Becky?" he asked.

"No, I don't think so," she said. She felt him relax his arm, letting his elbow straighten out, allowing his arm to fall to his side. Instead of letting go of his hand, she asserted her grip even more.

He stopped walking. "Becky?" He looked down at this hand; the same hand which now had her gloved hand wrapped around it. "What are you doing?"

"I'm holding your hand, foolish boy," she answered. Jacob turned away from her momentarily. He was instantly uncomfortable.

"I can see that, Becky," he answered. "Aren't you supposed to be in mourning? Aren't you supposed to ignore people like me?"

"Because you're Amish?" she asked, a note of surprise in her voice.

"No, not because I'm Amish," he answered with hesitation, "because….I'm a boy."

"What are you talking about, Jacob?" she asked. "It's because you are a boy that I am noticing you!"

Jacob was even more confused. He was confused why Rebecca, after all the time they had spent together over the past few days, had suddenly turned so aggressively forward with him. "Still," he replied, "I am sure that your parents would be shocked to hear that you were seen flirting with a boy while wearing black."

"That is probably true," she admitted, "but I can tell you what would shock them even more… "Jacob became even more concerned. "And what would that be, I wonder?" Rebecca let out a short, dry laugh. "They would be shocked to hear that I was discovered giving that same boy a kiss…while I was still dressed in mourning clothes."

"What?"

"You understood me, Jacob," she maintained.

"I suppose I did," he answered. Suddenly he felt trapped. He had never been in this position before. He might have been, had the family stayed put in Paradise. He could have very well have been betrothed to a young Amish girl by this time in his life. His parents would have already begun planning their future together. But he had almost completely put those thoughts out of his mind for the past two years – things being how they were. Even still, he had known instantly that he had been attracted to Becky. He hadn't realized until now that she was also attracted to him.

"Well?" she asked. "Don't you want to kiss me, Jacob?" "Yes," he said quietly. "The thought had entered my mind."

"Then what in perdition is stopping you?" she asked, a tone of frustration entering her voice.

He cleared his throat. He started to lean his face closer to hers, but then backed away quickly. "Becky...I must admit this to you," he said nervously, "but I have never kissed anyone before...except my parents... and that doesn't and shouldn't really count for much."

"Indeed it shouldn't!" she said.

"Have you?"

"Have I what, Jacob?" she said, toying with him.

"Have you kissed a young man?" he asked, embarrassed for his bluntness.

She smiled at him. "No, Jacob. I have not."

He felt relieved at her answer, but still had more questions for her. "Then I must ask you more, Becky. Why is it, with all the eligible young men in Gettysburg, that you find yourself wanting to kiss me...a poor, Amish boy...with no certain prospects...but certainly a person that could easily raise the ire of your own family?"

She reached up and grabbed the front of his wide-brimmed straw hat, pulling it from off of his head. Then, using her other hand, she took a large handful of his hair in her hand, letting it sift through her fingers. "Don't you know that I fell in love with your long, blonde hair, Jacob? Any woman would give her eye teeth to have hair as long and straight as yours."

"You are mocking me, Becky!"

Her face fell to the sidewalk. "No! Really no I am not! But I am serious about your hair, Jacob. You wear it so incredibly long, and yet it looks good upon you."

"Are you telling me that you are attracted to me because I have long hair?" he asked.

"Yes," she answered truthfully, "but there is a great deal more besides that feature that I have come to adore. You are intelligent and mature – far more mature than the other boys I know. And you are also the kindest and gentlest of young men. I could very easily do exactly what my parents want me to do and end up in an unhappy marriage, to a man who….in addition to being balding and overweight…also treats me with disdain and anger. I believe that you would never treat me in this way."

"No," he answered. "I would never do that."

"So," she continued, "then you should do what is normally done at a moment like this…and kiss me." She moved her face slightly closer to his. Jacob felt a tremor in the pit of his stomach; a knot that was forming somewhere beneath his trousers that he couldn't quite explain. He felt the urge to give in to Rebecca's request – or was that really more of a temptation, he asked himself?

He turned away from her.

"What is wrong, Jacob?" she asked, her voice suddenly sad.

"I'm not sure, Becky," he answered. "There is nothing that I would like more than to stay with you and see where our time together leads us." He turned back around to face her. "But I also think that, if I am to make something of myself, that I cannot allow myself the luxury of becoming involved with you."

"Involved?" she said, hurt by the insensitivity of the word.

He closed his eyes and shook his head. "That didn't come out the way I had intended it. I'm sorry, Becky. Look…as I see it…there are two big temptations awaiting me. I could accept the offer from General Sickles – which could have the effect of splitting my own family down the middle, or I could also stay here in Gettysburg…and I would stay here just to avoid the first situation, but in doing that I would find myself being drawn closer and closer to you – which is also a pleasant thought, I might add. Perhaps too pleasant! I would put my other desires on hold for the time so that I might court you."

"I see," she said.

"Do you?" he asked. "Do you understand that, if I go away, that I may someday return – my prospects being enhanced by my education; my career firmly established; the timing for us far better than before?"

"But what if I cannot wait that long, Jacob?"

"Then it wasn't God's Will, Becky!"

"God's Will?" she asked. "You would pin that blame upon God's Will?" Jacob could see that he had upset the girl. "I don't mean to hurt you, Rebecca."

"I know that you don't, Jacob," she said, "but…you have…just the same." Jacob had only met this young lady a few days prior to the battle, but he was very aware that he felt a special connection to her – even though their backgrounds and traditions were at odds. He looked back at her face.

She was crying.

He stepped closer to her again. He took both of his hands and cupped her face in his hands. He never gave it any thought or reasoning, but within a few seconds found himself kissing her gently on her lips.

"I think I love you, Jacob Zook," she whispered.

"If that is so," he answered quietly, "then we have a very big problem, Becky. I think that I love you, too."

CHAPTER 31

Rebuilding the Homestead

Jacob bade farewell to Rebecca and quickly walked back up to the Emmittsburg Pike. His stomach was twisted in knots in just about every imaginable direction. He hadn't planned to have their meeting go exactly in that manner – especially the kiss – even more especially, the profession of their love for each other.

"What was I thinking?" he muttered to himself, as he rounded the corner onto the Pike. The trouble was that he wasn't thinking; he wasn't thinking of how he wanted his life – particularly his career – to go. He had let himself give in to impulse…to the temptations of the flesh. He had told her, hadn't he? Yes…he had. It had almost turned into an argument…but, in the end, he relented. He couldn't bring himself to hurt her feelings…and he certainly couldn't break off any kind of friendship with her.

But Jacob felt that he had his priorities in order. He needed to get a good education first, then establish himself in his career, and then… and only then would he consider taking a wife and raising a family. He might have felt a great deal of affection for Rebecca Tilden, and yes… it might even be love…but this would have to be put on a back burner somewhere in his mind. Rebecca would have to be patient and wait for him. And if she didn't wish to wait…if she met someone else along the way…what then? God's Will, Jacob thought.

God's Will.

And suddenly the phrase that his father loved to quote came flooding into his mind – only this time it made him far more uncomfortable than ever before.

He realized that he had just become more like his father, and less like the independent son which he had always believed himself to be.

Jacob reached Reilly's Pharmacy and went inside to retrieve his brother, who he found at the counter, leisurely sipping on his second phosphate. "Are you almost finished with that, Abraham? We should be going!"

"Almost!" the boy answered. "How did your meeting go with Rebecca Tilden, Jacob? Did you kiss her?" The mere mention of that word as part of the question caused the younger boy to giggle.

"That's none of your beeswax, Abraham," Jacob scolded.

"Which is as good as saying that you did kiss her," said Abraham, with a sly smile.

"You have a vivid imagination!" Jacob retorted.

"And you have a hard time facing reality," said the boy. "Any fool can tell that she wants to get her hooks into you."

"Abraham," said Jacob, with a perplexed voice, "you are almost four years younger than me. How can you know this kind of thing? You almost never get away from the farm."

"Frustrating, isn't it?" the boy answered. "And what makes you think that I never get away from the farm?"

Jacob cocked his head to one side. Was his brother telling him, in a very cryptic sort of way, that he had resorted to sneaking out of the house in order to go into the town? "Can we go, Abraham?"

Abraham downed the last few drops of the phosphate and got up from the counter. "Those were really delicious, Jacob. Thank you for your generosity."

"You're welcome…now…keep your mouth shut!"

It was now just a little past midday. The two boys exited the pharmacy and headed in the direction of Seminary Ridge. Jacob felt confident that, even if they were a little late, they would have the vast majority of the afternoon to assist with the building of the new house. The boys walked at a much faster pace than when they had walked to the town that morning. Jacob was thankful that Abraham had wisely chosen not to discuss any further his brother's involvement with the aforementioned Rebecca Tilden. In fact, Abraham had become usually quiet – so quiet that Jacob was able to detect the eerie silence.

"Is everything alright, Abraham?"

The boy shook his head. "No…I guess I shouldn't have had that second phosphate, Jacob. I think that I am going to be…."

The boy ran over to a split rail fence and stuck his head between the second and third railing, vomiting a purplish liquid onto the grass that was growing of the other side of the rails. In between retching, the boy could be heard imploring his Maker, in the form of several very emphatic cries of 'O My God!'

As the boy began to straighten back up, the episodes now subsiding, Jacob put his arm on his brother's back. "As they say, Abraham…too much of a good thing is never really a good thing!"

The boy nodded. "Now I understand what that one means, Jacob." "You have a few little stains on your shirt," Jacob observed.

"Oh, no!" exclaimed the boy. "Muti will have my head!"

"Possibly," said Jacob, "but if we remove our shirts in order to work on the house, perhaps she won't notice it…and perhaps it will come out in the wash."

"That's good, Jacob!"

The boys continued their walk back home. Even at a distance of several hundred yards from the house they could how hear the sounds of construction. Especially noticeable at this distance was the sound of hammering, but this sound was always peppered with the sound of men's voices.

"Sounds like they are making some progress," observed Jacob. "It sounds like they are already working on the framing of the house."

"Then we had best pick up our pace," answered Abraham, "or else we will miss out on some of the hardest work."

"Right!" agreed Jacob. The two boys started running toward their homestead.

Suddenly, as they rounded the final bend in the little dirt road that led to the Seminary, the framework of a large home loomed into view. Jacob stopped dead in his tracks, which caused Abraham to crash into his backside. "Look!" said Jacob, pointing out the rising home."

"Is that for us?" Abraham asked, his voice filled with amazement.

"It must be," exclaimed Jacob. "We are the only ones who live up here." The framework of the new house outlined a building that, when finished, would surpass the footprint of the original house by more than three times the area.

Not only was it two floors in height, but the roof line contained space for a full attic.

"They are building us….a mansion!" gasped Abraham.

Jacob nodded. "It certainly doesn't look plain."

"It could be plain, Jacob. Perhaps it is just big…and plain."

But what was equally as shocking to the older boy was the fact that the house was not merely framed…it had also been sided. Jacob could see that the windows were being installed, and that there was already a front door. Several men were sitting on the roof, hammering on the shingles

– and there was a small army of men building two stone chimneys – one on each end of the house. The sight of the new house, so near to a completed state, was so overwhelming for the boys that neither of them remembered to remove their shirt in order to perform the ruse on their mother, but rather both were drawn toward the property, as if they were being pulled by magnetism. The sight was so grand that neither could stand back to observe the building – they both had to see it up close.

As they rounded the southern corner of the house, Jacob spied his father, Ishmael. His father was standing by a large table, which had been brought out from the seminary, and now acted as a platform to hold the papers and plans for the house. An engineer from the army was standing next to his father, but it was immediately clear to Jacob that his father was clearing giving the commands.

They were building the house to his specifications.

The boys continued to circle the construction, taking in other features of the new, large house as they went. A team of about twenty soldiers were building the porch. This was not to be the same porch as they had known on the previous house; this was a large, deep wrap-around porch that extended around three quarters of the ground floor. The uprights — the columns holding up the roof above the veranda, were very simple, but sturdy. There was not a hint of 'gingerbread' to be found anywhere on the façade of the building — an element that was incredibly popular in modern building techniques. Normally, these features would be incorporated at the top of the supporting structure, creating a decorative top that would blend into the roof line. This decorative feature might also be found elsewhere, particularly around the doors and windows.

Jacob left Abraham to ponder the wonders of the new house so that he could speak with his father. He crossed the twenty yards of grass to where the construction table was standing. His father smiled at him when he saw him approaching, but quickly caught himself and changed his countenance to a more austere look, not wishing to seem overly ebullient in front of the Federal officer.

"Jakob! Es ist gut! Ja?" his father asked in German.

"Fati," Jacob replied, also in German, "you don't have to speak in German in front of the officer. I am sure that he knows that you are happy with the house."

"It is that easy to tell?"

"It is, as they say…written all over your face." The boy smiled up at his father. "The house is magnificent, Fati!" he said….in English. "My only concern is whether or not it is 'plain.'

"Why do you ask such a thing, Jakob?" his father answered, returning to English, as well. "Why are you suddenly so concerned with the traditions of our forefathers? Are you planning on sticking to the ways of the Ordnung?"

"I am not asking for myself, Fati," explained the boy, "I am simply confused. I am surprised that you are moving in this direction!"

"And why not?" asked his father. "Doesn't your mother deserve something better than what I have given her these past few years?"

Jacob heartily agreed. "Without a doubt, Fati! Has Muti come out to see the progress? Has she seen the house?"

Ishmael laughed at his son's ridiculous questions. "Of course she has been out! She has been out to supervise throughout the entire morning!"

"And does she approve?"

Once again his father laughed at Jacob's question. "Of course she approves! I have not seen your mother this happy in years!"

Jacob nodded, as if he understood why this was the case. The boy knew that the friction caused by the shunning at Paradise had put a strain on his parent's relationship, as well. They never came out and said so…not in so many words, but Jacob could tell that there was something wrong between them. His father became more demanding, and his mother seemed to retreat to a safe corner of the house. The house that had just burned down was appreciably smaller than their house in Lancaster County, and Sarah had very little room to hide. But Jacob also knew that his father had changed – and changed drastically within the last week. If there was any reason to design the new house to be larger than before, than Jacob figured that this was it. His father was giving back something to his mother which she had sacrificed for the good of the family; her home.

Still, Jacob found the desire to further needle his father. "How so, Fati?"

"How so?" his father answered. "The kitchen is twice the size as the one that we lost. The bedrooms are far more spacious. There is more space for storage, and a very large pantry. She loves the size of the porch…and there are two sitting rooms."

"Two sitting rooms?"

"Yes," replied Ishmael, "one upstairs, and one downstairs."

Jacob was surely impressed with the new dwelling, but was still confused over one major detail. "I don't quite understand, Fati. I expected to see the cellar dug out, and…maybe the side walls raised. How did they accomplish so much in just a few hours?"

"How?" his father answered. "It is like we Amish always say, Jakob… Many hands…"

"…make light work," finished Jacob. He had heard that adage many times before. He wasn't sure if it was an Amish man who had come up with that expression, but it might as well have been. The Amish had proven that proverb to be so every time that they raised a barn in a neighboring farm.

"And speaking of light work, Jakob," his father continued, "I believe that most of the construction on the house will be completed by the end of this day. Perhaps the only thing I will need you and Abraham for will be to paint and to varnish. That certainly lightened your workload, didn't it?"

"Yes, Fati." Jacob wondered if this had any kind of significance to it.

"So that would mean that your time on the farm does not seem to have a very long future."

"Excuse me, sir?" said Jacob.

"I won't really be in need of you, Jakob…as I had originally thought."

"What are you saying to me, Fati?" asked Jacob.

"I am saying that I think I can make do around here without you to help me," answered Ishmael, who knew that he was saying a great deal to the boy without really saying everything at once.

But Jacob would have none of the cryptic answer. He wanted his father to answer his outright. "I still don't understand, Fati. If you don't need me here, then what am I to do?"

Ishmael smiled at his first born and laughed. "You know very well what you are to do, my son. You must go with the General and get your education!"

"Truly?"

"Truly!" answered Ishmael. "I only hope that I can do the same for Abraham, when his time comes."

Jacob felt the sting of a tear in his eye as the reality of the situation became clearer to him. "I must tell, Muti," he said, which was only an excuse so that he did not have to let his father see him cry. He quickly turned and ran flat out toward the seminary building. About fifteen yards into his run, Jacob stopped suddenly – still facing the seminary. He turned around and ran back to Ishmael, throwing his arms around his father's body and embracing him. "Thank you, Fati. Thank you!"

Ishmael ran his fingers through his son's long blonde hair. "You deserve a chance, Jakob. We are all very proud of you, already…but you deserve a chance to do something truly great!"

"Truly?"

"Truly!" his father replied. "In truth, I have always wondered if we were doing you a disservice by preventing you from going out into the English world. Perhaps I just needed a good excuse to allow this to happen. Perhaps, after all that has transpired in the last week, that I am finally seeing…"

"…God's Will?"

Ishmael tightened his grip on his son. "Yes, Jakob…perhaps that is exactly what it is…God's Will. And who am I to argue with God's Will? And who am I to flatly deny the possibility that God has actually had a hand in this?" Jacob began to sob. "What is wrong, my son? Why do you weep?"

"I am ashamed, Father," the boy replied. "I have been so wrong about you, and for that I am ashamed!"

"Nonsense!" said Ishmael. "It is I who has been wrong. I am sure that it has not been easy living here with me these past few years; living within the Ordnung, as if we still belonged to the community. I have learned that life is too short to waste on such matters. You, and your brother, Abraham, represent my finest achievement in this world. It would be wrong to not share it with everyone – including the English!"

"Then I may tell the General that I can accept his offer?" asked Jacob.

"You certainly may do that…and with my blessing, Jakob."

Jacob, at last, let go of his father's waist. He knew that it was his first duty to tell his mother of this turn of events – just in the event that his father had seen fit to decide this on his own. His second stop would be a visit to General Sickles to tell him the good news, which would be closely followed by a visit with Becky Tilden. He glanced over toward the seminary. He could see his mother standing by the door leading into the kitchen. She waved at him, beckoning him to join her.

Jacob was instantly aware that his mother also was in on the secret. He started to walk toward her.

"Jakob?" his father called.

Jacob stopped immediately and spun around. "Yes, Fati?" "Isn't there something you are forgetting to do?"

Jacob hadn't an inkling what it was that his father was alluding to, and so shook his head.

"No, sir…I have no idea."

"Isn't there something you must build for the General?" The question startled Jacob. "What, sir?"

"You heard me, Jakob! Isn't there something you must build for the General?" Jacob searched the grounds for his brother. He would give him a beating if he found out that he had told his father about building the coffin for his amputated leg.

"Ah…mm…"

"I didn't quite understand you, Jakob!" his father said.

"How did you come to know that I was asked to build him something, Fati?" the boy asked, slowly returning a few paces toward his father.

"Jakob," Ishmael answered, patiently, "I asked you the question. Don't answer me by asking another question."

"I am sorry, Fati," Jacob answered. "I was just…surprised."

"Surprised?" asked his father. "Surprised to hear that I know all about it?" "Well….yes."

"This is a small town, my son," Ishmael said, his voice never rising above that of a gentle father. "There are very few secrets that stay secret very long." Then he gestured with his head toward some of the workmen and officers. "Besides…they all seem to know that you are building a coffin to hold the General's leg."

"What?" exclaimed Jacob. "They told you? I thought it was Abraham!" "Jakob….Jakob….did you not know that your brother would never betray your trust? Do you not better know your own brother than to suspect him of that?" Jacob looked toward the new house. He could see his brother still investigating the new structure, as if he was the foreman of the crew. He laughed to himself, and shook his head. "I suppose that is the truth."

"Your brother would like nothing better than to grow up to become you, Jakob," his father observed. "He idolizes you!"

"Sometimes he has an odd way of showing it," said Jacob.

"All younger brothers are like that," said Ishmael.

"So then after I say hello to Muti, I will begin the building of the little coffin for the General," answered Jacob.

Ishmael nodded. "Do a good job, Jakob. Look at all the man has done for our family! Do you need me to help you?"

"No, I don't think so," replied Jacob. "It seems easy enough…I just need to find some good wood to work with."

"There is a good supply of hardwood in the barn…some maple, oak, and cherry."

"That's good! Thank you, Fati."

Jacob turned and head back toward the seminary. He spent a few minutes speaking with his mother, who, true to her husband's words, was very much both knowledgeable and supportive of Jacob's prospects. Jacob had a few of his mother's freshly baked Snickerdoodles before heading out to the barn in search of hardwood and tools to build a sarcophagus to a human leg bone. He was sifting through the woodpile when he heard the barn door open.

"Do you need any help?"

Jacob turned around, but, judging from the pitch and timbre of the voice, he was already aware that it was Abraham.

"Sure!" he replied, smiling across the large space at his brother. "You can be a big help, Abraham."

The younger boy quickly closed the distance between the door and his older brother. "I watched you come in here, Jacob. I knew that you were going to build that coffin for General Sickles."

"How is it that everyone seems to know my business?"

"It's common knowledge around here, Jacob," said his brother. "You are famous! Didn't you realize that?"

"No!"

"Well…you are!" Abraham joined his brother searching through the pile of scrap wood. "Here's a good piece of maple, Jacob," he said, holding up a large piece of the expensive hardwood.

"That's good, but I am thinking that the coffin would be best made out of oak," replied his brother.

"Any particular reason why?" asked Abraham.

"No, not really," replied Jacob. "I like working with oak…more than with maple…and I think that this should be a better box than the typical pine box used for coffins. It is for the leg of a General…don't you think?"

"Hm," agreed Abraham, thoughtfully.

"Besides…I am thinking that I will stain and varnish the wood, so that will turn it darker and richer looking."

Abraham went back looking in the pile, finally finding a large piece of oak. The boy extracted the plank from the pile and held it up to the light, checking it for imperfections. "I think this piece looks good, Jacob."

Jacob turned away from his examination of a piece of poplar to see the board that his brother had found. "Right you are, Abraham. This will make a fine box!"

The brothers worked through the afternoon on the request from General Sickles, completing the woodwork by suppertime, and getting it sanded, stained, and varnished before quitting for the night. Jacob planned to get up early in the morning in order to apply another coat of varnish, figuring to add the black decorative cloth to the inside of the box in the early afternoon.

CHAPTER 32

Sickles Notebook

What the boys hadn't realized was that the General had another one of his secret agendas already in the making. Well before the recent battle, Sickles had learned, through his good friend, Edwin Stanton, the Secretary of War, that the Army was planning on establishing a Military Medical Museum in Washington, D.C. The new museum would hold specimens that would serve to educate the military on the effects of war on the body. Sickles had been privy to a memo that had circulated asking for donations of amputated limbs for this cause. At the time, Sickles had never anticipated that he might be donating his own severed leg, but he was also more than slightly aware of the great political ramifications of doing such a deed.

The leg of a General was more valuable than the leg of a Private.

But that night, on the eve of his being transported back to Washington, Sickles had even larger thoughts in his mind. He knew that the loss of his leg was due mainly to his own insubordination to the orders given by General Meade. He knew that his own personal stubbornness had led to the decimation of III Corps. But he also realized that the Federal Army had now won the battle; that they had done this in spite of his actions.

This would result in a stronger position for George Meade; a result that was not particularly pleasing for Sickles.

But Sickles was also aware that Meade had chosen not to destroy the rebel army when he had the chance. He knew that Meade had taken too much time to muster a counteroffensive against the Army of Northern Virginia.

Sickles desired to get back to Washington as quickly as possible. He needed to see Stanton, and he wouldn't mind seeing the President, as well. He wanted to strike out at Meade before Meade could bring charges of insubordination against him. Sickles knew that timing, in this case, was everything.

General Daniel E. Sickles spent his final day on the Spangler farm planning his case. He started by writing notes to himself in a journal. He jotted down his own account of the battle, especially the details of the second day.

As he had in a bygone day, Sickles now had Meade in his crosshairs, just as he had with Phillip Barton Key. He really didn't have a desire to see the General dead, as he had with Key, but he didn't feel that it was out of bounds to see to it that the General's reputation as a strategist, leader of men, or Commander of an army was destroyed. He had the political contacts to make this happen. He and Edwin Stanton were very close. He had also had several audiences with the President, who had commented that Sickles' brash nature was more in line with what the Army of the Potomac needed than the genteel refinement of the gentlemen from West Point.

But Sickles also knew that timing was everything. If Lincoln had removed Joe Hooker from command after Chancellorsville for losing an extremely hard-fought and closely contested battle, then Sickles would expect Lincoln to vilify Meade for not seeing to the total destruction of the Army of Northern Virginia while he had his chance. On the other hand, Meade had won the day, but in the end he had done so because of General Lee's decision to engage so many of his men in that one final, futile assault on Cemetery Ridge.

Sickles found a blank page in his journal. He took his pencil and drew a line from the top to the bottom of the page, then labeled each column with the headings "For" and "Against." He was, in essence, coming up with his own version of a friends and enemies list, and he was attempting to predict where his other Corps Commanders would ante up in the debate that would rage in Washington. Would they be on his side, or on the side of George Meade? Or perhaps a better question would be…would they support the removal of Meade as Commanding General, or show their loyalty to the man? Sickles knew that some of the Corps Commanders might think that Sickles was unfit to command, as he had heard rumors circulating around the hospital tent, mostly when those whispering had thought he was asleep. But that didn't mean that those same Corps Commanders might not actually defend Sickles if the end result was the removal of Meade from command.

It was, purely and simply…politics. And politics is what Sickles did better than any other general in the field.

He began his list with General Winfield Scott Hancock, quickly writing his name down at the top of the column marked, "Against." If Meade had one strong supporter, it was Hancock. But Sickles had also heard that Hancock had been badly wounded on the final day of the battle, and that his status was still unknown. Remove Meade from command of the army, and Lincoln might well appoint Hancock to take his place. That, in Sickles' eyes, would be even worse.

Sickles turned to the "For" column and quickly jotted down a few names, including Joe Hooker and George McClellan. He didn't particularly like McClellan; he was, in many ways, the same type of general as Meade. He was arrogant and self-assured – and in this way was closer to the demeanor of Sickles than anyone else. But he had also lost quite a few battles – and was trounced by Bobby Lee. He was even threatening to run against Lincoln in the next Presidential election.

Hooker was his closest ally within the military, but he also had a run of bad luck on the battle field. Sickles drew a circle around both of the names, leaving them for future consideration. What he really wanted to find were allies that hadn't put themselves in a position where their own actions could be so scrutinized. He also needed men whose own personal hubris was their own ambition to command the army. In other words, he needed to find the officers who thought that they could have done a better job of command than George Meade.

He wrote down the name of Oliver Howard in the "For" column. Sickles knew that Howard had been passed over for the command of the army, and thus…was a malcontent. Howard was one of the most senior officers on the field the first day of the battle, and yet, after the sudden death of General Reynolds, command of the field was given to Hancock, rather than to Howard. The situation on the battlefield was starting to dissolve while the two generals argued over rank and seniority. But in the end, Hancock took command – and this command had been given by Meade.

He also wrote General Slocom's name down in the "For" column. Slocom had gained a reputation for being slow to react to battlefield pressures, earning him the nickname, "Slow Come." He was, however, the most senior officer on the field.

Sickles placed a question mark next to his name. He wasn't really sure where this naturally reticent man would stand when the chips were down.

He wasn't at all sure about General Sedgewick. Sedgewick was well-liked by his men, although he really wasn't much of a field general. As Sickles began to mull over his list in more detail, he realized that he was not looking at a list of detractors, as much as a group of malcontents and nay-sayers.

Then there was the Cavalry Commander, General Pleasonton – a man whose very name was a contradiction in terms. Pleasonton could actually be used, if Sickles could arrange it. Pleasonton was very young, and very ambitious. He was the youngest Major General in the Army of the Potomac, and was also well known for his aggressive commanding style – a style which sometimes bordered on the foolhardy, and often resulted in disaster, but Sickles also knew that Lincoln was more in favor of this type of leadership than the conservative approach favored by so many of his senior generals. Sickles could make use of the horse soldier, especially if the young man had an ambitious eye turned toward the command of the army.

There were other generals to consider, as well. Abner Doubleday, a veteran commander in several battles, had also suffered the same indignity as Howard on the first day of the battle, having fought hard to hold the untenable tract of land all throughout that first day. He had first taken command of the field upon the death of his Corps Commander, General Reynolds, but, at the end of the day, when his battle-weary corps was forced to drop back to Cemetery Ridge, was relieved of his command by General Hancock.

Sickles also wanted to confer with General Warren, the chief engineer of the army. It had been Warren who had noticed that the Federal left flank was exposed and undefended on the second day of the battle – especially the small mound of rock known as "Sugar Loaf Hill." He had noticed this oversight while standing on that same said hill, which also meant that he had a good view of the Federal center of the line – the same position that Meade would order Sickles to hold. Sickles quickly turned a page of his journal and jotted down a few words to describe his memory of that position. It had been Sickles opinion that Meade's positioning of his Corps had put him in an awkward place in the line, and that, instead of holding the 'high ground,' as the rest of the army enjoyed, his corps was now being forced to shoot uphill at the enemy. Sickles decided to abandon this position in favor of taking a higher terrain several hundred yards to the front of the Federal line – a move which allowed his corps to be attacked on both sides by the Confederates.

Sickles wrote down the single word, "BRAVERY?"

It was at this moment that Sickles decided upon his defense. He would have to admit that he had made a bad decision – that he was, in fact, insubordinate. But he would plead the case that his position, given by Meade, was also a bad decision; that his corps would not be able to defend itself, under the circumstances. There was only one choice, and that choice demanded something that was still held in high regard.

Valor!

By charging forward, ahead of the Federal line, Sickles and the men of III Corps, showed the rest of the army their fighting spirit; their aggressive and resolute nature. They had showed them bravery in the face of fire.

They had showed them real valor!

If, as he had conjectured, both positions were bad and could not be defended, then the only aspect that made them different was the bravery and daring that III Corps had displayed in the Peach Orchard and the Wheat Field on the hot, humid 2 July, 1863.

And what better proof than the small box which he planned to carry to Washington and bring to the office of the Secretary of War, and, hopefully, to the office of the President of the United States?

A box that contained his own severed, shattered right leg bone.

Sickles put the journal onto his lap and sat back, taking a long pull on his cigar. The vision of his opening up that box for Lincoln brought a smile to his face. That would be the ticket to success, he thought.

Meade….poor General George Meade, he lamented.

Poor General Meade didn't have such a box.

He still had both of his legs!

CHAPTER 33

Moving Up Day

Jacob finished the little coffin for General Sickles in the early afternoon of the seventh day after the battle. It was 10 July, 1863.

The last part of the process was lining the inside of the bottom and top of the box with black material. Even though it was 'fancy,' Jacob decided that he would use a black fabric with a silken sheen on it, so he choose a piece of taffeta which he picked up at the millenary store while he was waiting for the final coat of varnish to dry.

The crew had returned to the seminary in order to complete the work on the new Zook homestead. Most of this work was finishing work; painting, masonry, laying the hardwood floor, installing the bannisters, and things of this nature. General Birney had stopped by to check on the progress around noon. It was at that time that Jacob found out from the officer that General Sickles was scheduled to leave Gettysburg in the early evening by ambulance – perhaps around five o'clock. Jacob became immediately anxious to finish the general's requested box and deliver it to him. The boy had stained the outside of the box a dark oak color, and had, true to his word, put on two coats of varnish. As noontime passed, Jacob checked the box to see if it had dried sufficiently to work on the lining, but unfortunately, the varnish was still a little sticky. The sun had come out very strongly since about ten that morning, so Jacob decided to place the box on a table which was standing in the yard of the seminary to allow it to bake in the sunlight. He used this drying time to enjoy his lunch.

He returned to find the coffin almost totally dry by around one thirty, although there were still a few tacky spots. He enlisted his mother's assistance to lay in the lining of black taffeta; she was far better at gathering the tufts of lining, especially around the four corners of the box.

The entire project was finished around two thirty.

Jacob packed up the grim package and headed back toward the town, his destination once again being the Spangler Farm. He walked with a quick pace, hoping that he would not run into anyone that he knew; anyone that he thought might distract him, or delay him from delivering his commission. He especially did not want to bump into Rebecca Tilden.

He managed to get past the intersection of the Emmittsburg Pike and Baltimore Street without stopping along the way. He did speak to several members of the community, who hailed him as he passed by, or offered a word of praise for his actions during the recent battle. But that was the limit of his interaction with the people of the town, and within that limitation was the fact that he had not run into any member of the Wade/McClellan family – or any of the Tildens.

As he entered the property belonging to the Spangler family, he heard a male voice call out to him from across a small pasture. Jacob was sure that it was one of the Spanglers, but he couldn't be certain which one… so he simply waved back and kept moving toward the large hospital tent.

It was now almost three thirty in the afternoon.

Jacob greeted the guards outside of the tent; men who he had come to know by sight over the course of the past week, or so. One of the guards pulled back the tent flap and allowed him to enter without any formality. Jacob quickly entered the tent, keeping his head down and focused on the business at hand, his handicraft tucked neatly under his right arm. He had only walked about twenty paces from the tent flap when he noticed that General Sickles was not in his usual bed. He said nothing to anyone, and didn't even try to ask the orderly stationed in the tent if there was a problem with the General. Instead, Jacob quickened his pace and continued forward toward the empty bed.

As he drew closer to his destination, it didn't take a keen eye to discover that the General's personal affects had removed from the area; in fact, there was no trace of General Daniel Edgar Sickles anywhere to be found.

It was at this point that a knot formed in the base of Jacob's stomach.

"If you want to catch the General, you had better move quickly," said a voice from behind him.

Jacob turned to see his old friend, Doctor Sim. "Doctor! Is the General still here?"

"Yes, but not for long," replied the doctor. "They are loading him into the ambulance heading for Washington."

"But I was told that he was leaving around five o'clock," said Jacob.

"And that, my boy, is how the Army always works," answered the doctor. "Hurry up…but not too fast." Sim glanced at the box which the boy held tightly under his arm. "I see that you have made his…box. He will be very happy to see that you have done this for him."

"Does he have his leg with him?

"Yes," replied Sim. "He has it wrapped in a blanket. He wasn't sure that you would make it back here in time – but you did."

Jacob nodded. There was a brief silence while each man decided what to say next. "Where is he, Doctor?"

Sim shook his head, as though groggy. "Oh! I am very tired, Jacob. I need more help in this field hospital. I think I performed over twenty amputations this morning alone."

Jacob nodded politely…again. It wasn't that he didn't care about amputations, but the fact remained that he needed to find the ambulance that was taking the General away from Gettysburg. "I am sorry for your troubles, Doctor Sim, but could you tell me if the ambulance has left yet?"

"Have I not made that clear to you?" asked the groggy Sim. "Yes, he is still here. The ambulance is just out back. The General will be happy to see you, Jacob…which is good, because he is in an otherwise cantankerous mood." The doctor pointed toward the opening at the rear of the tent – the direction in which Jacob should move.

"Thank you, Doctor," replied Jacob, already moving toward the open flap. "I am sorry that I cannot stay to assist you today…but…if you are still in need of an assistant…I can be available."

"Thank you, Jacob," answered the surgeon. "I may take you up on your offer. Good surgical assistants are hard to find."

Jacob Zook crossed the expanse of the surgical tent in only a few seconds, reaching the opening in time to see the ambulance as it began to pull away. As he exited the hospital tent he passed several large piles of rotting amputated limbs – arms, legs, hands, and feet. The older piles – the ones that were created during the three days of the battle – were infested with flies and maggots. The fresher piles were in varying degrees of decomposition, depending upon their time in the sun and rain. Jacob took notice of the refuse, but kept moving toward the ambulance, which was now beginning to gain some speed. Even still, the ruts in the ground created by the rain that fell in the days after the battle, which had then hardened in the days that followed, made the going very slow for the large wagon. Jacob was easily able to catch up to the back end of the last ambulance.

"General Sickles?" the boy called out, hoping that Sickles was in that final ambulance.

"Is that you, Jacob?" answered a voice from within.

It was Sickles.

"Yes, Sir," answered Jacob, trotting behind the ambulance.

"Stop this wagon!" thundered the General. There was no immediate response from the driver, a private in the medical corps – an orderly. "This is Major General Daniel E. Sickles," the General thundered again, "and I am giving you a direct order to stop this damned ambulance….or by the heavens above…I will have you shot!"

The wagon immediately slowed to a stop.

An orderly hopped down from the front of the wagon and scurried around to the back. "This boy is here to see me off," yelled the General from inside. "Open up the gate and let him in."

"But General," pleaded the private, "we must keep up with the rest of the train."

"Don't worry, Private," Sickles answered, a bit more calmer than before, "I will take full responsibility for this unscheduled stop…and I won't have you shot, either."

"Thank you, Sir," replied the orderly, who then unlashed the gate on the rear of the ambulance. After the gate was let down, the orderly pulled back the canvas covering to allow Jacob access to the interior of the wagon. Sickles was not alone. There were about a half dozen other men inside the ambulance, however, they were all officers. This was an ambulance reserved for wounded officers.

"Come in, Jacob," said Sickles, his voice returning to normalcy. Jacob climbed up the gate and into the ambulance, taking care to avoid stepping on any of the other wounded men. Sickles was sitting up, but was located in the very front of the wagon, furthest from the tail gate.

"Is that my coffin under your arm, Jacob?" the General asked as Jacob approached.

"It is, sir," the boy replied, taking the box from beneath his arm and offering it to the General.

Sickles received the coffin with his open hands. "You made this by yourself, Jacob?"

Jacob nodded. "Mostly, General…I had a little help from Abraham."

"This is a remarkable piece of carpentry and craftsmanship," Sickles said.

"What kind of wood is this?"

"It is Oak, sir."

"Oak? Not Pine?"

"Oak, sir" answered the boy. "I thought you might appreciate a better grade of hardwood."

The General examined the exterior of the box a little closer, running his fingers along the grain. "And right you were about that, my boy! This box is fitting for the leg of a General!" He removed the cover, which was sanded down to fitting snugly over the bottom. The General let out a slight gasp when the tufted black taffeta appeared before his eyes. "Jacob!"

Jacob thought he saw Sickles' eyes begin to brim with tears at the sight of the elegantly crafted interior of the coffin. "Is it…satisfactory, General?"

"Satisfactory?" asked Sickles. "It is…perfect!" Sickles leaned to one side and picked up an army blanket. Unfolding the blanket, he lifted out his right legbone, now just a shattered piece of bone, the fragments of the shell still imbedded in the ivory.

"General!" Jacob exclaimed, shocked that the muscle, sinew and skin had all been removed.

"I had it….cleaned up a bit," said Sickles, noticing the boy's reaction. "I didn't want my rotting flesh falling off the bone for all the ages to see.

Besides, now you can see the damage caused by the cannonball. Here, open the box for me."

Jacob held the bottom section of the coffin, while the General gently lifted his shattered right leg and placed it in the box. Sickles then replaced the cover onto the coffin, closing in the appendage for the journey ahead.

He smiled up at the boy. "Thank you, Jacob. You have shown me a great deal of kindness and…mercy. More than most people would have shown me….have shown me…and probably a great deal more than I deserve." "I was happy to do this for you, sir," the boy replied.

The General cleared his throat, the emotion having caught hold there.

"So…how is the new house, Jacob? Is it…satisfactory?"

Jacob smiled at the General. "It is…perfect! I cannot thank you enough for all that you have done for my family."

"Yes…your family," replied Sickles, a bit embarrassed. "I really didn't do it for your family, Jacob. I did it…for you."

"I realize that also, sir," said Jacob very humbly. "You did it so that I could leave my family to pursue my education."

"Yes…I did…I must confess that you are correct."

"And now….I can," responded Jacob, his mouth broadening to a smile.

"What?"

"I am free to leave Gettysburg to live, as my father says, 'among the English.'" Sickles beamed with happiness. "This is wonderful news, Jacob! This will help speed me on the road to my recovery."

"I hope so, sir," replied the boy.

"You must come to Washington, Jacob," Sickles said, his voice becoming animated. "You must come as soon as possible."

"Yes, sir."

"Can you come next week?"

"Next week, General?"

"Yes," answered Sickles, his brain in overdrive as he thought of the way to proceed. "Yes…in about a week. I will send word for you to come, and where you should stay…and where I am at, because I am not really very sure at this moment."

"Yes, sir."

"We must prepare you for entrance exams, and write letters of application…and decide on a college…and find you a dwelling…and…well…we shall be very busy."

"Yes, sir."

"Is that all you can say, boy?" asked the General. "Yes, sir?" "Yes, sir, it is!" said Jacob, but quickly added, "and thank you!"

"This will be my pleasure, Jacob! So go home, get your affairs in order…" "My affairs, sir?" questioned Jacob.

Sickles shook his head. "I suppose that is a strange word to use. But you probably get the gist of it, anyway, don't you?"

"Yes…I suppose I do."

"Wait for my instructions. I will send information…and a train ticket. You will only need to get to Harrisburg. Is that clear?"

"Absolutely, General," Jacob answered.

CHAPTER 34

The Journey Begins

The workmen from the Federal Army, under the supervision of III Corps Commander, General Birney, finished up their work at the Zook residence on the following day. It wasn't so much of a case that their work was completed, but rather that Ishmael Zook had taken the stance that any further design on the part of the soldiers, be they woodworkers, masons, carpenters, and the like – would probably be in opposition to his concept of what a 'plain' house should look like. Even so, Ishmael had acquiesced to certain allowances, for Sarah's sake. The house was about as modern as any house in 1863, and the soldiers had worked, albeit quickly, to bring running water into the house. Moreover, in addition to the four fireplaces that could be found in the major rooms of the home, the workers had also installed a furnace in the cellar that would centrally heat the house – a very modern convenience for that day. The furnace would burn coal – which was plentiful, especially in Pennsylvania.

Most of the rooms in the house had already been painted, and Sarah Zook had supervised the selection of color, but even these tended to stray a bit from the average Amish color palette. The final details of the home would be left to the Zook family, and that was just fine with Ishmael, although he certainly was not ungrateful for the generous gift that the soldiers, and, in particular, that General Sickles had given to them.

But Ishmael was also more than aware that the General's largest gift was still in the making.

Ten days after delivering the small wooden coffin to the departing General Sickles a Federal courier appeared on the doorstep of the newly rebuilt Zook manse. The courier bore a letter from the General, addressed to Jacob – but with references to his parents throughout. Included with the letter was a train ticket from Harrisburg to Washington. The ticket was for July 25th, at 4:00 in the afternoon.

After reading it, Jacob placed the railroad ticket to the side. He gently opened the letter, which had been encased in its own envelope. As this was not, in any way, a clandestine maneuver on his part, he read aloud the contents of the letter while his parents and brother were in the room.

"Dear Jacob,

I hope that this letter finds you and your family healthy and happy. I have been told that the Zook family is now situated comfortably in their new home, and this information does nothing than to please me a great deal.

I have been making inquiries on your behalf, Jacob, at several institutions of higher learning. I have met with great success at some, and some resistance at others. Most of the resistance stems from the fact that you have had very little formal education up until this point in your life – a point which I have rejected quite enthusiastically. Even though you may not wish to attend these schools, for whatever your own reasons, I bristle at the thought that they can reject you without due process – so I continue the fight. I am sure that, once you have made the trip to the east, that we can conquer these nay-sayers with a personal visit to their campuses.

I have been in contact with the admission departments of some of the oldest and most respected universities and colleges in the country with you in mind, sir. I, personally, have rejected several – as I think is my right, under the circumstances. I would not have you attending William and Mary, or the University of Virginia – even though both have ties with our third President, Thomas Jefferson. Besides, the war is still raging strongly in the South, so I suppose the point is moot. I also will not have you considering any school in Baltimore, as the city is still a hotbed of violence and anti- government sentiment.

I think that your first choices may be the University of Pennsylvania in Philadelphia, or The College of New Jersey in Princeton, simply because of their proximity to Gettysburg – but I would caution you that you not rush to judgment for this reason. Harvard and Yale still enjoy excellent reputations, as does Columbia, Brown and Dartmouth. I personally like Dartmouth a great deal – but as it is practically in Canada, you may not wish to attend that school.

My leg is very much on the mend. The wound does not seep as much as it had, and I have been fortunate to have avoided the puss of gangrene.

We have much to do when you get here, Jacob. I will have my representative meet you at Union Station on the evening of the 25th. I expect that the train will arrive in the Capitol around nine o'clock.

Your obedient servant,

Daniel E. Sickles, Major General, United States Army of the Potomac

Jacob slowly lowered the letter. He looked over toward his parents and then to his brother. It was now official, so to speak; he was about to leave for his education among the 'English."

His mother spoke up first. "Well, Jakob…do you know of these schools?" "Most of them, Muti," Jacob replied. "They are all fine schools. Most of them were founded by various forms of the Protestant Church."

"But will they allow an Amish boy there, Jakob?" Ishmael asked.

Jacob had been wondering the same thing. He wasn't sure if that was the 'resistance' that Sickles had mentioned in the letter, or if it meant something else. "I don't think that they would reject me because I am Amish, Fati. No…I don't think they would do such a thing!"

"Still," his mother interjected, "if it was up to me I would see you go to the school most distant from this dreadful war. If we can have battles in Pennsylvania, then there can be battles in New Jersey and in New York. Perhaps you might like to look into that Dartmouth school?"

"I promise you that I will consider it, Muti," said Jacob, smiling at his mother's concern for his welfare. This, of course, was completely ironic, considering how involved Jacob had been with the war at the beginning of the month.

"This gives you about a week to prepare for your journey, Jakob," added his father. "We need to go into the town to get you some new clothes."

"New clothes, Fati?"

"English clothes, my son," Ishmael said, nodding proudly. "We don't want you going to the English Capitol looking like a farmboy!"

"But I am a farmboy, Fati!"

"Yes, you are," answered his father, "but I have learned, in my dealings with the English, that one's looks are very important. You will be judged by how you look, and by what you wear. This is a very sad commentary, I know, but this is just the way things are. So…we shall get you a trunk of new clothes to take with you to Washington."

"And won't Rebecca Tilden be surprised when she sees you dressed like that?" teased Abraham.

"And why not?" scolded his mother. "Why shouldn't your brother look like a proper gentleman, Abraham?"

"I was only joking, Muti," answered a contrite younger brother. "Joke or no joke," Sarah replied, "your brother will have his chance." "What do you mean, Muti?" asked Jacob.

"We shall have this Rebecca Tilden to our home for dinner…perhaps a night or two before you leave."

Jacob felt all the air inside of him leave his body. "I don't understand!"

"Of course you do," said Ishmael. "We are going to ask the young lady to join us here for dinner."

Jacob was confused. "But why would you do that?"

"Why?" asked his mother. "Because it will mean a great deal to you if we do." "You may pass along the invitation to her, Jakob," added his father.

"Are you telling me to invite a non-Amish girl for dinner at our house?" Jacob asked again, just to be absolutely certain.

"Of course we are," confirmed his mother. "Why else would we mention it to you?"

Jacob was bewildered. He had secretly hoped that this day would come, and now that it had, he was more confused than ever. "What time and day should I tell her?" he innocently asked, although this wasn't really the concern foremost on his mind. The fact remained that he was more than a little concerned about how the girl would react to his 'real' life. He was concerned that she would come to understand just how odd the Zook family really was.

"I think that Saturday would be best, and at about six o'clock," answered his mother. "Jakob? Is everything alright? You look a little strange."

"Shocked might be more appropriate, Muti," he said.

And thus it came to pass that slowly, but surely, the Zook family began the process that would complete their assimilation into the 'English' culture. There had been events in which they had actively played a role – the most significant being Ishmael's marriage to Sarah, which had eventually resulted in the shunning of the Zook family from Paradise – a more modern telling of the expulsion from the Garden of Eden. One might argue that, had this series of events not happened, the rest of the story of their lives would not have taken the decided turn that it had. But, then again, that same argument can be made for almost every life on the planet. From that point on, the Zooks – particularly Ishmael – had been pushed at every juncture. They had closer contact with the outside living in Gettysburg – including the influence of the German Lutheran clergy. They were forced to live outside of their homogeneous community, and thus had to deal more closely with the 'English.' But in 1863, in the little town of Gettysburg, Pennsylvania, their lives were brought to the brink of being ripped asunder, as war came to their village.

Now, with peace returning to the hamlet, the Zook family was already coming to grips with the change and, for the first time in several years, understanding that their entire way of life was no longer as staid as they once had thought it to be. But Jacob could still reply the he was 'shocked' by the revelations posed by his parents, because the change had come so suddenly to them – transforming their thoughts and belief system in less than one month's time.

Many of the local residents organized burial parties, consisting of small teams of men and some women, who devoted many hours during the weeks and months that followed the battle to bury the dead. In many cases, the unfortunate souls were buried right where they had fallen, and the work was done, for the most part, ignominiously; very few of the graves were distinguished with any identifying marks, other than a small pile of stones. Almost all of the bodies were buried without much pomp, but were always finished with a small prayer. Almost all of the bodies were buried just as they had fallen – without the luxury of a coffin.

The day after the Zook homestead was completed by Birney's men, Sarah Zook decided that she would join one of these burial parties. Her husband, Ishmael, was still too busy with the details of the new house to be included in the grisly work, but Sarah didn't really mind. When the direction of the wind changed a bit, she could already easily smell the stench of the rotting corpses. She arose early that day, collecting several of the Lutheran Seminarians to assist her in the tasks for the day. As she returned to the new house accompanied by the young men, she was surprised to see her first-born waiting for her, standing on the porch.

"Jakob? You are already awake?" she observed.

"Ja, Mama," he answered. "I thought I might go with you today. I think you will be shocked by what you see."

Sarah nodded to her son. He had been perceptive on that account. Sarah wasn't sure that she was up to the grim task ahead of her. She gazed at her boy. "Is there something in particular you have in mind, Jakob?"

"Ja, Mama," he said. "I want to find a friend of mine."

Sarah knew better than to question Jacob any further. He had already related quite a few of his battlefield experiences to his family. The young man stepped off of the porch and headed toward the barn, gesturing along the way to one of the seminarians that he should come along, as well. He reappeared moments later, a pine coffin being carried by the two young men.

As he approached his mother, he said, "I built this last evening. I built one for the General. That one wasn't very plain…but this one is." And with that said, the burial detail moved down the ridge.

Having spent the better part of the last two years roaming over some of the lush Pennsylvania farmland in Gettysburg, Jacob knew his way around the terrain – but the sights and odors of this familiar land had become foreign to him. The landmarks that he had grown to love, were either destroyed or altered beyond recognition. The wheatfield was no more; neither was the peach orchard. As far as the eye could see, the ground was littered with dead soldiers, both blue and gray. After about a fifteen minute walk, Jacob instructed the party to turn to the right and head down into the valley. He carefully eyed up distinguishing marks to his own rear; noticing the spot where he had dragged the hapless Major Winslow to safety. They walked past the wheatfield and into the open plain.

"Perhaps they have already taken his body away?" asked his mother.

"That is unlikely, Mama," Jacob replied, gently. "He would be the last one, in any case." They walked further into the open field. They were now well past the concentration of dead Confederates that had been killed in that last bloody charge on the third day. They were even out past where General Sickles' men had meet with disaster on the second day. Jacob looked forward. The tree line, where he had been captured just days before, now loomed closer to them. "We are getting closer," he observed. He side-stepped around a dead horse. The horse was still saddled and wore a gray blanket under the saddle. It had been a Confederate officer's horse. The hot weather had bloated the animal to the point of bursting.

"There!" shouted Jacob, pointing at a body just several yards away.

As if the body was naturally capable of such contortions, the lifeless body of Bobbie McLean sat as if he was posed in prayer. He seemed to be kneeling, but his upper body was crumpled over his knees. As if on cue, the seminarians brought their shovels to the ground to prepare the grave. "Stop!" ordered Jacob. "He cannot be buried here!"

"Jakob?" soothed his mother.

"No, Mama! He was my friend. I don't want him buried in such an angry place!"

"Where then, Jakob?"

"Near the grove of trees by our house, Mama." His mother calmly nodded his assent and the seminarians began the task of loading the poor boy into the coffin. His body was still in the effects of rigor mortis, but they were able to load Bobbie McLean into the casket. Jacob, very much affected by this scene, was able to find the rebel cap that had earned Bobbie the bullet to his head. He lovingly placed the cap in the coffin with the body.

Two days later Jacob appeared at the local haberdashery, accompanied by the rest of his nuclear family. Even though the Amish folk kept to themselves, for the most part, that had never stopped them from dealing with the 'English,' in fact, many had become quite wealthy because of it. This wasn't quite true for the Ishmael Zook family, because much of Ishmael's personal wealth was sacrificed during the move from Paradise to Gettysburg. Ishmael didn't consider himself as wealthy as many of his brethren, but he still did have quite a bit of the 'English' currency in his pocket. Most of this income came from woodworking; building tables, chairs, cabinets, and the like – such as he had for the Spangler Farm.

Now it was time to put all of that good hard-earned money to use.

The four members of the Zook family entered the men's clothing shop owned by Gettysburg resident Silas Green. Green, who was, in actuality descended from the English, greeted the family at the door and ushered them into his store. He had recognized Jacob at sight; the boy's fame around the town was undeniable. The manner in which the family dressed would have given him more than enough information to allow him to make that assumption, however. There were no other Amish families in the Gettysburg area.

"What may I do for you today?" asked Green, bowing from the waist and directing them toward the racks of trousers.

Jacob looked to his father to speak, however his father was too busy taking in the strange surroundings. "Fati," the boy began, speaking in

German so that Green wouldn't know just how uncomfortable they were, "the shopkeeper would like to know how he can assist us."

Ishmael seemed bewildered by all of the ready-to-wear clothing. No self-respecting Amish man would be found dead in any of this! The jackets and pants had buttons on them – not hook and eye. The shirts were very brightly colored, and some even had a bit of lace trim on them. Not very plain at all! There were undergarments laying out in the open, ready to be selected and purchased, a fact that both Ishmael and Sarah found upsetting.

His father waved him off. "You just find whatever you need, Jakob. We will wait for you to finish."

Jacob turned back to face Silas Green, and switched his language to English. "I need to purchase several sets of clothing for school, sir. I will be leaving for Washington in a few days."

As if to belabor the obvious, Green asked, "What is wrong with the clothes on your back?"

"Outside of the fact that they are getting very worn, that I don't quite fit in the trousers any more, and that they seem to cry aloud that I am Amish….nothing at all," proclaimed Jacob, with a smile.

Green's face immediately fell, as he realized that he may have insulted his newest customers. Jacob was nonplussed by the shopkeeper's reaction and pressed onward. "I will need several sets of trousers, several shirts… perhaps about five will do, two waist coats, two vests, some hose, a few neckties, and a nice hat."

Green looked from the boy to the father, as if to ask tacitly whether the boy was, in fact, in charge of all of these purchases. As if to answer the man's unspoken question, Ishmael Zook simply smiled at the man and nodded his head. "All of this will take some time, sir," Green replied, speaking again to Jacob. "Would you like some chairs so that your family can be comfortable?"

That notion had not entered Jacob's mind until that very moment, but it certainly did make a great deal of sense. He quickly turned, stuffing his right hand into his trouser pocket. "Abraham…why don't you take Fati and Muti over to Reilly's Drugstore?"

"We are not sick, Jakob," his mother replied.

"I know, Muti," Jacob answered. "Abraham will show you what it is to enjoy a cherry phosphate. Won't you, Abraham?" Jacob pulled out his hand and produced several coins, promptly handing them to his brother. Abraham immediately understood the implication; Jacob didn't want his parents hovering over him, perhaps questioning his choice of garment or color…or fashion.

"That is a wonderful idea, Jacob," his brother said, winking at Jacob. The younger boy took his mother's hand and led her toward the shop door. "Wait until you see what they can make, Muti! Last time I was there I had two sodas…which were delicious...but I drank them so quickly…because they were so delicious…that I spuked them out on the sidewalk."

"What?" exclaimed his mother. "And this is what you want me to do?" "No!" replied the boy. "You will only have to drink one!"

The rest of Jacob's family left the store, with Abraham leading his mother, and with his father, Ishmael, bringing up the rear.

"Good," said Jacob to Silas Green, "now we can get down to business." "I see," replied Green, who really didn't 'see.'

"I will also need at least a week's worth of suitable undergarments," Jacob said, in a suitably lower voice.

"I understand, sir," replied Green, nodding his head.

"I will also need some toiletries, and perhaps a clothing accessory, or two," continued Jacob.

"Will you be away during the winter months, sir?" inquired Green. Jacob gave it some thought. "Probably….yes, I imagine so. Why?"

"Because you might find it necessary to have an overcoat, and perhaps some gloves…oh, and don't forget the long johns."

"Good thinking!" replied Jacob. "We had better get going with this order, though. I can't imagine how many cherry phosphates my brother will be able to pump into my parents before they will return."

Green nodded in agreement. "Shall we begin with the basics…the trousers?" Silas Green escorted Jacob to a table filled with neatly folded men's pants. "I would say that a young man of your build would do very well with a pair of these Fall Front Trousers. I might suggest black, as you will probably want at least a black waist or tailcoat to match."

"Will I look too much like some English dandy?" asked Jacob.

"Where will you be wearing these clothes?"

"At the university," Jacob replied. "I don't know which one quite yet…maybe Harvard or Yale."

"Very good, sir," answered Green. "If that is the case, then with this style you would fit right in. I would suggest a tailcoat and a Griffith Frock Coat." He brought Jacob over to the wall of the store that had a clothes pole filled with men's coats.

"Here are the frock coats, sir. Why don't you try one on for size?" "Yes…thank you," said Jacob. "I like that one right there."

"Oh, yes," said Green. "That is a popular color this year. This is called heather green." He took the jacket off of a hanger and helped Jacob into it. "This one fits you very well…first time out."

"I really like it," said the boy, "but I am not sure my parents will approve of the color. Do you have one that is a little more…plain?"

"I have another one right here, sir," answered Green. He took down another frock coat, which seemed very much like the other jacket, except that it was a light gray color.

"That seems better," replied Jacob, "but I really like the other one. Let's keep the green one to the side, and then see which one they pick – although it will probably be the gray one."

"I understand, sir," said Green, taking both coats to the sales counter. "Now…about the tailcoat. You may want your basic black, however there are also some coats in Burgundy, Royal Blue, Dark Green….and, oh….look at this one!"

Green pulled a striking tailcoat off of the rack. It was a fanciful fabric, to Jacob's untrained eyes, and yet…it somehow appealed to him. The fabric was a golden tone brocade, with black lapels. "I can see by your expression that this coat meets with your approval."

"Perhaps," agreed Jacob, "but it might be a bit much for me right now. I think that if I am going to wear anything other than black, it should be a solid color."

Green re-hung the brocade coat back on the hanger. He seemed visibly disappointed that he wasn't going to sell this audacious coat. "What about shirts, sir?"

"Shirts?" asked Jacob. He looked around the shop, seeing a great many shirts on display, many of them in very non-Amish colors and styles. "What about a white shirt?"

"You can never have too many white shirts, sir," answered Green. "I might suggest that you vary the color of your shirt with the pin striping that decorates it." Green then proceeded to show Jacob exactly what he had meant by his suggestion, offering him Coulter shirts with black and blue pin stripes, as well as off-white versions of the same shirt. Jacob agreed that this would fit the bill and asked Green

to set eight shirts to the side for him. Green also pointed out that this type of ready-made shirt tended to come with a sleeve that would be long enough to fit any man's arm length, so the purchase of garters would be in order.

The coat, trousers and shirts were now out of the way. Jacob anxiously looked out of the window in time to spy his parents and Abraham exiting Reilly's Drugstore. He quickly asked Green to place a sufficient supply of undergarments in with the order, asking him to judge his size. The next selection was to be socks and hose, which Jacob selected to match his trousers.

The rest of the Zook family entered the shop. "How was your time at Reilly's?" asked Jacob.

"Such a place!" exclaimed his mother. "I have learned so much in just a little amount of time!"

"We all had cherry phosphates," explained Abraham.

"How is the shopping going, Jakob?" asked Ishmael.

"Fine, Fati. I have some choices to show you, if you'd like to see them." "Now why would you ask our opinion, Jakob?" inquired his father.

Jacob knew how he would have liked to answer his father, but chose instead to be diplomatic. "I am only still a boy, Fati. What do I know of the 'English' world?" "The 'English' are going to turn you into one of their politicians, Jakob," said Ishmael, smiling at his son. "Let us see what you picked out."

"I have picked out my trousers and shirts, but I have several tailcoats selected…and I need your opinion." Jacob walked to the sales counter and lifted the black tailcoat. "What do you think of this, Muti?"

"I suppose it is very nice, Jakob," his mother replied, "but don't you want to have something a little more colorful?"

"Colorful?" asked the boy. He then lifted up the heather frock coat. "Do you like this color?"

Jacob thought he heard his mother gasp, but even if he did not actually hear it, he did not miss his mother turn to his father for guidance. "Don't you think that is a beautiful shade, Ishmael."

"I would not wear it!" said his father.

"I know that, Ishmael," answered Sarah. "Can you put it on, Jakob?" Green quickly nodded and once again helped Jacob into the frock coat. "Oh, I think you look very handsome in that color, Jakob. It goes very well with your blue eyes and blonde hair. Don't you agree, Ishmael."

"Yes."

"Is that all you can say?" she asked her husband. "Actually…I think that color would be very becoming on you, as well."

"On me?" asked Ishmael.

"Why not?" she gushed. "You and Jakob share a great many similarities in your looks."

"I also like this burgundy tailcoat, Muti," said Jacob, holding up the other jacket.

"That is very nice, too," she observed. "The black one seems very formal, Jakob. You should keep that one for special occasions."

"Do you mean to say that I should buy three coats?"

"Absolutely!" answered Ishmael.

Jacob smiled at his parents broadly. This adventure was going far better than he had anticipated. "I still need to pick out a few vests, and then the accessories."

"What are accessories?" asked Abraham.

"I, for one, do not know," answered his mother, "but I will help you pick out the vests."

Sarah Zook worked with Green to match the selected frock coat and two tailcoats with matching vests. She then turned her attention to picking out several cravats and neckties, along with the necessary pins. Jacob, during the same interval, was looking at the great coats – the warmer outwear for the cold months ahead. He selected a charcoal grey great coat, and a pair of black leather gloves. While his mother had her attention drawn away in the selection of cravats, Jacob selected a single-edged razor with a mother of pearl handle, a shaving cup, and a bottle of men's cologne. He also chose a modest set of cuff links and a set of suspenders.

"Jacob?" his mother called, from the other side of the store.

"Yes, Muti?"

"Don't you think you need a hat? I don't think your straw hat is going to look very good with all these fancy clothes."

Jacob immediately wished that his mother had not used the term 'fancy.' "I'll be over there directly, Muti." He quickly added the toiletries to the pile of purchases, then crossed the floor to where his mother was standing, admiring the gentlemen's hats.

"Could you please try one of these hats on, Jakob?" she asked. "I don't know very much about men's clothing, but I must admit that I have always admired their hats." Sarah Zook took down a black bowler from a hat block and placed in on Jacob's head. She stepped back and gazed lovingly at her first born. "I am not sure about this one, Jakob. I think your hair is too long for this style. Why don't you look at yourself in the mirror?"

"What? The mirror?" Now Jacob was certain that the world had changed. He turned to look at himself. His reaction, although he did not say it in a many words, was that he thought that he looked ridiculous. He removed the hat from his head.

"You agree with me, don't you?" asked Sarah. Jacob nodded in agreement. She took down a different style hat – a John Bull – a short, squat top hat, also in black, and placed it on Jacob's head. Jacob immediately turned to look at himself in the mirror.

"That looks much better," observed Abraham.

"I think so, too," added Sarah. "You look….handsome!"

Silas Green stepped forward to offer some advice. "There is only one other thing that a young gentleman might want to have."

"Shoes!" said Jacob, realizing that his black work boots, while having served him well, were not going to match the elegance of his purchases. "I need to buy new shoes."

"You may want to consider that," agreed Green, "but I do not sell shoes. You will need to visit the cobbler for those, and he is right down the Emmittsburg Pike from here. No…I was talking about one of these."

Green selected a gentleman's walking stick from among a dozen different canes.

"Why would my son, a healthy, robust young man of eighteen years of age, have need of an old man's cane?" asked Ishmael.

"This is all the fashion these days, Mr. Zook," explained Green. "The cane isn't used for balance, or as a crutch…it is a decoration."

"It is a thing of fancy," observed Ishmael.

"You are correct, Fati," agreed Jacob.

"But it is more than that," continued Green. "It can be used to defend oneself. The city can be…"

"Dangerous?" asked Sarah.

"Challenging!" answered Green. "Look…this ferule is made of solid brass. A young man, dressed as handsomely as Jacob here, would be able to fend off any petty thief with just one rap."

"Oh!" exclaimed Sarah.

"The shaft is rosewood. It is a precious hardwood," continued Green. Ishmael nodded. He was opposed to violence of any kind, but he also wanted his son to be safe. He didn't think that Jacob would go around the city rapping people on the head with his cane without just cause. "Jakob should have this thing," he announced.

And that was that!

Green added up the bill and gave the amount to Ishmael, who produced the proper currency out of his coat pocket. "I will need to have Jacob try on the trousers and coats so that I can make any needed alterations. I can deliver them all to your home in two days.

"That will be perfect," said Jacob. "I should wear one of these suits when Rebecca comes to dinner on Friday."

CHAPTER 35

Dinner at the Zook House

Friday night dinner at the newly re-built Zook home was going to be a special occasion. It was not only meant to be the farewell dinner for Jacob, but it was also a welcoming dinner for Rebecca Tilden.

Sarah Zook spent the entire day in the kitchen. This was usually the case, as most days typically went, as Amish women spent very little time in any other room other than the kitchen – although there was always time set aside for quilting and for cleaning and tending to the rest of the house. But Sarah had spent the last few days preparing for this one particular meal. She had prepared large quantities of food for an extensive menu to be served all at one meal. It wasn't that she was under the impression that Rebecca Tilden would be able to eat immense quantities of any one selection, but she was concerned that the girl may not prefer certain of her typical Amish fare, so she wanted a large selection for the girl to choose from – just in case.

About two days out from the event Sarah began to make some of the items that would keep for several days. She made several varieties of relish, along with some cookies. She found a nice big piece of salted pork, which she promptly submerged in water in order to remove the excessively salty taste. She would change the water regularly over the course of the next few days in order to remove the saltiness. It was on this day that she also prepared a dough out of eggs and flour in order to make noodles.

On the morning of the dinner party, Sarah began the preparations by baking. She baked an apple pie, as well as a cherry pie and a shoe-fly pie. She wasn't sure if Rebecca would care for the shoe-fly pie, as the sweetness, owing to the inclusion of so much molasses, did not seem to please every palate. But the pie was Jacob's favorite, so she really was making it for him.

In addition to the pork, Sarah was also cooking a roasted chicken, as well as a dish that contained stewed pieces of beef over egg noodles. She also planned to serve a variety of vegetables – some of which had been rescued from the root cellar in the old house. She cooked some mashed potatoes, mostly out of fear that Sarah might not like egg noodles.

In addition to a fine, eat-in kitchen, the new house also had a feature that was completely missing in the old house – a dining room. Ishmael had first dismissed this additional room as unnecessary and ostentatious, but Sarah pleaded with him for a sum total of about ten minutes in order to change his mind. The farewell dinner, the Zook's first formal party, would be served in the dining room. Due to the relative proximity to the loss of the old house, the battle, and the scarcity of certain lumber, Ishmael could not hope to furnish the new, larger home with his own hand-made furniture – at least not in less than two weeks. Ishmael spent the better part of the first week after the battle building new beds for the new bedrooms. He built a large table for the kitchen, along with four chairs. Thankfully, the soldiers had already built several of the built-in cabinets in the large pantry and along the wall in the kitchen. Ishmael was currently working on several dressers for the bedrooms, working on the three in different stages.

But he was unable to work on the fancier pieces of furniture that would eventually complete the look of the house. He needed to be creative to furnish the house for the dinner.

He borrowed a large trestle table from the seminary, along with six strong side chairs. Sarah borrowed the special china that the minister, Reverend Meier, had locked away for special occasions.

By five o'clock in the afternoon the Zook household was in panic. Sarah was busy putting together the final touches on the meal. Ishmael was getting himself washed up in the new bathroom. Jacob and Abraham, who had both already bathed, (Jacob had even shaved for the event) were already dressing. Jacob had selected the heather colored frock coat to wear for his first public appearance as a young American gentleman. He had placed the clothing on top of his bed, and then invited his brother to come into his room to lend his opinion. One of the other benefits, and differences, between the old house and the new house was the fact that the boys no longer shared a bedroom. Jacob showed his brother his choice for trousers, shirt, vest, and tie – to which Abraham had only a slight suggestion of a change – and that was in the color of the cravat.

Having helped his brother choose his attire for the evening, Abraham repaired to his room to get into his best suit of Amish garb, the clothing which his mother had quickly made for him in the days after the battle. All of his clothing had been destroyed in the fire which had burned down the house. Sarah Zook had stayed up throughout the night in order to create new trousers and shirts for Ishmael and her boys. After Abraham had finished working on tying his black string tie, he left his room again and returned to his brother's room, knocking quietly on the door.

"Come in," said his brother from the other side of the door.

Abraham cautiously opened the door, keeping his eyes cast downward, as if he was trying to prevent himself from seeing his brother and his new clothing. He closed the door behind him, then turned to where his brother was standing, gazing at the young man who was obviously his brother, Jacob…but, in many ways, a total stranger.

"Well, Abraham," Jacob said softly and expectantly, "what do you think? How do I look?"

Uncharacteristically, Abraham was momentarily without words. The sight of his brother wearing these unfamiliar pieces of clothing was, for the time, overwhelming to him. He was so overwhelmed, in fact, that his eyes began to well up with tears.

"Is there something wrong, Abraham?"

Abraham quickly shook his head, then wiped his eyes. "No," he said. "You look perfect, Jacob! You look like a perfect gentleman!" Then the tears began to reappear in his eyes. "It's just that…" He stopped, unable to continue.

"What is wrong, Abraham?"

The boy inhaled deeply, clearing the emotion from his soul. "I just realized…when I saw you standing there…dressed like that…that you are going away. I may never see you again!"

Jacob took a step closer to his brother. "Nonsense! I am going away to college…not off to the war! Besides that…we are brothers, and we will always be brothers…forever!" Jacob opened his arms in an inviting manner, and Abraham knew exactly what to do, running the few steps that separated them and embracing his brother tightly.

"You promise?"

"Of course, foolish boy! In just a few short years you will have your turn, as well…and all of this will seem very silly."

"Do you think so?"

"Without a doubt. Now…go wash your face. You look like you've been crying."

"I have been crying, Jacob."

"I know." Jacob let his brother go, but ruffled his hair before he moved out of reach.

"Jacob!" his brother protested. "Now look what you've done! I have to comb my hair again."

"Yes, you do," replied his brother. "Isn't it a good thing that we finally have a mirror in the bathroom?"

Abraham left the room. Jacob readjusted his tailcoat one final time and then also left the room. He headed down the hallway and then descended the staircase to the ground floor of the house. It was almost six o'clock.

Just as Jacob reached the bottom of the staircase he was met by both of his parents. Sarah Zook immediately burst into tears, falling onto the shoulder of her husband, Ishmael. Jacob reached inside his tailcoat pocket and produced a white pocket handkerchief which was monogramed with a black "Z." He handed the cloth to his mother.

"Why is it that I have this effect on my family?" asked Jacob, with an anxious smile.

His mother took the handkerchief and wiped her eyes and nose. "Jakob! You look so handsome! You look just like your father when he was your age….before he grew his beard out." Abraham came bounding down the stairs. "Abraham! Do not run in the house!"

"I am sorry, Muti!" the boy replied. "Doesn't Jacob look like English royalty?" "Bah!" said Ishmael. "That is a bad choice of words, Abraham."

A soft knock was heard on the front door.

"Abraham," said Sarah, quietly, "you should go open the door and let our guest in."

"Yes, Muti."

The younger boy slowly and quietly moved to the front door, firmly grasping the brass fitting and slowly pulling back the door. The door swung inside to the right, concealing the rest of the family from Rebecca's view. She could only see the youngest member of the Zook family, and he was the only one who could see her.

"Good evening, Rebecca," said Abraham politely.

"Good evening, Master Zook," responded Rebecca, with the same degree of formality.

"Would you care to come in?" asked the boy.

"Why thank you," said Rebecca, stepping past the door frame. As she passed by him, Abraham gently shut the door, which allowed Rebecca to see the rest of the family – and they, she – for the first time.

Rebecca was wearing a sky blue gown that had been trimed in white lace. As was the custom of the day, she wore long, opera-length gloves and had a white linen shawl wrapped around her shoulders. Several hoops of various diameters, sewn into her petticoat, had created a voluminous triangulation of her lower limbs. She had curled her hair in long, wide curls, which now draped down her neck. She held a blue matching fan in her right hand, which, at present, was closed.

Rebecca gasped when her eyes fell upon Jacob. "Oh, my! Am I in the presence of Squire Jacob Zook?" She said this rehearsed line, which she had practiced all throughout the day, with a halting and nervous gait.

"You are," replied Jacob, bowing to her and returning her salutation.

But then breaking her character, Becky gushed, "My word, Jacob… you look absolutely…beautiful….no, handsome. I was not ready for this!"

Jacob stepped forward and took Rebecca's arm, leaning in and whispering in her ear. "You look very beautiful,too." Then he turned Rebecca to face his parents, who were still standing at the base of the staircase. "Rebecca Tilden…this is my mother, Sarah Zook."

Rebecca dipped toward the floor in a well-practiced curtsey, her legs seeming to collapse beneath the expanse of the hooped skirt. "Mrs. Zook…it is a pleasure to meet you," she said.

"And I think that you have already met my father, Ishmael," continued Jacob with the formal introductions.

"Yes," Rebecca answered, once again dipping to the floor, "but that was under far less joyful circumstances."

"Shall we go into the sitting room?" asked Jacob, nervously trying to move the evening along. Abraham cleared his throat. Jacob turned to see his brother frowning at him. "Oh, and you already know my brother, Abraham…don't you?"

Becky smiled at Abraham. "Oh yes…we know each other. He is quite the charmer, he is…and, until I met your mother just now, Abraham, I never realized where it was that you got your good looks from. You are the very image of your mother."

"Abraham may not thank you for that, Rebecca," offered Sarah, "but I will. Jakob takes after his father – in so many ways, I'm afraid – and Abraham is very much my son." And then Sarah smiled warmly at Rebecca, stepped forward, and took her other arm, pulling her away from Jacob and leading her out of the entrance hall.

The sitting room, or parlor, lay adjacent to the entrance hall. It was another large room in the house, which, in any other fashionable home in Gettysburg would have decorated and wallpapered in dark Victorian colors, and would have had several upholstered pieces of furniture – central of which being a large couch or sofa. The preferred covering would have been of mohair. In the Zook home this room was particularly sparse, with only a few wooden chairs set around in a conversational setting. Sarah had made an attempt at making the room seem a little less cold by throwing some quilting material over the backs of the chairs. Most of the people in the room were uncomfortable in this new setting, including Rebecca, who was very uncomfortable in the presence of the Zooks. The only one who seemed right at home was Abraham.

"That surely is an odd shape for a dress, Rebecca," the boy observed. "Why would a woman want to wear a dress that makes everyone think that she is shaped like a bell?"

"Abraham!" his mother interrupted. "I don't think that is a proper thing to ask a young lady."

"That is quite alright, Mrs. Zook," replied Rebecca. "This is the fashion, but I don't really understand why myself."

"Abraham? Why don't you get the relishes and lemonade from the kitchen?" "Yes, Muti," said the boy, who promptly left the room in the direction of the kitchen. Sarah had wanted to ask Rebecca the exact same question concerning the shape of her dress, but now knew that she could not ask it – not after reprimanding her son for doing so.

"Rebecca…how are the Wades doing these days?" asked Ishmael. "They seem to be holding up quite well, all things considered," replied

Rebecca. "They received terrible news just a few days after the battle." "Really?" asked Ishmael. "What bad news?"

Jacob seemed concerned as well. He hadn't been aware of any other developments at the Wade/McClellan house – but, then again…he had been purposely avoiding the place ever since the funeral.

"This may seem like a cruel twist of fate," said Rebecca, "or maybe it is just for the better, but several days after we put Ginnie in the ground, we received word that her finance, Jack Skelly, had died from his wounds in a Confederate hospital."

"Oh, no!" exclaimed Jacob.

"Yes," continued Becky. "We don't think he ever knew about Ginnie being shot. One could say that they are now united in heaven – but it seems another tragedy of the war, just the same."

Ishmael slowly nodded his head in agreement.

"Georgia's husband will be returning from the war any day now," she went on. "Georgia received a letter from him last week."

"That should help ease things a bit," offered Jacob.

"Yes, it should," agreed Becky. "The baby is doing very well, too." Abraham appeared at the door to the sitting room carrying a tray that was fully loaded with Sarah Zook's pickles and relishes, plus an assortment of dry crackers on the side. Fortunately, the boy had aired on the side of caution when loading the tray and decided to make a second trip to carry in the lemonade and glassware. He put the tray down on a small table in the middle of the conversational grouping and then left the room again for the liquid.

"Do you like relishes, Rebecca?" asked Sarah Zook.

"Oh, yes," she answered. "My mother loves to put up all kinds of things for the winter and relish is among her favorites to can."

This answer impressed both Ishmael and Sarah. Ishmael had been under the impression that most of the 'English' women were very lazy, and had now gotten to the point where the fine art of cooking had been lost; that they spent most of their time purchasing these items in the grocery store. Sarah was impressed that Rebecca did not seem to be a picky or prissy eater.

"May I get you something, Becky?" asked Jacob.

"Why yes, Squire…you certainly may." Becky let out a little giggle, which made Ishmael squirm a bit. Even still, he managed to begin a new conversation.

"Rebecca…you are the first guest we have had," he said, "not only the first guest in this new house…but also the first 'English' guest we have ever had under our roof."

Rebecca Tilden really didn't know how to respond to that observation. "Mr. Zook? Why do you refer to me…and the rest of us…as the 'English?' Even though we are descended from settlers from England, the Tildens consider themselves to be American."

"I am sorry if I have insulted you, Rebecca," Ishmael said, with great concern that he might have offended her written on his face. "We Amish always refer to the non-Amish as the 'English.' The word has nothing to do with where you came from – it has to do with the language you speak."

"But you speak English, too…and you speak it well."

"Yes," agreed Ishmael, "but only out of necessity. We would normally speak the German language – our native language in Alsace."

"So when Jacob calls you Muti and Fati…?"

"These are terms of affection for his parents…much like you say 'Mama' and 'Papa.'

Abraham entered carrying a pitcher of lemonade. In the days and weeks following the battle, lemons had been excessively difficult to come by, so this drink was to be considered a real treat. Abraham did the honors of pouring out a glass for everyone in the room. Rebecca took a sip of the yellow liquid. She thought it tasted wonderful; the perfect blend of tart and sweet.

After taking a sip, Ishmael took the initiative to begin a new conversation. "So…Rebecca…Jakob has told us very little about you. Do you have plans to go away to school….I mean to the university?"

"Oh, no…Mr. Zook!" she quickly replied. "I have no inclination to learning. I like working around here…in Gettysburg. I like to cook and bake and sew. This particular dress, for example…I made."

Jacob cleared his throat.

"Well, yes…actually I made the dress with a great deal of help from Ginnie Wade. She was supposed to wear it for her wedding to Corporal Jack Skelly. Her mother gave it to me."

"If that is the case, then you sew beautifully," observed Sarah Zook.

"Thank you, Mrs. Zook." Rebecca smiled at Jacob's mother, happy to receive an important compliment. She was overjoyed to think that she might be making a favorable impression in an otherwise ultra-conservative home. But she also knew that Sarah Zook's opinion did not wield very much weight within the home; that distinction fell squarely on the shoulders of her husband, Ishmael.

"I am happy to hear that a young lady outside of our Ordnung has these kind of sewing skills," added Jacob's father. "I was under the impression that young women these days were flighty and unskilled in the skills of the home."

Rebecca smiled at Ishmael. "You are probably correct in that assumption, Mr. Zook," she said, trying to hold her ground, "but this is not true for all of us. I can cook, sew, put up preserves, and tend to the house. My mother made sure that I could take care of whomever I married."

"It is always wise to plan for the future," answered Ishmael, but not in an insignificant manner.

"Fati, you sound as if you are interviewing Rebecca for a job," quietly, but nervously joked Jacob.

"Nonsense, Jakob!" Ishmael answered, followed by a quick burst of laughter. "You act as if I am trying to marry you off to the girl." It was as if Ishmael was attempting to hide something by hiding it out in the open.

"Fati!" Jacob exclaimed, but, in a very secret way felt nothing but relief that his father was beginning to take to the idea.

"Jakob, why are you getting so upset? You know that you are too young to even consider getting married. And now that you are leaving to pursue an education, these thoughts must be put on hold for many years more. I am doing nothing but conversing with Rebecca. You are making too much of small talk!"

Jacob sat back in his chair. Perhaps this was his father's method all the long, he thought. Perhaps all he wanted to do was demonstrate how ridiculous and love-sick his son had been acting as of late. Perhaps it was to allow Jacob to make a clean break of his relationship with Rebecca when he went off to college.

His mother must have been wondering as well, because she soon stood up and announced that she was going to the kitchen to see about the dinner.

And then she left the room.

Jacob looked over at Rebecca. She was staring down at the floor. "Anyway, Jacob," she said, "we are rushing to judgment here. We are

speaking of things that are years away…for both of us."

Sarah Zook re-entered the sitting room. "Ishmael? Would you please come assist me in the kitchen?" All present in the room, with the exception of Rebecca, realized just how odd this request had been – for it had never, ever been made before this evening. Sarah Zook was master of her domain, and, even though it was never spoken of, it was almost unwritten law that she did not need assistance in the kitchen, nor was it ever offered before.

To Jacob's surprise, he witnessed his father rise, and then go dutifully to the kitchen.

"I think Fati's going to get a earful," observed Abraham, getting up and moving toward the door to the kitchen.

"Abraham?" called Jacob, signaling the younger boy back toward the sitting area. "Would you sit down with us, please?" Abraham looked surprised to hear this request from his brother, and asked for clarification with his eyes. "I would like you to join us…while Muti and Fati are out of the room." Abraham walked back to his chair and sat down.

"I thought that maybe you would like the privacy," suggested Abraham. "You have been reading too many of the 'English' novels, Abraham." "Is something wrong?" asked Rebecca.

"No, nothing is wrong," replied Jacob. "I simply want my brother to witness something, and then swear that he will never repeat any of this." Jacob looked at his brother. "Swear to it, Abraham!"

"What if I don't want to, Jacob?"

"Then it will be Hell to pay!"

"Really? For how long? You leave here in only another day," his brother said, smirking.

"Swear it!"

"Do I need to get the Bible?"

"No," answered Jacob. "Your word is your bond! Swear it!" Abraham relented. "I swear it…just get on with it."

Jacob once again smiled at his brother, then turned back to Becky and took her left hand in his own hand. "Rebecca Tilden…before this witness…would you consent to marry me? Would you marry me….in a time in the future to be arranged?"

Rebecca looked toward the door to the kitchen, then back at Jacob. "Of course I will, Jacob. I will marry you at a time to be determined in the future, and we shall raise a happy and large family together." Rebecca leaned into Jacob and kissed him gently on his lips, sealing the compact.

"What just happened here?" asked Abraham.

Jacob turned to his brother. "We have simply pledged ourselves to each other – that's all. We will marry when the time is right, but until that time arrives, we will be faithful to each other."

"And you have witnessed this, Abraham," added Rebecca. "We trust that you will keep this a secret?"

Abraham gave his characteristic smirk, as if to ask if they really knew who they were speaking to. "Of course I will."

"When the time comes," said Jacob, "you will be my best man."

"When the time comes," answered Abraham, "you will need me to wheel both of you down the aisle in your wheelchairs, and I will be old and gray, myself."

CHAPTER 36

Moving Out

The day after a very successful dinner party, the Zook family loaded up a wagon in order to transport Jacob to Harrisburg. It had already been determined that the entire family would see him off at the train station in the Capitol City of the State, and that they would take him there on Saturday – the day before the train was scheduled to leave.

Ishmael was worried that they might, in some way, be delayed in making the thirty mile trip to the city. Sarah simply wanted to spend the last few hours with her first-born son, and to give him a proper send-off.

To accomplish this, however, the Amish family would need to spend the night in a residence in the all-to-English-city of Harrisburg.

This would be another new experience for all involved.

By nine o'clock in the morning, Ishmael had loaded the back of the wagon with their baggage, including the large wooden trunk which he had recently constructed to hold Jacob's new wardrobe. He had made the trunk out of a sturdy, but thinly cut pine. The box was strong, but light – at least when it was empty.

Just before the hour of ten the family was ready to leave for Harrisburg. Not wishing to make them into any more of an obvious target than they already were, Ishmael had made the suggestion that they not dress in traditional Amish fashion, but should rather wear clothing that would help them 'blend in.' Sarah had gone into the town of Gettysburg several days earlier and had purchased some suitable 'English' clothing for Ishmael and she to wear.

In his letter to Jacob, General Sickles had also arranged accommodations in a large manse in the city. This was arranged through his connections with Secretary of War, Edwin Stanton. They were to stay in a large house that had been recently used as an all-female college, but had closed its doors as such in 1861, at the start of the war. A member of the board of trustees of the school, Simon Cameron, who had been President Lincoln's Secretary of War prior to Stanton, had quickly snatched up the property, planning to convert the old house to his new private residence. Lincoln had given Cameron the post of Secretary as a way of thanking him for his support during Lincoln's recent election, but the first few years of the war had not gone favorably, and Cameron left the office soon thereafter. He was then appointed as Ambassador to Russia. Stanton stepped into Cameron's position, and into his social and political connections, as well. The house in Harrisburg was already under construction, with Cameron out of the country, but there were several rooms that were already fit for entertaining guests, so Stanton suggested that the family stay there. At any rate, they would be more comfortable staying in a private residence than in a hotel.

Harrisburg was several hours away by wagon. The Zook family took a main road heading northeast toward Mechanicsburg, which was just outside of the city. It had been conjectured that Harrisburg, with its railroad center, had been one of the main objectives for the Army of Northern Virginia on this most recent campaign. If Lee had been able to take Harrisburg, he could have tapped into the northern industrial might to enable him to invade Washington. Unfortunately for Lee, he ran into the Union Army at Gettysburg.

Sarah Zook had prepared a hamper of food for the journey, and at around noon Ishmael pulled the wagon off to the side of the road so that they could enjoy her lunch. In the two hours of travel they had gone almost fifteen miles, by Ishmael's estimation, and were almost halfway there. Ishmael predicted that they would be seeing Harrisburg by around two o'clock. There were several unscheduled stops along the way, mostly to find an available outhouse or other facility. This formality was reserved almost exclusively for Sarah, as the males would have just as easily found relief off the road in the brush.

As predicted, around two o'clock the tall buildings of Harrisburg started to loom into view, particularly the church spires and the dome of the State House. Ishmael turned the wagon southward, looking for the way across the Susquehanna River, which was at its widest point as it passed by Harrisburg. He located the access to the Market Street Bridge, which used some of the channel islands in the middle of the river as a means of creating stability for the long expanse. Once across the bridge, Ishmael turned the wagon northward, once again, as he travelled up Front Street – a fashionable road which had large, stately homes looking out across the river.

The family reached their destination around three o'clock in the afternoon. Abraham unhitched the horse from the wagon and led it around to the rear of the large house, where he found a stable. Jacob and Ishmael unpacked the wagon, bringing the luggage and the trunk into the vestibule of the home. They were met by the caretaker of the residence, a tight-lipped older gentleman by the name of Dithers, who welcomed the family Simon Cameron's name. He showed them the two bedrooms which they would have for the next two nights – with the exception of Jacob, who would already be on a train to Washington by the second night.

"I am sorry to say that our kitchen is under extensive renovation," said Henry Dithers, although his voice did not really seem all that unhappy to say it, "but there are some very nice taverns and restaurants along Front Street. I hope that you enjoy your stay in our city."

"Thank you," said Sarah, smiling at the sour little man. "We have had a long ride today, so any suggestions you might make would be greatly appreciated."

Sarah's gentle nature seemed to warm the soul of the mousey little man. "I might suggest you try the River Inn, madam. It is only about three minutes from here. Walk along Front Street and you will not be able to miss it. They have a very good stew; not to mention some of the other fine meals which they serve."

"Thank you," answered Sarah. "Do you have facilities for us to wash up?" "Oh, yes," smiled Dithers. "You will find that we have indoor facilities in each bedroom."

"That is very convenient," remarked Sarah.

"My apartment is to be found on the back side of the first floor, in case you have need of me," offered Dithers, who was now warming greatly to Sarah Zook.

"Thank you," she answered, "but I am sure we will be able to manage." Dithers bowed formally to them and departed. Jacob carried his trunk into the room which he would be sharing with his brother for the night. A few minutes later, Abraham appeared at the door. Jacob noticed that his brother seemed more antsy than usual.

"What's wrong, Abraham?"

"Wrong? Nothing! Isn't it exciting, Jacob? We are in the center of one of the biggest cities in the country.

"I don't know if I would go that far, Abraham – but, yes…it is certainly the biggest city that you and I have ever seen, so I guess that it is a pretty good adventure."

"I can't wait to explore it, Jacob!"

"Neither can I. I wonder if Muti and Fati would care to join us on our quest." Once again, the smirk appeared at the corner of Abraham's mouth. "Don't you think that they might be tired after that long wagon ride?" "Are you hoping that they might be tired, Abraham?" "Well…. yes."

"Alright, then," Jacob said, "you wash up a bit, and I will go speak to them. Maybe we can explore a bit before we have to go for dinner."

As it turned out, Sarah and Ishmael were not planning to walk around the city at this time. They had discovered that the mansion had a beautiful veranda, which held some very comfortable chairs. The veranda looked out across Front Street and had a beautiful view of the river. It was the perfect place to relax after the long journey.

The boys bade their parents farewell and headed north on Front Street. Abraham was particularly attracted to the river, which was running rapidly past them. He soon felt compelled to cross Front Street to get a closer look.

"Be careful, brother," called Jacob. "We don't have rivers such as this back in Gettysburg!"

"Come join me, Jacob," his brother called back. "It is very exciting!"

Jacob crossed Front Street and caught up with Abraham. "Do you think we could go in swimming?" Abraham was already heading down the embankment toward the river's edge.

Jacob shook his head. "This isn't the type of river for swimming – not at this spot, at least. Look at how quickly the water is moving. That is a current, Abraham. As soon as you would step into the water it would wash you away downstream."

"It's dangerous?"

"It's really dangerous! Let's just keep to the path and see where it leads." The boys walked a little further along Front Street until they reached the intersection with one of the main streets in the city, Market Street. They turned right on Market Street and continued their walk, gazing at the many shops and activities to be found in a city of that size. As the continued their walk, they saw more and more people. It was obvious that they were approaching a far more commercial area of the city than were they were staying on Front Street. The city was already developed into obvious square blocks. There were streets that were numbered going one direction, and there were streets that had names, such as Market Street, going in another direction.

Always the talker, Abraham had dozens of questions for his older brother – some of which he was able to answer, or give an educated guess – others he would simply shrug off, as if he hadn't heard them in the first place. Jacob was, in actuality, trying to hear some of the things that the locals were saying. As they continued walking, Jacob thought he heard one man mention Gettysburg to another, and it seemed that the war was most commonly the subject of conversations.

And then, as they turned another corner, there was the Capitol Building – standing directly in front of them.

Neither of them had ever seen a structure as large as the Pennsylvania Capitol Building. In their simple rural upbringing, the boys had never travelled further than the quaint village of Gettysburg, except for a spell living in the even quainter hamlet of Paradise.

"Can we go inside?" asked Abraham.

"I don't see why we can't," replied Jacob, which was, of course, quite true. The Capitol was a public building, and even though the legislature was in session, the main concourse of the building was open for the citizens to see. Sitting over the grand court, between the bi-cameral wings of the legislature, was built a large dome. This added a cathedral-like ambience to the area below, and the spaciousness akin to the heavens above. The boys were particularly taken by this architectural feature.

Jacob had only seen pictures of buildings like this one in books – and this one made him long to see the massive dome which was now under construction above the United States Capitol Building in Washington.

After looking around the Capitol building for a while, Jacob reminded his brother that it was time to head back to Front Street. They had been out exploring for over two hours, and dinner time was quickly approaching. The boys beat a hasty retreat back to the Cameron Mansion to see what plans their parents had made for the evening.

When Jacob and Abraham arrived back at the manse, they soon discovered that, to their disbelief, their parents had no plans solidified at all. Abraham had felt sure that his parents would have been taken with the excitement of the big city, just as he had been, and that, having spent a few hours resting up on the veranda, they would now be ready for their adventure to begin.

That may have been true; perhaps Ishmael and Sarah were eager to begin an adventure in the big city, but more likely was the fact that they were so overwhelmed by what they were seeing on that front porch that they had been transfixed for over two hours. They had watched several large barges float past them, filled with all kinds of goods, headed to the ports of Philadelphia or Baltimore. They watched several peddlers and street vendors come by, hawking their wares. They watched a procession of Nuns and novices, as they passed by them on their way to a nearby convent. And they heard murmurs of talk on the street in front of them, as they came to realize that this area of Harrisburg was one of the main hubs in the Underground Railroad.

But their dinner was definitely not a priority.

Not until their sons returned to them, several hours later.

Abraham wasted no time grilling them on where they were going to eat. At fourteen years of age, Abraham was constantly concerned with the source of his next meal. Ishmael looked at Sarah, with concern in his eyes, as they were both aware that the kitchen in the house was being renovated. Sarah would not be able to provide the dinner, and even if she could have used the kitchen, there would have been no provisions stored up there for her to use.

Sarah shook her head. There was only one recourse – other than going without dinner…

…they would have to eat in a tavern or restaurant.

But the boys already knew that!

As sensitive as Jacob was to the fact that this experience was going to make both of his parents uncomfortable, Abraham was relishing every moment. It wasn't that he was hoping to see his parents, particularly his father, squirm at the discomfort of a new situation, he was rather looking forward to seeing his parents engage in a totally new learning experience. He was looking forward to them becoming 'Americanized.'

But the boy was obviously disappointed when Ishmael conceded that dinner out was the only solution. He had expected more resistance. In a not too bygone day – perhaps only several weeks prior – his father would have expected his wife to make the most of any possible bad arrangement, and would have expected dinner on the table at six o'clock come hell or high water.

"So then," Ishmael announced, "we shall eat somewhere else tonight." Abraham tested the waters. "Where, Fati?"

"Where? Hm? Jakob….did you pass any eating establishments on your walk?"

"As a matter of fact, Fati, we did pass a few very nice places along the way. I took note of their menus, which were displayed on boards outside."

"Would you suggest that we try one of these places, then?"

"I think that will be agreeable, Fati," Jacob answered, giving a nod to his brother.

"Then we shall go," said Ishmael, "oh, and jungen…I think you had better stop calling us by Fati and Muti."

"What?" asked Abraham.

"Yes…" his father answered. "Perhaps it is time that we all started to act like we actually live in this country. I think 'Papa' and 'Mama' are perfectly presentable." Jacob smiled; first at his father and mother, and then at his brother, who, for the first time in recent history – was totally speechless.

CHAPTER 37

Leaving

Jacob woke early the next day, rising before the Sun was above the hills in the distance. He tried to get his effects together without waking his brother, who seemed for all intents and purposes to be dead to the world. Jacob was once again wearing the same old, borrowed nightshirt that he had worn in the seminary just a few weeks back – that same nightshirt that he had been wearing – and then not wearing – when he disturbed his brother last; when his brother had given him a piece of his mind.

Jacob didn't want that to happen again.

The train was scheduled to depart the Harrisburg station at four o'clock in the afternoon. Sickles had picked that departure time to allow Jacob enough leeway to get to Harrisburg from Gettysburg, never figuring that the entire Zook family would accompany the boy on the journey, especially coming over a day earlier. But Jacob had written back to Sickles, telling him of the plans, and Sickles had pulled a few strings to get them their overnight accommodations.

Jacob dearly wanted this final day with his family to be flawless, and memorable. He wanted them to see the city. He wanted them to understand that the English were not to be as feared as they had originally been taught. Above all, he hoped that they would not encounter anything along their way that would change their mind in this regard; a riot, a robbery, a violent crime. These events would not hold well for Jacob, and, even though he was now bound and determined to leave for Washington, he knew he would be once again saddled with an enormous amount of guilt.

He simply wanted the day to go perfectly....and that was all.

Jacob walked over to the trunk his father had made for him and lifted the lid. He selected a clean pair of undergarments, then lifted his legs successively to pull them on. Jacob had purchased several pair of these at the haberdashery in Gettysburg. They were definitely different from those he was used to as an Amish boy. They fit his legs snuggly, and they had been made in a factory instead of by hand. He pulled the leggings up to his waist, lifting his nightshirt out of the way as he did. Jacob then moved to the large dresser that stood in the room, quietly pouring out some water into a waiting basin. He returned to the trunk and found his toiletry kit, selecting the shaving cup and soap and then carefully removing the straight-edged razor from its case. Taking a few drops of water from the basin, he used the brush to lather up the shaving soap. He had gone to visit a barber in Gettysburg several days before in anticipation of the dinner party, and the visit of Rebecca Tilden. This would be Jacob's first attempt to shave his own face using his newly purchased tools.

He was quite nervous.

Jacob scooped up some of the lather and applied it to his face. He tried very hard to keep it from going into his mouth, but to no avail – it was going to happen, and that was that. He didn't need to strap the blade to sharpen it because it had just been sharpened back home. It was already ready for his face...so he thought!

Jacob gazed at himself in the mirror. This was the moment of truth. He said a silent prayer that he would not cut his own throat and then gently…very gently…began to shave his right cheek. He used a towel to wipe off the blade, and then proceeded to his left cheek. Having finished the sides of his face, he carefully approached what he perceived to be the most difficult part of the procedure – his chin. He managed to knick his chin just at the natural cleft formed above the chin bone and the lower lip. It wasn't a very deep gash – more of an irritation than anything else – but it did bleed a bit. He moved down to his neck, and working a little faster and more confidently, removed the soap and what few whiskers were growing there without any further incident. Now there was just one other place to shave – his upper lip.

This was the only place on his entire face that had anything close to a real stubble…and even that was comprised of very light, almost gossamer-like platinum colored hairs. He gingerly removed the growth, making sure that he didn't cut his nostrils in the process. The morning ritual complete, he first closed the razor and then dipped his hands into the basin, lifting the water to his face in order to clean off the remaining soap. The bleeding on his chin had already stopped.

He took the opportunity to use more of the water to wash off his upper body, then returned again to the trunk to find the rest of his clothing for the day. He didn't want to overdress, but he really didn't bring very much of his old wardrobe, so he didn't have much choice.

"What are you doing, Jacob?"

Jacob closed the lid of the trunk, looking over it toward the bed. Abraham was sitting up, still half-asleep. "I'm trying to get dressed. I am sorry that I woke you, Abraham."

"Why are you up so early?" the boy asked, through a stifled yawn.

"I couldn't sleep," Jacob replied. "Too excited, I suppose."

Abraham nodded. "I would be, too, if I were in your position." He threw back the covers and crawled to the foot of the bed so that he was face to face with his brother. "Where did you get that underwear,

Jacob?" He was asking the question because both of them rarely wore any underwear at all, unless it was the dead of winter and they were wearing long johns.

"At the haberdashery in Gettysburg. Don't you remember?"

"I remember a great many things, Jacob, but I don't remember you buying undergarments. Why all the secrets?"

"I just want to be able to completely fit in where I am going, Abraham. I don't want to be outwardly 'English,' but inwardly Amish. I think Fati will think this is going a step to far, don't you?"

His brother agreed with him.

"Are you going to tell?" asked Jacob.

"Tell what?" asked Abraham in return, his face broadening to a wide grin. "Are you going to dress like a dandy today, Jacob?"

"Not if I can help it. But it seems that is pretty much all the clothes I brought for the journey. I don't want to make our parents uncomfortable on our last day together for a while."

Well, then…" said his brother, hopping out of the bed and approaching the trunk, "why don't you simply wear a pair of your trousers and a nice shirt…and you can wear one of my jackets?"

"One of your jackets?" asked Jacob. Abraham had come to Harrisburg with the only clothing that he owed, which was all typically Amish…and made by his mother. He did happen to bring an extra coat, but Jacob was skeptical that he could fit into the jacket, given the difference in their age.

"Muti just made me a new coat, Jacob. She said that I grew out of the old one." Abraham crossed the room to a wardrobe that was standing on the opposite side of the bedroom and removed a black jacket. He carried the coat back to his brother and handed it to him. As he stood facing his brother, Jacob was able to see just how much his brother had grown over the summer of 1863. They were virtually eye-to eye in height. Jacob put the coat on. It was a little tight in the shoulders, owing to Jacob's more developed upper body, but otherwise it fit him well.

"This will do, I think," he said, smiling at his brother. "Thank you."

Abraham collected his clothing for the day from the wardrobe. This included a clean white shirt and the trousers which he had worn the day before, plus a clean pair of socks. He walked back to his bed with the clothing, keeping his eye on his brother as he put on his fancy white shirt. "Do you like the way they feel?" he asked.

"What?"

"Your underwear! Do you like the way they feel on you?" "Yes," replied Jacob. "They feel....comfortable."

Abraham stared at the floor for a moment. "Do you think I could try on a pair?"

Jacob lightly laughed. "Certainly you can." He opened his trunk and took out a pair of the pants and tossed them to his brother. "I won't give you the shirt, because Fati might be able to see it."

"Good thinking." Abraham pulled off his nightshirt. Among many of the Amish sub-sects, the wearing of nightshirts was also prohibited, except for the unmarried children, in which case this was considered being modest. He quickly stepped into the borrowed pair of undergarments.

"Well?" asked Jacob.

"It's...very different," replied Abraham. "Not bad, or good...just different." "That was my first reaction, as well," said Jacob.

Both young men continued to dress; Jacob looking somewhat eclectic — a cross between the modern and the ultra-conservative; Abraham looking — outwardly, at least — like a typical Amish youth, but wearing a more modern secret beneath the façade. Before leaving the bedroom, Abraham went to the large dresser and picked up Jacob's hairbrush, straightening his hair out.

"Don't worry, Abraham," Jacob teased, "you look very handsome."
"Do you think so?" Abraham innocently asked.

Jacob became more serious, realizing that his brother was only trying to emulate his older brother. "Absolutely! You are a Zook male, don't you remember?"

"Right!" nodded his brother, replacing the brush on the dresser.

Jacob headed for the door. "Shall we go see if our parents are ready for breakfast?"

"Yes," replied Abraham, "I am starving!" He took a step to follow his brother and then suddenly stopped. "Wait!" he said, with a note of urgency.

"What is it?" questioned Jacob, turning back toward his brother. He quickly noticed that Abraham's face had completely lost any sign of joy or happiness. "What is wrong, Abraham?" he asked taking a few steps in the direction of his younger brother.

Abraham quickly closed the distance between them, throwing his arms around Jacob and hugging him with all his strength. "Ich liebe dich, mein Brüder!" Abraham whispered.

Jacob understood. This would be the last time that they would see each other for some time. It would be the first time that they would be separated since Abraham was born. They hadn't realized it until this moment, but this had become a rite of passage for both of them, which, in and of itself was something very non-Amish. Jacob gently kissed his brother on his forehead. "Ich liebe dich, Abraham." Then he returned his brother's embrace. He thought it quite fitting. He wasn't sure they would get the chance to say this kind of good-bye at the train station later that day. It might be awkward…and very public.

This was fitting!

Finally letting go of each other, the two brothers patted each other on the shoulders and headed out of the room. When they arrived at their parent's bedroom, Jacob knocked on the door. Hearing no response from the other side of the door, the boys then headed downstairs for the living area. The sun was now beginning to rise in the sky and Abraham was the first to spot the back of his mother's head as she sat in a rocker on the veranda. She was watching the sunrise.

Approaching the doorway, Abraham could see that she was sitting with someone else. He could hear them speaking quietly, as in conversation. He couldn't see who the other person was – not distinctly – but it was definitely a man. He had light colored hair, but, other than that similarity, did not seem to be his father. Even though his face was almost totally obscured by the doorway, Abraham could tell that this man didn't have any facial hair. The boy turned and shrugged to his brother, as if the scene was a great mystery.

Abraham and Jacob walked through the door and out onto the veranda. Seeing them, the gentleman rose and spoke to them. "Ach! Guten morgen, jungen!"

Both boys let out a gasp.

The strange man was, in fact, their father.

He had shaved his beard off.

"I can tell by the expressions on your faces that you are shocked at my appearance," Ishmael observed.

"Yes, Fati," agreed Jacob. "Shocked would be the word I would use." Abraham didn't say a word.

"I decided that it was time to rid myself of the beard," Ishmael continued. "I've had it for so long that I was beginning to worry that my skin might have disappeared. Your mother seems to think that I look a bit younger."

"You do look younger, Ishmael," counseled his wife. This observation was not all that surprising. Ishmael didn't seem to have a thread of grey on his head. The only visible signs of his age were to be found in the whiskers on his chin, and now they were gone.

"I just thought that there was no sense to keeping up those appearances anymore," Ishmael said. "If we are going to be a modern, 'English' family, then I should appear that way. Shouldn't I?"

The boys looked at each other, searching for a good answer. "You are probably correct, Fati," offered Jacob.

"Absolutely!" added Abraham.

"Good! We are in agreement....now let's go get some breakfast, shall we?" said Ishmael, who seemed far more ebullient than his usual demeanor. "I noticed that the Inn we ate dinner at last evening also serves breakfast. Would you care to eat there again?"

"Wherever you would like, Fati," replied Jacob.

"You should choose the place, Jakob," interrupted his mother. "This is your last day with us for a while, and we want it to be a special day for you."

Jacob noticed that his father was also agreeing to that statement. "Very well. We can eat breakfast at the Inn...but I reserve the right to choose our place for luncheon."

His father smiled at him. "There you are...playing the politician again, Jakob. Once the General is finished with you, I believe you will find your way into the United States Senate."

Jacob shook his head, mystified by the remark. "Fati," Ishmael raised a finger in his face, "Papa...since when are you interested in the United States Senate?"

Ishmael shrugged off the question. "Many things have changed, Jakob. My eyes are now open to the ways of the world. We are no longer stuck in the fifteenth century."

Jacob looked at his mother; she, too, was smiling. It was then that he noticed that she wasn't wearing her white Amish bonnet. "What is happening here?" he asked.

"I don't understand, Jakob," his father said, "I thought you, of all people, would have been happy to see that your mother and I have left the Ordnung."

Jacob was flustered. He wasn't sure if this was some form of crazy trick that his parents were playing on him, or if they had really, truly left the Ordnung. "Papa...Isn't this all going too quickly? One day you are devoutly Amish, and the next you are....what...English?"

Ishmael laughed. "English, Jakob?"

"Sorry, Papa...that was unfair."

"Look..." his father said, undeterred by Jacob's apology, "this didn't happen overnight. We have lived in Gettysburg for over two years. Before that, your mother and I had to endure several years more than fifteen years of snide comments and insult hurled at us – mostly your mother – back in Paradise. We were the ones who were shunned, Jakob. We carried on for two years, hoping in vain that the elders would have the compassion to ask us back. And when they didn't, we still carried on as if they might still do so."

"I know, Papa," Jacob said sympathetically.

"Yes, but Jakob...that battle changed everything. It forced me to see who we were, and where we were living...and, most of all, the young men that we had raised. So, we decided that it was time to move in a totally new direction....and now...here we are."

Jacob still didn't understand, but he also knew that this could take more than one take to comprehend. "I'm hungry, Papa. Are you ready to go for breakfast?"

"We are both hungry, Jakob," his father answered. "Half of the morning has already passed."

"Papa...it is only about six thirty."

"We have been up since before five, Jakob. Our bodies are on cow time. We are very late for breakfast."

Jacob nodded. "Then let's go." The Zook family walked down Front Street toward the little Inn where they had eaten their dinner the previous evening. After breakfast, they spent the rest of the day walking around the city. They headed back to the Cameron house by three o'clock, hitched up the wagon, and brought Jacob's trunk down from the room and loaded it onboard. They arrived at the train station at about half past the hour, and gave their farewells to each other. Jacob found a porter, who took his trunk to the platform. The train for Washington was only two minutes behind schedule.

Jacob was soon comfortably sitting in a railroad car on his way to the nation's capitol.

CHAPTER 38

New Acquaintances

The train from Harrisburg to Washington arrived at a little after eight o'clock pm. As this was the end of the line, the passengers had plenty of time to disembark and leisurely picked up their personal belongings. Jacob was confident in his decision to make the move to the Capitol, but his excitement was clouding his thinking at this moment. He didn't know what to do next, or where to go. He knew that General Sickles had planned to meet him at the station, but he had no idea exactly what he meant by that. He was also worried that his trunk might not be taken off of the baggage car, leaving him alone in a strange city, with no other belongings than the ones on his back.

Jacob stood up. He reached up and into the overhead storage area and retrieved his hat and his walking stick. He drew in a deep breath and headed for the nearest exit. Jacob stepped off of the train and onto the platform at Union Station. The platform was very crowded with soldiers, businessmen, families, and a host of other people who seemed to be searching the faces of those getting off the train – looking for their loved one, or their visitor, or…whomever.

"Jacob! Jacob Zook!" a voice thundered out. Jacob could easily pick out that particular voice in any crowd. It belonged to General Sickles. Jacob scanned the crowded platform again. The voice seemed to come from his right, so he turned in that direction. He couldn't see the General, in spite of his efforts to do so. He walked back toward the railroad car and hopped up onto the stairs, getting himself above the heads of the crowd. Then he saw him.

The General was in a wheelchair, so he was much lower than everyone else. A nicely dressed man of color was standing behind the chair, ready to push it wherever the General ordered. Jacob immediately assumed that the man must be the officer's servant. Jacob raised his arm and hailed the General, tacitly communicating to the man that he had indeed seen him through the crowd. He once again stepped down from the train and headed in the direction of the General, side-stepping the rushing and weaving of many a person on the platform, each of whom were rushing about tending to their own personal business.

Finally, he reached the General. He stretched out his hand and offered it to Sickles. "General Sickles….it is a pleasure to see you once again."

"Likewise, Jacob," replied Sickles. "You are looking very much the part, I must say. You have on some very elegant clothes…for an Amish lad."

"Thank you, sir," said Jacob.

"Jacob…this is Henry Smith….a very dear friend of mine."

Henry Smith extended his hand to Jacob, who grasped it firmly. Obviously, this man was not the manservant he had assumed he was. "It is a pleasure to finally meet you, Jacob. Daniel has spoken of you many times since his return to us a few weeks ago."

"It is a pleasure to make your acquaintance," said Jacob. This was not the first black man that Jacob had ever seen. He had encountered quite a few in Gettysburg, including several who were passing through the community as a part of the Underground Railroad, or had just plain run away from their masters in the Deep South. But this man was the first he had ever seen dressed in fine dress wear – clothing that was every bit the match for the fashions that he himself was wearing. He looked back down at Sickles. "How is your leg, sir?"

"The doctors all say that it is mending very well. No infection- which is good." Suddenly, the General seemed impatient. "Come! Let's get off of this damned platform and get to my cab. We can reminisce on the way back to my place."

"Your place, sir?" asked Jacob.

"My house, Jacob," answered the General. "Surely you didn't think I was going to let you stay in a hotel?" Jacob simply shrugged his shoulders. "Come now, Jacob…friends just don't do that! It isn't hospitable."

"I will happily go wherever you take me, General," Jacob said.

"That's much better."

After a few minutes of weaving and dodging the crowds, the threesome found their way to the outside of the station, where a cab stood at the ready. Henry assisted Sickles into the cab, while the driver assisted Jacob with his trunk. Once both Sickles and the trunk were securely on board, the driver hopped back up to his position, and the cab lurched ahead.

The cab headed north, hugging the Potomac River bank, heading toward a fashionable community known as Georgetown. Sickles had once lived very close to the center of the government, not far from the Capitol Building. It had been at this address that he had shot Philip Barton Key. He had divorced his young wife, claiming adultery. Of course, he never bothered to mention the many incidents when he had been unfaithful to her in the process. But he also didn't want the memory of that house, so he sold it just prior to the beginning of the war. From his bedroom window in Georgetown, he could practically see Alexandria – and the Confederacy.

Sickles made small talk on the ride to his house, asking Jacob about his family, and about Gettysburg and its recovery after the battle. He didn't really seem surprised when Jacob explained that there were still many bodies lying scattered on the battlefield – which was, in actuality, the fields belonging to many of the local residents. The cleanup process was ongoing, and slow. But even as Jacob explained these details to Sickles, he had the impression that everything he was saying was information that the General was already aware of; that there was no real news from that area that the General needed to hear. The General seemed both interested and aloof – all at the same time.

The cab pulled up outside of a large brownstone. "We are home, Jacob," announced Sickles. "Henry, if you could go get my man, he will see to Jacob's trunk. Jacob, would you be so kind to assist me getting out of this cab, please?"

"Certainly, sir," Jacob responded, "but I am not sure that I know what to do." "Have no fear, my boy," laughed Sickles, "I am sure I can tell you what to do." Henry quickly alighted from the cab, quickly moving to the front door of the brownstone. Jacob could see the front door open. Henry was greeted by Sickles' butler, who was, to Jacob's surprise, not a man of color. The man quickly ran down to the cab and received Jacob's trunk and carried it to the house. Henry returned to the cab.

"Daniel…the trunk is on its way to Jacob's bedroom. May I assist you to the door?"

"No, thank you, Henry," replied Sickles. "My houseguest will need to know how I am functioning these days, so this is as good a time as any, I suppose. After we are out, you may take the cab home."

"Fine, Daniel," Henry said. "Jacob…let me give you some advice. The General is still very strong. He is not helpless – even though he might want you to think that occasionally. Do not cater to his every whim!"

"Did I ask you to give him any advice, Henry?" Sickles bellowed.

"Fine! Not advice, Jacob. These are the facts!" answered Henry.

Sickles pulled himself toward the door of the cab, swinging his leg so that it was out of the door. "Just get out of the cab first, Jacob, just to make sure that I don't end up sitting in the mud of the street. I can pretty much do the rest." Jacob used the street side door of the cab to exit, rather than trying to push past Sickles, and quickly ran to the curb side to offer his assistance.

Using his upper body strength, Sickles turned himself completely over. He positioned himself so that he could place his leg on the first step on the outside of the cab, then grabbed the two side bars so that he could hop down, one step at a time. The General used a great deal of effort and energy to complete this task, but Jacob's role was reduced to that of a 'spotter' – just to make sure that nothing unplanned had the chance to happen. Almost immediately after landing on the street with his good leg, Henry was standing next to the General, handing him a set of crutches. The General accepted the crutches and said his good-bye to his friend. Another servant had also arrived at the curb, this one responsible to get the General's wheelchair from the cab.

Henry re-entered the cab and gave the driver the orders to take him to his home. Sickles hobbled toward the steps of the brownstone, with Jacob bringing up the rear. When they reached the stairs, Sickles handed one of the crutches to Jacob, then used the other crutch to help balance himself to that he could use the leverage of the hand rail to ascend the stairs to the house. All this, and only a few weeks after having one of his legs removed from his body by a cannonball.

Jacob entered the General's home. The interior was decorated in earth tones – all in all very masculine colors. There were paintings that were either originals, or very good copies of battle scenes throughout history. There were also a great many framed photos of the current war, purchased, no doubt, directly from Matthew Brady's Photographic Studio in New York City. Sickles stopped just inside the vestibule and turned around to face Jacob.

"I will return in just a moment, Jacob. The sitting room is just through the archway. Please make yourself comfortable." Sickles then hobbled along down the hallway. Jacob looked toward the sitting room, which beckoned invitingly to him after the long journey. The sitting room was a continuation of more of the same, except now the furniture was large and overstuffed, covered with a combination of mohair and leather. Jacob placed his hat and walking stick on a rack that stood near the doorway in the hall and entered the sitting room. He walked over to the wall that backed up against the main hallway. The wall was covered with photographs, mostly of III Corps and Sickles. Jacob moved in closer to the wall so that he could better scrutinize the pictures. He easily recognized the staff officers of III Corps in one of the photographs, particularly Generals Birney and Humphreys. There was a picture of Sickles taken with General Zook. Sickles still had both legs in that picture, which made a great deal of sense to Jacob, as General Zook was mortally wounded on the same day that Sickles had lost his leg.

Jacob moved down the length of the wall. He noticed a picture of their chief adversary, Robert E. Lee. Although Jacob didn't think it was very odd, he also discovered that there was no picture that included the likes of General Hancock or General Meade. The wall was a collection of photographs of people that Sickles liked and respected.

On the far end of the room stood a large fireplace, now standing without a fire due to the unusually warm weather. Jacob remembered the fact that he had seen pictures of such rooms as these decked out with the heads of wild animals which had been shot and then stuffed, then hung to display for all to see. There was no such thing above the fireplace, which indicated to Jacob that Sickles was not, nor was he ever, a hunter. But something was sitting on the mantelpiece…

…it was a dark oaken box.

It was the coffin he had constructed for Sickles shattered leg.

The box was standing upright on top of the mantelpiece for all to see, or at least all that entered this particular room. Jacob wondered if the leg was still encased in the box, just as he had last seen it the day the General was taken away by ambulance. He shook his head in silent wonderment, still thinking of this possibility, when he discovered that there was another display to be seen on top of a sideboard that stood against the outside wall of the house.

It was the leg!

It was the leg, set out on a display stand, with a small iron cannonball for added effect.

Jacob walked over to the display and reached out to touch it, but withdrew his hand before it made contact – as if it could jump off the stand and bite him.

"Pretty impressive, isn't it?" said Sickles, entering the room behind him. Jacob quickly turned around so that he could speak to the General. Sickles was in his wheelchair, attended by one of his servants. "General…I…."

"You are surprised to see how I have put your handiwork on display, Jacob?" But Jacob remained speechless.

"My macabre offering will not be mine much longer, I'm afraid," Sickles continued. "There is going to be a museum dedicated to all forms of war history. I am going to donate my leg to the museum to show off just what can happen on the field of battle."

"Yes, sir," was all that Jacob could say.

"You look…disturbed, Jacob," observed Sickles.

"General…I thought that you were joking. I thought that you were putting on a show of bravery for the sake of your men. I never thought that you would keep the thing!"

"I am a man full of surprises, Jacob," Sickles replied. "Come…sit down on the settee for a while. Let us talk about your future." Jacob moved away from the dismembered leg and approached the couch. "Where are my manners? You must be hungry! When was the last time you ate anything?"

"This afternoon, sir….around one o'clock."

Sickles turned to his servant and barked some orders as if he was speaking to a Private in his Corps, he then turned to Jacob again. "I have arranged to have us visit a few institutions of learning over the next few days, Jacob. I have been in contact with the governing bodies of each of these schools. Each of them cannot wait to meet you face-to-face."

"Is that a fact, sir?" Jacob asked, skeptically.

"It is, my boy. It is! Have you given any thought to which particular school you would like to attend?"

"I have been thinking on it, sir. The University of Pennsylvania is surely attractive, but possibly for the wrong reasons," Jacob said.

"Because of its proximity to Gettysburg?" Stickles wondered aloud. "Exactly! So I don't think that Penn will do me or my family much good in that regard – but it is a fine school."

"That it is," agreed Sickles. "And what about the College of New Jersey?" "Princeton, you mean?" asked Jacob. "That isn't all that much further away than Philadelphia, but it is in another state."

"So your chief object is to put distance between yourself and your parents?" Sickles asked.

"No, not really," answered Jacob, "especially not in recent days. I'm really looking to do this for my own reasons. I want to see more of the country."

"That's a fair reason," said Sickles. "So…the next choice is in New York. That would be Columbia College."

"That is certainly a possibility, General," Jacob stated, "but I am really thinking more in the area of New England."

"Harvard?"

"Or Brown…or Yale…or Dartmouth," listed the boy. "Truth be told…I would like to go to school in Vermont."

"That is very adventurous of you," declared Sickles. "Have you discussed this possibility with your parents?"

"In a way, I have," the boy replied, "but they have already told me that the choice is completely up to me. My mother actually mentioned that she would rather like to see me attend Dartmouth, because it seemed most distant form the war. My father said that he doesn't want to interfere with my selection. He feels that he is unqualified to make that kind of decision for me."

"So he is allowing you the right to fail on your own?"

"Exactly!" the boy said, smiling. "If I am a success, then he will boast of my achievements, but if I fall on my face, and have to return to Gettysburg, then I will have no one else to blame for my failure than the person I see in the mirror."

Jacob looked down at the floor momentarily. Sickles could see that his last remark had taken an emotional toll on the boy. The General softened his tone, losing the edge that he was so famous for displaying. "He is allowing you to grow, Jacob. Your father is enabling you to mature; he is allowing you to make your own decisions."

"Perhaps…" replied the young man, still looking down at the floor.

A cart containing a substantial meal was wheeled into the sitting room. Jacob looked at the food and immediately began to salivate. He looked from the food and then back to Sickles, as if to ask if he was permitted to eat. "Don't wait for me, Jacob…You should begin." Jacob helped himself to a large plate of food.

"So then…we should be off in a few days to visit each of these schools. It is now time to make that first big decision, Jacob."

"Yes, sir," mumbled Jacob, his mouth already stuffed with roast turkey. "But first…I have a few people who I would like to have the pleasure of introducing to you."

"Really? Who?"

"Just some friends, Jacob," Sickles answered. "…just a few of my Washington colleagues."

"Politicians?" asked Jacob.

"And some members of the military," added Sickles.

"Oh," pressed Jacob, "anyone that I know?"

"Perhaps…but it is not very likely, Jacob. Most of those whom you have already met are still off fighting the war."

"That is true I suppose," admitted Jacob.

"We have an appointment at the War Department tomorrow at ten o'clock in the morning. We will have a carriage here to pick us up at nine thirty," explained Sickles.

"At the War Department?" asked the boy. "How am I to dress for a meeting at the War Department?"

"For my money, I would have you dress like a typical Amish lad," lamented Sickles, "but I have a feeling that you did not come to town with much of that clothing in your trunk. Did you?"

Jacob laughed. This was about the last thing he would have thought to have packed! He had been convinced that the General wanted him to become a modern American, whether as a student or as a farmer in Gettysburg. "Why would you think I would bring my Amish clothing, General?"

"I'm not sure if I really did expect you to do that, Jacob," Sickles explained. "It's just that I built you up as this folksy Amish kid - a little naïve, but a great deal interesting. They are all fascinated by your story, Jacob. When you show up looking like you just stepped off of Pennsylvania Avenue they will think that I concocted the whole affair."

"But General," Jacob argued, "isn't this what you expected me to wear to the University?"

"Of course it is," soothed Sickles. "I must have been deluding myself."

Jacob closed his eyes and considered his situation for a moment. He thought back to earlier in the day when he dressed very simply in order to fit in with his parents while they were in Harrisburg. "I could dress more simply than this, General."

"How is that?" asked the General.

"I could wear a simple white shirt, black trousers, and a black tie. I have brought along my black boots, which I thought might come in handy during the winter months. I won't wear a vest or a frock coat. If I could get my hands on a straw, wide-brimmed hat, then that would probably complete the ruse."

"Brilliant, Jacob! I can send one of my men out first thing in the morning to search the city for a hat."

Jacob smiled at the General. He didn't quite understand the man's elation over his manner of dress. He had never considered himself particularly vain, but he definitely felt a pang of disappointment at the prospect of going to such a lofty venue as the War Department, but not be wearing some of the 'fancy' clothing that he had purchased; clothing which he thought really made him look and feel…handsome.

But there was also something else that was nagging at him something that the General had also said in passing. "Why did you refer to me as -naïve?"

Sickles looked down at the floor. The last thing he wanted to do was insult Jacob Zook; he had a great regard for the boy. "Please don't react to the word as if it shows you as something other than what you are,

Jacob. Your character exudes a gentleness and sincerity that has been long missing from the big cities of this country. You display a natural innocence; an innocence which is directly a result of your upbringing. It is a big part of what makes you…you."

Jacob took another mouthful of the food from his plate, attempting to fill his stomach, while, at the same time, holding a discussion with one of the strongest and willful personalities he had ever met…even stronger, in fact, than his father's personality.

"Jacob, you must be getting tired, "observed Sickles. "You don't have to finish every morsel on that dish, you know. You have been travelling almost all afternoon. It takes a great deal out of a person… I can tell you that."

"I am a bit bushed," replied the boy, stifling back a yawn.

"We will have plenty of time to catch up over the next week," said Sickles. "Your bedroom is to the left at the top of the stairs."

Jacob nodded. He stood up and slowly headed toward the staircase, momentarily forgetting his manners. He reached the base of the stairs and placed his left hand on the newel post, but then turned back to the General. "Pardon me, General," he said, "but may I ask where you sleep?"

"I stay in the room that is down the hall to the right on this floor, Jacob. I'm afraid that I don't navigate stairs very well anymore."

Jacob smiled at the General's self-deprecating comment. "I understand, sir." Jacob released the newel post and dismounted the bottom stair, turning back toward Sickles, who was already wheeling himself out of the sitting room. "And General, I would once again like to thank you for all of the kindness that you have shown me…and especially my family…the house, and all."

"You are quite welcome, Mr. Zook. I hope that you will find your stay here with me very comfortable."

Jacob smiled again and bowed his head to the officer. "I shall, sir… and with that, I will bid you good-night."

Sickles returned Jacob's bow by lowering his head toward his chest. "Good-night, Jacob. I will see you tomorrow morning, at breakfast."

CHAPTER 39

The War Department

By nine o'clock the next morning, Jacob had risen, washed, dressed and eaten his breakfast. General Sickles' butler was not to be found anywhere on the premises, as he was already out and about, attempting to find a suitable straw hat that might lend credence to the boy's Amish upbringing.

Sickles arrived for his breakfast at about 9:15. Jacob was enjoying a second cup of the most delicious coffee he had ever tasted - it was so much better than anything he had experienced in Gettysburg – when the General entered the breakfast room. Jacob was almost surprised to see, given the circumstances, that Sickles was not in his uniform. Even though his fighting days were now over, Sickles was still on active duty. And they were going to visit his bosses at the War Department. Surely, he thought, this visit would warrant him wearing the uniform of a Major General in the Army of the Potomac.

"Good morning, Jacob," greeted the General, as he rolled himself into his position at the small, round table.

"Good morning, sir," answered the Amish boy – who was now dressed to be equal to the part.

"You are looking right Amish this morning, Jacob," admitted Sickles. "Now all you need is the damned straw hat, which you should be getting at any minute now. My man is out getting you one."

"Yes sir…I know."

"You know?"

"Yes sir," answered Jacob. "I spoke with the butler as he was going out of the door. He asked me to describe it to him."

"Good. Good," replied Sickles. "But we have to leave here in about fifteen minutes, so he'd better hurry himself along."

"I am sure that he is doing his best, sir," answered Jacob, calmly.

Sickles nodded. He was well aware that it was only a little past nine and that most shops would not have opened yet. Still, he expected immediate results. He shook off his morning anxiousness and turned pleasant again. "How was your breakfast, Jacob?"

"Very good, sir," the boy replied, taking advantage of his new-found company at the table to help himself to another sweet roll.

"Yes," agreed the General, "Mary is quite a cook…I must admit that. If I am not careful, I am going to put on an enormous amount of weight from all of her cooking… what with my inability to get around as I was used to doing." He gently patted the stump of his right leg.

Jacob smiled back at the General with a mouth full of sweet roll, but he was also made uncomfortable for the moment; uncomfortable to be reminded of the permanent nature of the man's affliction. "I am greatly looking forward to seeing some of the buildings in the Capital today, sir," he mentioned, attempting to change the subject.

"Ah, yes," puffed the General. "This is a magnificent city, Jacob. But even still, there is much work to be done around here. That's part of the reason for our visit this morning."

"Sir?"

"This visit will mix business with pleasure, Jacob," Sickles explained. "I have a list of projects up my sleeve that I wish to address – both at the War Department, as well as on Capitol Hill."

Jacob, who didn't know much about the man, other than the fact that he was a wounded officer, had just had his first glimpse at Sickles, the politician. "Pardon me, sir," he asked, "but aren't these men too busy fighting the war to listen to you at this moment?"

"Nonsense, my boy," Sickles sighed expansively, "our visit is an outgrowth of the war! Don't worry…you will see. You will see." And then the General left the boy hanging; leaving his last phrase dangling in the air, as if Jacob was required to guess the meaning of the cryptic statement. "And we had better be going, if we are going to make our ten o'clock appointment."

"Yes, sir," answered Jacob, who promptly stuffed the remaining piece of sweet roll into his mouth. "May I assist you by pushing your chair?"

"That would be very nice of you," answered the General. "Just be sure that you don't push me down the front steps!" Jacob was so shocked by the General's crass answer that his jaw dropped. Getting the reaction that he wanted, Sickles broadly smiled and let out a loud, short burst of laughter, which instantly broke the tension.

They headed toward the front door of the brownstone. Sickles crutches were positioned against the wall adjacent to the door. Jacob stepped from behind the wheelchair and handed the General the crutches. The boy held the chair firmly in place while the officer used his upper body strength to raise himself out of his sitting position. That accomplished, the General opened the door, while Jacob continued to take care of his rolling transportation. As he had done the previous evening, Jacob watched the General manage the front steps, only now in reverse. A cab was already waiting for them in front of the home; the driver already moving to assist the General to his accustomed place in the cabin. Jacob gently lowered the wheelchair to the street level, giving it to the driver to secure on the rear of the cab before entering the cabin to sit with the General.

They were just about to pull away from the curb, when they heard a rapping on the door of the cab. It was the General's butler.

"Pardon me, General Sickles," said the butler, obviously trying to catch his breath. "I found this for the young man, sir." He raised his right hand, which held a fine, new wide-brimmed straw hat. The only adornment on the hat was a band of black felt.

"What do you think of this, Jacob?" asked Sickles.

Jacob studied the hat. "It is perfect, sir. It is just like the ones we wear in Paradise."

The General nodded to the butler. "Well done, John. Well done!"

"Thank you, sir!" John replied, smiling at his success. "Will you be returning for luncheon, sir?"

"That is a fair question. I will think not, John," said Sickles. "I think that Jacob might like to see a bit of Washington today. It looks like it is going to be a nice day for a drive."

"Yes, sir," answered John.

Sickles rapped the roof of the cabin with one of his crutches and within a moment the cab jolted ahead. "Well, we may be a little late, Jacob. But they can wait, now can't they? They all have both of their legs."

Jacob could only nod, considering that the General had made a statement the natural reply to which he could not possibly agree or disagree to its fact. The only bit of information that Sickles had offered which could actually be debated was, in fact, the weather. "General? It seems a bit cooler today than yesterday. Don't you think so?"

"And you should be grateful for that, Jacob," Sickles replied. "There is nothing as awful as Washington in the summer, especially when it is humid – except perhaps Charleston…or Atlanta."

"Have you been to those places, sir?" asked the boy.

"Oh, yes," replied Sickles. "Before the war, of course. Charming cities, they were…but too hot for my taste. New York is no picnic during the summer months, but it is a far cry better than Charleston."

The driver of the cab turned the horses to the left and they rounded a corner. They were now driving along a main avenue, the Potomac River was clearly visible on their right side. Jacob could see the Confederate city of Alexandria across the river. The driver cracked his whip and the horses responded by accelerating to a much quicker canter. "That's the spirit, Jack!" Sickles yelled to the driver. "See that, Jacob? Jack knows we are in a great rush."

The cab now raced along the banks of the river, quickly passing through the little community of Georgetown. "Look over there," said Sickles, pointing with an outstretch hand, "that house over there belongs to the Key family."

"The man you shot?" asked Jacob.

"Well…it was first the home of his father, Francis Scott Key…the writer of that famous poem, 'In Defense of Fort McHenry.'" Sickles looked Jacob squarely in the eye when he said that, but the boy had no sign of recognition in his eyes. "You don't know that poem, I suppose?" Jacob shook his head. "I thought that every schoolboy knew that poem, Jacob!"

"I didn't go to school, sir," Jacob said. "Don't you remember?"

"You're right! I'm sorry!" answered the General. "Key was a good man….but even good men can raise a bastard as their son!" The cab entered the confines of the Capitol city. The avenues now were named after the States of the Union. They were now driving on Pennsylvania Avenue, a fact that had not escaped Jacob's mind.

Suddenly, there were hundreds of similar cabs darting in and out of the side streets. Jacob could see a great many soldiers, all of them wearing the dark blue uniform of the Federal Army. By leaning out of the window, Jacob could make out the tallest buildings in the city, including the partially completed dome of the Capitol Building, as well as the lower portion of the obelisk that was being built to honor the first President of the United States, and the man for whom the city was named, George Washington. He was so fascinated by the sites within the city that time literally slipped out of his control. Even though it seemed but just a few minutes, he had been preoccupied by the vistas provided by the Capitol that he completely ignored Sickles for almost fifteen minutes.

The cab pulled up to the building that served as the headquarters for the War Department. Jacob pulled his head back inside the cab.

"I thought you said it would take almost a half hour to get here, sir?" Sickles gave the boy a wry smile, and then said, simply, "It did." "What?"

"You were so involved with your new surroundings that I didn't want to disturb you," answered Sickles. "Don't worry, Jacob…I love this city, too."

Their driver, Jack, appeared at the door and positioned himself as Henry Smith had done the previous evening. Sickles descended from the vehicle, with very little help from Jack. Within a few minutes time, both Sickles and Jacob were standing in the main corridor of the War Department building.

Jacob was holding his new wide-brimmed straw hat in his hands.

"You're a bit late," called a booming voice from behind them.

Jacob turned the General around in his wheelchair so that he could face the man who had accused him so. "Your pocket watch is fast, Edwin. We are right on time!"

The man laughed at this retort, even though he was absolutely correct. The General and Jacob were, indeed, late for the meeting. The man was tall, and wearing a gray suit. His beard, as well as the hair on his head, was a salt and pepper gray – with some of the gray seeming to match the color of his suit perfectly, and the beard was quite long. Jacob's first impression of the man was that, given different circumstances, location, and the rest of his dress – the man could easily have passed for an Amish man. The man approached Sickles and extended his hand, warmly shaking hands with the General. "How is the leg, Dan?"

"It has good days and bad, I'm afraid. It still is oozing a bit." "They tell me that is normal, I'm afraid," said the tall man.

"Hm," said Sickles, his grunt merely agreeing with the awful truth of the matter. "Ed....I would like you to meet Mister Jacob Zook, from Gettysburg, Pennsylvania. This is the young man who assisted in the procedure that placed me in this precarious position."

The man offered his hand to Jacob, who took it and shook it cordially. "So this is the young man that you have been talking about. It is a pleasure to meet you, Mister Zook."

"Jacob…this is Secretary of War, Edwin Stanton."

Jacob instantly felt his knees buckle. This was the man who was in charge of the Federal effort to win the war. There weren't a great many people associated with either side of the conflict that Jacob knew by name, or reputation, but Edwin Stanton was certainly one of them. "A pleasure to meet you, Mr. Stanton," stammered the boy.

"Secretary Stanton," corrected Sickles.

"Excuse me?" asked Jacob.

"Secretary Stanton," repeated Sickles. "Not Mr. Stanton, Jacob. Our Cabinet members are addressed as 'Secretary.'"

"Don't trouble the boy with all of our mumbo-jumbo," protested Stanton. "He is allowed a few breeches of protocol, under the circumstances."

"Thank you, Mr. Secretary," said Jacob.

"There…you see?" observed Stanton. "The young man is already skilled in the ways of Washington. What more could you ask for in two minutes time? Now…we should head into my office. The others are waiting for us in there." Stanton turned and led the way, with Jacob pushing Sickle's wheelchair down the hallway. Stanton turned to the right and opened a door, he then stepped to the side to allow Jacob the ability to push the wheelchair into his office.

Stanton's office was a large room, almost perfectly square in dimension. There was a fireplace on one side of the room, which was unlit due to the time of year. There was a very large, elegant wooden desk on the opposite side of the room, with windows behind it. The windows let in a great deal of the morning sun, but Jacob could clearly see a large, white building only a city block or so away. It was the Executive Mansion - the White House. Jacob remembered seeing pictures of the President's home back in Gettysburg. In many respects, Stanton's office had a similar feel and décor to Sickle's sitting room back in Georgetown. The furniture was mostly covered with mohair, and the styling was large and cumbersome - absolutely masculine in appearance. The walls contained paintings, and some of the newer photographs, of some of the military leaders of the war. There were models of new armaments, particularly cannon, which were in the room for either approval or some form of discussion. There was a large table, near the center of the room, which held a large map of the country. Upon the map were moveable, dimensional figures – some in blue and others in gray – meant to represent the opposing armies and their positions around the country. Some of the larger figures contained Roman numerals, signifying the particular Corps assigned to that area. Even the waters surrounding the land mass contained these figurines, as it also showed the placement of the naval vessels of both sides of the conflict.

As he became more aware of his new environment, Jacob noticed that they were not alone. There were several other men in the room. Two were carefully studying the map and troop placements; another was sitting in a large armchair. The armchair was one of a matched set, placed in close proximity to the hearth of the fireplace – a place to have a quiet, or even secret conversation, especially in the colder months of the year. The high back of the armchair precluded Jacob from fully seeing the man sitting in it; he could only see the bottom of his trousers and his black shoes, as he was sitting with his one leg crossed over the other.

His observations were put to an immediate halt when Sickles suddenly spoke. "Gideon…still trying to keep the rebels at bay?"

A shorter, stocky man with gray hair and a white beard straightened up from his position, where he had been studying the map. "Daniel…. it's good to see you again. How is the leg?"

"The leg is fine, and on a table in my home," replied the General. "The stump has its good days and bad days. Today….is a good day."

The older man smiled at Sickles. He seemed perfectly accustomed to the General's wry sense of humor, and seemed to already know that Sickles was keeping his macabre souvenir at his house. "And who is this young man?" he asked.

Sickles wriggled in his wheelchair, attempting to face Jacob. "This is my Amish friend, Jacob Zook. Jacob….this is Secretary of the Navy…. Gideon Welles."

As Welles made no attempt to move from the side of the map table, Jacob bowed to the gentleman by nodding his head. "A pleasure to make your acquaintance, Mr. Secretary."

"And, I might add," inserted Sickles, "an extraordinarily quick study!"

"So you are the young man who helped the surgeon amputate Daniel's leg?" asked Welles, still standing by the map table.

Jacob was astonished. It seemed that everyone in the Washington inner circle already knew of the story. "Yes, sir," replied the boy, "….I mean to say…I was there to help…so…I helped."

"You are too modest," added Stanton. "I hear that you were also the one who saved the life of one of our other officers…a Major…who happened to be carrying vital information back to the line."

"Yes, sir…," answered Jacob, "but…once again…I just happened to be there. Gettysburg is my home, sir…I knew my way around the area very well. I couldn't just leave the man there on the open field to die from his wounds." Jacob decided to leave out the details about Major Winslow forcing him at gunpoint to get him to safety, or his own sad opinion about the death of his Confederate friend, Bobby McLean.

"And still you stayed to help," added a voice from the far end of the room. It had been spoken by the man in the armchair.

Jacob turned toward the armchair. "There was nothing else for me to do, sir. It was God's Will that I help the Major…just as it was God's Will that I help the General. But," he paused, thinking again about Bobby McLean, who he considered an innocent victim of the war, his voice faltering a bit, "I tell you, quite honestly…I would have done the same for any man…Blue or Gray…had I been given the opportunity."

"What?" asked Stanton, his voice filled with righteous anger. "You would help the enemy?"

"I did not see them as my enemies, Secretary Stanton," replied Jacob, "only as men. We Amish do not look at your war with the same eyes as you do, sir."

Stanton's face flushed with rage. "Daniel….did you know about this boy's political views?"

Sickles remained uncharacteristically calm. "Of course I did, Ed. And they are not political views…they are…humanitarian. The Amish are simply a peace-loving people…and a people whose views are very misunderstood by the 'English.'"

"The English?" yelled Stanton. "What the Hell do the English have to do with this?"

Sickles crossed his right hand over his body, passing it over his left shoulder. He found Jacob's left hand, still gripping the back of the wheelchair and gave it a pat. "This boy represents the basic good that we all have …somewhere….within us, gentlemen. He represents a neutral stance. In many respects, his view of the war may be compared to the way the Maker is looking down upon us right now. He sees two armies of his own creations…who are blowing each other to Kingdom Come.

Jacob Zook is no more an enemy to the Union than he is to the Confederacy. He has been a friend to both sides."

"And this is something we all need to remember, gentlemen," said the voice in the armchair, "as this war grinds to a halt. We must heal this nation with kindness, not with malice." The man now stood and faced the others in the room. He was wearing a black suit. Jacob could tell that the man was extremely tall – perhaps even over six foot in height. He wore a straggly black beard, but no mustache – very much the style of the Amish married men – which made Jacob wonder if the man was, in fact, Amish.

The tall man now approached the center of the room, and the wheelchair occupied by Daniel Sickles, and pushed by his young friend, Jacob Zook. Jacob watched the man closely – there was something ungainly and awkward about him, and yet awesome at the same time, but he also noticed Stanton, who was reacting negatively to what the man had just said, as if he was diametrically opposed to that philosophy.

"Mr. President," Stanton began, but if Jacob heard anything that followed by way of a rebuttal, it was quickly squelched.

"Mr. President?" Jacob muttered, looking at the tall man.

"Hold on a moment, Edwin," said the tall man, interrupting his most salient thoughts on reconstruction. "We are forgetting our manners, are we not?"

Stanton seemed flustered, but acquiesced. "You are correct, Mr. President. May I have the honor of presenting Mr. Jacob Zook, of Gettysburg."

The President extended his hand to Jacob, who took the President's hand and shook it gently. "Are you…President Lincoln?" he asked.

"The very same," Lincoln answered, "but not for long, if we don't get this here war won. I understand George McClellan is seeking the nomination for my job."

"That snake in the grass," cursed Sickles, who was never a supporter of McClellan when he was General-In-Chief. "He thinks that he's smarter than the rest of us."

"Yes," replied Lincoln, "but we will have to see about that. Gettysburg helped our cause, gentlemen, but Vicksburg helped us even more."

"Vicksburg?" asked Sickles.

"Yes, General," explained Stanton. "We have won a tremendous victory on the Mississippi River. General Grant has taken the city of Vicksburg. The Mississippi River is ours. We have cut the Confederacy in two."

"That is correct," continued Lincoln, "but more importantly…I have found, at long last, a General who knows how to fight."

"I know you are considering Grant to command your armies, Mr. President," warned Stanton, "but don't you think that he is a bit too reckless? Remember all the blood shed at Shiloh!"

Lincoln nodded in agreement. "That is true, and unfortunate. But we have had more than our share of cautious Generals, Mr. Secretary. I think it is high time that we tried some "reckless" Generals. I hear that Grant and his friend, Sherman are quite a pair."

"They will make the South pay dearly," said Sickles.

"The South will have to pay dearly, General," replied Lincoln, "until the war is over…but it is at that point that we must be willing to accept them back into the Union with open and loving arms." The President looked over at Stanton, who silently dropped his gaze to the floor. "Now…General Sickles…what brings you and Mr. Zook here to this office this fine day?"

Sickles cleared his throat, preparing to make his presentation to the President and the two Secretaries. "Gentlemen…as a person recently returned from the field of battle, I would like to propose several ideas to you – projects, if you will."

"Continue, please," said the President.

"Mr. President…if there was one thing that was ever-present in my mind during my time of recovery, it was the fact that our military hospitals are too few…and that the ones that exist are but a little better than deplorable. I would like to suggest that we build a series of new military hospitals, perhaps even here in Washington." Sickles looked over at Gideon Welles. "You might consider a hospital here in Washington for the wounded from the land battles, and then, you might consider building a hospital for the injured seamen, as well."

Lincoln stroked his black beard, heavy in thought. "You have given this a bit of thought, General?"

"I have, Mr. President," Sickles answered. "My idea is this: If a General, such as me, was made to endure the suffering and conditions, such as I did, then what suffering must be in store for a Sergeant, or a Corporal…or even a Private? Are these men not entitled to fair and equal treatment?"

"You make a very good argument, Daniel," agreed the President. "This war has taken a terrible toll on the people of this country. The government needs to provide some sort of relief for the thousands of young men who made this sacrifice in defense of their country."

"May I ask a question, sir?" asked Jacob.

"Certainly, Jacob," replied Lincoln, "we are just having a conversation here, like ordinary citizens."

"Very well," said the boy. "Would these hospitals be open to all Americans, regardless of which side they fought on in the war?"

A silence fell over the room that was palpable. Jacob looked over at Stanton, who was already seething. He then looked at Welles, who was dropping his eyes toward the floor again. He had obviously hit a nerve.

"You ask the tough questions," said Lincoln.

"But he asks the correct questions," interjected Sickles. By standing behind the General's back, Jacob had no idea how Sickles had reacted to his question – but he was about to find out. "Mr. President, I spent the last two years watching brave young men dying on battlefields in Maryland, Virginia, and Pennsylvania. I was often put in the position of having to order company, regiment, battalion, and even corps into the direct fire of the enemy – but just as often it was the enemy that was facing our guns. When this is all over, we shall have to rebuild this country, and much of that rebuilding process will involve the repatriation of these southern men – men who fought as bravely as they could, without question… without reserve. What if there is another war…an international war instead of a civil war? Where would you get the manpower to fight this war? Would you only ask those from the northern states? I doubt it! These hospitals can help heal a variety of wounds…but they can also help heal the wounds that have afflicted this country."

Sickles sat back in his wheelchair, having delivered the first of two speeches he intended to give that morning. He felt Jacob reach forward and affectionately squeeze his right shoulder. Sickles reached up with his hand and, before the boy could remove it, grabbed his hand in his own.

"Well spoken, Daniel," said Lincoln, obviously impressed with Sickles gift of oratory. "You have made a fine argument….one that I must consider."

"Thank you, Mr. President," answered the General. "I think that this will mean a great deal to the men who have spilled their blood for this country."

Jacob suddenly felt a warm rush coursing through his veins. He knew immediately what that feeling was all about; it was pride. He felt very proud to know the General, something that he never really felt up until this very moment. He replaced his right hand on Sickles' shoulder and gave it a light pat, thinking that the General had accomplished his mission for the day.

"But there is something else that I wish to discuss with you, Mr. Lincoln," Stickles continued. Stanton and Welles gave Sickles an odd look, as if too indicate that he was overstepping his bounds.

"Another request, Daniel?" asked Lincoln. "Have you been saving them up for this one special day?" Sickles let out a short, dry laugh – realizing that he was treading on politically unstable ground. "Well... you have my attention, General," continued Lincoln, "so you may as well go on."

Sickles exhaled with relief. "I witnessed a great deal of carnage during my service to the Union, sir," he began, "and through much of this action saw many a brave young man die on the field of battle – never to return to his loved ones. I don't think I will ever forget that which I witnessed at Gettysburg, sir."

"I am sure that you are not embellishing that truth, General," answered Lincoln.

"Before I was taken away from the field hospital...which was several days after the conclusion of hostilities...I received a final report on the condition of III Corps, Mr. President," said Sickles. "Much of the Corps which I once commanded lay dead in the middle of the field; in a Peach Orchard, a Wheat Field, and in a Hell-hole called "Devil's Den.""

Stanton took a step forward toward Sickles. "General Meade has already submitted his report on your part in the battle, Daniel. He claims that many of the losses suffered by your Corps were the direct result of you countermanding his orders as Commander of the Army."

"Damn that man," thundered Sickles, forgetting the company he was with for the moment. "Meade had placed me in an indefensible position. I had to move my Corps forward, or else be caught in a crossfire."

"Which seems to have happened anyway," added Stanton.

Sickles nodded slowly. "Yes."

Lincoln interrupted the conversation. "But this is not what you wish to ask me. Is it, Daniel?"

Sickles once again let out his breath. "No, sir…it is not. My part played in the battle aside.…I discovered upon my removal from Gettysburg that many of my men still lay rotting on the farmland of Gettysburg. Sir.…they may still be lying there, even as we speak."

Lincoln turned slowly toward Jacob. "Well, Mr. Zook.…is the General correct?"

Jacob's face turned immediately grim, while he nodded slowly. "There are still many bodies – from both sides of the battle – strew all around the fields, sir. It has been a hot, humid summer…and you can't evade the stench of rotting flesh that is everywhere in Gettysburg. The Army has been gone for weeks, so the citizens have organized details to bury the dead, giving them as much of a Christian funeral as they can manage – but the going is very slow, sir."

"I don't understand," said Lincoln. "Where are they burying these poor boys?"

Jacob shook his head. "Many of them are buried right where they fell in battle – which means that they are being interred in the middle of Mr. McPhearson's farm, or on the land of some other farmer in Gettysburg. The citizens have attempted to mark the gravesites, and, in some cases… they are able to discover the identity of the soldier in order to mark their grave with a name. But often they are simply marking down the name of the state, or company, or Corps…depending upon what they can make out on their uniform."

"This is inexcusable," exclaimed Lincoln.

"But, sir…" added Jacob, "there is more. There is a great fear that the dead might also spawn an outbreak of some dreadful disease, such as cholera. For this reason, the citizen's detail is kept very small. Fewer and fewer men are volunteering for this job, as they fear that it is like a death sentence. Most of the farmers in the area…especially those most affected by the battle…have not returned to care for their fields. We have lost most of our livestock, which were either killed or plundered during the battle. Our town is on the verge of economic ruin, sir." Jacob had spoken from his heart, but with a purpose, even though he had not been aware up until that very moment that he had been brought to this very room by Sickles just so that he would have the chance to speak his mind. Even so, a large tear now coursed down the side of his face; a tear which did not go unnoticed by the President.

Lincoln crossed the room and placed his hand on Jacob's shoulder. "You have spoken well, Mr. Zook. How old are you? Seventeen?"

"Eighteen, sir."

"Eighteen!" Lincoln said, correcting himself. "That is the same age as many of the boys fighting in the field….some, I am afraid…are even younger."

"Yes, sir," answered Jacob. "I met quite a few, myself." "And what of your parents, Jacob?" "My parents, sir?"

"How did they fare during the battle?" asked Lincoln.

Jacob cast an eye in Sickles direction. He noticed the General squirm a bit in his wheelchair, causing Jacob to assume that he should not mention the new house, or the fact that the army had rebuilt it for them. "My parents…as well as my younger brother, Abraham…all survived the battle, sir. The situation was difficult, but we managed. But recently, they have been assisting the Lutheran seminarians and ministers – helping them to bury the dead – because very few others will do it. The battle has changed my parents, Mr. Lincoln – especially my father. I would not be here today, was that not so."

Lincoln turned to Stanton and Welles. "We should do something about this situation, gentlemen."

Stanton cleared his throat. "Mr. President…this is the same situation that we face after every major battle. Very often the dead are left behind for the locals to bury."

"This is unacceptable," replied Lincoln.

"Indeed, it is!" commented Sickles. "And that is why, Mr. President…I would like to propose that a National Cemetery be created."

"A National Cemetery?" asked Lincoln.

"Yes," answered the General, "to receive the remains of the gallant fallen." Lincoln pondered this concept for a moment, pacing back across the room toward the hearth. "This may be a very good idea, Daniel. Do you have a location in mind?"

"Well," interjected Stanton, "if he doesn't, then I certainly do. I have had my eye cast across the Potomac River for some time now. Isn't that right, Gideon? On a clear day, you can see that traitor Lee's home… Arlington House, I believe it's called….sitting atop his property; acres and acres of lush hills. It would make a fine cemetery."

"You are speaking of the Custis-Lee Mansion, are you not?" asked Lincoln, "the ancestral home of the wife of our first President?"

"The very same," answered Welles, who also agreed with Stanton's idea. "Edwin," Lincoln counseled patiently, "we have already had this discussion many times. I do not plan to punish the South for our disagreement. We need to embrace these men, not create more animosity. Besides that, this property has deep historic significance for the entire nation."

"But….Mr. President…" pleaded Stanton.

"Mr. President…" Sickles interrupted. "I do have an alternative suggestion for the location."

Lincoln turned to face the General. "And for some reason, Daniel, I can honestly say that I am not all that surprised. What is your suggestion?"

"Well, sir," began Sickles, "as the dead are already there in the first place, why don't we simply create the National Cemetery right there at Gettysburg?"

Lincoln stroked his bead pensively. He sat back down in the armchair by the fireplace to mull over the suggestion. Jacob stepped away from the back of Sickles' wheelchair for the first time since entering the room, getting himself to a position where he could see the General's face. He now realized that he was there for a specific purpose. He could detect a slight smile on the General's lips, as if he was tacitly thanking him for the role he had just masterfully played.

Sickles looked over at Stanton and Welles. Welles had a confused look on his face, which, truth be told, was far from abnormal for the man. Stanton had more of a glare in his eyes, as if he had just been outmaneuvered by a master. Sickles nodded his head in deference to the Secretary of War, and then Stanton nodded back, as if to acknowledge the well-played move.

"We should acquire a tract of land in Gettysburg," said Lincoln, still sitting in the armchair. "Who is the Governor of Pennsylvania, Jacob?"

"I have no idea, Mr. President," answered Jacob, honestly. "We Amish tend to separate ourselves from knowledge of your government… or of any government."

"Oh, yes…I had forgotten that point," said Lincoln.

"Andrew Curtin is Governor of Pennsylvania," interjected Sickles. Stanton quickly raised an eyebrow at the General's concise knowledge of Pennsylvania government. He had obviously done his research on the matter.

"Thank you, Daniel," answered Lincoln. "We shall contact the Governor's office to see whether or not we can acquire a tract of land large enough to be effectively used for this purpose."

"Mr. President?" Jacob spoke up. "There are already several men in Gettysburg who are interested in pursuing the same idea. They are…like yourself, sir…lawyers….and leaders within the Gettysburg community."

"Excellent!" exclaimed Lincoln. "This idea already has grass-roots beginnings. This should make it easier to act quickly, gentlemen."

"Yes, Mr. President," said Stanton.

From behind the armchair, Lincoln then asked Sickles, "Do you have any other suggestions for us this morning, General?"

"No, Mr. President, I do not."

"Very well," Lincoln answered, "then I should very much like it if you would allow me to confer with Mister Zook for a few minutes, Daniel." The President paused for a moment. "…Unless you are in a rush to go someplace?"

"No, sir," answered Sickles. "You may speak with the lad for as long as you desire. I will take the opportunity to catch up with Edwin and Gideon."

Welles quickly took the cue given by both the President and the General, stepping up to Sickles' wheelchair, and, along with Stanton by his side, pushing the General out of the office of the Secretary of War.

If he had been nervous or apprehensive prior to this moment, Jacob was certainly nervous and apprehensive now. He had never expected to even see the President of the United States on his visit to Washington, and now he was about to speak with him, one on one.

"Come…" said Lincoln in a gentle voice. "Come over here, Jacob, and sit with me."

Jacob slowly crossed the width of the large, square office. He rounded the side of the second armchair, but halted at the side, looking at Lincoln for his approval. Lincoln looked up and smiled at the tentative nature of the young man. "Sit down, Jacob. I won't bite, you know."

A smile filled Jacob's face. He had heard stories of the very homespun and gentle nature of this particular President; how he was different from many of those who had come before him. Jacob lowered himself into the armchair.

Lincoln looked over at the boy and then smiled. "So…Jacob Zook… you seem like an extraordinary young man. I know how you and General Sickles got to know each other….the amputation of his leg, and all…but why is it that you have come to Washington?"

Jacob wasn't sure how to answer the President's question. He wanted to tell him about the generosity of the General, but didn't want to overstep his position with Sickles, if that was, in fact, what he would be doing by answering. Still, he thought, it was the President of the United States asking the question. "The General is assisting me, Mr. President, so that I may get a proper education."

"Is he, now?" questioned Lincoln, in a surprised tone of voice.

"Yes, sir," confirmed Jacob, more confidently than before, as the secret was already out. "The General has offered to pay for my education."

"Well I'll be!" exclaimed Lincoln.

"General Sickles thinks I could be a physician."

"A physician?" asked Lincoln. "Perhaps even a surgeon…like the one who removed his leg?"

"Doctor Sim" added Jacob. "That was Doctor Sim. He is very skilled, indeed!" "I am sure," confided the President, "but is that what you want to do, Jacob?" Jacob lowered his head a bit. "I don't really like blood, Mr. Lincoln. It makes me nauseous."

"Really? And yet you assisted with amputations during the battle!" "That was because it was something that had to be done, sir," explained Jacob. "I don't like blood, but I got passed it. I saw a great deal of blood, I'm afraid." "So you really don't want to go into medicine?" questioned the President.

"I didn't say that, Mr. Lincoln," replied Jacob.

"I don't understand."

Jacob shifted his position in the armchair, creeping up a bit more toward the edge of the chair, leaning in toward the President. "It is true that I assisted quite a bit in the field hospital during the battle. But it is also true that I witnessed many men and boys die….and not from their obvious wounds."

"I still do not follow you," remarked Lincoln.

Jacob nodded. "It is difficult to explain, sir. There was this other General…he was a Confederate officer….General Lewis Armistead."

"Ah, yes," acknowledged the President, "the Armistead family is well-known in American history for their military service. Too bad this Armistead was fighting for the other side."

"Yes," continued Jacob, "but the General should not have died in our hospital. He was seriously wounded…but he should have recovered. He just suddenly…died."

"Go on."

"I witnessed this type of thing many times, sir," said Jacob. "Men were expected to live, and then they died. Many of them developed gangrene, which was worse than their actual wound. There are many mysteries surrounding illness and wounds that need to be discovered."

"And you want to be the one who finds the answers to these mysteries?" asked Lincoln.

"I think so," answered Jacob. "At least that's the way I feel right now."

"That is very noble of you, my boy," said Lincoln, but, having said this, sat back in his armchair, seeming to slump into an instant state of melancholy.

Jacob could easily see the change that had come over the President. "Is there anything wrong, sir?"

Lincoln slowly nodded. "You explanation set my mind turning, Jacob. Just last year, one of my sons….Edward….Eddie…fell sick. He seemed to be recovering, but then…on a night when Mrs. Lincoln and

I were entertaining many guests, he lapsed into a coma and was dead by the morning. His doctors called his illness…a mystery…" Lincoln ceased speaking, his emotion waking within him.

"I am sorry, Mr. Lincoln, to learn of your loss." Jacob had no idea that the President had lost a son. The fact of the matter was that Jacob had no knowledge of any aspect of the personal life of Abraham Lincoln; that the President was married – or the fact that the loss of Eddie was, in fact, the second child that the couple had lost during their marriage. Their son, Willie, had died several years earlier.

Lincoln nodded to the boy, graciously accepting his thoughts. "Dan Sickles is an odd duck, Jacob. He is a very complex and complicated man. I trust you are already aware of his brush with the law?" Jacob nodded. "Good! I am happy to hear that you know at least that much. Perhaps you represent the General's chance at…redemption."

"Redemption?" Jacob asked.

"Yes," replied Lincoln. "Forgiveness for his sins."

"Oh!" answered the boy, understanding Lincoln's deeper meaning. "Whatever Daniel's ulterior motives, Jacob…I believe that he has chosen wisely. I believe with all of my soul that some things are predestined. I believe that your path crossed with Daniel Sickles' path for a reason."

"My father has a way of expressing the same idea, sir," Jacob replied. "He always says that everything is God's Will, although I am not so sure that he still feels that way after the recent battle."

"And why is that, do you think?"

"I believe that he finds it difficult to believe that it was God's Will that allowed thousands of young men to die on our fields; that it was God's Will that allowed my friend, Ginnie Wade, to be killed by a sniper's bullet. Nor do I think that he now believes that it was the hand of Providence that guided the Elders of our sect to shun us out of our home and way of life back in Paradise, Pennsylvania."

"That is a very strong statement, Jacob," cautioned Lincoln.

"I am sorry, Mr. Lincoln, if I am offending you or your belief system, but I believe that my father feels that there is another form of will at work in the day to day business of running the world – and that will is man's free will. Men make these decisions – sometimes in the name of God; sometimes in the name of the country. They may ask for guidance or direction from on high, but they will still pursue their own appointed course. And when things do not go as planned, they chalk it up to "God's Will." Why does God have to take the blame for causing the death of thousands of young men? Did God's voice enter General Sickles' brain and tell him to advance his Corps into the Peach Orchard, a place where they were to be cut to ribbons by the Confederate troops? No! For whatever reason, General Sickles decided that it was more prudent for him to attack than to follow General Meade's direct orders. He made that decision of his own free will – and many of his men died that day, or soon thereafter, because of that decision. God had nothing to do with it!"

"And this is your father's opinion, not yours?" asked Lincoln, quietly.

Jacob sat back in the armchair. "I share the opinion, sir." Jacob knew what he wanted to ask Lincoln, but wondered about the sensitivity of the question. He decided to ask it anyway, because his free will and questioning mind demanded it. "Sir…do you believe that it was God's Will that your son, Eddie, was taken from you?"

Lincoln closed his eyes. His wife, Mary, had been under the constant watchful eye of a doctor for the past year because she was so distraught over the death of Eddie. "I have asked myself the same question many times, Jacob."

"I, for one, do not believe that God is a vengeful God, or a hateful God…or even a God that would punish someone for their sins by taking one of their children from them," said Jacob.

"And yet," Lincoln muttered, "he is gone."

"But what if there was another answer, sir?" Jacob asked.

"I don't follow you," answered Lincoln.

"What if God's Will was more of a challenge to us?" "A challenge?" asked the President.

"A challenge to our resourcefulness…to our intellect…to our ability to solve our own problems," said Jacob. "What if God put us on this Earth so that we could develop our own God-given minds so that we would be able to solve our own problems?"

"An interesting notion, I must admit."

"Look," explained the boy, "even though we Amish don't involve ourselves with many of these things…the fact of the matter is, that here, in 1863, we have many advantages at our disposal than our ancestors did several hundred years ago. We now have the telegraph…and we have trains. We also have better cannon and rifles. We have been given the intelligence to communicate better; to get from place to place faster – but we have also been given the intellect to kill each other more efficiently."

"I see your point," said Lincoln.

"That is why I want to discover the mysteries that are still locked away in medicine, Mr. Lincoln. The surgeon is following practices that are already in place. I want to find new practices."

A smile crept over Lincoln's otherwise melancholy face. "Your parents must be very proud of you, Jacob."

"Thank you, sir," replied Jacob, "I believe that they are." The boy stood to leave, shaking hands with Lincoln before saying his goodbyes. As he crossed the expanse of the large office, headed for the doorway, he turned back to Lincoln. "Mr. Lincoln? I should also like to express to you that I agree that no man should be held in slavery by another. If there is anything that is contrary to God's Will, then the institution of slavery is certainly it. It would certainly not be God's Will to enslave an entire race, even if an entire society believes that to be the case."

CHAPTER 40

Tests, and More Tests

Jacob and Sickles set off for their whirlwind circuit of the finest colleges in the Union early the next morning.

After their discussion of college choices on Jacob's first night in Washington, Sickles had made several appointments, via the telegraph, at the institutions which Jacob had mentioned in his conversation. What Jacob was unaware of was that Sickles had already been in contact with many of these same schools, and had used some of his political power to insure that Jacob would be given a more than fair chance of being accepted into them, regardless of how he fared on their standard admission requirements. Sickles had chosen to keep this information hidden from his younger friend because, had the actual truth come to light, he was afraid that Jacob's pride would get in the way of him attending.

So, on a clear and warm late summer morning, Sickles and Jacob boarded a train at Union Station and headed north. As the main rail line easily connected them with a large hub in Philadelphia, Sickles had arranged to have their first stop at the University of Pennsylvania.

The University of Pennsylvania sat a few miles north of the city, built upon the banks of the Schuylkill River. Like many things inherently

Pennsylvanian, the University took its name from the founder of the original colony, William Penn, and at this juncture of time the school was affectionately dubbed, simply, "Penn."

Jacob and Sickles arrived for their appointment at the Admissions Office at around 3:00 on that same day. After the usual formal introductions, Jacob was escorted into an adjacent room, leaving Sickles to wait for him in the office. A young man, perhaps in his early twenties, was given the assignment of interviewing and testing the new candidate. Jacob was surprised to see that such a young man would be given this responsibility; he had expected someone much older – someone bent over, and with a flowing white beard.

When they had reached their destination, a conference room containing a large wooden table and leather-covered armchairs, the young gentleman finally spoke. "How do you do, Mr. Zook? My name is Jeffrey Gordon. I am a teaching assistant here at Penn."

"Teaching assistant?" inquired Jacob.

"Yes," the young man replied. "I am a graduate student here. I am working on my doctorate." Jacob nodded. He understood the terminology. "I need to find out exactly what you know and what you don't know."

Jacob smiled at the young man. "I am afraid you will find that there is a great deal more on the side of what I do not know than on the side of what I know, Mr. Gordon."

"You speak rather candidly about your lack of knowledge, Mr. Zook," answered Gordon. "Most young men, under similar circumstances, will usually choose to mask their inabilities, rather than confess them. Do you not wish to attend Penn?"

"It is not that, sir," Jacob confessed. "I would very much like to attend this school – or any other school that would have me – it's simply that I truly lack any kind of formal education."

"I….don't understand," stammered Gordon.

"I have never been to school, sir," replied Jacob. "Not in my entire life." Gordon looked at the young man sitting across the conference table from him

with bewilderment. "Are you telling me that you are…illiterate?"

Jacob could have taken offense to Gordon's use of the word, which had immediately sounded condescending. "Oh no, sir…not at all. I can read and write in English and in German…as well as in a German dialect. I have been entirely home-educated – mostly by my mother."

"I see," muttered Gordon, while writing down a few notes in the margins of the stack of papers he was organizing. "What about mathematics, or the sciences?"

"I am able to add, subtract, multiply, and divide." "What about Calculus….or Geometry?"

"I have no idea what those things are, sir," Jacob answered.

"I see," Gordon muttered again, and again wrote more notes in the margins. "Do you have any idea what you would like to study here at Penn, were you to be accepted?"

Jacob nodded quickly at that question – the first question asked that he actually had a decent answer at hand. "I would like to study medicine, sir."

"What?" Gordon asked, his eyes wide open with amazement. "Do you realize how much advanced mathematics and science are required to become a medical doctor?"

"Yes, sir…I do," Jacob answered, his euphoria instantly deflated.

Gordon pushed his chair back from the conference table. "Will you excuse me for a moment?" he said, and exited the conference room. He returned to the Admissions Office, where he found Daniel Sickles reading a journal. "Excuse me, sir," he said, interrupting the General in his reading.

"Yes?"

"Might I be as bold to inquire why the young man is under the impression that he is prepared for an academic career here at Penn?"

Sickles slowly closed the journal, never taking his gaze off of the young scholar. "Might I be as bold to inquire why you think the young man is unable to fulfill the requirements of that career here at Penn?"

Gordon noticed that there was a slight smile on Sickles' face as he asked that question, but there was also a fire in his eyes, as if he was already anticipating this moment. "Sir," he continued, unperturbed, "the boy has virtually no formal education."

"Yes," agreed Sickles, "of that you are correct."

Gordon could tell that there was something very contentious about this man; the man in the wheelchair with only one leg. A new thought quickly entered his mind. "Is the young man related to an alumnus of this school, sir?"

"No," replied Sickles. "Why do you ask?"

"It had occurred to me, sir, that you might be bringing the son of a wealthy magnate, the scion of a socially well-placed family, to enroll in our school."

"And why should that make any difference, Mr. Gordon?" asked Sickles.

Gordon, feeling that he had just uncovered the truth in the matter, continued with confidence. "The school is always happy to enroll the 'entitled,' sir."

"The entitled?" asked Sickles. "You think that Jacob Zook, a poor Amish farmboy from Gettysburg, Pennsylvania, is entitled? I never heard of anything so humorous in my entire life!"

"Sir," continued Gordon, unabated by the fact that Sickles was beginning to raise his voice to him, "for Mr. Zook to be accepted into this school, he will...."

"Accepted?" interrupted Sickles, using his trademark thunderous vocal chords. "The boy has already been accepted, you buffoon! We are here to see if he will accept the University of Pennsylvania!"

"I beg your pardon, sir," answered Gordon. "What are you talking about?" "Jacob Zook has already been accepted into your school. He was accepted, sight unseen, by your Board of Governors, based on letters of recommendation from six Major Generals in the Federal Army, the Secretary of War, and…oh yes…I almost had forgotten. You should probably take a look at this letter." Sickles brandished the letter before the young man's eyes.

Gordon took the letter from the General and read it to himself, his eyes opening wider and wider as he read. When he was finished, he could nothing more than, "I…don't understand, sir."

"I know….I know," said Sickles, his voice returning to a peaceful tone, "it must be very confusing for you, but I do not think you will be dissatisfied in any way with the boy's performance at this institution."

Gordon shook his head, still bewildered. "Who is this young man, sir?"

"Never you mind," said Sickles. "Now I suggest that you return to your interview. I would suggest that you give him any barrage of tests that you deem necessary, but I will also caution you that the boy is not to know that he has already been accepted into the school."

"Excuse me?" asked Gordon.

"Sir…this conversation never happened!"

Gordon nodded his head, understanding the meaning of the General's words. He returned to the conference room, and to the waiting Jacob Zook. "I am sorry for the delay, Mr. Zook. Have you, by chance, ever read some of the classics of English Literature?"

"Yes, I have," answered Jacob, proudly. "I have read a great deal of Shakespeare, as well as Hawthorne, Melville, Chaucer, Milton, Keats, and Shelley."

"Very good," said Gordon. The young man produced a testing booklet and handed it to Jacob, along with several pencils and a small knife for sharpening them. "You will have two hours to complete your answers. I will have it reviewed by early evening, and you will know the results by early tomorrow morning."

"That is good," answered Jacob, "because we have another appointment in Princeton tomorrow afternoon."

"Where? At the College of New Jersey?" Gordon asked.

"Precisely!" said Jacob, with a smile. "We are visiting six or seven of the oldest schools in the country over the next week, or so. I am undecided as to which one I would like to attend."

"For medicine?" asked Gordon.

"For medicine," answered Jacob, with a nod, as he opened to the first page of the testing book on English Literature.

*   *   *

After the testing was concluded, Sickles and Jacob headed back toward the city to spend the night. They took a carriage from the University toward the banks of the Delaware River, stopping in the area of Independence Hall and the United States Mint. Sickles took the opportunity to give Jacob a guided tour of some of the historic sights in the 'City of Brotherly Love," using the time and the location at hand to inform Jacob about the writing of the Declaration of Independence. Teacher and pupil had dinner at the City Tavern – an old establishment that had been in business on 4th Street from before the time of the Revolution. Only a few city blocks from the Old State House, the back rooms of the tavern had hosted all of the members of the Continental Congress at one time or another, with the possible exception of those who had preached temperance. Among the regular guests during that historic time period however, was the most famous man in Philadelphia, the Colonies, and in most of Europe – Benjamin Franklin.

After dinner, Sickles and Jacob checked into their hotel – a large, wooden framed building that sat on the commercial hub of the city, Market Street. Sickles had arranged for a suite of rooms for the night, to allow himself to have maximum privacy as he prepared for the evening, and then in the morning that followed. They were to head over to Princeton in the late morning, taking the ferry across the Delaware River, and then a carriage to the college, but, prior to leaving Philadelphia they would check back in with the Office of Admissions at Penn to see how Jacob fared with the admissions testing.

Making certain to rise early, Sickles and Jacob ate breakfast by eight o'clock and headed back to meet with Jeffrey Gordon at 9:00; all done with the idea that they needed to be at the river wharf by eleven to catch the ferry. Unlike the previous day, Gordon seemed genuinely happy to see them again. His actions and his mannerisms gave away his ebullience when he saw Jacob. "Mr. Zook….Mr. Sickles…it is wonderful to see you again. I hope that you had a restful evening in our fair city."

"Quite restful," replied the General, unperturbed by Gordon's revised attitude.

"Very good," answered Gordon, turning to Jacob. "Shall we step into the conference room so that we may analyze your test scores?"

Jacob nodded, turning an eye toward Sickles, as if to ask silently ask him if he would be joining him inside for the verdict, but the older man simply smiled at cocked his head to the side, showing him the direction toward the doorway to the conference room. Alone, Jacob now followed Gordon into the room. Gordon closed the door behind them, and proceeded to take his folder to the head of the table, pulling out a chair and sitting in it. He gestured to Jacob, signaling him to take a seat at the side of the long table.

"Let's see here," said Gordon, leafing through the test papers, "I know that your test scores are in here…somewhere."

"Mr. Gordon," prompted Jacob, "I have a feeling that you can tell me my exact score without locating the paper."

Gordon looked up from the pile of papers. "You are probably correct, Mr. Zook…although I must say that I was quite surprised by your academic abilities."

Jacob shook his head. "You needn't try to soften the blow, Mr. Gordon. I am prepared for what it is you have to tell me."

"Are you?" asked Gordon.

"Yes," replied the boy, "you were completely correct. I have very little education. I don't see how I could ever hope to live up to the high expectations of this school."

"Really?" asked Gordon. "Are you absolutely sure about that, Mr. Zook?" And then Gordon smiled at Jacob. It was a toothy, crocodilian smile. "Ah!

Here are your results." He glanced down at the paper just for effect. "Have you been pulling my leg, Mr. Zook?"

"I beg your pardon, sir?"

"Is this all a put-on, Mr. Zook?"

"I don't understand," replied Jacob.

"I am baffled as to how you managed to achieve the score you did, Mr. Zook." "What score?" asked Jacob.

"A perfect score," answered Gordon.

"Perfect?"

"Perfect!" said Gordon. "We have Graduate students who would not be able to score that high."

"Let me see that paper!" demanded the boy, grabbing the test score out of Gordon's hand. Gordon was flustered, but said nothing, hoping that the young man was, in fact, as ignorant as he thought. Jacob sat back in his chair. "So then….what does all this mean? This does not indicate that I scored a perfect score!" "Well….we have no basis to judge your Mathematics and Science knowledge, which comprises the balance of the test - but your verbal ability is off of all our charts. We think you would make an excellent candidate for Penn."

Jacob couldn't believe his ears. "Just yesterday afternoon you had plenty of doubt in my abilities to survive here, and now you are telling me that I am an excellent candidate?"

"I know it seems a bit odd, but your scores really do say it all, Jacob. Congratulations!"

"Thank you," replied Jacob, "but I still have quite a few schools to visit before I make my selection…that is….if you are actually offering me a place here at Penn for the fall term."

"We are," said Gordon, a bit surprised by the boy's candor, "but I was under the impression that you wished to attend Penn?"

"Possibly," answered Jacob. "I will have to let you know my decision." And with that said, Jacob stood up, pushed back his chair, and left the room. Jacob quickly and deliberately walked to where Sickles was waiting. He took the handles of his wheelchair in his hands and directed him toward the building exit.

"What are you doing, Jacob?" asked Sickles.

"We are leaving, General," answered Jacob, his voice filled with anger.

"Leaving? Aren't you going to tell me what you received on your entrance exam, Jacob?"

"Why don't you tell me, sir?"

"What? Now how can I do such a thing as that?"

Jacob abruptly stopped pushing the wheelchair. "You had this all figured out, didn't you, General?"

Sickles turned around as best as he could so that he could face the boy. "What the hell are you talking about, Jacob?" For a moment their eyes locked, as Sickles took quick notice of just how angry Jacob seemed to be. "Well?"

"You planned this, did you not?" argued the boy. "This trip isn't really all that necessary, is it, sir? I would be accepted in any one of the schools I desired…or all of them, for that matter. Isn't that correct?"

"You seem to be feeling very confident about your prospects."

"I am not confident about my prospects, General," the boy said, raising his voice, "because good or bad you have made sure that I will find a place at the school of my choosing."

"I don't know what you are talking about, young man."

"Don't you?" questioned Jacob. "Tell me that you haven't used your political power to insure that I get access to a fine education? Tell me that you haven't used your influence to make sure that Jacob Zook – a poor, uneducated Amish boy from Gettysburg, Pennsylvania – gets his chance to fail; to fall on his face! Oh….dear

God….what was I thinking?"

Jacob walked away from the wheelchair, leaving Sickles by himself in the middle of the hallway of the Administration Building. The boy walked over to a large window that overlooked the campus and stared out into the distance. "Jacob?" Sickles called, but the boy refused to face him. Sickles grabbed the wheels of his chair and forced himself toward the window. "Jacob?"

Jacob waved the General away with a sweep of his arm, but Sickles was determined to continue pressing the boy. The Sickles calmly uttered a quiet and serene question, speaking in hushed tones as he sat just to his young friend's rear. "Jacob…what score did you get on your entrance exam?"

"I scored 180 points out of a possible 800," replied Jacob, quietly.

"Oh…I see," said Sickles. "Well…perhaps you will do better at Princeton." Jacob whirled around and gazed into Sickles eyes. If there was one thing he had become quite adept at, he knew when the man was telling him a fabrication. "You really don't know, do you?"

"Know what?"

"That Gordon told me that I scored beyond his expectations."

"Really?"

"And you didn't fix this for me?" the boy asked.

"Jacob," Stickles explained calmly, "I confess that I used my political might to get your foot in the door at these schools – otherwise they might not even give you the time of day. I know you are very smart, but I also know that you are very proud."

"Are you telling me that I scored a perfect score on my own merits?"

"I suppose that must be true, Jacob," answered Sickles. "At any rate, I had nothing to do with it."

Jacob lowered his head toward the floor. "I am truly sorry, sir, for not trusting you. Evidently my mother did a great deal more than teach me my basic education."

"Indeed," remarked Sickles. "Now…if you have finished ranting at me, can we please call for our cab? We have only about twenty minutes to make it to the ferry."

"Yes, sir," answered the boy, happy to be past this rocky moment in their relationship. But the fact of the matter was that Jacob had actually scored a 180 on his entrance exam; that Jeffrey Gordon had lied about the true score - a score that was below the 700 score needed, on average, to get him accepted into the program at Penn – and that only accounted for the verbal portion of the exam; the mathematics and science portions were not even factored in. Sickles knew that the boy need not know the complete truth. He was banking on the possibility that this success would give him even more confidence as they proceeded from school to school. No, he thought…there was no good reason for him to know the complete truth.

It was a gamble that Sickles was willing to take.

CHAPTER 41

The College of New Jersey

With a timetable almost a carbon-copy of the previous day, Sickles and Jacob arrived at the Admissions Office of The College of New Jersey at around three in the afternoon. Their carriage had delivered them to the front door of the school, dropping them on Nassau Street in Princeton, directly in front of Nassau Hall.

Jacob felt an immediate attraction to this particular school. He couldn't really say why, but a comparison was instantly drawn in his mind, pitting what he had seen and experienced in the application process at Penn, compared to what he was now experiencing in Princeton. He had no way of knowing, however, that the General's political connections were even stronger at this school than at their last stop; that the two schools most strongly aligned to the wishes of General Daniel Sickles was that of this school in Princeton, and at Columbia College in New York City – their next stop.

In a similar manner to their experience in Philadelphia, Jacob first had an interview with the Director of Admissions, then proceeded to take his entrance exams; this time taking several shorter tests, including two tests that quizzed him on his knowledge of mathematics and natural science. Unlike the previous day, they did not plan to spend the evening in Princeton, but were scheduled to catch an evening train into Jersey City. They would have accommodations there for the night, and would rise early in order to catch the ferry for lower Manhattan. The college would send the test results, as well as the acceptance or rejection letter, by post as soon as it was available. Among other things, Jacob had been fascinated by Princeton's involvement in the American War for Independence and the battle which was fought on these streets. The American Revolution was one of his favorite subjects when reading about the country; a country which, up until this point in time, he had little to do with.

*   *   *   *

After Rebecca Tilden returned home from the Zook house, following her attendance at Jacob's farewell dinner, her parents called her into the parlor for a family discussion. Mary Elizabeth and John Tilden were both aware of the good fortune that had befallen the Zook family as of late. They certainly did not begrudge them their good luck; that would not have been very Christian of them. The fact that their home for several generations had escaped the battle unscathed, compared to the burning of the Zook home, was thanks enough. Both Mary Elizabeth and John liked and enjoyed the company of Jacob Zook, especially in the aftermath of the battle. To Mary Elizabeth, it was a sign of Divine Providence itself that General Sickles had taken the boy under his wing and had offered to pay for his college education. Until that point in time, they had been under the opinion that Jacob would never have amounted to anything more than a farmer.

Now his prospects for success had changed....and, with that, if the relationship was to continue, so would change the prospects for their daughter, Rebecca.

So… prior to this evening…Mary Elizabeth had started the slow, gentle process of counseling her husband. After more than two decades of marriage to the man, she was knowledgeable of the fact that John was not one to make snap decisions, nor was he one to allow emotions to play a part in the decision-making process.

Rather than resent the fact that Jacob had been chosen from on high to fulfill his destiny, Mary Elizabeth looked at his circumstances as a golden opportunity for her daughter. But there was also a negative side to this scenario, and she had mulled over this possibility for quite a few sleepless nights before deciding to bring her husband into her thought process.

Her argument was simple:

If Jacob Zook, by way of a superior education, social and political contacts, and opportunities only presented to those living in the large cities of this country, could raise himself up to success and prominence – and yet still remained loyal to his bond with their daughter, Becky – then this would prove to be the easiest and most convenient road for them to travel.

However, if Jacob Zook, because of his superior education, social and political contacts, and opportunities only presented to those living in the large cities of this country, having raised himself up to success and prominence – happened to then regard Becky as backwater or provincial – or if he, as chance may have it, happened to meet another young, educated young lady while staying in one of those aforementioned large cities – then this might spell disaster for their daughter.

Something had to be done about this!

Therefore, about one week prior to Jacob's departure – at about the same time that he was beginning to purchase the clothing that he would take with him to school – Mary Elizabeth started to plant the seed – the germ of an idea in her husband's mind.

She knew that she would have to tread lightly. John was not about to care whether or not Rebecca and Jacob had a bright future together – not at eighteen years of age. But Mary Elizabeth knew that John was very proud of his daughter.

Rebecca was a very bright, intelligent young lady – and of this fact, John Tilden was extremely proud. This was the card that she decided to play.

Over the course of the next few nights, amid all the excitement generated in their household – mostly by their daughter – concerning the fact that Jacob Zook would soon be leaving for Washington, Mary Elizabeth began to inject tiny thoughts into her husband's mind. The first action was a thorough, but calm, discussion on the rights of women – and the fact that the world was changing rapidly. John, forever a liberally-minded individual, was also the father of a daughter, and whole-heartedly agreed with his wife that the male-dominated society they lived in left much to be desired.

The next evening's discussion would be slightly more pointed. Mary Elizabeth pointed out to her husband that, while it was extraordinarily fortuitous that Jacob Zook had been given this wonderful opportunity by the Union General, it was also a shame that their own daughter, Rebecca – being a female, of course – would never have received such a largess. She went on to say that, although she was sure that Jacob was an exceptionally bright young man, she was positive that Becky had a great deal of intelligence at her command, as well. This point did illicit a stronger response from her husband than the previous conversation; it was, after all, all about hitting a nerve in her husband's psyche. John Tilden was extremely proud of his daughter. He responded by saying that it was unfortunate that 'even smart girls, like their daughter' were allowed to languish as second-class citizens, when, with some good education, they could be on a parity with the gentry. Satisfied that she had planted the seed, Mary Elizabeth extinguished the candles and they went to sleep.

Proving to Mary Elizabeth that her seed had indeed been planted, John initiated a conversation on the third evening by beginning the discourse with information that they were both already well aware of; that the family dry goods business had experienced a boon in sales and in profits – due entirely to the recent battle that had raged throughout the town and surrounding countryside. When Mary Elizabeth asked her husband why he chose to repeat information of which she was already knowledgeable, John hesitated, then cleared his throat, before continuing his point. When he finally decided to venture forth, he mentioned, as if needing approval from his wife, that this windfall profit had garnered them a great deal of extra income - income that might be well-served by spending it on the education of their own children.

Mary Elizabeth took this moment to act as if this was a most shocking revelation. This was a very tricky business. John was having great difficulty justifying the expenditure on his own daughter, and it was also obvious that he expected some resistance to his idea to come from his wife. Mary Elizabeth understood her husband well enough to know that if she met his idea in an overly enthusiastic way, he might actually be led to believe that it was she who had put that idea there in the first place. She also knew that if she tried to feign too much resistance, that tactic might also backfire upon her, as well, for John might back off rather than argue about it.

So, in order to keep her husband's hopes alive, as well as to play her quietly conceived coup, Mary Elizabeth told her husband that she would need to sleep on the idea; that this would not be a decision that would be taken lightly; which meant, of course, that Mary Elizabeth would need to prepare her thoughts for the fourth evening, because it would be on that night that all would be decided.

Mary Elizabeth spent the morning of that final, fateful day in the library building. She was researching schools which specialized in the education of young women. She found several schools which she felt would do justice for her daughter, Rebecca, but kept all knowledge of her research concealed and to herself. She returned home in the afternoon and prepared a fine supper for her husband and children; a dinner that featured her husband's favorite vegetable – turnips - and then waited patiently for John to re-open the conversation of the past few nights, which he finally did as they were settling down in their bed for the night's sleep.

"Well, Mary Elizabeth," he began, "have you given any further consideration to my thoughts regarding Rebecca's education?"

"Yes, I have, John," she quietly replied. "I must admit, however, that still have some reservations about the topic."

"In what way?"

And in asking this simple question, Mary Elizabeth was now ready to spring her carefully constructed trap. "My problem is this, John. Are we doing what is right by Rebecca?"

"How do you mean?"

"Do you think it is right to simply bundle her off to boarding school – as if we had nothing better to do with her than to get her out of Gettysburg – or are we expecting her to get a real education?"

"A real education?"

And then it was time…."An education that would compete with any offered to a young man, John."

"You are speaking of a college education, my dear?"

Mary Elizabeth slowly nodded. "That is exactly what I am speaking of, John. If our Rebecca is as intelligent as she seems to be, why shouldn't we want the best for her? Why shouldn't she have every opportunity we can give her?"

Mary Elizabeth allowed her husband time to mull over her questions. "I think that we should give her that opportunity, Mary Elizabeth."

"You do?" she asked.

"Absolutely!" replied John Tilden. "You have, no doubt, already picked out several women's colleges that may be appropriate places for Rebecca to study."

"Excuse me?"

"Mary Elizabeth," he continued, "I know you well enough by now to know when I am being played like an old violin. Never fear, my darling…I had every intention of sending Rebecca to the finest school my money can afford."

A smirk began to appear on Mary Elizabeth's mouth. "You are a devil, John Tilden."

"Yes," he agreed, "I will admit to my deception…but I learned from a Master." In the end, John and Mary Elizabeth decided on a short list of quality schools that seemed to fit their standards for educational content in the curriculum, as well as high standards for morality and behavior. Sitting on the top of the list was a women's college in Poughkeepsie, New York, by the name of Vassar College. The school was virtually brand new, having just been founded in 1861, but, unfortunately for their consideration, the campus was still under construction and would not be ready to accept students for a few more years. It was somewhat affiliated with Yale University, and was quickly joining the ranks of several other notable schools for women that were academically rivaling their male-dominated counterparts. And now, as Rebecca entered the house, after an evening saying good-bye to her friend, now turned beau, Jacob Zook, they decided that this would be the perfect time for them to inform her of their plans for her education.

Rebecca was surprised to see her parents still up and in the parlor, considering the fact that she arrived home from her dinner party at the Zook home at a little after eleven o'clock. Both of her parents usually were in bed before ten o'clock on most nights. She removed her bonnet and walked into the parlor to see if there was a problem – perhaps, she thought, someone in the family had died.

"Rebecca," her father called out, nervously, "come join us in here for a moment."

"Is anything wrong, Papa?" she asked.

"Wrong?" he repeated. "No, dear….nothing is wrong. Please come in, and join us."

Becky walked across the room and found an armchair to sit in. She noticed that her parents looked apprehensive, almost care-worn, as if they were keeping a great burden from her.

"Rebecca," her mother said, "how was your special night at the Zook house?" "It was very pleasant, Mama," the girl answered. "It was surprisingly pleasant."

"I suppose Jacob is very excited about leaving for Washington in the morning?" her mother continued.

"Oh, yes…he is very excited," Rebecca answered, smiling at her friend's good fortune. "He is looking forward to this adventure very much." And then she cast her eyes to the floor, as if Jacob's good luck was also her bad luck, for as much as she was overwhelmingly happy for him, she also wished that she could go with him in the morning.

Her mother looked across the room to her father. This was her signal to him that he should bring up the proposal.

"Rebecca," he began, "how would you like to have a similar adventure?" "Excuse me?"

"How would you like to attend a college for women?"

Rebecca quickly looked from her father to her mother, her face filled with a mixture of both confusion and excitement. "I don't understand," she finally answered. "What exactly are you asking me?"

"We are asking you if you would like to go away to school…just like Jacob Zook?" asked her mother.

"Really?"

"Of course, dear," assured her father. "It's high time someone from this little town got themselves a proper education…and now we will have two…Jacob….and you."

Becky nearly jumped out of the armchair and raced across the room to embrace her father. Having accomplished this feat, she turned and embraced her mother.

"I think she would like to go," observed Mary Elizabeth.

"I think that I am feeling flushed," mentioned Becky, taking out her lace fan to cool herself.

"You are getting yourself all worked up, Rebecca," cautioned her mother. "This is almost too good to be true," she said, waving the fan furiously. "I don't know what to say. Where will I be going to school?"

"A fair question," remarked her father. "We have several fine schools in mind."

"Tell me, please," Becky anxiously pleaded.

"Well, dear," her mother said calmly, "we were thinking about Bethlehem Female Seminary."

"Bethlehem?" she asked, quizzically. "You mean…where Christ was born?" "No, dear," answered Mary Elizabeth. "I mean Bethlehem, Pennsylvania. It's north and east of here."

"Oh," Becky replied. "That doesn't sound very far away, does it?"

"No, dear," continued Mary Elizabeth. "It's run by the Moravians."

Becky knew about the Moravians. These were the followers of John Huss, who decided to stand up to the practices of the Roman Catholic Church perhaps a century before the time of Martin Luther. For this action, Huss was burned at the stake. The Moravians hailed first from the regions in Europe of Bohemia and Moravia – hence the name – but they also gained a foothold in some of the areas of Austria and Germany. And it was the Germans who would bring the faith to this country, founding towns in Eastern Pennsylvania with decidedly biblical names: Bethlehem, Emmaus, and Nazareth.

Becky nodded her head at the prospect of her education.

"It's the oldest college for young women in the country, Becky," interjected her mother.

"Really?" she answered, half listening, and half deep in her own thoughts. Her father, noting her hesitancy, then added, "Of course…we have thought of a few others, as well." Mary Elizabeth shot him a glance, as if to say that his statement was not appropriate to their discussion at the moment.

Rebecca turned quickly to face her father. "Other schools, Papa?"

"What your father means to say, Rebecca," countered her mother, "is that we have looked into a number of fine schools… just as a matter of necessity."

"Necessity?"

"Well, dear….you must apply and be accepted in order to attend these colleges. You can't simply put all of your eggs into one basket, you know." Becky nodded again. She wished that she knew where Jacob was going to end up – but that could still be weeks, maybe months away. If he went to the University of Pennsylvania in Philadelphia, then the Moravian school would be reasonably close…but what if he went to Yale, or Harvard…or even Dartmouth?

Still…it was a college education, she thought.

"Well, dear…." Her mother continued, "there are some wonderful schools for women in the south…but those are certainly out of the question."

"Certainly," replied Becky, hopeful that her mother was simply opening the door to other possibilities. To ensure that more colleges were named, Rebecca looked expectantly at her mother.

"There are two fine schools in Massachusetts," her mother mentioned, almost as if saying it very offhandedly. "One is called Wheaton Seminary and the other is Mount Holyoke."

"Massachusetts?" asked Becky. "You would allow me to go to school in Massachusetts?" She looked her mother in the eye, but could instantly see that Mary Elizabeth was not very accepting to the idea. Becky then turned to face her father. His expression told an entirely different story.

"First you must apply, Rebecca," her father counseled. "If you are accepted, we shall make that determination at that time."

"There is also a fine school in Connecticut, as well as one in New Jersey," said her mother, now grasping at straws.

"Thank you," gushed Becky, embracing both of her parents. "I will spend some time at the library tomorrow doing my research on these schools."

"I have their addresses, in case you wish to write to them," added her mother.

"Thank you both so very much," said Becky, barely able to contain herself.

She rushed out of the room and up the stairs to her bedroom. She considered tying her bonnet on again and running back to the Zook house to tell Jacob of her good fortune, but then thought better of the idea. For what purpose, she thought? What would she tell him; that she was able to apply to a women's college and that she might possibly be near him for the next four years? How extremely vague! No, she would bide her time and wait. It would take weeks for her letter of application to get there, and then another few weeks to be reviewed, and a few more just to learn of the results.

Besides, she thought, the rest of the evening, as well as the next few days, were the exclusive property of the Zook family. They needed to say their good-byes to Jacob, and there was no need for her to poke her way into that small, close-knit family circle.

But that didn't mean to imply that she was not excited about her future. Even if things did not work out with Jacob, she knew that she would be able to attract any numbers of eligible suitors; young men who also possessed college educations.

More than anything else, Becky was amazed how much things had changed over the course of the summer of 1863. She had met Jacob Zook – but her parents didn't very much like the idea of her friendship – however casual it was, with an Amish boy; which wasn't all that surprising, because Jacob's parents didn't like the idea that their son was speaking with an 'English' girl. The battle changed much of that – but there were serious consequences to that, as well. Her good friend, Ginnie Wade, had been killed during the struggle, even though it seemed a casualty of war. Jacob's actions during the battle had earned him fame, respect, and a great opportunity. His parents – for the most part, his father – also underwent a change. They accepted the fact that Jacob would leave them soon, with or without their blessing, and did their best to smooth out this transition by seeing the world through his eyes. And as opposite as her parents were to the Zooks, Rebecca could easily discern that they had done very much the same thing.

It made Rebecca Tilden wonder what the year 1864 would bring.

CHAPTER 42

The Search Continues

Over the course of the next week, Sickles and Jacob visited almost a half dozen schools, traveling up and down the Middle Atlantic States in the northern part of the Union. Jacob would meet with the Director of Admissions for an interview, he would take a battery of tests, and they would have a short tour of each campus. After leaving the College of New Jersey in Princeton, they headed into New York City in order to visit the college where Sickles held the most political sway – Columbia.

This stop proved to be the longest of the journey, as Sickles took the opportunity that his visit allowed to catch up with his old political cronies at Tammany Hall. As tedious as these reunions were for Jacob, the additional time gave him a wonderful opportunity to see the city, as well as the college, which he had placed high on his list of possible schools. The school was located near the northern edge of the developed city on Manhattan Island, at the intersection of 49th Street and Madison Avenue, and since its move to this location several years ago, was growing in leaps and bounds. Jacob found this city to be fast-paced and exciting – so very different from that which he was used to. He even found time to visit Mathew Brady's photographic studio, where the photographer had just created an exhibit showing the aftermath of the Battle of Gettysburg. Many of the photographs were of the dead soldiers; victims of the battle from both sides. To Jacob, as well as to hundreds of others spectators, the exhibit was horrifying, but something that he could not turn away from viewing.

Two days later, they were on a train bound for New Haven, Connecticut, and Yale University. The following day they boarded another train which brought them to Providence, Rhode Island, and Brown College - and the next day they took a train to their final destination - Boston. Jacob would be able to meet with the representatives of two colleges in Boston; Harvard College and Dartmouth. Because of the great distance and difficulty in making the long trip up to Hanover, New Hampshire, the college had decided to send a representative down to Boston to meet with Sickles protégé.

This also allowed the boy to have a few more days to enjoy a new American city, especially one as famous as the seat of the Revolution with England. Jacob resumed his usual college activities on the morning after arriving, spending most of the day at Harvard Yard. When he returned to the hotel, he found Sickles mulling over a pile of telegraph messages.

"Jacob…I have just received your test scores from The College of New Jersey and Columbia," Sickles announced, as Jacob removed his hat.

"Oh?" replied the boy. "What did the school in Princeton say about my performance on the English Literature exam?"

"Splendid!" answered the General. "You have quite a knack for the great works of literature, Jacob. You have once again scored a perfect score."

"Is that a fact?" said Jacob, glumly.

"What is wrong? I thought you would be pleased."

Jacob walked across the hotel sitting room, finding his place near a large window that looked out on the Boston Common. "General….I was skeptical about my performance on the test at Penn. I suppose I simply couldn't imagine me getting a perfect score on any college admission test – not with my limited education…."

"Yes…go on," prompted the General.

"So as I was taking my entrance exam at Princeton, I decided that I would initiate a little test of my own…"

"Oh?"

"Yes…" continued Jacob. "There was a question that concerned itself with 'Macbeth,' a story which I happen to know quite well, sir."

"I know you do, and that's a fact."

"Yes…but I purposely answered the question incorrectly, sir." "Excuse me?"

"I chose the wrong answer for that question. If that is so…then either the Admissions Office was not accurate in marking the exam….or…."

"What are you saying, Jacob?"

"….they gave me a mark that I didn't earn, sir."

"I see," said Sickles, bracing himself for the inevitable barrage that was surely to come.

"Why would they do that, sir?" Jacob asked, but he already knew that answer.

"I can't imagine," mumbled Sickles.

"I think you can, General," answered Jacob. "In fact, I think there is a great deal about this that you already have imagined."

"Calm down, Jacob," replied Sickles. "It was just a bit of insurance, that's all." "General," said Jacob, quietly, "I have already told you. I will only go to a school that finds me qualified to attend."

"I know…I know," Sickles answered. "I knew you were smart, my boy….I just didn't know how you would do this well on these tests."

Jacob could feel his face getting redder as his temper began to boil over. "General…you lied to me."

"What? When did I lie to you, Jacob?"

Jacob shook his head violently and raised his hands towards Sickles. "You lied to me in Philadelphia, sir. You told me that I scored a perfect score on that test."

"And so you did! That was the score that they said you earned, Jacob." "That is true," replied Jacob, "but I think they may have been prompted to give me that score, sir."

"Jacob," Sickles said in an injured tone, "I may be many things…but I am not a cheat!"

Jacob turned to face the General, raising his right eyebrow at the man's vow in disbelief. "General Sickles…I am not certain about cheating, but I do know that you would do anything to get your way."

Sickles shrugged his shoulders, as if caught in the act of lying. "Jacob…I know that you are a brilliant fellow…but I just wanted to be sure that you were given every opportunity to prove yourself to these crusty academics. They tend to give great credence to students descended from some form of American aristocracy. I suppose that this helps pay the bills on the school – but, in doing so, they turn their backs on some really good talent. America is not meant to have class distinction, Jacob. 'All men are created equal.' Remember? You have every right to attend any one of these schools, Jacob, and I intend to make sure that happens…come Hell or high water!"

"Oh, so then you did it to simply prove a political point about class distinctions in America?" he lashed out. But Jacob calmed down a bit during the General's monologue and quickly his tone softened. "General…I appreciate everything that you have done for my family, and for me. Please do not think me ungrateful, sir. It's just that I wish you didn't take this matter into your own hands."

"You think I did this by myself?" Sickles asked.

Jacob was confused at the question. "What do you mean? You had help?" "Of course I had help, Jacob," the General bragged. "I have in my bag over a dozen letters written on your behalf."

"What? From whom?"

"From whom? Let's see….we've got one from Generals Birney and Humphries… and Major Winslow…there's one from Gideon Welles….and one from Edwin Stanton…."

"The Secretary of War?" asked Jacob.

"And the Secretary of the Navy," added Sickles. "There is one here from Harry Halleck….he's the Army Chief of Staff…General Halleck, to you…" Jacob nodded, dumbfounded that a total stranger would write such a letter. "…and then….there is the coup d'grace, Jacob."

"The what?"

"The letter that should open every door imaginable…the letter from Abraham Lincoln, himself."

Jacob took a step backward – not because of fear, but because his knees had buckled beneath the weight of his body. "President Lincoln wrote a letter on my behalf?"

"That's right. He did." Jacob couldn't believe his own ears. How did this come to be? Why would the President of the United States….the most powerful man in the country…take time out of his busy day to write a letter about a poor Amish boy? "He wrote two, actually," Sickles said. "He wrote the first after I explained my plans to him when he visited me in the hospital in Washington. He wrote the second letter right after we visited with him, and then had it sent over to my townhouse by messenger later that evening. Jacob…your actions during the battle have made you famous in Washington. The fact is…any one of these letters, taken alone, would probably have gotten your foot into the door of one of these schools. All of these letters means that you just have to pick the school you wish to attend. They all really want to be the school that you pick. Trust me on that fact, Jacob."

Jacob nodded. He, too, had done some research on the various schools that were up for his consideration. He was, indeed, attracted to one particular school more than the others. Up until this moment, he hadn't realized that his first choice was within his grasp. "I don't know what to say, General."

"What a pleasant surprise!" answered Sickles, with a bit of sarcasm.

"Now…which school would you most like to attend?"

Jacob was startled by the question. It was as if Sickles had been reading his mind. "I am still not sure, sir. We still have one more appointment for tomorrow." "Yes…Dartmouth College," said the General. "You'd better be prepared for a long winter if you go there, Jacob. It's so far north, you might as well be in Canada."

"Hm," grunted Jacob, deep in thought.

"It's a good school, though," admitted Sickles. "Daniel Webster went there, you know?"

"Who?" asked Jacob.

"Never mind."

*   *   *   *

Jacob met with the representative from Dartmouth College the following morning at ten o'clock. The gentleman's name was Andrew Withers. He was a middle-aged man with a very tired looking countenance. He met with Jacob in the sitting room of their hotel suite overlooking the Boston Common. Withers brought with him several entrance exams, which Jacob dutifully took after their interview. After Jacob finished the first exam, Withers marked the paper while Jacob took the next exam, and so the pattern continued for several hours. Sickles, in the interim, had gone downstairs to the hotel bar for some liquid libation.

As Sickles was almost certain that Jacob hadn't made up his mind on his choice of school, he decided that he would use their time together that evening – after Withers had departed again for parts north – to politic with Jacob on his choice. Sickles was hoping that the boy would choose to go to school in New York City…and Columbia College. The General had already decided that he would do his level best to sway Jacob to his way of thinking, but he also knew that the boy had a very strong will, so this task may not be all that easy. Sickles was particularly impressed with The College of New Jersey, and he knew that Jacob had been impressed with that school, too. The school in Princeton was probably the front-runner, Sickles thought. If that was the case, and he couldn't turn Jacob from Princeton to New York, Sickles didn't think that would be the end of the world, either. Princeton was only a few hours from Washington by train, and about the same distance from the school to Gettysburg. It seemed like a logical choice for the boy to make. To add fuel to his list of reasons, he remembered that Aaron Burr, the third Vice President of the United States, was a graduate of that institution. But that recollection also caused him to reconsider using Burr as a reason for selection, as Burr had not only been tried for treason, he had also shot down Alexander Hamilton.

The General was most worried that Jacob would opt for either Brown or Harvard – and he completely discounted Dartmouth, because of the tremendous distance between the school and the boy's home. Sickles wasn't fond of the New England political machine that was in place during this time; it was counterproductive to his way of doing things. The New York machine had people like William Seward, the current Secretary of State. Sickles knew where he stood with Seward; he had no idea where he stood with the people from Boston or Providence. Not that it mattered…not really. This wasn't really about Sickles…it was about Jacob Zook.

Wasn't it?

Sickles had polished off about a half bottle of Irish Whiskey by three o'clock in the afternoon. He was interrupted from downing his next glass of the potent liquid by a bellman, who politely told the General that Mister Zook had requested that the General come back up to the suite. Under normal circumstances, Sickles would have been a belligerent state by this point in his drinking, but his behavior, in this case, was tempered by the fact that this meant that Withers had gone and the debate over school choice could now begin. The bellman helped Sickles out of the bar and to the lift, safely delivering the General back to his room.

Upon entering the suite, Sickles was unpleasantly surprised to see Withers sitting on the sofa, still in conversation with Jacob. Jacob instantly smiled when he noticed Sickles entering the room, getting up to greet him and taking the command of his wheelchair from the bellman. Jacob could also detect the strong smell of alcohol surrounding the General, which gave him a bit of a cause for alarm, for he knew that the General would be at his most outspoken worst in this condition.

"Jacob….I thought you were finished with your exams?" questioned Sickles, who was fighting off his own personal demons in an attempt to remain civil.

"I have finished, sir," Jacob answered. "Mr. Withers and I were just having a talk about the program at Dartmouth."

"Oh?"

"General….did you know that the Dartmouth Medical School is the oldest in the country?"

"No," grunted Sickles, "I had no idea. Does that also imply that it is also the best in the country?"

"General!" replied Jacob, shocked at the man's lack of tack in front of a representative of the school.

"I beg your pardon," said Sickles. "I would merely like to point out that several other schools – schools that are in question, as well – also have fine medical schools, Mr. Withers. I mean no disrespect to your institution, sir. Medical Science is constantly changing. For all I know, the way your school teaches medicine may not have changed in several hundred years."

"I am sure that you will find us very much in pace with the standards of 1863," commented Withers, calmly.

But Jacob was not as forgiving of the General's behavior. "General…sir…did you know that Dartmouth also has in place an agreement with some of the great medical schools in Europe? Medical students from Dartmouth have the opportunity to study with some of the finest medical minds overseas."

"That is impressive," Sickles answered, with a note of sarcasm in his voice. "Does that mean that European doctors are able to quell the speed of one's demise more ably than our American doctors?"

"Not at all, General," answered a very patient Withers. "Medical research is more established in Europe than it is over here – that is all. Mr. Zook had expressed a desire to study medical research…and I merely pointed that opportunity out to him."

"I see," responded Sickles, quickly understanding that Jacob might have already have made up his mind on this, the most distant of the schools in question. "Is this true, Jacob?"

"Yes, sir," replied the boy. "I am interested in learning as much about medicine and medical research as I can possibly muster over the course of the next few years. Dartmouth seems to offer what I most would like to do."

Sickles looked crestfallen. The boy had taken the wind out of his sails. His first instinct was to lash out; to argue with the boy, but even he knew that would be a slippery slope. He looked over at Withers, who, for the first time since he had seen him, was smiling. "Thank you for your time, Mr. Withers," expressed the General, graciously. "The young man and I have a great deal to mull over."

"My pleasure, sir," answered Withers, bowing from the waist. "The young gentleman is filled with great hope and promise."

Jacob rose and shook Withers hand. "Thank you for your advice, Mr. Withers. I look forward to seeing you again." And with that said, Withers left the suite. Jacob turned to face the General. "You are angry with me, are you not?"

"Angry?" asked the General. "No…I wouldn't call it that, Jacob. More like…deflated. Are you sure that you wish to go to school in Vermont?"

"New Hampshire," Jacob corrected.

"Does it really matter, Jacob? I didn't realize that you wanted to remove yourself from the rest of civilization."

"You **are** angry with me."

"Frustrated is a better word, son," replied Sickles. "You seem to have chosen the school that is the farthest away from both Gettysburg…and Washington."

"Are you hinting that I am doing this to get away from the reach of my parents, sir?" Jacob asked. "One could make the argument that I am doing this in order to please my mother. It was she who suggested going to Dartmouth, as it would be completely removed from the war."

"I didn't mean to imply that," answered Sickles, quickly. "If anything…I would say that you are looking to put a great many miles… between us."

Jacob walked over to the General, looking him squarely in the eyes. "That would be about the last thought in my mind, sir. Besides, with the transportation system as modern as it is, I could be in New York or Washington in just a day's ride by train."

"That is true, I'll admit."

"Besides," continued Jacob, "in selecting Dartmouth I will also be putting a great many miles between myself and Rebecca Tilden. Who knows what will become of our relationship once we are that far apart?"

"Jacob…let me give you a bit of advice," smiled Sickles. "It doesn't matter how close or how distant you are…a beautiful woman always needs minding."

Jacob smiled back at the General, knowing exactly what part of his own history the man was referencing with that statement.

CHAPTER 43

Schooling Begins

As Sickles had already guaranteed, all of the schools on Jacob's list quickly responded that they would accept Jacob Zook into their incoming class in the fall of 1863. Jacob busied himself over the next few weeks preparing to make the move up to Hanover, New Hampshire. He wrote several times to Rebecca, explaining his decision for the move. She hesitated to write him back – mainly because her own decision was yet to be affirmed. She wanted to keep her plans a secret from him until they were a little more set in stone. Jacob also wrote almost daily to his parents and to his brother, Abraham. He spent at least an hour each night writing the correspondence, making sure that the content of Abraham's letter was exciting enough to make him want to experience the same thing in only a few more years. He kept his parents missives, however, a little more on the conservative side.

Jacob boarded the train for New Hampshire in the first week of September. The ride took more than a full day, but was otherwise very pleasant. Some of the foliage was already starting to change colors as he viewed the Northern New England landscape from the window of the railway car. Upon arriving in Hanover, Jacob gathered his belongings, including the large trunk which his father had made for his clothing, and found a livery to take him to Dartmouth College.

The college had been built directly adjacent to the town green, and had its roots dating back to the time that the community was originally founded in the 1760's. Considering himself as a New Englander for the first time in his short life, Jacob immediately felt something warm inside his chest. The people spoke differently – many of them broadening the "A" vowel, among other attributes. Jacob found the accent somewhat humorous, although truth be told, within a year he would adopt that way of speaking as part of his own, so much so that lifelong friends would comment upon the change in his manner of speaking.

Jacob discovered that his new residence would be in a dormitory known as Wentworth Hall, which was built in 1828. He would share his room with one other freshman student, Oliver Bartlett, who hailed from the same state as the college, New Hampshire. In only a few minutes of casual conversation, Oliver quickly informed Jacob that he was directly descended from Josiah Bartlett, member of the Second Continental Congress, and therefore a signer of the Declaration of Independence. His pedigree aside, Jacob thought that Oliver was a very genuine and friendly fellow, and the two became immediate friends. Besides, Oliver had found Jacob to be an altogether interesting person, as well. He was unabashedly Amish – and was not embarrassed to speak plainly of his beliefs – and, as he soon discovered, came from the Pennsylvania town of Gettysburg; the same town that had hosted one of the bloodiest battles of the war to date. Little did Oliver understand at the time of their first encounter just how much Jacob had been closely involved in the battle, or their opening salvo of conversation would have never ended in time for their first dinner in the campus dining hall.

But Jacob had found Oliver to be an interesting character, as well. Oliver was physically almost the same build as Jacob. They both stood a few inches short of six foot tall, but Oliver seemed to care nothing of his outward appearance. He had hair that was a dark blonde, almost sandy color that was almost never combed, although always clean. He wore expensive clothes, but always looked somewhat disheveled. Jacob would comment later that he always felt that his friend, Oliver, was a handsome young man who never had the time or the inclination to realize that he was, in fact, a handsome young man.

Oliver Bartlett was a brilliant academic scholar. He was very much the match for Jacob, intellectually that is – but his easy-going demeanor made it possible for the two young men to work together on academic pursuits without turning it into some sort of competitive event. Perhaps because they lived within the same dormitory room, or perhaps because they were so individually different in nature, the two boys began fast friends, and spent most of their waking hours in the same classes, and in many of the same activities around the campus.

Jacob received letters from his friends and family about three times per week. He usually heard from his parents about twice a week – a letter that often also included a note stuffed inside the envelope from his brother. He heard from the General about once every two weeks, and would also hear from Rebecca at about the same interval. Rebecca had spaced her letters that far apart to allow sufficient time for Jacob's reply to reach her before she would pen another. In this regard, Jacob was extremely diligent. The young man was very surprised to learn, however, that his young lady had also taken up academics, and was now enrolled at Mount Holyoke College for Women. He wondered why it was that she never mentioned this to him before he left for Washington, but even this question was answered in one of her earliest communications with him. But he was very happy that she was also working to advance herself, and that her parents had seen fit to educate their daughter beyond the scullery details of running a household.

By the end of September, Jacob was firmly entrenched in the college society. Even though Oliver Bartlett was studying the law and he medicine, they did spend much of their time together. Jacob discovered that, within the college itself, a strong intramural sports program existed. Organized sport was something which Jacob had never become in any way involved in while in Gettysburg, as he was considered an outsider within that community, and his parents would have looked down at his association with the 'English.' Here, at Dartmouth, he enjoyed his chance to become involved with activities that appeared to him as new and exciting. He joined a singing club, and became actively involved in team sports. Chief among his interests in this regard was a relatively new game, fashioned off of an older sport called 'rounders.' The game had supposedly been around for a decade, or more, but those scholars at Dartmouth who seemed to be in the know declared that it was an 'American' game, and that it had been 'invented' by a soldier while studying his military craft at West Point. When Jacob inquired who the soldier was, he was surprised to hear that it was one of the Generals from the battle of Gettysburg, Abner Doubleday – one of the heroes of the first day of the battle, later to be somewhat vilified and overlooked for his contribution to the battle.

Jacob spent a week, or so, playing the game with his fellow students. He discovered that he needed to specialize in a particular position; that all skills in the strange new game – which was called 'baseball' – were not equal. Of the eleven positions to be played defensively, Jacob found that he was most at home being the 'catcher' – the position played behind the home plate. His job was to 'catch' the pitches thrown by the 'pitcher,' who hurled the baseball passed the opposing team's 'batter,' who attempted to clobber the thing with a wooden bat. Jacob found that his farm boy legs were very adept for the long periods of squatting that was required to play this position, owing much of his success to the many hours he had spent milking the cows on their farms in Paradise and Gettysburg.

Whatever his physical attributes, Jacob enjoyed playing the game of baseball. Over the course of his first few weeks at the school, he played in over a dozen games. In addition to his skill behind home plate, where he soon discovered that he was in both a primary and final position of defense, he also became almost legendary with the bat. His quick eye enabled him to hit the ball into the outfield, keeping it down on the ground in order to score needed runs. On the other hand, Jacob could also hit the 'long ball,' placing several hits over the fence at the rear of their playing field – a feat which he learned was called a 'home run.' Jacob had the occasion to hit one of these at one of his first games, the end result of this accomplishment was that his team won the game, making him a 'hero' for that moment in time.

But more than this, Jacob found that his involvement with his team also changed his social status around the campus. After a game, both teams would adjourn to a local tavern, the choice of which belonging to the winning team. He soon discovered that it was not only socially acceptable, but rather socially expected, as well, that he raise a pint, or two, of ale in celebration of the event – something which he had never done while living in Gettysburg. He found the taste of the brew surprisingly strange, and, once tasted, wondered what all the fuss was about in the first place. But after several more trips to the tavern, discovered that he had started to nurture his taste to appreciate the substance.

Oliver Bartlett, on the other hand, was not one for organized sports. He preferred more academic pursuits, especially those which involved debate and forensics. He spent a great deal of his time in the college library; time that greatly exceeded the allotment that most of the other students did not devote, including, to a limited degree – his good friend, Jacob Zook. He would, however, attend as many of the baseball games that his friend played in as he could, and, quite often, found himself tagging along to the local tavern, as well. In many respects, Oliver had a quirky personality. He tended to speak in a very formal manner, and his mannerisms often seemed very stiff and almost uncomfortable. But, in spite of his family heritage, he was a very genuine and caring young man – and soon became extremely devoted to his new friend, Jacob Zook. Like his friend, Oliver had spent very little of his free time visiting the taverns of New Hampshire, but he was also anxious to discover the freedom that living away from Montpelier would bring – so he was overjoyed to join the team when asked to go out with them. After the first few times, he was considered a regular, along with the members of the team. The other young men found Oliver's banter especially comical; he had a very humorous way of turning a phrase and expressing an opinion.

By mid-October, both young men had been totally assimilated into the fabric of college life in New Hampshire.

As the weather turned colder toward the end of October, and the leaves and the trees turned radiant colors, later to fall to the ground, the baseball season came to an end. Jacob was surprised to see how early in the season they were experiencing snow flurries, and how much colder the average temperature was than in Pennsylvania. Even so, the camaraderie of his newly found social life continued to proceed unabated. He would join his friends about twice a week in the local pub, often joined by his most willing compatriot, Oliver Bartlett. The tavern was more than a local watering hole – it was also a place to learn the news of the day – especially on the progress, or lack of it, concerning the war.

Jacob was concerning over Abraham Lincoln's popularity in recent months. According to most sources, Lincoln's chances for re-election were becoming slim to none, with General George McClellan's candidacy weighing very heavily into this process. Lincoln had received a bit of a shot in the arm from the twin Union victories at Gettysburg and Vicksburg, but the Confederacy didn't seem any weaker than it had at the beginning of 1863.

Then, in the final week of October, Jacob received two letters.

The first was a letter from General Sickles. In his letter, the General informed Jacob that Lincoln would be making a trip to Gettysburg in early November. The motivation for this trip was to dedicate a National Cemetery on the grounds of the battlefield. Sickles had been politicking with Lincoln in order to accomplish this, even though Secretary Stanton wished to see the site on Robert E. Lee's property across the Potomac River. Sickles letter was more informative than anything else. He explained to the young man that he was planning on attending the dedication ceremony. Jacob smiled when he read the letter, seeing the General's deft hand at work behind the scenes.

The second letter was more personal. It was a letter from his brother Abraham.

Abraham, who had now turned fifteen, had written to his brother with alarming news. Their mother, Sarah, had taken ill. She had been ministering to the many dead still laying out on the battlefield even months after the conflict. The number of town volunteers had dwindled since the early days after the battle, so that by the end of the summer on a few dozen remained to accomplish the grisly task of burying the dead. Disease, or the possibility of becoming ill from working with the rotting corpses, was a reality.

Sarah Zook had contracted cholera.

Jacob read the letter several times over, each time trying to digest the importance of the words. He resolved immediately thereafter to return that evening to Gettysburg, hoping that his arrival was not too late. As Oliver Bartlett was in the room at the time, he needed to explain his actions… and his tears. Oliver proposed that he accompany his friend to Pennsylvania, an offer which Jacob accepted with great humility and gratitude. They quickly packed and caught a train to New York, and then caught another to Philadelphia. The next day they boarded a train for Harrisburg, and when they arrived, they hired a horse and wagon to make the final leg of the journey to Gettysburg.

The young men arrived at the seminary property in the late afternoon. They were immediately greeted by Abraham, who, even though he had heard nothing from Jacob, had assumed that his brother would return out of concern for his mother. He also knew that if he had departed New Hampshire upon receipt of his letter, which he had, that he would have gotten to Gettysburg far faster than any reply he had sent by post.

Jacob hopped down from the buckboard and embraced his brother.

"I knew you would come," blubbered Abraham.

"How could I not?" asked Jacob, gently patting his brother on the back. They broke their embrace and stared into each other's tear-streaked faces. "I think you have grown a bit since I last saw you," observed Jacob.

"Maybe an inch," replied his brother. "Who is this?" he asked, noticing the stranger still sitting in the wagon.

"This…is Mr. Oliver Bartlett," announced Jacob. "Oliver is my friend….and my roommate."

"Oh!" exclaimed Abraham, with a charm that sounded friendly enough. "Why don't you come down from there, Oliver? I will help you get settled while Jacob visits our mother."

"How is she?" asked Jacob, nervously.

"Not very good, I'm afraid."

"Where is Papa?"

"He is up there….with her," explained Abraham. "He hasn't left her side for the past two days."

Jacob nodded to his brother, understanding just how serious the disease could be. Even in this simple conversation, he could tell that his brother was extremely upset by the circumstances. He knew it was good that he had come home. He looked over at Oliver, who gently returned his gaze with a weak smile and a slight nod. Bartlett jumped down off of the wagon and led the horse toward the barn, following Abraham. "This is a beautiful part of the Country," he said to the boy, striking up a meaningless conversation.

"Are you one of my brother's friends?" asked Abraham.

"I am proud to consider myself as one," Oliver answered.

"You speak a little oddly," observed the younger boy.

"I have been told that quite a bit," laughed Oliver. "Your brother finds that to be a very endearing charm about me." But Abraham, unlike the young men at Dartmouth, did not find much humor in Oliver's manner of speech. He found it…annoying.

Jacob turned and went into the house. He knew that Oliver would keep his brother occupied for a few minutes, at the very least. He didn't stop to remove his outer coat and hat, but rather proceeded immediately up the flight of stairs to his parent's bedroom. He knocked gently on the door, but then pushed the door open, not waiting for a reply. He could see his mother lying in the bed, and his father kneeling in prayer beside her on the floor – his prayer so intense that he failed to notice the knock on the door or his son entering the room.

"Papa?"

His father looked up. "Jakob! You have come home?" "Of course, Papa!" the boy replied. "How is Mama?"

"Not very good, I am afraid," Ishmael replied. "The English doctor is confused. He doesn't understand why God has not taken her already. He says that it looks like she has Cholera, but she keeps hanging on…. far too long for most Cholera victims."

"So…maybe it isn't Cholera?"

"Maybe…but if it isn't, then what is it?" asked Ishmael. "I have seen Cholera before this…and this is what it looks like…but then again, there is something different about it."

"Is she asleep?"

"If you can call it sleep," his father answered. "She has been like this for more than a day. She did not want me to send for you. She didn't want to draw you away from your studies, Jakob. How did you know to come?"

"Abraham wrote me."

"Ah…Abraham. I should have known! Well, it is a good thing that he did that! You made that long trip from New Hampshire by yourself?"

"No, sir…a friend of mine from school accompanied me on the journey. He is in the barn with Abraham…taking care of the horse and wagon."

"Good…good," answered his father. "It will be good to have some more people in this house again, Jakob."

His father rose from his kneeling position and embraced his first-born. "Father," Jacob said, "I will stay here with Mama for a while. Why don't you go get something to eat, or take a bit of a rest. You look very tired."

"I am tired, Jakob. This has been very draining for me." His father turned to leave the room.

"Papa?" Jacob questioned. "What shall I do if Mama wakes up?"

"Speak to her a bit…. And then come get me, Jakob," answered his father.

And Jacob knew exactly what his father had meant by this answer, for he really had no idea what to do if she did, in fact, wake up. He could hear his father lumbering down the hallway. He heard a door open and close. His father had gone into one of the other bedrooms on the second floor of the house. Evidently, he was going to take his son's advice and get some rest. Jacob thought this was a good plan, although part of him knew that he was also a bit worried how his father would take to Oliver Bartlett, especially under the circumstances. Ishmael Zook was not known for his sense of humor, in fact, he was one of the more humorless people in Gettysburg. Jacob could imagine that his father might not take quickly to Oliver's personality – and he would most certainly not understand his use of the language, or of his use of wit and sarcasm.

He sat down on the side of the bed and looked at his mother. Her pallor was a strange color. Her eyes seemed to have sunk into their sockets, and there were wrinkles of loose skin on her arms and hands – the classic symptoms of Cholera. He lifted his mother's hand off of the blanket and held it between his two hands, praying. "Dear God…please do not allow any harm to come to this good woman;" and, having said that, Jacob burst into tears.

Meanwhile, down in the barn, Abraham was wrapping up the grand tour of the building, showing Oliver each of the stalls for the horses and cattle, as well as the

various and sundry pigs, goats and sheep that were raised there. When this was completed, Abraham brought Oliver over to the Lutheran Seminary and introduced him to Reverend Meier. Oliver had expected Jacob's brother to be a younger, smaller version of same, but this was not to be the case. Where Jacob was quiet and reserved, Abraham was always energetic and ready to ask a million questions. Where Jacob had moments of shyness, Abraham was effervescent and outgoing. Within moments of knowing him, Oliver was certain that Abraham was the type of person who could easily speak to whatever was on his mind.

Never was this clearer to the young man than when they were returning to the house following their visit to the seminary, Abraham asked, "Will you be leaving tomorrow morning, or will you be staying for a while?"

Oliver was taken aback by the question. "Well…I suppose that depends on your brother, Abraham."

"Of course," the boy answered, "but what is it that you want, Oliver?" Thinking for only just a moment, Oliver answered, "I think that I would like to stay here for the time being."

"And do you really think that is wise…I mean, with the Cholera in the house, and all?"

Once again, Oliver was taken by surprise. "I don't want to be in the way, Abraham. I can always find a room at the hotel in the town."

"And what would you do then?" the boy continued. "Surely you must realize that Jacob could be here for quite some time?"

"I just want to offer him my support, Abraham."

"That's my job, Oliver!"

Oliver stopped walking, instantly realizing from where this comment had arisen. "Abraham…I didn't come here to replace you. I can never replace you…don't you know that?"

"You! You're his best friend, I suppose?"

"That may be," answered Oliver. "Actually…I hope that is so." "Hmm," grunted Abraham.

"Yes," countered Oliver quickly, "but you are his brother. That is a bond much stronger than friendship."

"Sometimes," said Abraham.

"Almost always," replied Oliver. "If Jacob is to be my friend, Abraham…then I need you to be my friend, too. Don't you think?"

"That may be true," answered the boy, "but my mind is too filled with other matters right now. I'm sorry, Oliver."

"Yes, you are correct, Abraham," he replied. "Your mother's health should be your first concern."

"It *is* my first concern, Oliver!" screamed Abraham, rushing out of the barn. Oliver felt instantly awkward and uncomfortable, a mixture of emotions and ideas running rampant through his mind. Should he leave, or should he stay? Should he support Jacob, or try to win Abraham's confidence? And what about their father? Surely he would have a say in all of this, as well! Unable to think in his usual calm, clear manner, Oliver found a nearby bale of hay and sat down upon it, resting his head in his hands – as if this action would help him think more organized thoughts.

But for the first time since getting on the train in Hanover, New Hampshire, Oliver started to re-think his decision to travel to Pennsylvania with his friend. He now had second thoughts; thoughts that weren't quite as obvious a day or so before. He realized that he was treading on foreign soil; that he was an obvious outsider in a very close-knit family.

He felt out of place.

But part of the reason he felt that way was because of his own upbringing. He had been born into a family of privilege; a family that could lay claim to some form of American birthright – if there even was such a thing. Oliver was aware that there was a form of American aristocracy in the Deep South, but his New England background never had really suggested a similarity to those customs – yet he knew that this was somewhat the case. He knew what was expected of him – a member of the Bartlett family; that he could trace his ancestry back past the signing of the Declaration of Independence – and then back to England.

Once again, he wondered what had possessed him to hop on that train to agrarian Pennsylvania. But he didn't have to consider it very long; it was because of his friendship with Jacob Zook. He didn't want to say it – not in so many words, of course – but he had never had a friendship as close as the one he now felt for Jacob. The Bartletts were mostly about appearances and expectations; the Zooks were about family…and tradition. It was so different that it had become attractive to him – almost magnetic.

If he was to make his visit become anything of value – both to the Zook family and from his own personal point of view – then the first thing he had to do was to convince Jacob's brother that he wasn't as much of an outsider as he seemed; that he wasn't as awkward as he now felt – even though he actually was quite awkward.

*   *   *   *

Jacob stayed with his mother until almost suppertime. He sat on the side of her bed and spoke to her as if she was fully conscious and able to return his banter. He spoke to her in German and in English.

Abraham came into the bedroom at about five thirty. He asked Jacob to go downstairs to the kitchen and to have something to eat, and that he would stay with their mother until he returned. Jacob reluctantly left the side of his mother; the woman who had instilled in him the desire to be something more than a simple farmer – the woman who had inspired him to become something more than his fate would allow.

Jacob walked down to the kitchen to find that Oliver Bartlett had, in fact, prepared the dinner for the family. For some reason, Abraham had neglected to mention this to him when he relieved him at his mother's bedside. He had also failed to mention that their father, Ishmael, was now engrossed in a full-fledged conversation with Oliver. The topic, as Jacob entered the kitchen, had turned to, of all things – religion. As Jacob turned the corner, rounding the base of the staircase, he could easily recognize Oliver's booming voice coming from the area of the house which held the kitchen.

"We Bartlett's are…and have been for many generations…. Congregationalists, Mr. Zook."

"What does that mean, young man?" Jacob heard his father ask, in a not unpleasant sounding voice.

"Well," Jacob heard Oliver reply, "that means is that we do not follow a particular system of hierarchy…like the Roman Catholics or Episcopalians…or even the Lutherans…with a system of synods and bishops…and so on. Every congregation is its own governing body, acting independently of the general organization."

Jacob had reached the doorway to the kitchen when he heard his father reply, "Then that sounds very much like the way that the Amish community is organized."

"Indeed, it is!" agreed Oliver, who had discovered this similarity when in conversation with Jacob during their first week at Dartmouth. "Of course, if you ask a Congregationalist, he will probably proudly explain that our main claim to fame is that we were the people that landed at Plymouth in 1620."

"You are the descendants of the original Pilgrims?" asked Ishmael, in a tone of awe.

"A fact which I have heard innumerable times already," added Jacob from the doorway.

"Jakob!"

"Jacob!"

"Your college friend, Oliver, has prepared a meal for us," said Ishmael. "Look! He has cooked up some sausages and made some potatoes and carrots."

"It smells very good, Papa," answered Jacob. "Oliver…I had no idea that you knew how to cook."

"And why would you?" asked Oliver. "We eat at the dining hall or at the tavern. When would I have had the opportunity to cook? It's just part of my charm…that's all!"

"And I am starving to eat some of your charm, Oliver," replied Jacob, grabbing a plate off of the table. "Papa…I see that you and Oliver are getting along just fine."

"And why not?" asked his father. "He is a fine young man…and even more than that…if he is a friend of my son, then why should I not like him, too?"

"A very solid argument," agreed Oliver. "I only wish that your brother could see it the same way."

"Why?" asked Jacob. "Is there a problem with Abraham?"

"It is delicate," answered Oliver. "I think that he may resent my presence here….especially at this time."

Jacob nodded, knowing his brother's penchant for being overly dramatic. "He will get over it. He is a little jealous, I suppose…but give him some time and he will warm up to you, Oliver." He took a mouthful of Oliver's food. "Good job on the potatoes, Oliver!"

"Thank you….it's an old family recipe."

"Jakob?"

"Yes, Papa?"

"I have an idea. When you go back upstairs to see your mother again, why not ask Abraham to show Oliver around the town? That way they can get to know each other a little better."

"I don't know," said Oliver, cautiously. "I don't wish to upset him more than I have already done in coming here as I did."

But Jacob ignored the observation of his friend, however insightful it may have been. "It is a bold idea, Papa…but I think it will help. How about if you hitch up the wagon…like you are going out for a ride all by yourself…but then you plead with him for his assistance, Oliver? I don't think that he will refuse you."

"Maybe…"

"And…I'll tell you….if you make a stop at Reilly's Drugstore…in the middle of the town….Oliver loves Cherry Phosphates."

"He does?" gushed Oliver. "So do I!"

"There! You will have plenty of time together to get to know each other. Just don't be too overbearing, Oliver. Be yourself!" Having given this homily, Jacob sat back in his chair chewing on a piece of the sausage.

"Jacob! When am I overbearing?"

Jacob put down his fork and merely raised his right eyebrow in Oliver's direction. The point was taken, and Oliver graciously nodded his head in defeat. "Ask him to show you some of the places where the battle took place, beginning with right here on Seminary Ridge. Ask him to show you how our friend, Ginnie Wade, was killed while standing in her own kitchen. Just don't let him take you down to the wheat field or the peach orchard…or anywhere that had heavy causalities…because they are still trying to bury the dead."

"What was that?" asked Oliver.

"They are gathering up the remaining bodies for burial in common graves on Cemetery Ridge," explained Ishmael. "Evidently it is going to be turned into a national cemetery. I hear that Lincoln is coming out here next week to dedicate the ground."

"That is so! I had nearly forgotten about that," said Jacob. He immediately thought that the possibility existed to see General Sickles, as he would very likely try to attend any sort of dedication ceremony for the cemetery, seeing how it was very much his idea in the first place.

"Yes," continued his father. "There is even a rumor going about that the entire battlefield – or most of it, I suppose – is going to be purchased by the government as a memorial to those who fought and died here."

"But doesn't that land belong to people already?"

"That is so, Jakob. It belongs to the MacPhersons, the Trostles, the Spanglers….and quite a few more. But that ground now contains hundreds…maybe even thousands of shallow graves. It's more of a graveyard than farm land…and the owners haven't been able to produce a crop this season on it…and they probably won't be able to do much of anything next year, either. The money that the government will pay will help them to survive."

"I suppose," answered Jacob, putting another piece of sausage into his mouth.

"But there are other rumors, as well, Jakob," continued Ishmael.

"Oh?"

"The town has already been flooded with many inquiries about putting up monuments…statues…markers…anything that will show where certain events in the battle occurred."

"Why would they want to do that?" asked Jacob.

"I am not sure, myself," confessed Ishmael, "but I have heard that the three day battle was the most costly of the war…to date; that there were more lives sacrificed in those three days than in any other battle."

Of that fact Jacob was not at all surprised. He had been a first-hand witness to the utter futility of the battle. He had witnessed Generals ordering rank upon rank of brave young men into the unspeakable horror of battle. He had seen the results of their efforts in that field hospital – many of them have their limbs amputated by Doctor Sim, and by others. He had experienced it most from the vantage of the Federal troops, but he had also witnessed it from the perspective of the Confederates. He had watched General Armistead die. He had seen Major Winslow kill his friend, Bobby MacLean.

He had heard the screams of the wounded and dying.

"They are correct," Jacob said. "It is one massive graveyard. It shouldn't be touched."

CHAPTER 44

An Unhappy Ending

Toward the end of the first week of November, it became obvious that Sarah Zook was beginning a downward spiral. Her coma was deeper; her breathing more labored. It was around ten o'clock in the morning and Ishmael was taking a turn sitting with Sarah when he noticed a big change in her appearance. Her color had become almost ashen, as if the blood had drained away from her face. Her eyes were even more sunken into her head than earlier. Ishmael quickly arose and called his sons to the room. Jacob and Abraham sprinted up the stairs from the parlor below as quickly as they possibly could, standing then at the foot of the large bed. Ishmael waved his sons over to his side, but Abraham would not move from the foot of the bed. Jacob rounded the side of his parent's bed and slowly sat on the edge, as he had so many times before. He took his mother's hand in his and gently patted it.

Sarah Zook's eyes opened.

Jacob looked up at his father, astonished at his mother's reaction. "Speak to her, Jakob," his father said.

"Muti... Mama...can you hear me?"

"Jakob?" his mother asked hoarsely. "Is that you?" "Yes, Mama.... here I am."

"You came all the way from school to see me?"

"Yes, Mama," assured Jacob. "I came home to see you."

"I was hoping that you would, Jakob." Then Sarah reached up with her hand and touched the side of his face. "You look older already, Jakob." Tears began to stream down the side of Jacob's face, but he would not take his eyes off of his mother. She turned away from him, however, and looked toward the end of the bed. "Abraham...come here." Abraham shook his head. "Abraham!"

And then, with that second request...which sounded more like the way Sarah usually spoke to her younger son, the boy did move around to the side of the bed opposite his brother. "You must be very brave now, Abraham. Do you know that?"

Abraham could not bring himself to answer his mother – he could only shake his head.

"Abraham? What will your father do once I am gone? He will need you to help him, don't you know that? Jakob will be away at school...so it will be up to you. Promise me that you will help him."

Abraham continued to shake his head, as if by denying the reality of the situation it could suddenly bring about a change. But then, when Sarah momentarily closed her eyes, Abraham quickly changed his mind and began to nod in the affirmative. The Zook men could see a slight smile pass over Sarah's lips.

"I've waited for you to come, Jakob," Sarah said slowly, "but now I think I am going to have to leave you."

"No, Mama!" Jacob dropped to his knees at the side of the bed, quickly reaching out to grasp his dying mother's hand. This, in itself, was a foolish move on Jacob's part, and he already knew this to be so. Jacob was already aware that if his mother had contracted Cholera, or Typhus, that any contact at all – even being in the same room with the victim – could easily spread the disease to bystanders.

"No, Mama!" cried Abraham, now pleading with his mother to survive this ordeal.

But it was already too late – she had gone. With one final breath, Sarah Zook departed this life. Abraham immediately broke down into uncontrollable sobbing, which he further punctuated by stomping his foot on the floor out of anger and frustration. Ishmael moved toward the bed and to his younger son, embracing him with both of his immense, strong arms, trying desperately to sooth that which could never, ever be soothed.

Even though the doctor never confirmed the cause of Sarah Zook's death, the possibility that it might be from Cholera called for special precautions. She was buried almost immediately – before sundown on the same day in which she died. If there had been an actual epidemic, there would have been cause to cremate the body instead of the traditional burial. Even so, all of the bed linens were burned, as well as the curtains from the bedroom. As Sarah was Amish, she did not have a large wardrobe of clothing. In fact, according to the Amish Ordnung, she wore the same house dress for much of her adult life. She was buried in this dress, and the balance of her clothing, including her undergarments were also burned. The entire house was then washed down with a mixture of lye and water. The Lutheran Seminarians accomplished this task as the family prepared to bury their mother and wife.

Owing to the nature of her death, the mourners and well-wishers were few. The Tilden family paid their respects, along with some of the town fathers, and the entire staff and students at the Lutheran Seminary. Oliver Bartlett was, of course, on hand – as was, for the first time in many months, Georgia McClellan's husband, who had returned from the war. He came to the funeral out of gratitude for the kindness shown by the Zook family during their time of need back in July.

As the Zook family, along with Oliver Bartlett, walked from the open maw that now contained the coffin containing Sarah Zook, Jacob noticed a man that was all too familiar to his eyes.

It was General Daniel Sickles.

The General was standing on a slight rise above them, propped up by crutches, his wheelchair pushed off to the side. "General?" Jacob said, with surprise.

"Jacob," replied the General, speaking very softly. He then cast his eyes toward the earth.

"Papa," Jacob explained, "General Sickles is here."

Ishmael was also taken by surprise at the news, turning quickly to see the man on the hillside…the man with only one leg. "General Sickles."

Jacob walked up the slight rise to greet his benefactor. "General…it was good of you to come."

The General reached out with his right hand and grasped Jacob's hand. "Jacob…words cannot express the degree of sorrow which I feel for you and your family at this moment."

"How did you come to learn about this, sir? My mother died just today." Sickles shifted awkwardly on his crutches. "Jacob…as much as I would like to say otherwise, the fact that I am here is purely coincidental. I came in this morning for the dedication of the national cemetery tomorrow, and I decided to take a ride out to the Spangler farm to see the place where they…" The General looked down at his leg and uncomfortably broke off the sentence. "I know it is a bit macabre, Jacob…but I just had to do it. Anyway, Old Man Spangler told me about your mother."

Ishmael walked over to the spot where Sickles and Jacob were talking. "General…I am honored to see that you have come at this time." Sickles was about to repeat his explanation to Ishmael, but Jacob raised his hand and waved him off. "General…we are all going to go to the tavern for dinner. Would you care to join us?" asked Ishmael.

"I would be honored to join you, Mr. Zook," replied Sickles.

"This is good, General," replied Ishmael, smiling at the officer. "I don't wish to rush back to my own house…not right now…and I am sure that Jacob has much to tell you about school."

"Thank you for your hospitality, Mr. Zook," answered Sickles. "There is much I need to tell Jacob regarding the proceedings of tomorrow."

But that conversation could wait for the time. Sickles was sensitive enough to the situation to realize that such topics were not fitting to be spoken of standing at a graveside – even though the chief topic was to concern itself with the dedication of the national cemetery. Sickles quickly looked at each face standing by the open grave. He recognized Jacob's brother, Abraham – but there was another young gentleman with him who he did not recognize from his last visit to Gettysburg. He looked at Jacob and his father, Ishmael, once more. As if the shock of the battle, the loss of their house, the destruction of pasture and farmland – if these events were not enough – they now had to deal with the loss of the matriarch of the family.

Sickles gestured to his right, showing Ishmael that he had a carriage waiting for him. "We can all ride together into the town," offered the General.

"Thank you," responded Ishmael, happily taking the officer up on his offer. Ishmael turned to call to Abraham and Oliver, who, at last glance, were still standing over the grave. To his surprise, his younger son and his older son's new friend were now walking toward them. Oliver had his arm over Abraham's shoulder, comforting the boy after he had said his final farewell to his mother. It had taken more than a full day for Abraham to warm up to Oliver Bartlett; a full day, and a long ride into the town after dinner one night – plus several cherry phosphates at Reilly's. Oliver had come to appreciate what made Abraham so very different than his brother, Jacob – and Abraham had come to understand Oliver's strange, but humorous way of speaking.

They, too, had become friends.

And, in this friendship Abraham had discovered that he was receiving support from someone other than his father, Ishmael, and his brother, Jacob. There was someone he could turn to outside of his own nuclear, Amish family; someone who viewed the world from a very different perspective.

The three Zook men, Oliver Bartlett and Daniel Sickles all crowded into the General's carriage and headed off to a tavern on the Chambersburg Pike. Ishmael and Abraham were both surprised to see that Jacob had developed quite a taste for ale over the past few weeks - although this wasn't much of surprise to Oliver, who had developed a similar vice. Sickles really didn't notice that the young men were drinking; he was too busy swilling back shot after shot of Kentucky Bourbon.

Ishmael, usually one for temperance, decided that he would break his long-standing, self-inflicted rule by having a mug of beer, along with a shot of bourbon. Abraham had to make due with cider, which was plentiful in the autumn months.

The tavern was unusually crowded; there wasn't a room to be had anywhere in Gettysburg, owing to the fact that the dedication of the new national cemetery was being held on the next day. Many members of the burgeoning press corps were taking up many of the rooming accommodations, including those offered at this particular tavern. The politicians had already reserved the few nicer hotel rooms in the small town, and the rest seemed swallowed up by the military personnel and curiosity seekers. It had been publicized that the President would be on hand to give a speech at the dedication, but the town fathers had seen fit to make sure that the most famous orator of the day, Edward Everett, was on hand to give the keynote address.

Because of the overcrowded conditions, the food order was taking a much longer time to be completed, so the small party from the cemetery had more time to sit and converse…and drink.

"When do you expect President Lincoln to arrive?" Jacob asked Sickles. "Arrive?" the General answered back with his own question. He took out his pocket watch and checked the time. "I believe that this food has taken so long to get here…that Lincoln is already here."

"Today?" asked Jacob, bewildered. "Isn't the ceremony tomorrow?"

"Yes…but Lincoln is the guest of one of your big shots….a lawyer named David Wills. He is supposed to spend the night at the Wills house before heading over to the cemetery in the morning."

"I know of this man," said Ishmael. "He is the one who pushed the town council to create the national cemetery. It was his idea!"

Sickles slammed his fist onto the table. "It was my idea! Damn it!" he thundered. Even in the crowded, noisy tavern his exclamation brought an instantaneous silence in the room. Sickles immediately realized that his pride and temper – not to mention the alcohol – had gotten the better of him. He spoke quickly to Ishmael in a much more hushed tone. "I am truly sorry, Ishmael. I did not mean to raise my voice at you the way I did. You have suffered enough for one day, without me adding to it with my boorish behavior."

"You do not have to explain yourself, General," replied the elder Zook. " In one of the letters he sent home to us – after he first left home to stay with you – he told us of your visit with the President, and that you had suggested the very same thing at that meeting. It is often a very difficult thing to watch another man take credit for your own hard work – such is the nature of our pride."

Sickles nodded. "Yes…it has been difficult." Jacob gave the General a long, hard look. He seemed genuinely hurt, and, for one of the first times since they had met – utterly sincere. "Warfare is a hellish business, Ishmael. Even after the heat of battle is over, there are always questions to be answered. Reasons must be found why the fighting went a certain way…or didn't go any way at all. Sergeants ask this of their Privates. Captains ask it of their Lieutenants. Colonels ask it of their Majors. And Commanders in the Field ask it of their Generals."

"And why is that?" asked Ishmael, innocently.

"Why?" repeated Sickles, taking a gulp of his whiskey…"Because someone must always be held accountable! One moment you are being praised for taking the initiative; for charging into the fray when other men were either too afraid or too cautious to proceed – and the next moment you find that you are being set up as a scapegoat for all the woes of the day. That's the thing about the army, Ishmael – someone must always be there to take the blame."

Jacob knew exactly what the General was speaking about; he had heard some of the rumors flying about during his brief stay in Washington. Now, almost two full months later, Sickles himself was confirming that which he had heard.

But Ishmael was not as enlightened as his son. He allowed a slight smile to form on his lips, took a sip of his whiskey, and then asked the question that no one else at the table dared to ask. "General Sickles, are you being blamed for something?"

"Indeed I am, Mr. Zook…."

"Ishmael…" corrected the Amish gentleman.

"Sorry…Ishmael," said the General softly. "George Meade had to take the heat from Lincoln for not pursuing the Confederates back into Virginia and ending the War at that very instant, so he, in turn, decided to point the finger of blame on some of his own subordinates. I get the blame for the Union losses on the second day of the battle, and Abner Doubleday gets the blame for giving up the high ground on the first day."

"The high ground?" Oliver asked.

"A military advantage, Mister Bartlett. The high ground, in this case, was located at Seminary Ridge – exactly where your friends, the Zooks, lived…and still do to this day."

"Ah, yes…" nodded Ishmael. "Thanks to you for that, General."

"That was my distinct pleasure, Ishmael," smiled Sickles, "and I would do it again tomorrow, if the occasion presented itself."

Ishmael smiled graciously at the General. Jacob couldn't help but smirk at the reality of the scene being played out before his very eyes. His father, once a stern, immovable Amish man – was now sitting in a tavern with one of the most irascible officers ever to don a uniform – who was, in fact, already two sheets to the wind.

"Could you be more specific, General?" asked Oliver, who had little knowledge of the explosive nature of General Sickles.

But Sickles was more ready to teach than to preach. "Abner took command of the field after John Reynolds was killed by a sniper. They held off the Confederate army for most of the day…against far greater numbers, I can tell you…and then….when Meade finally arrived on the scene late that night, poor Abner was relieved of his command, because he finally had to retreat to higher ground on Cemetery Ridge. To add insult to injury, Meade appointed a junior office to take his place." Sickles looked directly at Ishmael. "You know…Abner aimed the first volley

at the Confederates from Fort Sumter. The Confederates may have fired the first shot, but it was Abner Doubleday that returned the fire." But this aside left little reaction with Ishmael, who had absolutely no idea what the General was talking about.

"It sounds to me as though the military is very political," observed Oliver.

"Certainly it is political, Oliver!" agreed Sickles. "Rank has always been determined by who you know…at least up to a point. It worked for me. It will work for Abner, as well."

"What makes you say that?" asked Jacob.

Sickles let out a short laugh. "Doubleday is a good friend and ally of President Lincoln. He was supposed to ride with the President on the train from Washington today. He is coming with the President to dedicate the cemetery."

"Really?" asked Jacob. "The man who invented the game of baseball is coming here?"

"What is this 'baseball,' Jakob?" Ishmael asked his son.

"Umm…"

"It's just a game, Papa," said Abraham, in a very off-handed way, as if it really didn't matter what the game entailed, or how much time Jacob had spent during his first few weeks at school playing it.

"And I am not sure if Doubleday actually had anything to do with it," answered Sickles. "I do know that he is interested in being transferred to California, which will probably happen, because Lincoln likes him a great deal."

"Politics," said Jacob to his father with a nod, as if to explain the procedure to the elder Zook.

"I see," said Ishmael. "So….Oliver? Do you play this…baseball?"

"Me, sir? Oh, no…I am not very athletic," quipped Oliver. "Your son is very adept at playing."

Ishmael turned back to his son. "So, Jakob…you play this game a great deal, do you?"

"Are you asking me if I am forsaking my studies in order to play a game, Papa?" Jacob responded.

"Not exactly….but are you?"

"No, Papa...I am doing very well at school." Jacob shot Oliver a glance that drained the color from the young man's face.

But it was Sickles who broke the tension of the moment. "Ishmael... relax a bit, won't you. First of all, there is a social element involved with going off to college. It is all part of the process of growing up. Second...I can't imagine Jacob being that irresponsible that he would allow a game to interfere with your generosity in allowing him to attend Dartmouth."

"That was your generosity, General," corrected Ishmael.

"Only the money, Sir....the rest was up to you. He would not be there at all, were it not for you...and your wife."

Ishmael nodded in agreement, but turned back to Jacob anyway. "And remember, Jakob...it was your mother who sat up with you and helped you learn to read...who helped you learn all of those things out of books. Remember that!"

"I will, Papa! I will never forget what Mama did for me!"

Ishmael glanced over at his son. Jacob's eyes were beginning to well with tears at the recollection of all the home education that his mother had given him; that she would never get to see him graduate or to fulfill the dreams she had for her son. But seeing his son's reaction, Ishmael took his son by his arm, drawing him with surprising force out of his chair until he embraced him.

And for the first time since his mother died, Jacob broke down into uncontrollable sobs, as he held his father's shoulders.

Ishmael felt compelled to utter the phrase...the phrase he had not uttered often to either son ...before the battle, "Ich liebe dich, Jakob."

Jacob pulled back from his father's embrace, his cheeks streaked with tears. "Ich liebe dich, Fati," – a phrase which Jacob, too, had a great difficulty emoting and saying. And the sight of his father and older brother emoting in that way had a similar effect on Abraham, who immediately bolted from his chair and embraced his father's left side. In just a matter of seconds, the remaining members of the Gettysburg Zook family were reduced to a puddle of emotion.

Oliver Bartlett, too, was overcome by the scene that he was witnessing. Even though he had only know Jacob's father for a few short days, Jacob had been very forthcoming in his description of his father to Oliver; especially when relating the details of how he almost ran away from home at the beginning of the summer. In this moment of catharsis, even Oliver was close to breaking down – something that did not go unnoticed by Sickles, who decided that the mood was getting far too maudlin for his own taste, so he turned to Oliver and said, "You take one step out of that chair towards me and you will never live to see nineteen years, Oliver Bartlett!!" The statement was delivered with perfect execution, and had the desired effect on the Zook men. In just a blink of an eye, the tears were turned to laughter again.

CHAPTER 45

Later

After a seemingly endless wait for their food, it was finally delivered to Sickles, Bartlett, and the Zooks – who were, with the exception of Abraham, now quite inebriated. They all ate ravenously, even though, were the truth to be told, the food was not up to the usual standards served by that particular tavern; the overcrowding had taken its toll on the level of quality from the kitchen. But it really didn't matter; the adults taste buds had been sufficiently dulled by the amount of alcohol that they had consumed, and Abraham's palate was still too immature to notice – he was simply satisfied to be eating dinner in a tavern.

The dinner completed, the party rose from the table to leave the pub. Ishmael complained to Sickles that he did not look forward to returning to his dark, empty house; not that it would be truly empty – it would be without his Sarah. Sickles countered with the suggestion of a carriage ride through the town.

"Do you know where this David Wills lives?" asked the General.

"No, I do not," replied Ishmael. In actuality, he had very little knowledge of the whereabouts of the 'English' in the town.

"I know where he lives," inserted Jacob. "He lives over on Baltimore Street…just a bit past where Rebecca lives, and even further past Ginnie Wade's house."

"How do you know this?" asked his father, surprised by Jacob's thorough knowledge of the town.

"Rebecca pointed the house out to me when we went for a walk before I left for Washington," replied Jacob, rather sheepishly. "She told me that the Wills house was one of the largest in the town. She also mentioned that Mr. Wills was a very successful lawyer, and that he had studied law with one of the President's colleagues, Thaddeus Stevens."

"That's not the half of it," added Sickles. "Wills is hosting most of the dignitaries from Washington at his house tonight. I understand that there will be at least thirty, or so, for dinner. Of course…even though I was involved in the battle…lost my leg…know Edwin Stanton personally…and have even had dealings with Lincoln, himself…I have been passed over for an invite. It looks like Dan Sickles is not very welcome around Gettysburg these days. I am a bit of an embarrassment to the administration."

"Why is that?" asked Abraham very innocently.

Sickles looked over at the younger boy and smiled. "Just some things that I've said, Abraham…and quite a few things that I've done, I suppose." He thought it better not to descend to the depths of his soul and wallow in self-pity, so he quickly changed the subject. "So…why don't we take a ride over to the Wills house to see what is going on there?"

"Do you think that is wise?" asked Oliver. "I mean to ask, sir… considering what you have just told us."

"Certainly!" said Sickles. "Why not? I am a veteran of this conflict… and I have the wounds to show it. Let's go over and see what it going on."

Of course there was no further discussion to be had; the General had already made up his mind to move his troops forward – just like he had done this past July 2nd, when he moved III Corps forward into the Wheatfield and Peach Orchard.

The party rose to leave the crowded tavern. Sickles was busy collecting his crutches, which he had placed to the side of his chair. Abraham, wishing to be polite – or perhaps because he had started to feel an affinity toward the man, quickly rushed to assist the General – but, in the process, tripped over a chair leg at an adjacent table. He went sprawling to the floor, howling in pain.

"Abraham…are you alright?" asked a concerned Oliver.

"I hurt my foot," replied the boy. "I think I might have broken a bone."

"Good Heavens!" shouted Sickles, concerned that the boy had hurt himself on his account.

"Don't pay him any mind," responded Jacob. "He's probably not all that hurt." "Jacob!" Oliver said, reprovingly. "He just fell over a chair!" "Oliver…don't you think I know my own brother?" Jacob said with a sneer.

This question took Bartlett by surprise, but what was even more surprising was the somewhat callous tone which Jacob had spoken it. Oliver looked over at Ishmael, who didn't really seem very concerned; even this was surprising to him. "Get up off the dirty floor, Abraham. You are embarrassing us!" reprimanded his brother.

To the amazement of all at the table, it was General Sickles who ultimately came to the aid of the boy, reaching far beyond the limits of his wheelchair to lift Abraham off of the floor. He pulled the teenager close to his side, patting his head affectionately – then he glared across the table at Jacob. "What is the matter with you, Jacob? You…more than anyone…should have an appreciation for the value of another member of your family – especially on this day! Even if your brother is actually exaggerating his pain – which I assure you he is not – then you could have overlooked that and have come to his assistance." He looked over at Bartlett and smiled at him. "Friends may come, and friends may go, Jacob…but you will only ever have one brother. Treat him well."

Jacob felt the flush of embarrassment fill his face. Sickles was right! What had come over him? He tried to think of an excuse for his behavior, but couldn't. "I am sorry, Abraham. I don't know what came over me." Abraham looked over at his brother – his feelings, as well as his foot, still hurt. But then he graciously nodded back to his older brother and forced a slight smile. "Come on," said Jacob, "I'll help get you to the carriage – even if I have to carry you out."

"Now that's more like it!" said Sickles.

Jacob pushed himself back on his chair, rose from the table and circled it to where Abraham was half-standing, half-leaning on Sickles' wheelchair. "Can you put your weight on it?" Jacob asked his brother.

"I think so…but it hurts," replied Abraham.

"I will check to see if you broke anything once we are outside of this place," said Jacob, now back to his normal, accommodating self. "Put your arm around my shoulder." Abraham complied so that he could hobble through the tavern toward the door. The other three men in the party brought up the rear. Once Jacob cleared the front door of the tavern, he scooped his brother up from behind his knees and carried him the rest of the way to the carriage. Even though he knew that there was no way that Jacob would ever drop him, Abraham took this opportunity to hold onto his brother's neck tighter. It was more than just for safety – it was a hug.

Jacob carried his brother to Sickles' carriage, placing him gently inside – then he climbed inside, as well. He removed his brother's shoe carefully, amid stifled grunts and groans from Abraham. Jacob figured that, considering all the fuss that his brother was making over the injury, that he probably had sprained his ankle. He carefully removed the stocking on his right foot. He was surprised to see that there wasn't any sign of swelling – not even the slightest. He took his brother's foot in his hand and started to squeeze gently around the juncture of the ankle and the foot. "Does this hurt more when I do this?" he asked his brother.

"Not any more than before," answered Abraham.

"Hm," was all that Jacob could muster, as he moved his fingers down toward the rest of Abraham's foot. He had no experience from either the farm or the battle that would help him diagnose if his brother's foot was broken or sprained. His one medical experience had come from the Dartmouth baseball league, when one of his teammates had taken a bad fall rounding third base. A doctor had been called in, and Jacob had watched intently as the doctor examined the young man's foot. The player had broken one of the bones in his foot, and, upon asking the doctor some probing questions on site, the doctor allowed Jacob to feel the place in the foot. Jacob now knew what a broken bone felt like – only he still didn't feel anything of the sort in Abraham's foot. "I don't think you broke any bones, Abraham…it may be a sprain, that's all." He moved his hands back up his brother's leg to his ankle. "Are you sure that this doesn't hurt?"

And then…for the first time since he began to examine his brother's foot…Jacob looked up at his brother's face.

He was smiling.

It only took a few moments for Jacob to realize that he had been played. "Why you little…"

And then Abraham laughed. "I'm sorry, Jacob, but you were getting far too full of yourself for my taste. I had to bring you back to Earth. You may have met some pretty important people out in the English world, but today…today is about the fact that our mother has just died…we have just buried her. I think that you may have forgotten that fact…I think that you may have forgotten that we are related."

"I could never forget about either one of those facts, Abraham."

"I suppose I know that…deep inside, but I just had to remind you… that's all." Jacob nodded and smiled at his brother. "It's like the General just said in there…you are the only brother I will ever have."

Abraham smirked and shook the shock of hair which half covered his eyes. "So then…you had better take good care of me."

Jacob grabbed Abraham behind his neck and pinched his thumb and middle finger together in a claw-like movement, but, at the same time, pulled his brother toward him so that Abraham's head was forced against his chest. He roughly rubbed the younger boy's head with his knuckles; an act which he knew Abraham disliked. But instead of the predictable reaction, Abraham wrapped his arms around his brother's torso. In just a moment, Jacob stopped rubbing his head, noticing that the boy was already beginning to sob. Jacob removed his hand from Abraham's head and slid it down to his back, holding his brother with affection. And then…he also started to weep. In all that had happened, he had failed to recognize that he had yet to mourn properly for the woman who had given him life; for the mother who had gone that extra mile to insure that he would be educated. And before much time elapsed, Jacob's chest was heaving as rhythmically as Abraham's.

When Abraham felt the warm tears fall onto his face from above, he slowly pushed himself up and away from his brother's embrace. Looking at his brother, the younger Zook said, simply, "Good! I see that you finally remembered why we are here today, Jacob."

Jacob re-embraced his brother tightly. "Thank you, Abraham." Suddenly, Oliver Bartlett's face appeared at the door of the carriage. "Is everything alright? Is your brother's foot broken, Jacob?"

Jacob gave his brother one final pat on his back before breaking the embrace, but answered Oliver without turning to face him – his face still streaked with tears. "It's fine, Oliver. Would you please tell my father that his foot is fine."

"Certainly, Jacob," Oliver replied. "We weren't sure what was going on in here, so the General asked me for, as he put it… 'a report.' Are you ready for the rest of us to join you?"

"Yes," said Abraham. "Tell the General that we are ready to go see President Lincoln." And with that, Oliver bounded off. "I have decided that I really like him, Jacob," said the boy of Oliver. "He really seems to care about you…and your feelings…almost as if he was a member of our family. I am very happy that I got to know him better."

"So am I," remarked Jacob. "He is a true friend. I can't wait to introduce him to Becky."

Abraham shook his head in disgust. "Becky!"

"And one day, little brother, it will happen to you, too." Abraham wiped the tears from his face with his sleeve and simply wagged his head, as if to imply that it was not going to happen as Jacob had predicted. But their moment had come to an end; the rest of the party had reached the carriage.

"If you healthy young lads could come out here, you could help an old cripple into his carriage," bellowed Sickles. The fact of the matter was that Ishmael Zook was more than capable of placing the General into the carriage single-handed. But Sickles, in addition to his irascible temperament and his dogged pursuit of his own personal agenda, had also moments of real wisdom, and he was in the middle of one of these now.

Even though he was still showing the remnants of his recent bout with emotion, Jacob dutifully descended from the carriage. He allowed the General to place his hand firmly on his shoulder, while he pulled himself up into the cab – but not before taking notice of the track lines on the young man's face. He made no mention of his observation, but simply sat down on the rear bench seat. Jacob, Oliver, and finally

Ishmael all boarded the livery, and, within a few moments Sickles gave the command to the driver to move toward Baltimore Street. Sickles happened to be sitting directly across from Ishmael, who hadn't seemed to notice that both of his sons had been upset just minutes prior. "You know, Ishmael," said the General, "I think the world of Jacob."

Ishmael laughed good-naturedly. "I think that you have made that more than abundantly clear through your generosity, General."

Sickles nodded in agreement, but held up his hand, as if he was not yet finished with his statement. "What I mean to say, Ishmael, is that Jacob is like a son to me." Ishmael stopped laughing. "I must also add that I have developed quite a fondness for Abraham, as well – and I see quite a few merits with young Mr. Bartlett, here, too."

"Yes," agreed Ishmael, "Oliver is a fine young man."

"Yes, but Ishmael," Sickles continued, "I must say that I am very jealous of you."

"Jealous of me?"

"Yes…that would be the emotion, I think," said Sickles. "I am jealous of you, my friend. You see, my child is still very young…and is my only child. Because of my estrangement to my wife, I don't get to see him very often…practically not at all. But when I look at your son… excuse me, your sons…I see everything that I hope my child grows up to be…and then a bit more. I am sure that the same will hold true for Abraham when he reaches the same age as Jacob, but I can safely say that I am extremely proud of all that Jacob has accomplished, and that I am anxious to see what other great things he will accomplish in the future. I think that he is quite remarkable!"

"Thank you, General," answered Ishmael. "I…I think that he is quite remarkable, too." His father had a difficult time saying the phrase; it had gotten stuck in his throat momentarily. When it did finally come out, Jacob was astonished to hear his father actually say those words.

His father was not one to compliment his children. He turned to Jacob, who was sitting next to him, and then patted him on the knee. Ishmael looked back across the cab of the carriage at Abraham, who was sitting very close to the General. "I am very proud of both of my sons, General." But then, realizing that he might have shunned, so to speak, the third young man in the carriage – even if totally by accident – Zook took into account that Oliver Bartlett, who he hardly knew before the past few days, might have been excluded by his remark. Ishmael leaned forward and turned to Oliver, who was sitting next to Jacob, and said, "And I am sure that your parents are very proud of you, Oliver."

"It is sometimes difficult to tell," answered Bartlett, "but, in my heart, I do believe that you are correct, Sir." The reply was quintessentially Oliver Bartlett.

"Nonsense, Oliver," roared Sickles. "I have only just met you, but I can already tell that you, too, are a remarkable young man… and Jacob is fortunate, indeed, to have one such as you as a friend." Sickles paused briefly, looking over at Jacob. "And I can tell that it is a very strong friendship. Isn't it?"

"Yes, sir," answered Oliver. "I believe that it is."

In just a few shorts minutes, the carriage approached the intersection of the Chambersburg Pike and Baltimore Street; the site of the David Wills' house. Still several hundred feet away from the property, the cab was thwarted by a throng of people gathered outside of the house; on the lawn, in the street, hanging in trees – all with the same purpose; to see the President of the United States, Abraham Lincoln.

Lincoln had arrived by train in the late afternoon, around the same time that the Zook family and Oliver Bartlett had been in the process of burying Sarah Zook. Wills was accommodating most of the principal participants in the ceremony for the evening at his house. In addition to the President, keynote speaker Edward Everett was also staying the night in the house. Mrs. Wills had given up her own bedroom for the President. Lincoln had not felt well for the past few days. On the morning of the trip out of Washington, he considered canceling the journey because of his health, but reconsidered because of the immense political pressure to attend. He also knew that he had to address the gathered masses – especially the press. Even though he knew that Everett was the featured orator for the ceremony, he also realized that a great deal of focus would be placed on what he would say for the occasion. He had written down some scattered thoughts before leaving Washington, had put a few more ideas down on paper on the train ride up to Gettysburg, but the speech was far from complete; at least not by the standards of Abraham Lincoln, who was a notoriously impeccable writer. He would draft and re-write, and then polish and self-edit many times before settling on a final version. He believed whole-heartedly that every single word and every bit of punctuation carried its own weight. In this regard, he was more of a quality versus quantity man – airing on the side of quality. Everett, on the other hand, in keeping with the style of the time, would probably use a great deal of time to develop his oration.

The driver of the carriage informed Sickles that he was unable to get any closer to the intersection of Chambersburg and Baltimore. They would have to walk to get a better view. "Well…come on, then," encouraged Sickles, as he threw open the carriage door. "If you want to heckle the President, we are going to have to get much closer."

"Heckle the President?" asked Oliver. "Are we going to heckle the President?" Sickles shook his head. "Mr. Bartlett…I do hope you grow accustomed to my sense of humor soon. I would hate to think of you going through the rest of your life thinking that I am serious about everything that I say." "Oh," replied Oliver, "it was just a joke."

While their patient driver once again tended to the horse and carriage, the small party headed up Chambersburg Street toward the

Wills' house. The streets were filled with onlookers; both curiosity seekers and members of the press. Many in the crowd were wearing the dark blue uniform of a Federal soldier, and many of those were officers. They were stopped several times along the way by some of these same officers, who recognized Sickles and had to have a few words with one of the most infamous men connected with the battle.

But even this somewhat negative connotation had its privileges, for they found the crowd willing to part in order to allow the General a closer access to the Wills' house. They made it as close as fifty feet from the front door of the house, when a great shout went up from the crowd.

The front door was opening.

Someone was coming out of the house.

To everybody's surprise, that person turned out to be Abraham Lincoln, himself, who had acquiesced to the request to speak at this moment. The President walked slowly out to the edge of the porch and began to speak. Very few people, including the Zook family, and their associates, could hear what the man had to say. His voice was very weak, and he seemed somewhat confused. "He does not look well," remarked Sickles. "He does not seem like himself."

Jacob agreed with that observation, even though he had only spoken with Lincoln but once. The man to whom he had spoken was a very serious man, but he displayed a vitality which was clearly missing from the man on the porch. Another man stood near Lincoln on the porch. This was, clearly, a man assigned to guard the President; a bodyguard. The President spoke for less than a minute, then turned and went back inside the house.

"He didn't seem to make any sense," remarked Sickles. "That's not typical for Lincoln."

"Perhaps he was just tired from the trip out here," observed Jacob.

"Perhaps," answered Sickles. "Look!" said the General, with a note of surprise in his voice. "Over there! Walking toward us….it's Abner. Abner Doubleday!"

"Abner Doubleday?" asked Jacob. "General Doubleday?"

"The very same," answered Sickles, before calling out in his usual thunderous manner, "Abner Doubleday!" Doubleday immediately turned upon hearing his name. "Over here, Abner. It's Dan Sickles!" Doubleday managed to spot Sickles in the large crowd and made his way through the well-wishers and curiosity seekers. Unlike Sickles, Doubleday was dressed in his Federal uniform. The two Generals shook hands.

"How are you, Daniel?" Doubleday asked.

"As good as can be expected, Abner," Sickles answered, gesturing down at the void on his side. "They giving you back a command again?"

"That's why I'm here, I suppose," answered Doubleday. "I'm hoping that our political friendship will help them see past what Meade has done to discredit my leadership in the field. You know what they're calling me, Dan?" Sickles didn't answer. He didn't want to confirm the nickname, but Doubleday continued anyway, unabated. "'Old Forty Eight Hours'….because that's how long I was in command."

"Damn shame!" agreed Sickles. In fact, Sickles also longed to get back in the saddle and command a Corp again – but he knew that his days in the army were numbered – at best. In all likelihood, they were already over. "Damn that Meade! He's just making a lot of noise for being replaced. I hear that Grant is taking over in a few weeks."

"That's correct, Dan," answered Doubleday. "Grant is a good man… when he's sober."

"He was near the bottom of his West Point class," noted Sickles with a wry smile, "which means he will probably fare far better than the rest of those men that graduated near the top." And even though Doubleday, himself, was one of these men, he had to laugh at Sickles' bluntness.

Grant was already known as a tough fighter; one who would never give up – and one who would never hesitate to attack.

Doubleday then realized that Sickles was not alone. He didn't recognize the young man that was standing at his side, even though he had, in fact, seen him some months before, when Jacob had entered into the Federal Headquarters on the evening of the first day of the battle. At that time, Doubleday was still considered a bit of a hero; Meade had not started to discredit him, although he had already removed him from command of the field. It was also at that time that Jacob had experienced his first encounter with General Daniel Sickles, and it had not been a very pleasant experience. "Who is this young man, Daniel?" asked Doubleday.

"You may not remember him," said Sickles, "but this is the young Amish boy that delivered Major Winslow back safely to our side on the evening of July first."

"This…" replied Doubleday in amazement, "is Jacob Zook?" Jacob extended his hand, which the General eagerly shook. "You are quite a living legend, sir… especially considering your age."

"Thank you, sir," answered Jacob. "I am studying medicine at Dartmouth College presently…thanks to General Sickles."

"And partially thanks to you, General Sickles is still with us to send you to Dartmouth," added Doubleday. "But it is a fine school."

"I particularly like…." He paused a moment, debating whether or not he should mention what was on his mind, but then continued… ."baseball."

"Baseball?" Doubleday asked, laughing. "Even I don't know who invented that foolish game…but if they want to pin it on me, I will be happy to oblige. What position do you play?"

"Catcher, sir."

"A vital, defensive position, Jacob. Do you hit well?" "I think so, sir…at least that's what I am told."

Sickles grew impatient. "Where are you staying for the night, Abner?" "Right here, Dan. I have a mattress on the floor in one of the sitting rooms.

And yourself?"

"I have a room in one of the fancier hotels in this little town," smiled Sickles. "But I can tell you this…it surely beats the accommodations that I had the last time I visited Gettysburg."

"Will you be at the dedication in the morning?"

"Wouldn't miss it!" said Sickles.

In just a few more minutes, the men would part company. Jacob was already attempting to find Oliver, Abraham and his father in the thick and boisterous crowd. He led Sickles toward the place where they had left the carriage, and, in doing so, they also ran head-first into the rest of their party.

"Papa," said Jacob, upon reaching his father, "the General is staying in a hotel tonight. Shouldn't we have him stay at our house?"

"Yes!" agreed Abraham, quickly.

"I should say so," replied Ishmael. "General…you must stay with us." "But I have a room prepared, Ishmael."

"Nonsense!" replied Ishmael. "They can sell that room a dozen times over considering this crowd. You will be more comfortable in our house."

"Perhaps…" mused the General.

"Perhaps?" questioned Ishmael. "Of course you will be happier staying with us. We can stop by the hotel on the way back up to Seminary Ridge to pick up your things."

Sickles finally relented. There was just no arguing with common sense.

CHAPTER 46

Another Sunrise

Jacob Zook had a difficult time sleeping on the night of November 18. The fact that his mentor, if you could call him that – General Daniel E. Sickles, was asleep in a bedroom down the hallway from his own room was scarcely reason for his apparent insomnia. It had been the first time that the General had set foot inside of the home that he, himself, had ordered built for the Zook family. But even that topic had been thoroughly discussed among the five members of the burial party – once they returned from the tavern and the Wills' house. Jacob had never seen his father so ingratiating; he virtually bubbled with words of praise and thanksgiving for the generous gift – as well as for the generosity shown by the General to his oldest son.

Jacob had turned in for the night at almost midnight, convinced that he was exhausted from the events of the day, and sure that he would immediately fall asleep. He did, in fact, fall quickly to sleep – but he found himself awake again at just a little past one in the morning. The bedcovers and sheets were thrown almost completely off of the bed, indicating to the young man that he had been having a restless sleep – possibly one filled with a nightmare, or two.

And what would be so odd about that, he thought?

He had just buried his beloved mother the day before. It had been the day before, because it was now the early morning hours of November 19, 1863. Jacob collected the bed linens off of the floor and attempted to reorganize his bed. Having completed this task, he crawled back under the loosely gathered material – shivering slightly in the cool of the late autumn night. He turned onto his right side and stared out of the black maw that was his bedroom window. He could see the moon and some stars. He hoped to relax and drift off to sleep, but he found that his mind was too filled with thoughts to let him sleep.

The first thoughts that entered his sleep-deprived mind were memories of his mother, Sarah. As much as he wanted to keep these memories alive, Jacob knew that these thoughts would keep him up all night, so he purposely thought of other things to push those thoughts to the rear. This seemed to work positively for him; at least the most unpleasant thoughts were gone.

Jacob used his brother, Abraham, and his encounter with him in the carriage to jettison the sadder thoughts. As much as he had wanted to remain angry at his brother for playing him as a fool, he knew that he could not. His admiration of his brother turned into a veritable mental showplace of many memories from their past together. He had to quietly laugh to himself over some of Abraham's antics, especially those of late. This kaleidoscope of older memories was also blended, and this blending often included memories that featured Oliver Bartlett. But these thoughts did nothing to help Jacob get back to sleep – in fact, he was even more wide-awake than he had been an hour earlier.

Jacob rolled over onto his back.

Clearly – this was not working as he wished. He began to think back to the battle – those three days in the beginning of July – and suddenly his brain activity seemed to intensify even more than before. He wondered why – after a hiatus of over four months – that it was on this night in the middle of November that these memories had come crashing down upon him. He mulled over the many acquaintances that he had made over the three day period; Major Winslow, Bobby McLean – who had died in his arms after the Major had shot him; General Armistead – poor, unfortunate General Armistead, Doctor Sim – the man who had more to do with him choosing a career path in medicine, and, of course, General Sickles.

But those thoughts led to other thoughts. He began to re-live his brief relationship with the Wade-McClellan family. He thought of poor Ginnie Wade, now dead and buried for several months. He hadn't really seen anyone from the household since he, Abraham and his father had helped put Ginnie in the ground.

But even those thoughts segued into a final series of thoughts; a group of thoughts that were even more persistent than the thoughts that had come before.

He thought of Becky Tilden.

It was a natural progression, was it not? Or so he thought!

Had it not been for Becky, he never would have made contact with the Wade family. Had it not been for Becky, he would not have felt the urge to disobey his father; to consider running away from home – a decision which he had actually made at the time, only to be thwarted by the start of the battle.

But that was another whole set of thoughts… and then his mind quickly returned to the problems within his own family.

He mentally put those to the side to concentrate more on Becky. He put his hands behind his head and stared up at the ceiling of his bedroom. A reflection of moonlight illumined the area above his head.

It had been more than a week since he had last written to his young lady. It had been more than two weeks since he had last received a letter from her.

Although she still seemed to write affectionately to him, he wondered if she hadn't met another young man while away at school. He was well aware of the temptations.

Jacob had caught the eye of a young woman – a local in Hanover – who had started to attend his baseball games as a spectator. Even though he didn't feel any particular attraction to the young lady, she seemed to have the determination to find out more about who Jacob was, and what his daily routine entailed. She even managed to find her way to their local tavern after a game. It was obvious to Jacob that the young woman wanted to get to know him – even if he had no desire to return the favor.

He wondered if Rebecca had ever been in that same situation.

The very thought of that idea made Jacob squirm in his bed. It sent a shiver up his spine – although he really didn't know why that was. The thought of Becky being chased by another young man was not a pleasant one for Jacob, in fact, it made his face flush and his pulse race.

He swallowed. He already knew about respiration. He knew that his respiratory system could react to stressful situations in a similar way. But why the stress? What was it about these thoughts that, under these particular circumstances, was now creating a physical reaction?

And then a new idea entered his mind.

Could he possibly be showing signs of jealousy?

That must be it, he thought. This was all too new for him to fathom at this time. This was the same day, or at least the same twenty four hour period, when he had helped bury his mother. Couldn't he simply just get through this horrible time, and then worry about Becky Tilden at some other occasion?

No…he could not! This was the one thought that would not let him be. Suddenly, the world had changed…the worm had turned. Suddenly, lying there in the bed, it was all so clear and obvious. That young lady… the girl who had so very obviously flirted with him on the sidewalks of

Gettysburg just a few months earlier… was the object of his affections. And not just by way of a teenage infatuation. This was something a great deal more than that; at least that was what every fiber of his body was screaming at him at this very moment.

And…finally…he recognized it for what it truly was.

Jacob Zook was in love with Rebecca Tilden.

A warm feeling overtook his midsection, as he still struggled with the deeper meaning of his mental commitment to Becky. He would write to her in the morning, he thought. He would pour out his heart into that letter; telling her…and perhaps her roommates…of his undying love for her. He would then make sure that the letter found its way to the afternoon post.

One thing was clear; crystal clear. He had seen people come and go in his life; some through natural causes, other through a more violent end – but this was clear. He was not going to allow Rebecca Tilden to slip out of his life. And just as his decision seemed to take on a life of its own, Jacob turned onto his right side, and, happy that he had made this commitment – at least in his own mind – Jacob fell asleep.

His sleep was to be short-lived. He woke around five in the morning, resuming the thought process just about where he had left off on the previous session. How Jacob wished that the morning would come.

After about a half hour of restless dozing in and out of sleep, Jacob deciding that, as the sun was beginning to rise, he would move from his bed to the rocking chair that sat by the window. He removed the quilt from the bed; one of the last things that his mother had made for the new house were quilts for all of the beds. Jacob's quilt featured a geometric patchwork in shades of purple, blue and green. He wrapped the quilt around his body – the realization that this quilt could easily represent the arms of his own mother wrapped around him. His eyes welled up with tears, which rolled down his cheeks and fell onto the quilt. He looked out of the darkened window toward the horizon. He could barely make out the top of McPhearson's Ridge in the distance; the same ridge that had played such an important role just months earlier in July. But even though his thoughts could have easily swayed back to the memories of the battle, the tears continued to flow from his eyes, and, as his emotions steadily grew, he felt a deep sob rise up from within him, as he quietly cried the words, "Oh…Muti!"

As if to answer his call, Jacob heard a soft knock on his bedroom door. The knock was not to seek admission, or permission to enter – it was rather to say, 'I am coming in…like it or not.' And within the course of just a few heartbeats, the wooden door swung slowly open, revealing the shape of his brother, Abraham, silhouetted in the pale moonlight.

"Jacob?"

"What is it, Abraham? Are you not feeling well?"

"I couldn't sleep anymore, Jacob," his brother answered. "Actually…I didn't sleep very much all night."

"Neither could I,: replied Jacob. "Come on in, Brüderchen."

Abraham crossed the expanse of the room. Even in the dim light, Jacob could see that his brother was wearing his long underwear. He wasn't wearing a nightshirt. As he drew closer, Jacob could tell that the boy was shivering from the cold. "Come over by me, Abraham. Sit with me by the window." Abraham gave no reply; he simply walked to his brother's side. "Here…there is plenty of warmth beneath this quilt. I am happy to share it with you." Jacob stood up and spread out his arms like a large pair of wings. Abraham quickly moved to his brother's side. Jacob wrapped his quilt and his arms around his shivering brother and then they both gently sat down on the large rocker. Like all of the other furniture in the large house, the rocker had been built by Ishmael in the barn, following the destruction of the old farmhouse.

Though he was considerable warmer than before, Abraham continued to shiver slightly, his body taking time to warm itself beneath the thick quilt. "Why couldn't you sleep, Jacob?" he asked.

"I'm not entirely sure," Jacob replied, while rubbing his brother's arms, trying to speed up the warming process. "My mind was just too busy to sleep, I suppose."

"Mine too," said Abraham. "I kept thinking about Mama." And then Abraham broke down and cried, just as Jacob had done only minutes before.

"Let it out, Abraham," comforted his brother. "I did the exact same thing but a few minutes ago…in fact…I was weeping heavily when you knocked."

"You were?"

"Certainly! Just because I'm older doesn't mean that it hurts any less."

"I suppose not," answered Abraham. Jacob felt Abraham's arm slip around his waist, still under the quilt. "Jacob…do you think it will always be like this?"

"What do you mean?"

"Us….I mean….as brothers. Do you think we will always be as close as we are right now? I don't mean just under a quilt together. I mean…as brothers." "Would you like us to be?" asked Jacob, gently.

"More than anything in the world," Abraham replied, tightening his grip around his brother's waist.

"That's funny," chided Jacob, "considering all that you put me through earlier this evening.

"You must admit that it was very funny…especially your reaction." "For a moment, I considered hitting you," responded Jacob, "then you wouldn't have thought it funny." Abraham smiled up into his brother's face – but it was a mixture of imp and devil that made up his countenance. He took his left hand, which was still tightly wrapped around his brother's waist, and suddenly jabbed him under his rib cage, attempting to tickle him. "Stop it, Abraham…lest I need remind you of which one of us is the truly ticklish one among us." Abraham immediately stopped the attempt. "But…in answer to your question…I think that our lives will both change quite a bit over the next few years. In some respects, we will grow apart….but, in others, we will always be close. We may even live very far apart from one another…maybe even in different states."

"Different states?" asked Abraham. "Then how will we be able to remain close?"

"That will require a great deal of work on both our parts," replied Jacob. "I can do that," replied Abraham, once again squeezing his brother's side. Just then, there was another faint knock on the door. "Come in," said Jacob, quietly. The door opened to reveal the figure of Oliver Bartlett, wrapped similarly in an Amish quilt, head to toe.

"I heard talking, and found the source," he said, softly. This, in and of itself, was not all that surprising. In the layout of the house, the bedroom which Oliver now occupied was placed directly between Jacob's room and Abraham's room.

"Join us," invited Abraham.

"I don't mean to intrude," explained Oliver.

"Nonsense," replied Jacob. "You are becoming like one of the family." "Come over here….Obie," said Abraham, his voice rising with delight.

Oliver crossed the room and sat on the side of Jacob's bed, facing the other two young men. "Wait! What was that you called me, Abraham?"

"Pardon me?" asked Abraham, quietly but with a purpose.

"You distinctly called me a name," answered Oliver. "What was it? Opie?" "Opie?" laughed Abraham. "No, not Opie! Obie! Obie!"

"Alright…Obie! Now I understand," said Oliver. "But what does that mean?"

"Obie," explained Abraham, "is my new name for you. It is made up of your initials…O and B…for Oliver Bartlett. Do you get it? Obie!"

"Oh!" observed Oliver. "Yes…now I understand what you said, but I don't know if it sounds very dignified."

Abraham blew out some air from between his lips in frustration. "It's not meant to be dignified, Oliver. It's meant to be humorous."

"I see," he replied. "I will have to give that some thought."

Abraham looked over at Jacob and smiled broadly. He really liked Oliver's quirky and overly formal way of expressing himself. "Why are you awake, Oliver? We weren't making that much noise…not enough to keep you up."

"True enough," answered Oliver. "I usually hit these feather mattresses of yours and fall directly to sleep…and then sleep on until the morning, but this night was different. I suppose my mind was racing a bit too much…or maybe I had a bit too much to drink earlier."

"My mind was racing, too, Oliver," said Jacob.

"Truly?" asked Bartlett. "But you have every reason to be upset, Jacob. You, as well, Abraham. I don't know what my problem is…except that I felt really badly for you and your father."

"Thank you," replied Jacob. "It was actually very nice to have you here, Oliver. I appreciated your company more than you know."

"That is…once you were able to get Abraham to tolerate me," added Bartlett.

Abraham laughed at this remark, which was, of course, quite true.

"In truth," Oliver said, in a low and serious voice, "I would do anything for you, Jacob. You are my best friend." Oliver looked at Abraham, who was looking down at the floor. "I don't mean to take your place, Abraham. I know that your brother means a great deal to you."

"Him?" But then Abraham flashed his smile again, "I'm glad that he has a friend like you, Oliver – especially when he is in New Hampshire.

You will keep him out of trouble. When he goes out on his own he ends up in the middle of battles."

The three boys had a good laugh at Abraham's candid opinion. "We shouldn't be so loud, gentlemen," observed Bartlett. "We will wake your father and the General."

"I don't think so," replied Jacob. "My father and the General had quite a few glasses of schnapps before turning in. My father will be out until morning, as will the General."

Just as he was saying this, a thin ray of light landed squarely on Oliver's forehead. The sun was rising over the top of McPhearson's Ridge. Within a few minutes most of the bedroom was illumined by an increasing number of sunrays. All three turned toward the window in silence and watched the sunrise on the morning of November 19, 1863. Jacob thought back to a similar morning in early July; the same morning in which he had decided to run away from home. It had been a decision that had changed his life. Now, in the company of his brother and his very closest friend, he watched the dawning of a new day as the sunshine broke over Seminary Ridge.

He wondered to himself what this day would bring.

He wondered if his life would change again after this day had run its measured course.

CHAPTER 47

Fourscore, and Seven Years Ago...

After watching the sun come up over McPhearson's Ridge, the three young men adjourned to the kitchen to make some breakfast. Taking the lead in the situation, Oliver started to issue commands to the others, giving instructions on how to properly make griddle cakes. By six thirty, all was prepared. The smell of coffee brewing, along with the savory smell of bacon, and the aromatic aroma of the food being cooked, was enough to wake both the General and Ishmael, who wandered into the large kitchen shortly thereafter.

They all enjoyed the breakfast, even though some of the food had been slightly overcooked. They were all going to go to the dedication of the new national cemetery later that day – and they were especially going in order to listen to the speech that President Lincoln was certain to deliver. General Sickles had more of a vested interest than the others, but all were very anxious to be there for the event nevertheless. The Zook men wished to go because it was a significant event in the life of their community; a community which had now embraced the Amish family as one of their own. Oliver Bartlett wanted to go because, as a student of political science – and as a future law student – he was very interested in the career of the backwoods, self-educated Lincoln.

Their breakfast had been leisurely – with the exception that the smell of the lye, which had been used to disinfect the house following Sarah's death, was still everywhere within the home. Ishmael had been relieved from his duties around the seminary and in the barn due to the death of Sarah, so he did not feel obligated to tend to any chores. They relaxed around the kitchen table, telling stories and enjoying pleasant conversation until about the hour of eight o'clock, when Sickles mentioned that he would need to leave in order to get ready for the events of the day. That cue given, the three younger gentlemen cleaned up the kitchen before retiring back upstairs to begin the same preparations, too.

They knew that the ceremony would begin around noon, which gave them ample time to wash and dress. Oliver stopped by Jacob's room again, interested in gaining additional information on what to wear for the occasion.

"I think it will be a formal affair," announced Jacob, who was selecting an array of clothing from his trunk. "I imagine that many dignitaries will be on hand for this ceremony."

"You are probably correct," admitted Oliver, although he was still not completely convinced. He harbored the opinion that Gettysburg was still a very rural and unsophisticated location; that national attention would not be focused on this little hamlet, and that the ceremony would be far from formal – not that he would attend in work clothes…if, in fact, he actually owned work clothes, which he did not. He found it hard to believe that, in the middle of this cursed war, that Washington would come to Gettysburg.

He was, of course, totally incorrect in this assumption.

Now approaching the end of his teenage years, Jacob had indeed started to look more and more like his father, Ishmael. His hair was still very light blond – very Germanic – but his facial hair was also starting to come in, and that was also, like his father's – very blond. Jacob was a strikingly handsome young man, who, on occasion would purposely avoid taking care of some of the more foreign personal grooming habits; habits that most Amish young men wished did not exist, such as shaving. Typically, an Amish youth will remove the early growth of facial hair, even up until it truly becomes stubble, until the time when they marry – and then they are forbidden, by the Ordnung, to ever remove it again. Jacob had never really wanted to wear a full beard, such as his father did, but he also did not enjoy removing any hints of his fast-approaching manhood. It was, in a very large sense, a badge of honor.

But today…today was going to be a special occasion. He had not used his razor for several days, and a visible coat of blond whiskers had grown on his neck, cheeks and upper lip. He knew that it was expected that he look the part today, so after selecting his wardrobe for the ceremony he mentioned to Oliver that he was going to shave before dressing. "And… so should you," he mentioned to his friend.

Oliver, on the other hand, was not the naturally handsome young man that his Amish friend was, but it also didn't help his appearance that he subjugated his looks by neglecting his personal grooming. Whereas Jacob would purposely ignore the task of removing his facial hair, Oliver, although the same age, carried on as if the situation never even existed – as if he were perennially twelve years old. Oliver's face was a disorganized jumble of errant whiskers and downy hair, all of which tending to detract from his appearance. Moreover, he tended to also ignore his hair, having convinced himself long ago that he was an academic and a philosopher; that physical appearance meant little – only his mind mattered. It was, perhaps, for this reason, that Oliver had not attracted the attention of any of the young ladies in the town of Hanover the way Jacob had done.

"What difference would that make?" he asked Jacob, with a very dismissive attitude.

"Don't you think it would be the right and respectful thing to do, under the circumstances?"

Oliver considered his friend's question. "I suppose you might be correct." But then he added, "However…I did not bring my razor on this trip. I didn't expect that we would stay this long…and I, generally speaking, have very little stubble to remove."

"So you have said," remarked Jacob, with a smile. "You should try looking in the mirror, my friend. Abraham may not have anything to remove, but you certainly do."

Oliver rubbed his face. "You also make another fine point, Jacob. Thank you." "You may use my blade, Oliver. I will go get some hot water for the basin." The situation was not all that different from almost any morning at Dartmouth, except that it wasn't Dartmouth – it was Gettysburg. Oliver had his own way of looking out for Jacob, as Jacob had his own way of looking out for Oliver. In many respects, Oliver was far more meticulous about certain aspects of school – and life – than Jacob was – growing up in a family of both heritage and privilege – but there were other examples in which Jacob, the newcomer to society, so to speak, had a definite advantage. Oliver was, to say the least, socially awkward. Jacob was embraced instantly by the academic community at Dartmouth as an instant favorite.

But that had not stopped the two roommates from becoming the best of friends.

Jacob made the trek down and back up from the kitchen in under a minute. He re-entered the room carrying a pitcher of hot water, which he then carefully poured into the basin on the dresser. Jacob took a little water from the basin in order to create the lather in the shaving cup and began to mix it with the brush. "You can go first," he said to Oliver, now turning his attention to the blade and strap.

"No…you go first," replied Oliver.

"No…I insist." Thus commanded, Oliver stripped off his undershirt while Jacob continued to work on the blade. Oliver grabbed the shaving cup and started to apply a thick coat of the soap to his face. Seeing him ready, Jacob handed his friend the single-edged blade carefully. Jacob re-positioned the mirror on the dresser so that Oliver had a clear view of what he was doing. Perhaps it was because it was a borrowed blade, or perhaps because he didn't normally shave his face with Jacob paying such close attention to detail – for whatever the reason, Oliver was exceptionally slow and methodical that day. As he drew close to finishing the job, Jacob reached over and took the shaving cup, beginning the preparations to remove his own daily growth. After he removed his undershirt, he turned to Oliver and asked, "Would you mind if I made a casual observation?"

Oliver, in the process of shaving his neck, did not turn to reply, but rather simply grunted, "And what might that be?"

"Well…it's just between us…as friends, you know…but…well…I think that you would look much better if you cut your hair differently."

"If I cut my hair differently?"

"Correct!" answered Jacob. It was already far too late to retreat, so he continued. "I think that your hair hides too much of your face." He decided to cover his tracks. "I was just thinking that, you know."

"No…I don't know exactly what you are getting at, Jacob."

Jacob started to lather up his face, but he also knew that he had just opened up a can of worms, so he felt pressed to continue. "I just think…that you would look far better if we could actually see more of your face, Oliver."

"But that was the idea, Jacob," Oliver answered, beginning to wipe the excess soap from his face. "Who would want to see my face?"

"Am I detecting a note of self-pity, my friend?" asked Jacob.

"Pity? No! Reality is more of the case….and you know it! We are friends, Jacob…but in some respects we are vastly different. We have both been blessed with intelligence, but you have been blessed with good looks and a winning personality, while I have been blessed with a quick wit, and…"

"And…?"

"And a quick wit!" Oliver said. But the response had a flat finish to it, as if he had acquiesced to the fact that he was living his life hiding behind an arsenal of sarcasms and quick jibes.

"Nonsense!" countered Jacob. "Becky groomed me a bit, before I left for Washington. She didn't want me looking like such a country bumpkin. She never said that, by the way…but I knew she was thinking it. It was she who helped me look more like the dandy you see before you today. I wasn't born this way!" Jacob let out a short laugh. "You do remember that I grew up in a strict Amish household, don't you? How much do you think we Amish really thought about a sense of fashion and good taste?" Oliver laughed at Jacob's self-deprecating manner. "I am very aware that I changed my style of dress and the manner of my carriage in order to prosecute my career…but I also did it because…of Rebecca."

Oliver finished wiping off the soap. "I don't think that I follow you."

And with that comment, Jacob had arrived at the crossroads with his friend – that moment when he would need to test the bounds of his friendship by saying something that needed to be said. "All I am saying, Oliver…is that you are a wonderful young man…you are my best friend…but I also think that you are lonely…and that you want a companion – other than me, of course."

"And you think that cutting my hair is going to garner me the company of a young lady?"

"I can't guarantee that…but, yes…I think that if you take the appropriate steps, people will discover that there is another side of Oliver Bartlett."

Oliver considered what his friend had said for a moment before answering. "Fine…if you think it will work. What did you have in mind?"

Jacob picked up the blade in his right hand, as if he was going to begin shaving, but instead he turned toward his friend. He grabbed some of the wayward hair on the right side of Oliver's face. "We should cut this off…and then do the same on the other side…then cut this up here, and shorten this over here…."

"Wait!" protested Bartlett. "Don't you think it would be easier if we just went to a barber?"

"Certainly…but we can't do that now, Oliver."

"True."

"Let me just trim a bit back, and then we'll have a look." Oliver agreed to the procedure and Jacob set in to cutting the unruly hair back. Even though it was not a perfect job, it was a step in the right direction. "Sooner or later we will both be remarkable catches for any number of women in society, Oliver. Don't you wish it could be sooner, rather than later?"

Oliver had to agree with that logic.

At eleven thirty the carriage arrived to take them to the dedication ceremony for the new national cemetery. The members of the town, along with some Federal troops assigned to this particular task, had spent several weeks exhuming the bodies of the dead which had been buried where they fell on the battlefield, in order to re-bury them on the new Federally-designated land. Fortunately, the vast majority of the battlefield graves had been marked with identification – if such information was present at the time of burial. In almost all cases, however, even if the soldier could not be exactly identified because he was not carrying papers, then at the very least he could be placed in a grave in the new cemetery that had been created for others from his own state in the Union.

By mid -November, a great deal of this work had been accomplished – but there still were thousands of bodies to dig up and move. It was ghastly work!

The dedication ceremony would begin at around noon, and would feature a keynote address by Edward Everett – perhaps the most famous orator in the country at the time – and closing 'remarks' by the President.

Edward Everett was a staunch 'Unionist,' and a great supporter of the President. He was a graduate of Harvard – in point of fact, the valedictorian of his graduating class. He served terms in the United States Congress and in the Senate, serving his home state of Massachusetts. He was Secretary of State and Minister to Great Britain. In the 1840's, he returned to Harvard to serve a term as the President of the college.

The planners of the dedication ceremony had expected Everett's speech to 'run long,' expecting it to last more than an hour. It lasted over two hours. Spectators noted that, while the crowd was not unruly, the length of the oration caused some in the audience to go for walks around the cemetery property, or to simply grow restless.

The Zooks, Oliver Bartlett, and General Daniel E. Sickles arrived at the new cemetery, which was laid out adjacent to the existing Evergreen Cemetery, at around noon. Sickles was already aware that Edward Everett was the first speaker on the docket for the day, and thus elected to stay put in the carriage, keeping a way back from the crowd. Not one for crowds, especially English crowds, Ishmael decided to stay with the General to keep him company. Jacob, Abraham and Oliver set out to wend their way through the crowd of people, with the hope that they might be able to catch a bit of the President's speech.

Jacob knew the terrain of this section of Cemetery Ridge quite well. The ridge had been named for the plot of land that had been designed as the final resting place for most of the citizens of the town. It was on this raised bit of topography, however, that the Union Army had enjoyed their finest hour of the battle on the third day, July 3.

Jacob led his brother and his best friend around the back of the group, negotiating a flanking move on the reviewing stand. They were standing off to the left of Everett's peripheral vision – not the most ideal of places to hear a speech, but at the same time – not very far away from the dais.

Jacob felt a tap on his shoulder. "You boys will have to keep moving," said a gruff voice from behind. Jacob turned around quickly to face the voice. In his view was a large man with dark black hair and whiskers on his chin. Jacob had no way of immediately know this, but he was face to face with Ward Hill Lamon, the man who was serving as bodyguard to the President. "This area is off-limits to civilians," Lamon said calmly. "You boys just go back down from where you came."

"I am sorry, truly I am," said Jacob. "We just wanted a better view for when Mr. Lincoln gets his chance to speak."

"Jacob? Is that you?" said another voice – a voice from behind where Lamon was standing.

Jacob recognized the voice immediately. "Mr. Lincoln?" "Mr. President…you know this young man?" Lamon asked.

"Indeed I do, Hill," replied Lincoln, stepping forward toward the young men.

As the President came further into view, Oliver felt his legs buckle underneath him.

"This is Jacob Zook – a resident of Gettysburg, and a hero of the battle." The President shook Jacob's hand warmly. "A pleasure to see you again, Jacob." Lincoln then turned his attention to the other two young men. "And who might these young gentlemen be, Jacob?"

"This is my brother, Abraham Zook, Mr. President." "Ah…I can see the family resemblance."

"Thank you, Mr. President," replied Abraham, smiling broadly at Lincoln. "My brother is very good looking, isn't he?"

Abraham's quick thinking and wit instantly charmed Lincoln, who reached out to the boy to shake his hand. "Very clever, Mr. Zook. Very clever, indeed. I must also tell you…I admire your name."

"Zook?" asked Abraham.

"No…Abraham!" said the President. Lincoln turned to face Oliver Bartlett.

"This is my friend, Oliver Bartlett, Mr. President. He hails from New Hampshire."

"Are you a relation to Josiah Bartlett…a signer of the Declaration of Independence?" asked Lincoln, shaking Oliver's hand.

"I am, Sir…but I am doing my level best to carve out my own way in spite of this honor" answered Oliver.

Lincoln laughed. "Another wit! Jacob, you are surrounded by clever young gentlemen."

"Yes, sir," Jacob replied, proudly.

Suddenly, Lincoln swayed a bit. He attempted to balance himself by extending his long arms to correct his equilibrium. Hill Lamon grabbed the President's arm and helped stabilize him. "Mr. President…are you feeling up to giving this speech?" asked Lamon.

"I have no choice, Hill. It is not a long speech…I should be just fine. We best be moving up to the dais," explained Lincoln. "Jacob and company…until we meet again." And then Lincoln set off to the speaker's platform.

"General Doubleday was correct about the President. He said so last night outside of the Wills' house," commented Jacob. "He said that he thought the President was not well."

They watched as Lincoln took his place, sitting on a chair almost directly behind where Everett was speaking. Ward Hill Lamon sat down next to the President, on his right side.

It was after two o'clock when Everett finally finished his oration. The crowd applauded loudly, although Abraham would later comment that the ovation was probably due to the fact that they were happy to see the end of the speech. It was now Lincoln's turn to speak to the assemblage. He stood up and walked to the front of the platform, then waited for the crowd to quiet down.

He began his speech, speaking in a frail voice.

"Four score and seven years ago our fathers brought forth on this continent a new nation, conceived in liberty, and dedicated to the proposition that all men are created equal.

Now we are engaged in a great civil war, testing whether that nation, or any nation, so conceived and so dedicated, can long endure. We are met on a great battle-field of that war. We have come to dedicate a portion of that field, as a final resting place for those who here gave their lives that that nation might live. It is altogether fitting and proper that we should do this.

But, in a larger sense, we can not dedicate, we can not consecrate, we can not hallow this ground. The brave men, living and dead, who struggled here, have consecrated it, far above our poor power to add or detract. The world will little note, nor long remember what we say here, but it can never forget what they did here. It is for us the living, rather, to be dedicated here to the unfinished work which they who fought here have thus far so nobly advanced. It is rather for us to be here dedicated to the great task remaining before us—that from these honored dead we take increased devotion to that cause for which they gave the last full measure of devotion—that we here highly resolve that these dead shall not have died in vain— that this nation, under God, shall have a new birth of freedom—and that government of the people, by the people, for the people, shall not perish from the earth."

The speech lasted less than two minutes. When it was over, some members of the crowd burst into applause, but some remained silent – confused by the brevity of the oration. Some instantaneously compared Lincoln's speech to Everett's – based on length alone. But the crafting of the two minute speech did not escape Everett, himself, who was very much taken with the sculpting of each phrase and sentence. Whereas he had developed his thesis over a slow-burning fire, as one might cook a multi-step, complicated soup, Lincoln's speech was dependent upon every word bearing weight in the argument.

Within a few more minutes, the ceremony was at an end – the spectators, members of the press, the representatives of the military, as well as public dignitaries, all started to disperse. Many stayed behind to greet the President, who, owing to his health was allowed to slip away without much ado. By the time all had concluded, it was almost three o'clock in the afternoon. Lincoln had another stop to make before leaving to go back to Washington. He had been surrounded by well-wishers, among them – Everett, but now had other obligations to attend before boarding the train. Allowing Limon to plough the way, Lincoln retraced the steps he had taken to get to the speaker's platform. Once again, he came face to face with Jacob Zook. Lincoln smiled weakly at the young man. Jacob was taken aback at Lincoln's profound sadness – what Lincoln would describe as 'his melancholy.' The President shook the hands of the three boys, he then turned to Jacob. "You do not necessarily need to remember, Jacob, what you heard and saw here today…but you should always remember what you witnessed here in the beginning of

July. Study hard at school…and make this a better country than when you first found it." Lincoln patted Jacob on the shoulder, as he did to each of the boys, and then strode off.

Jacob turned quickly; quick enough to hear the President say, "Daniel…do have a safe trip back to Washington." General Sickles and his father had come up from behind them. Jacob watched as Lincoln paused by his father, shaking his hand warmly. As they were only a few steps from where he stood, he could clearly make out what the President was saying to his father.

"You must be Mr. Zook?" Lincoln inquired.

"Yes….yes I am, Mr. Lincoln," replied his father.

"I am sure that there is no need to tell you that you should be proud of your son, Mr. Zook," assured the President, "but I would just like to mention it again to you…just to underscore the fact that our nation is indebted to anyone who acts as selfless as he."

"Thank you, Mr. President," Ishmael replied, with all sincerity.

"I hope that I will be able to watch his growth over the next few years. It should be interesting to see the man he becomes," said Lincoln. Lincoln turned and smiled one last time at Jacob. It was, perhaps, laded with the sadness of one who had already suffered the loss of two of his own sons – never to see them reach adulthood, or to achieve the promises and ambitions that their young lives had sought. "Next time you are in Washington, boys," he said to all three young gentlemen, "stop in at my house on Pennsylvania Avenue for a visit."

The boys nodded eagerly to the President, who turned and walked away with Limon in the lead. Jacob looked over at his father, who was in the process of wiping away the tears from his eyes. It was the first time in which Jacob had seen his father weep. He wondered if anything else was wrong. "Papa?" he asked, with a note of concern in his voice.

"I....I....just wish that your mother could have been here to hear that," he said.

"If pride is one of the deadly sins…then I am surely a sinner bound for the fires of Hell…because I can feel nothing but pride for my sons at this moment."

Sickles placed a hand on Ishmael's back and patted him gently. "Aye!"

*   *   *

Jacob and Oliver were back in New Hampshire before another week elapsed. In a letter written less than a week after his return to the college, Jacob asked Rebecca Tilden if she would consider some sort of permanent romantic arrangement between them. He came just short of proposing marriage, which was, of course, a totally ridiculous idea, considering the fact that they both had years of schooling to complete, and considering the fact that they had already made such a pledge to each other the evening before he left for Dartmouth. But he was more interested in having her know of his feelings; that they had not changed, but rather intensified – and he was just as interested to learn of her feelings toward him. A week later, his suspicions were confirmed. Rebecca wrote back, telling Jacob that she would remain faithful to him until that time when they could be together.

Near the end of his sophomore year at Dartmouth, Jacob was elated to hear that the dreadful war was drawing to a close; that the Confederate Army was about to surrender. By the middle of April, 1865, the Confederacy was ready to collapse. Only days after General Lee surrendered to General Grant at Appomattox Court House, President Lincoln was assassinated by John Wilkes Booth. In his reflections on the life of the great man, Jacob was constantly reminded of Lincoln's invitation to visit him in Washington, and the fact that it had been the last time that he had seen Lincoln alive.

Oliver and Jacob both graduated from Dartmouth College in the spring of 1868. Oliver then went to Harvard to study Law. The two young men, always the best of friends while at Dartmouth, remained the best of friends for the rest of their lives.

Jacob received a fellowship to study medicine in Edinburgh, Scotland. He became the protégé of Dr. Joseph Lister, the man who pioneered the concepts of antiseptic practices on the operating table. Jacob would return to the United States two years later and help to implement these same practices in America.

He had fulfilled his quest to change that which he had witnessed in the surgical tent at Gettysburg.

Jacob Zook married Rebecca Tilden in October of 1871. They would have six children together; Jacob, Abraham, Sarah, Virginia, (also known as 'Ginnie') Robert (for Bobby McLean) and, last but not least…Oliver.

CHAPTER 48

Years Later

General Daniel Edgar Sickles retired from active duty in the army several years after the hostilities ended, but the controversy that had followed him throughout the early years of his career continued to follow him into old age.

The General continued to fight to preserve the National Cemetery at Gettysburg, as well as the National Battlefield Memorial. He was most instrumental in creating a divider – a fence, of sorts – that served to mark the boundary of the cemetery. Ironically, the materials for this wall came from masonry dismantled at Lafayette Square in Washington, D.C. – very close to the same spot where the General had shot down Philip Barton Key many years earlier.

When General Oliver Howard died in 1909, Sickles became the lone surviving Corps commander from the conflict. Sickles was now approaching 90 years of age; but his health was rapidly deteriorating. He was almost blind, and was very often incoherent. Nevertheless, as the summer of 1913 loomed on the horizon, the General began to make plans to travel to Gettysburg to attend the 50th Anniversary reunion of the veterans of the battle. His personal affairs still a complete mess, he had once again managed to alienate himself from his wife, Caroline, and their grown son, Stanton. Instead, he chose to spend his time with his live-in housekeeper, Eleanor Wilmerding. As the first few days of July, 1913 arrived, Sickles arrived at the battlefield, accompanied by Wilmerding, who pushed the fragile man around in a wheelchair.

Reminiscent of the actual days of the battle, the weather was extremely warm and oppressive, and great care had to be taken that the aging veterans did not secumb to heat stroke and the like. On July 2, 1913, exactly fifty years from the day that he lost his leg to a Confederate cannon ball, Sickles had Eleanor push him to the edge of the ridge that overlooked the site of his last few moments of glory.

"Look down over there, my dear," commanded Sickles, but in a quiet and peaceful tone. "Can you see it? The orchard, I mean."

"Yes, Dan," she replied.

"That is the cursed peach orchard where I…" But he faltered, as he had so many other times in recent years, as the fleeting sparks of memory seemed to fade away.

"It is alright if you cannot remember, Dan," soothed Eleanor. "Damn it, woman! Of course I can remember it!" thundered Sickles,

surprisingly lucid. "This is where I purposely disobeyed that nincompoop Meade's orders to hold the line and charged out on my own. Do you think I could ever forget such a monumental blunder? It cost me my leg, you know?"

"Yes, Dan…I know," she replied.

"And yet," said a voice from the General's rear, "General Longstreet has credited your bold move with the ultimate success of the Union army."

"That is correct, sir," said Sickles, awkwardly trying to turn his upper body around to look at the speaker. "You, sir, are very well informed."

"I have made it my business, General," said the gentleman, now moving to the side of the officer's wheelchair.

Sickles looked up at the newcomer, squinting into the bright sunlight in order to ascertain the identity of the speaker. Whoever it was, Sickles thought, the fellow is well-dressed and well-mannered. At the same moment, he noticed that the man was accompanied by a woman – who he assumed must be his wife; although that was a large assumption on his part, considering that his companion was not his own spouse. "Have I had the pleasure of your acquaintance, sir?" he asked, still trying to clearly see the man's face.

"Many times, General…especially in these hills and fields…in 1863," was the reply.

"Were you a member of III Corps?"

"General Sickles?" And having said this, the man dropped down on his knees beside the wheelchair so that the officer could look him squarely in the face. "Do you not know me, sir?"

Sickles knit his brow, pondering the familiar question that so often provoked him into fits of rage. But this man's face was different, so he quelled his anger and frustration and concentrated on looking. He noticed a gentleness; a kindness…a….

He felt something move inside of him at the pit of his stomach. The man's hair was greying…but once upon a time, it had been…blonde.

"I once knew a young man from around these parts," said the General softly. "I could never forget that young man…or the distinguished gentleman he has become."

"Do you know this gentleman?" asked Eleanor.

"Yes…I believe I do, Eleanor. I believe that we are standing in the company of Doctor Jacob Zook," answered Sickles, his eyes sharpening – along with his mind. He was completely lucid once more.

Jacob reached out with his hand and patted the General's arm warmly. He knew that there wouldn't be many more times when he would be able to see Sickles alive, and he was grateful that the General still could remember his identity. "And do you recognize this lady, here?"

Sickles leaned forward, slightly, gazing past Jacob to the fashionably dressed woman on Jacob's arm. "Ah yes…this must be the lovely Rebecca Tilden."

Becky smiled at the General. "Rebecca Zook, General. Don't you remember?" The General returned the smile. "Of course I remember, young lady. I danced at your wedding…well…it felt like I danced at your wedding." A bit more of the old Daniel Sickles slowly returned to his countenance. "And you, young man…why haven't you stayed in touch with me? Of all the ungrateful wretches…you take the lot!"

"Dan!" cautioned Eleanor, with a reproving tone in her voice. "The doctor visited with you just last week…"

"Nonsense!" bellowed Sickles. "I have no reason to come back out here to the farmland of Pennsylvania….other than to come to this reunion. Are you going to tell me that this Amish boy came to the City of New York?"

"Dan!" repeated Eleanor.

"General," said Jacob in a soothing tone, "I live in New York City… we do…Becky and I."

"Nonsense!" argued the General. "That's against your 'Ordnung.' You live right over there a piece…in a beautiful house that I had my men build for you after the battle."

"General," Jacob explained, "that house was struck by lightning and burned to the ground almost twenty years ago – but Becky and I, along with our children, have lived in New York for the past thirty years."

"Ha! So they shunned you, after all," replied Sickles with an all-knowing smile.

"Sir…I was already shunned when you met me. Don't you recall?"

And it was at that moment that Jacob witnessed the General do something which he never seen him do in the fifty years he had known him; the General began to weep. "No, I can't recall…damn you! I can't recall that you visited me last week. I can't recall what I ate for breakfast this morning! The only thing that I vividly remember are the events of the second of July, 1863."

"The day you lost your leg," prompted Jacob.

"And most of my Corps," admitted Sickles. "I do recall asking you to make me something…but I can't even remember what that was."

"Ah…yes," said Jacob. "The box for your leg bones."

The General looked quizzically at his old friend. "Could that be it? That sounds very gruesome and strange."

"I thought so, too…at the time," agreed Jacob. "It's sitting in your living room, General."

"Odd…I don't recall anything about such a thing." Sickles looked out over the battlefield. From this promontory he could easily see the Round Tops (Sugar Loaf Hill had been renamed long ago) and Devil's Den, which was the name for the outcropping of boulders in the middle of what once was McPhearson's farmland.

"Somewhere out there," he pointed, "there is a rather flat marker that designates the spot where I marched out with III Corps, which led to me putting the corps into a salient, which caused the death of so many of my brave men."

"Yes, sir," said Jacob. "I have seen the marker. It seems a bit on the small side, I think. You are the only corps commander to not have a statue or monument placed on the battlefield – and that includes those who fought for the Confederacy."

Sickles nodded his head, acknowledging the slight, but then laughed it off in a style reminiscent of his bygone personality. "What need have I of a monument, my boy? The whole battlefield is my monument."

"Perhaps," replied Jacob, satisfied with his enigmatic answer.

"So…if you live in New York City…what brings you back out to Gettysburg? Are you here for the reunion?"

"Partly," said Jacob, "but Becky and I are also here to look at a piece of property over by Seminary Ridge. I am planning to retire from practice in a few years and we would like to move back out here.

"You are planning to give up the big city so that you can move back out here?" Jacob nodded. "Well…if that isn't the most stupid thing that I ever heard!"

The General suffered a cerebral hemorrhage in April of 1914, lingering in a coma until his death on May 3. He was just short of his ninety fifth birthday and, at that time, was the longest surviving officer from the Union or the Confederacy that had fought in the Battle of Gettysburg. His funeral service was held at Saint Patrick's Cathedral in New York City, and was well attended by many of the surviving members of III Corps.

Jacob Zook, nearing the end of his career in medical research, had spent the last few years on the staff of St. Luke's Hospital in Morningside Heights. As the General lived in close proximity to the hospital, Jacob spent many an afternoon or evening in his company, but in the last few months these visits had tapered off; mostly because of his busy schedule, but also because of the various scandals – both monetary and personal – which the General still had the misfortune to create. The fact of the matter remained that his conversation with the General on July 2, 1913 was the last time that Sickles had remembered his relationship with the younger man. When he heard of his death, he made plans to attend the Funeral Mass in Mid Town.

Jacob arrived at the great church at a little before ten o'clock in the morning, finding his way to a pew about halfway down the expanse of the nave. Even though he had spent the majority of his adult life as a member of the Congregationalist denomination, he was not unfamiliar with the traditions of Roman Catholicism, and quickly kneeled to say a prayer for his recently departed benefactor and friend. Having finished his meditation, he sat back in the pew – waiting for the Mass to begin. Soon thereafter, a cart holding the flag-draped coffin of General Sickles was wheeled out to the center of the Chancel railing. An honor guard positioned itself on both sides of the coffin. All now was in readiness for the final ceremony to this paradoxical man.

Jacob was just a few weeks shy of his seventieth year. He had worked diligently and as one inspired for all of his adult life, but he now realized that his own body was beginning to send him messages that he needed to slow down. Perhaps it was only that at that moment in time – sitting in a large cathedral, waiting for a funeral to begin – it gave him a moment's pause to reflect on his own life – and his own mortality.

Jacob felt a hand placed on his shoulder. He turned to the left to see just who had recognized him among the hundreds of people in attendance that day.

It was his brother, Abraham.

"I didn't know you would be coming to this," remarked Jacob, after embracing his brother warmly in the aisle of the church.

"I would have missed the event entirely, were it not for the fact that I received a wire when the General lapsed into a coma a few days ago. I figured that the end wasn't too far away and made plans to come to New York."

Jacob nodded to his brother. "How is the family?"

"I have another grandchild on the way," Abraham answered in a matter-of-fact manner.

"Fantastic!" replied Jacob. "But I will still have you beat in that department, you know."

"My children are still younger than yours, Jacob. They are still having children of their own. Give them time"

Jacob quietly laughed to himself. It had been a quiet competition between the two brothers for years, with Jacob drawing the first blood.

Abraham inclined his head toward the coffin. "When was the last time you spoke with him?"

"About a month ago…or so. He was totally bankrupt, Abraham. I had to give him some money just so that he could pay his bills."

"I thought that he had inherited a large fortune a while back?"

"He had," Jacob answered, "but he somehow squandered the whole thing on bad investments, women, liquor…and who knows what else?"

"You became the benefactor to your benefactor!"

"I suppose you could say that…but he changed so much since we knew him as boys. I used to be able to reason with him. Lately…it was just no use. We….had grown apart in recent years."

"I know, Jacob," nodded Abraham, understanding his brother's meaning, "but you can't really blame yourself."

"And yet I feel… guilty."

"Even after all of these years, Jacob?"

"Even still." Jacob dropped his head and looked at the floor between the pews. He suddenly raised his head back up, as if a shock had been sent flying through his body. "Wait! You said you received a wire about the General's condition?"

Abraham smiled at his brother, watching the revelation fill his brother's face, and relishing every moment of the experience. "That's right. I did, didn't I?"

"Who sent you the wire, Abraham?"

A deep, resonant voice answered the question from behind Jacob's right ear. "The only person that cared enough to keep your brother informed…that's who." Jacob whirled around in his seat to discover the smiling face of his old friend, Oliver Bartlett, now a successful New York attorney. Oliver and Jacob had many occasions, especially during the previous thirty years, when they had both resided in New York, to get together socially. They were still the best of friends.

"I should have known," said Jacob, with a smile. "You always had the best interests of the Zook boys tucked deep within that heart of yours, Oliver."

"I do what I can, my friend."

Oliver Bartlett was a senior partner in a large New York City law firm. He, too, was almost seventy years old, although unlike his friend, had no immediate plans to retire from his practice. Oliver was married, had four adult children, and twelve grandchildren. He had been an advisor to several Presidents, including Theodore Roosevelt. He was also primarily responsible for seeing that the final wishes of Major General Daniel Sickles were carried out, as per the General's final requests.

"Did you arrange all of this?" asked Jacob, referring to the funeral arrangements.

"The General made all of the arrangements, Jacob. I merely made sure that his wishes were followed, as per his orders."

Jacob nodded to his friend. He surveyed the cathedral nave, watching it fill up with guests. Many of the men in the congregation were wearing some form of their III Corps uniform. "Do you think that they really knew the General like we did, Oliver?"

"I sincerely doubt that anyone knew the General as we did, Jacob… especially as you did."

"He was an enigma!" responded Jacob.

"May he rest in peace," added Abraham, quietly.

"Amen to that," answered Oliver.

The three men were distracted from their conversation, as there seemed to be more movement up by the Chancel area. Priests were beginning to enter, preparing for the Mass. The Archbishop of New York, himself, was to give the eulogy. Just a the moment when the entire body of clergy had entered and taken their seats, an altar boy entered the nave, carrying a small wooden pedestal, which he proceeded to place in front of the General's casket. It was a pedestal designed to hold a large vase of flowers. A moment later, several soldiers appeared, following the same path as the altar boy. It seemed to be another small honor guard. There were four soldiers, two by two, in the lead, followed by a fifth soldier. The fifth soldier was carrying something.

It was another coffin – a small, flag-draped coffin.

Upon seeing the second coffin, Jacob immediately gasped, "Oh, no!" He once again turned to face Oliver, who simply shrugged his shoulders and said, "It was part of his last requests, Jacob." The final soldier proceeded to place the small coffin on top of the pedestal. "I do hope that it is going to remain closed." He turned again to look at Oliver's expression, which was suspiciously blank.

The honor guard separated. Two stood guard on either side of the small casket, while the other two removed the flag and began to fold it with military pomp. As the two soldiers snapped the flag tight in order to create a smart fold, Jacob became more and more visibly agitated. As the soldiers began to fold the flag into the familiar triangular shape, he could now make out the wooden coffin below…and it was all too recognizable to his eyes.

It was the small oaken coffin which he had made in the summer of 1863 at the request of Daniel Sickles.

It was the small coffin designed to hold his shattered right leg.

Jacob felt Oliver's hand on his left shoulder. "Brace yourself, my friend. It will get worse before it gets better."

"What?" Jacob wondered what his old friend meant by that cryptic remark. The soldier that had carried the casket into the cathedral now approached Jacob's handiwork and opened the latch. He propped open the lid and positioned the contents so that they could be seen by the congregation. In this, the final scene of Daniel Edgar Sickles, he would play the part with his entire body present – one last time!

A priest stood and began the Mass. The vast majority of the Mass was said in Latin, which was not much of a problem for either Jacob or Oliver, as they had studied classical languages while at Dartmouth. Abraham had, indeed, followed in his brother's footsteps, and four years after Jacob had left Seminary Ridge to study at Dartmouth, Abraham set out to study at the University of Pennsylvania. His inspiration to achieve his goals in life had come directly from the influence of his older brother, but his career path was a result of his friendship with his brother's friend, Oliver. Abraham was now a successful lawyer, practicing in Philadelphia.

The liturgy of the Mass came to a natural resting place. At the end a short preamble, the priest called several gentlemen to the chancel to relate some personal insights about the General. Occasionally the nave would erupt with laughter as an anecdote unfit for retelling in a sacred space would be told. Jacob noticed that most of the speakers were much younger than the General; in fact, they appeared to be very much younger than Jacob or Abraham. It led Jacob to wonder the extent in which the speakers actually knew the General.

"I am beginning to wonder if these men really knew Sickles like we did," observed Jacob. "I'll bet not a one was ever in the war with him."

Oliver leaned forward and placed his hand on Jacob's shoulder. "Don't worry, Jacob…we've saved the best for last." Jacob turned around and gave his old friend a quizzical look, as the priest began to announce the next speaker.

"It was one of General Sickles most adamant requests that Doctor Jacob Zook speak to this assembly today – even though, as the General wrote in his own words – we would have to arrange this completely by stealth in order for it to happen."

Once again, Jacob turned to face Oliver, his eyes brightening with indignation.

He turned toward Abraham, who was obviously enjoying his brother's discomfort.

"Would Doctor Zook please come down front and speak to us of his memories of General Sickles?"

Jacob sighed; it seemed useless to argue – and this was no place to create a public display. He slowly stood and began to move toward the aisle, crossing over the legs of his brother as he sat chuckling in the pew. For just one fleeting moment, he noticed that same gleam in Abraham's eyes as he had seen more than fifty years prior when they were in Sickles' carriage at the tavern on the Chambersburg Pike – the time Abraham had feigned injuring his ankle. Once again, Abraham was enjoying the last laugh. Jacob reached the aisle and walked toward the altar area. His mind was whirling, as he tried to plan his extemporaneous remarks – which, in itself, annoyed him greatly, as he much preferred to work out his comments in written form. He did not like to speak off of the cuff.

But what really took him by surprise was his reaction to Sickles' coffins – his two coffins – as they grew larger and larger as he approached the chancel. He stopped thinking about his reflections of the man and began to only consider this sight – the sight that all would face eventually.

He stepped up to the lectern and cleared his throat. He allowed his eyes to move and change focus as he sought out Abraham and Oliver, who were sitting beneath the rear gallery. He raised his eyes into the gallery, looking at the magnificent pipe organ and the rose window. He knew that his father would have declared the entire church as 'fancy.'

"Good afternoon," he began. "I first met General Sickles when I was but eighteen years old. I met him in the Headquarters of the Army of the Potomac on July 1, 1863 – in the town where I grew up…Gettysburg, Pennsylvania." A murmur arose from the assembled audience. "Our first meeting was anything but auspicious. I considered him boorish and ill-mannered, and…I can tell you…it didn't seem that he cared too much for me, either." A few laughs were elicited by this remark. "I met the General after the first day of fighting; fighting which I avoided but was dragged into at any rate – on both sides, I might add – a day after I had run away from home. I can tell you that on July first, that there was no place I would rather be than home in my own bed. But that was not to be – not just yet. I spent the next day working in a field hospital, assisting the army surgeon, Dr. Thomas Sim. It was at that moment that I decided that I wished to study medicine. While I was there, lo and behold, a General was brought in from the field – most of his right leg severed by a cannonball. I assisted Dr. Sim with the amputation of the leg – the very same leg that you see in the box before you." Jacob paused as the gathering reacted to what he had just said.

"I spent a great deal of the next day tending to the General as he recovered from the surgery. He was cantankerous, opinionated, stubborn, a hard drinker, and could cuss more than any man I had ever known – but, having said that – the General and I became close friends. He requested that I make a coffin-like box for his amputated leg – which I did – and <u>that</u> is the box that holds his leg right now. As the war shifted into the South, the General arranged for me to go to college. I went to Dartmouth – where I met my best friend, Oliver Bartlett, Esquire – who is hiding in the shadows back there under the balcony, along with my brother, Abraham. All three of us got to know the General, and, even though we were well aware of the kind of explosive personality he could display, we all were able to see a very different man, as well.

General Daniel Sickles was…my mentor and…my friend. I also am aware of the fact that he was many other less savory things to many other people, but I can safely say that he changed my life, as well as the life of those other gentlemen sitting back there in the shadows. We will miss you, General."

His remembrance concluded, Jacob turned and headed back to his seat in the back – in the shadows. Even though he had been initially annoyed that Oliver and Abraham had set him up as they had, Jacob was ultimately very happy that he had the opportunity to speak. It had felt like the right thing to do.

The Mass Proper concluded, the Archbishop of New York delivered the final eulogy. He spoke of Daniel Sickles and his many accomplishments during his long life as if he really knew the man…personally – which, in fact, couldn't have been further from the truth. He spoke of his valor at Gettysburg and Chancellorsville – about him winning the Medal of Honor – about his service to the Court of the Queen of Spain – about his years in the United States Congress. What was also apparent, in addition to those things being said by the cleric, was also those things not being said; the murder of Phillip Barton Key, his many mistresses, (including the deposed Queen of Spain) his military blunders, his hard drinking and quick temper.

The final bit of information provided by the Archbishop in his eulogy concerned the piece of bone fragment that lay on display for all to see. For this, it seemed, was how General Daniel Sickles wished to be remembered; as the man who forfeited his leg in service to his country. Looking around the cathedral, Jacob could see that most of the men in attendance were moved by this tribute; that the sacrifice of his limb was a testament to the man. But Jacob – as well as his brother and Oliver Bartlett – knew differently. Jacob listened, with discomfort, as the Archbishop continued praising the now departed Sickles; lamenting his loss to the country which he loved so dearly. He remembered back, some fifty years earlier – to 1863, when he and Sickles were at their closest. He remembered how Sickles had explained politics to him. He remembered that, at the time, the discussion was about as useless as anything he had heard. Imagine – attempting to explain the American political system to an eighteen year old Amish farm boy?

But, pondering again, he realized that this was also the man that had made such a tremendous difference in his life. Were it not for Sickles, he never would have had the opportunity to attend Dartmouth – so everything that followed in his life, perhaps even his marriage to Becky, would have also been at a loss. Despite his negative attributes, he owed General Sickles a great deal. But even thinking of these things brought back painful memories; the death of his mother, Sarah – the loss of his father, some five short years later.

The eulogy ended, the Archbishop moved back to the Cathedra, the large chair in the chancel from which a 'cathedral' draws its name. The Honor Guard sprang into action, preparing the casket for removal from the cathedral and then to hearse – to be followed, at some later date, with interment in the ground. The smaller contingent of soldiers – the one in charge of the small coffin with Sickles' leg bones – moved first. They replaced the shattered leg back inside the box and then recovered the small casket with the flag, then moved the coffin and the pedestal out of the way so that the pallbearers could now carry the General's body out of the cathedral. The six soldiers assigned to this task hoisted the large casket onto their shoulders and began to carry it down the center aisle of the cathedral, heading for the main exit onto 5th Avenue. Falling in behind the pallbearers, the smaller Honor Guard walked out as they had come in an hour earlier, two-by-two, with the single soldier bringing up the rear, carrying the small coffin.

But unlike the other soldiers appointed to the Honor Guard, the soldier carrying the amputated leg was animated; he seemed to be looking for someone in the crowd of mourners. These actions on his part did not go unnoticed by Jacob, who found the soldier's behavior curious, if not downright disrespectful – considering the circumstances.

But then Jacob, ever intent on watching the actions of this particular soldier, happened to lock eyes with the man. The soldier remembered Jacob instantly, from his part in the memorial portion of the mass, as if he had known him his entire life.

Seeing the pew directly in front of Jacob vacant, the soldier crossed out of the center aisle and through the empty pew, all the while carrying the macabre little box. Immediately upon seeing the soldier leave the main aisle of the cathedral, heading in his direction, Jacob nervously spun around to face Oliver. "What is going on here, Oliver?"

"You will see, my friend."

"You know about this?"

"You forget, Jacob," Oliver said, smiling, "I helped the General with all of these arrangements." He paused. "And I do mean…all of them!"

The soldier stopped in front of Jacob, turning to the left with military precision. He extended the entire box - coffin, contents and flag – toward Jacob. "Mr. Zook – With General Sickles' compliments. He wishes to return this to the original owner."

"Pardon me?" asked Jacob, incredulously.

The soldier spoke softly. "Please take the box, sir."

Jacob rose from his seat and took the coffin out of the arms of the soldier, who saluted and then turned smartly, heading for the rest of the funerary party. Jacob gently placed the box and its contents on his pew. He turned to face Oliver. His brother, Abraham, was wearing a wide grin. "You could have warned me, Oliver."

"I was sworn to secrecy…under pain of death," Bartlett replied, "… and you know the General…he would have killed me if I had breathed a word of it."

"Are you going to bring it home to Rebecca, Jacob?" asked Abraham, sarcastically.

"Funny, Abraham!" Jacob shot back at his younger brother. "Perhaps you wouldn't mind taking it home to Frances."

"Not in this lifetime! Besides…you made the thing. Remember?" "I remember you helping me quite enthusiastically."

"Yes," Abraham replied glumly. "I do somewhat remember that, as well." The mourners now started to file out of the cathedral. There was to be a funeral procession down 5th Avenue until they reached Grand Central Station at 42nd Street. "Where is he going to be buried, Oliver?"

"Arlington."

"Arlington National Cemetery? On General Lee's old property?" "That's correct," said Oliver, smiling vaguely at Jacob.

"Not at Gettysburg? Not in the National Cemetery he helped to create? Not at the place where he lost…this?" He patted the box on the pew.

"That was his choice, Jacob," explained Oliver. In one of his last conversations with the press, Sickles had explained that the pervasive opinion of the day has placed a great deal of the blame for the debacle of the second day of the battle squarely on his shoulders, even though Confederate General, James Longstreet – second in command on the field only to Robert E. Lee – had publicly defended Sickles actions that day, commenting that by moving away from the Federal line, Sickles drew rebel troops away from their intended target – Sugar Loaf Hill (Little Round Top) – and, in doing so, changed the course of the battle. Longstreet, himself, had passed away in 1904.

"I still don't understand," replied Jacob.

"He felt that he was more respected by Lee and his Generals than by the Senior Staff of the Union Army. He decided that, as there are no memorials or plaques to him on the battlefield – and that he remains the only Union General that does not hold that honor – he will be buried elsewhere."

"Isn't there a plaque to him somewhere on the field?" asked Abraham. "It only mentions the General in a negative light," responded Oliver. "It shows where he struck out on his own, and how his corps was decimated because of his decision."

"Well, then…," observed Jacob, "our friend, the General, went out just as cantankerous as he lived his entire life. What am I to do with this thing, Oliver."

"He doesn't expect you to put it in your home, Jacob."

"Thank God for that!"

"He wants you to put it in the Smithsonian."

"Really? The Smithsonian?"

"I have already petitioned President Wilson on that subject…but the General wished that you would act as caretaker of his….property…..Dr. Zook."

Jacob let out a large sigh. "I suppose so. It is the least I can do."

Abraham affectionately patted both of his companions on the shoulders. "I think we should repair to a local watering hole for some lunch."

"Some lunch, Abraham?" asked Jacob.

"To have something to eat," the younger Zook replied, "and to raise a glass, or three, to the memory of the General. He was, in many respects, the benefactor to all three of us."

Jacob and Oliver nodded in agreement to Abraham's plan. Jacob picked up the box that he had constructed, with some assistance from his brother, back in 1863. They walked out of the cathedral and found a local tavern on 5th Avenue. They all raised a glass of ale to the memory of Major General Daniel Edgar Sickles, a man who had changed their lives in so many ways.

Jacob brought the coffin and the shattered leg of the departed Sickles back to Washington, D.C. shortly thereafter. The leg was placed once again in the Army Medical Museum, along with a card that read, 'With the compliments of Major General D.E.S."

After he purchased a large tract of land in Pennsylvania in 1913, Jacob spent several months designing his new home. He meticulously researched the details of a home that had once stood adjacent to the Lutheran Seminary; the same home which had be rebuild for the Zook family in 1863, after it had been destroyed during the battle. When Jacob retired from his practice in the year 1915, the couple moved into the large, rambling farmhouse that they had been built on the outskirts of Gettysburg, Pennsylvania…

…in clear view of the Lutheran Seminary on Seminary Ridge.

EPILOGUE

While the entire Zook family, the Tilden family, and Oliver Bartlett are all fictional characters, most of the other characters are of historic significance, and played an important role in either the Battle of Gettysburg, or thereafter.

While the timeline of the battle may have been altered for dramatic content, most of the settings and scenarios are accurate.

Some of the principal players include:

Abner Doubleday – This West Point graduate was, in fact, the general to assume command of the field on the first day of battle following the death of General John Reynolds from a sniper's bullet. He was relieved of this command by Union Commander, George Meade, for failing to hold the high ground at Seminary Ridge, in spite of the fact that his corps was being overrun by vastly superior Confederate forces. As Meade would go on to blame Daniel Sickles for his insubordination on Day Two of the battle, so would he also lay the blame for the near disaster that developed over the course of Day One at the feet of Abner Doubleday. For this action, Doubleday received the nickname of "Old Forty Eight Hours," which demonstrated the length of time that he spent as a Corps Commander. He would never command a division again.

After the war, Doubleday traveled to California, where he engineered the only moving National Historic Monument, the San Francisco Cable Car System – it is in his name that the patent was issued. He returned to the East Coast for the remaining days of his life, living on Church Street, in Mendham, New Jersey. He became a leading member of a philosophical/religious organization.

But his single greatest achievement seems to be, according to legend, the 'invention' of the National Pastime, Baseball. Even though many scholars would disagree about Doubleday's involvement in the development of the sport, the Baseball Hall of Fame in Cooperstown, New York, named the baseball field contained therein as 'Doubleday Field.'

'Ginnie' Wade was, in fact, the only civilian casualty during the battle of Gettysburg. She was shot while standing over the dough which she was preparing to bake. It is believed that Confederate snipers had stationed themselves on either the rooftops or in the attics of buildings that faced up the Baltimore Street hill, looking toward Cemetery Ridge. It is assumed that these snipers had witnessed as many men as a company traveling down the hill to visit the Wade/McClellan home in order to have some of Ginnie's homemade bread. This could have precipitated the gunshot that found its way into the Wade house. The bullet passed through a wooden door and severed her spinal column, killing her instantly. Her house still stands in the center of the down, at the base of Baltimore Street, in mute testimony to her life and death.

Her sister, Georgia McClellan, did, in fact, give birth to a son just prior to the battle. Her husband was away at the time, fighting the war. He returned in the late summer of 1863 and was immediately put to work, repairing the house, as well as many other structures in the town. Georgia would go on to fight to memorialize her sister's grave, which by that time had been moved from the temporary grave behind the house to the Evergreen Cemetery on Cemetery Ridge. It now flies a perpetual American Flag over the gravesite – the only other such memorial to a civilian flies at the Betsy Ross House in Philadelphia.

One of the great friendships recounted during the Civil War was that of Lewis Armistead of the Confederacy and Winfield Scott Hancock of the Union. The two officers had become very close friends while serving in the West prior to the beginning of hostilities. A statue now stands on the Gettysburg battlefield commemorating this friendship between the two men. The statue, the "Friend to Friend" Monument, depicts the fallen Armistead being supported by Union Captain Bingham moments after the General is wounded. His battlefield words have been somewhat convoluted over the years, but a synthesis of the versions has Armistead sending greetings to Hancock, asking for his forgiveness, and possibly requesting that his watch be sent to the Union General. He had not been aware, at the time, that Hancock had also been seriously wounded in the battle. Hancock would, unlike Armistead, survive to live a long life.

Historians can always speculate over what would have been had Abraham Lincoln not been assassinated by John Wilkes Booth. It is quite clear that Lincoln favored a gentle and forgiving return to a unified nation, and would have probably dealt with the former rebels with charity and grace. In the wave of renewed animosity following the President's death, much of this was buried with the President. A great deal of this ill-will was harbored by Secretary of War, Edwin Stanton, who almost single-handedly led the reprisals against the South. Included in this was the creation of Arlington National Cemetery on the property of General Robert E. Lee, directly across the Potomac River from the Capitol. Lee was forced to live the remaining years of his life in his home, the Custis-Lee mansion, looking out from the promontory view that the builder had provided him, but now looking at the row upon row of Federal dead. If ever there was a case of 'the punishment fitting the crime,' then this was it.

Wesley Culp did, indeed, move away from his ancestral home on the Culp Farm in Gettysburg, to Western Virginia. Even though that portion of the 'Old Dominion' would eventually break away from the Confederate state out of political dissention, Wesley supported the Confederacy, and joined the Army of Northern Virginia. He was mortally wounded trying to capture the very hill he had climbed and played on as a boy – "Culp's Hill."

Major Robert Winslow was, in actuality, a member of the 68th Pennsylvania Regiment, and was wounded during the battle of Gettysburg.

General Ambrose P. Hill was one of the Confederacy's most valiant generals, having participated with a great deal of success in many of the major battles of the war leading up to Gettysburg. Even though two of his divisions participated in the final assault on Cemetery Ridge, command of the attack fell to General Longstreet, who, in turn, placed General George Pickett in battlefield command of the plan. The final charge of the battle of Gettysburg could easily have marched into the history books as "Hill's Charge," rather than "Pickett's Charge." But it really doesn't matter in the long run, as all of the divisions that made that final charge were decimated.

Hill would continue to lead his Corps for the remainder of the war, until – during the siege of Petersburg, Virginia – he was killed in action.

General George Meade was appointed to lead the Army of the Potomac just three days prior to the Battle of Gettysburg. Considering the enormous political pressures brought to bear in this change of command, it is a wonder that the army, and its commanding general, were able to function at all. Meade was appointed in relief of General Joseph Hooker, who had ineffectually led the army to disaster at the Battle of

Chancellorsville. Meade had been an outspoken critic of Hooker, which then somewhat backfired on him when he was appointed to the post, as he was surrounded by many of Hooker's friends. Chief among his critics was General Daniel Sickles.

History records the Battle of Gettysburg as a 'turning point' during the Civil War – not to mention a great victory for the Union forces. Even though they were considered the victors by the end of the third day of battle, the Union army had suffered more casualties than the Confederates – even with the debacle that was Pickett's Charge. If Meade is to be rightly credited with this modest victory, then it should be for taking the wind out of the sails of the Army of Northern Virginia and Robert E. Lee, for this was the first time that they had been truly defeated in battle. This defeat also closed the door on the notion that a victory for the Confederacy could be achieved by invading the North, or by capturing the Capitol, the Congress, and/or the President. What had started as a skirmish outside of a small town in Pennsylvania quickly turned into a mighty three day battle, and, by the end of the battle the momentum of invasion was clearly brought to a halt.

Meade did not, however, choose to pursue Lee back into Virginia; a decision that became his undoing as a commander. Meade remained in his position until later that fall, when he was replaced by General U.S. Grant. With this action, President Lincoln created his own 'turning point' of the war, for he finally found the man who would doggedly battle the rebels to a successful conclusion. Grant, the new and final General-in-Chief for the Union forces, allowed Meade to remain as Commander of the Army of the Potomac.

Sugar Loaf Hill, which was the given name for a small hill near the larger "Round Top" hill, was later renamed 'Little Round Top.' The defense of the Union position, especially that under the command of Colonel Joshua Chamberlain, became one of the legends connected with the battle. The outcropping of boulders and rocks adjacent to the Peach Orchard and Wheatfield would later become known as 'Devil's Den.'

General Samuel Zook was wounded mortally at the Battle of Gettysburg, lingering as described in the story for almost a day before succumbing to his wounds. The general was one of the more colorful commanders in the field, and was well-liked by his men. Zook happens to be a very common last name among both the Amish and the Mennonites.

General Daniel Sickles was a living contradiction of terms. He was trained as a printer, but educated to be a lawyer. He served several terms in the United States Congress, and also served overseas in England during the Pierce Administration. He married a fifteen year old girl – against the wishes of both families.

Sickles, did indeed, kill Philip Barton Key, son of Francis Scott Key, author of the words to our National Anthem, as Key was calling on his young wife at their home. He shot him five times at point-blank range – flying into a jealous rage after learning of his wife's infidelity. The man who would become Abraham Lincoln's Secretary of War, Edwin Stanton, would be his defense attorney, and he would successfully argue that Sickles had become so incensed when he learned of their misconduct, that he couldn't help himself; that he had become temporarily insane.

Sickles would beat the murder charge by using successfully, for the first time, the please of temporary insanity.

Sickles would cash in on his political favors once the war began, asking the Congress for a commission in the Army. He quickly rose through the ranks, and ended up commanding a corps. He was promoted by Hooker, who made him a Corps commander – becoming the only one of his kind on the field that did not have a West Point education, which also caused animosity among the general staff. He had a spotty performance at Chancellorsville, under his good friend and drinking companion, Joseph Hooker, and resented the way Hooker had been openly criticized for his leadership – or lack thereof. Part of the reason for Sickles rise through the ranks of the general staff was the fact that he had spent much of his efforts raising volunteers in New York – successful because of his ties to the Irish immigrants, as well as to the political machine of the time – Tammany Hall.

But it was at Gettysburg that Sickles would live forever in infamy. Either acting in a complete act of insubordination, or because he felt that his III Corps was actually in danger of decimation if they stayed put, Sickles moved his entire Corps forward and created a Salient – a triangular shaped formation which was then free to be attacked by the Confederates from two sides simultaneously. His Corps extended from Devil's Den, located just below Little Round Top, through the Peach Orchard and into the Wheatfield. At first, the Corps was successful in their attack, but this was to prove short-lived, as the entire Corps was ripped apart by heavy fire. It was at this point that Sickles received his famous wound – a cannonade virtually removed his leg from his body. He was carried from the field smoking a cigar and cursing the rebels.

A marker now stands at the high point of Sickles' Salient. It reads, *"Sickles's movement practically destroyed his own corps…; and with what result? - driving us back to the position he was ordered to hold originally."* This quote is by General Meade, who became the man who most criticized Sickles' actions, or rebuffed Sickles own criticism of his own. Other than that one marker on the battlefield, Sickles is the only Union officer of any importance to have been overlooked when placing monuments and statues. Sickles was removed from Gettysburg the day following the battle and moved to an army hospital in Washington, where he was visited by Abraham Lincoln and his son, Tad.

Sickles did ask for a coffin to be constructed to carry his amputated leg – a practice which he continued for several years, until he donated the leg to the Army Medical Museum in Washington. He would, however, occasionally take visits to the same hospital in order to pay a visit on that which was once attached to him.

In the years which followed the war, Sickles returned to Congress. His most important contribution may well have been helping to pave the way, through legislation, to set aside the land upon which the battle had been fought in Gettysburg as a National Historic Park.

Sickles did serve a term as Ambassador to Spain, but rumor also has it that he became involved in an affair with the deposed Spanish Queen.

Sickles argued for the rest of his life that his radical move on the second day of the battle had actually helped to win the day for the Union army. To this day, historians debate whether or not this was true, even if it was accomplished unwittingly.

Sickles lived out the remained of his life in New York City. When he died in 1914, his funeral was well attended, and included a procession down Fifth Avenue from St. Patrick's Cathedral.